PRAISE FOR ST.
BEING A JANE AUS   ...IES

Jane and the Barque of Frailty

"Barron does an admirable job not only with the [Jane Austen] mysteries, but also in mimicking Austen's style."
—*The Tampa Tribune*

"Satisfying right to the last revelation...Like Regency great Georgette Heyer, the author excels at both period detail and modern verve. Aping Austen's cool, precise and very famous voice is a hard trick to pull off, but Barron manages it with aplomb."
— *Publishers Weekly*

"Charming, literate and unequaled in its dissection of Regency-era social injustices."
—*Kirkus Reviews*

Jane and His Lordship's Legacy

"Considered by some as the best of the 'neo-Austens,' Barron gets high marks for authenticity and wit."
—*Booklist*

Jane and the Ghosts of Netley

"The latest installment in Stephanie Barron's charming series . . . [is] a first-rate historical mystery. Barron writes a lively adventure that puts warm flesh on historical bones. The nice thing is she does so in a literary style that would not put Jane Austen's nose out of joint."

—*The New York Times Book Review*

"With elements of an espionage thriller and a Regency romance, [this] is a book Barron fans have been awaiting. The suspense is superb. . . . Barron brings historical mysteries to a new level."

—*Romantic Times Bookclub*

"A wonderfully intricate plot full of espionage and intrigue . . . The Austen voice, both humorous and fanciful, with shades of *Northanger Abbey*, rings true as always. Once again Barron shows why she leads the pack of neo–Jane Austens."

—*Publishers Weekly* (starred review)

Jane and the Prisoner of Wool House

"There's plenty to enjoy in the crime-solving side of Jane. . . . [She] is as worthy a detective as Columbo."

—*USA Today*

"A carefully written, thoroughly researched novel . . . An enjoyable, authentic portrayal of this classic author, a strong setting and a thoroughly enjoyable plot will convert new readers to the series as well as satisfy longtime fans."

—*The Mystery Reader*

"The mores and manners of Jane Austen's 19th-century world are brought skillfully to life in *Jane and the Prisoner of Wool House*. A skillfully told tale with a surprise ending."

—*Romantic Times Magazine*

Jane and the Stillroom Maid

"Barron does a wonderful job of evoking the great British estates and the woes of spinsters living in that era . . . often echoing the rhythms of the Austen novels with uncanny ease."

—*Entertainment Weekly*

"This work bears all the wonderful trademarks of the earlier titles, including period detail, measured but often sardonic wit, and authenticity."

—*Library Journal*

Jane and the Genius of the Place

"This is perhaps the best 'Jane' yet. The plot moves smoothly and quickly to its denouement. Barron's mysteries also educate the reader, in a painless fashion, about the political, social and cultural concerns of Austen's time. Jane [is] a subtle but determined sleuth."

—*Chicago Tribune*

"Barron tells the tale in Jane's leisurely voice, skillfully re-creating the tone and temper of the time without a hint of an anachronism."

—*The Plain Dealer*

By Stephanie Barron

THE WHITE GARDEN

A FLAW IN THE BLOOD

The Jane Austen Mysteries

JANE AND THE UNPLEASANTNESS AT
SCARGRAVE MANOR

JANE AND THE MAN OF THE CLOTH

JANE AND THE WANDERING EYE

JANE AND THE GENIUS OF THE PLACE

JANE AND THE STILLROOM MAID

JANE AND THE PRISONER OF WOOL HOUSE

JANE AND THE GHOSTS OF NETLEY

JANE AND HIS LORDSHIP'S LEGACY

JANE AND THE BARQUE OF FRAILTY

JANE AND THE MADNESS OF LORD BYRON

JANE AND THE CANTERBURY TALE

Jane and the
Madness of Lord
Byron

Jane and the Madness of Lord Byron

BEING A JANE AUSTEN MYSTERY

STEPHANIE BARRON

BANTAM BOOKS TRADE PAPERBACKS
NEW YORK

A Bantam Books Trade Paperback Original

Copyright © 2010 by Stephanie Barron

Published in the United States by Bantam Books, an imprint of The Random House Publishing Group, a division of Random House, Inc., New York.

BANTAM BOOKS and the rooster colophon are registered trademarks of Random House, Inc.

Library of Congress Cataloging-in-Publication Data
Barron, Stephanie.
Jane and the madness of Lord Byron: being a
Jane Austen mystery / by Stephanie Barron.
p. cm.
ISBN 978-0-553-38670-7
eBook ISBN 978-0-553-90780-3
1. Austen, Jane, 1775–1817—Fiction. 2. Byron, George Gordon Byron, Baron, 1788–1824—Fiction. 3. Women novelists—Fiction. 4. Poets—Fiction. 5. Upper class—England—Fiction. 6. Brighton (England)—Fiction. I. Title.
PS3563.A8357J338 2010
813'.54—dc22   2010010513

Printed in the United States of America

www.bantamdell.com

8 9 7

Book design by Caroline Cunningham

Jane and the Madness of Lord Byron

CHAPTER ONE

Summons from London

25 APRIL 1813
SLOANE STREET, LONDON

MR. WORDSWORTH OR SIR WALTER SCOTT SHOULD NEVER struggle, as I do, to describe Spring in Chawton: the delight of slipping on one's bonnet, in the fresh, new hour before breakfast, and securing about one's shoulders the faded pelisse of jaconet that has served one so nobly for countless Aprils past; of walking alone into the morning, as birdsong and tugging breezes swell about one's head; of the catch in one's throat at the glimpse of a fox, hurrying home to her kits waiting curled and warm in the den beneath the Park's great oaks. Spring—in all its rains and clinging mud, its sharp green scents full-blown on the nose, and a newborn foal in the pasture below the Great House!

And in this glorious season, too, a splendid change has come upon the little Hampshire village I call my own—for my elder brother, the rich and distinguished Mr. Edward Austen *Knight*, as he and all his numerous progeny must now stile themselves, having acceded to his benefactor's surname as well as his estates in Kent and Hampshire—has descended in state upon Chawton Great House, with his full retinue of trusted servants, under-gardeners, grooms, coachmen, and what I am pleased to call Edward's Harem: a hopeful clutch of motherless daughters, most too young to marry and still at home.

Edward intends to spend the better part of the summer in the antiquated pile that once was let to our dear neighbours, the Middletons, Mr. John Middleton having determined to give up the place when his treaty was run. While the Austen Knights idle away June and July in Hampshire, their principal seat—Godmersham Park, in Kent—will submit to refurbishment, the interiors having grown sadly shabby without Edward's late wife's care. It is quite a treat to have one's relations—and all the elegancies of table, coach, and society—but a stone's throw from one's door; and I spun many happy webs for myself that bright April morning, as I walked through the meadows, and listened to the song of a blackbird hidden somewhere in the hedgerow. Edward's eldest daughter, Fanny, is full twenty years old—and although a trifle *subdued* for my taste, and possessed of starched notions quite appalling in one so young, she must be adjudged a welcome addition to the Cottage circle, whenever she may venture through the village in search of trifles and laughter. It was possible, I thought, that Martha Lloyd and I between us might be of use to poor dear Fanny, in enlarging her spirit and mind—or at the very least, her capacity for wit. There is nothing so quelling in a young woman, I find, as a want of humour; but much must be forgiven the girl—she was thrust too young into the rôle of Mother, when Elizabeth died. Fanny cannot have been more than fifteen, then; and at twenty, must feel already as though she has lived two lifetimes, in managing her father's household. She is certain to find Chawton unutterably dull, however; the Assemblies in Alton are not such as she has been used to, in the elegant

Kentish circle she frequents. Was there, I wondered, any young man in the neighbourhood capable of engaging her interest?

Considering and discarding the various scions of local families as I walked amidst the dew-laden grass, I was full of pleasurable schemes that dreadful morning. Once Fanny was dismissed as too dear a prize for Alton's youth, my mind revolved the various attractions of an altogether different cut of gentleman—one Henry Crawford: for I have reached a most delicious point in the writing of my third novel, which is to be called *Mansfield Park*, when I must decide whether another Fanny (a sober and rather humourless young woman entirely of my own invention, though *not quite* my niece) is to make the roguish creature the Happiest of Men, or cast him into the Depths of Misery at a single word.

I had turned towards home after a brisk half-hour of exercise and rambling thought; when all at once it was as though a cloud moved swiftly across the sun, and my pleasure in the day was blotted out. The very air felt chill. I stopped short a good thirty paces from the Cottage door, a feeling of deepest dread in my heart—and for why? Only that a handsome chestnut hack was tethered to the post in the lane, one I recognised as my nephew Edward's mount. Why should a morning call, even one paid so unfashionably before breakfast, have the power to stop my heart?

I ran the final distance to the door.

My brother's eldest son and heir was standing before the fire, dressed not for hacking about the countryside in buckskins and boots, but for Town; his cravat meticulously tied, shirt points terrifyingly starched; a striped waistcoat trimly buttoned over primrose-coloured pantaloons. An Oxford lad of nearly nineteen, he had stiled himself a Corinthian of the First Stare; and it was this unwonted grandeur, as well as the expression of scared dignity on his young countenance, that informed me my heart had not erred. Disaster was in the air.

"What is it?" I whispered.

Cassandra came to me then, and enfolded me in her arms.

"An Express from Henry, to the Great House," she said.

"Has she gone?" I faltered. "And none of us aware?"

Edward cleared his throat. "Not quite gone, Aunt. But failing, Uncle Henry says. She is asking for you, I believe. Father says you are to travel up to London as soon as may be—in his chaise—and I am to bear you company."

"Edward!" I stared at him. "I am sure you should much rather be hunting rabbits on such a fine morning."

"So I should, ma'am," he stammered, "but under the circumstances—no exertion too great—should consider it an honour—wish most earnestly that you will accept my escort." He bowed stiffly, his face flushing with embarrassment. "Not the thing, you know—lady travelling entirely alone. Might very well be offered an intolerable insult. Besides, m'father commands it."

Edward, whom I cared for and cajoled so many years since, when his own mother died—to be offering me escort! I understood, then, the punctiliousness of his manner and dress. My nephew was representing his House—and paying off a debt of gratitude. I should be churlish to protest further; and besides, the hour was already advancing.

I uttered not another word, but dashed upstairs to throw what swift provision I could into a carpet bag. My beloved Eliza, Comtesse de Feuillide, wife of Mr. Henry Austen of Sloane Street—was *dying*. It seemed far too bitter a truth for Spring.

WHEN DID SHE FIRST APPREHEND HER MORTAL SICKNESS, I wondered for the thousandth time as the chaise jolted and swayed over the Hog's-back an hour later?[1] Was it so early as my descent on London some two years since, for the proofing of the typeset pages of *Sense and Sensibility*? She suffered then, as I recall, from a trifling cold, and took to her bed on the strength of it; but surely that was a deliberate indulgence, to avoid the necessity of attending Divine Service of a particular Sunday?

Eliza was never very fond of Divine Service; she had seen too much of Sin, to place her faith in either repentance or redemption; and she felt certain that the clergy were the very *last* sort of men to lecture their brethren—indeed, she declared the whole pious enterprise an essay in hypocrisy. Eliza preferred to live her life and leave her neighbours to live theirs, without the benefit of unwanted advice or inspection; and on the whole, I confess I admire her philosophy. There is a great deal of disinterested benevolence in it.

If not April of 1811, then, the illness came upon Eliza soon after: a mass in the breast, that grew until it might almost have formed another—with tenderness, increasing pain, and suppuration. She had watched over her mother's dying of the selfsame malady, years since. She recognised the Enemy.

My incorrigible Eliza. My *gallant* friend. A word for gentlemen of high courage—but courage she brought to this final battle, knowing full well she would never triumph. The summer months of 1812 she spent in travel—relished two weeks in the sea air of Ramsgate in October—wished me joy of *Pride and Prejudice*'s sale to Mr. Egerton in November (which met with decided success at its publication this winter among the Fashionables of the *ton*!)—and by Christmas was rapidly declining.

---

[1] The Hog's-back is a narrow ridge that runs between Farnham and Guildford; the road traveled by the Austens on their journey to London ran along the summit and offered excellent views of some six counties.—*Editor's note.*

And Henry?

I might have said that he has not the mind for Affliction; he is too busy; too active; too sanguine. All the increasing cares of banking—my Naval brother Frank being now a partner in Henry's concern—and the activity necessary to a gentleman in the prime of his life, must inevitably attach Henry to the world. Add to this, that Eliza is fully ten years my brother's senior, and that the gradual progression of the disease has offered an interval for resignation and acceptance—and we may apprehend the steadiness with which Henry meets his impending loss. And yet—his summons to me surely augurs an unquiet mind, a soul in need of comfort. To part with such a companion as Eliza! —Who, though she gave him no child, brought him endless cheer and laughter from the first day he met her, as a boy of fifteen, when she descended *à la comtesse* on the Steventon parsonage, and dazzled us all within an inch of our lives.

"I believe Uncle Henry intends to give up Sloane Street," Edward observed as we rolled into Bagshot. "He claims he cannot bear to meet with my aunt's memory at every stair and corner."

"Better to remove from London, then," I managed, my throat constricted, "for Eliza shall haunt every bit of it."

I HAVE KNOWN THE JOURNEY FROM CHAWTON TO RUN FULL twelve hours, when leisure permitted; but we were to have no dawdling nuncheon, no walking before the coachman in admiration of April flowers, no pause for fine views as we descended the final stage into the Metropolis. Barely eight hours elapsed from the moment I bade farewell to Cassandra at the Cottage door, until I found myself alighting in Sloane Street.

We met the surgeon, Mr. Haden, on the threshold—

Madame Bigeon being on the point of ushering the good man out, as we ushered ourselves within—and paused, despite a scattering of rain, to learn his opinion.

"I fear she is sinking, Miss Austen," he informed me somberly. "A matter of hours must decide it. I have left a quantity of laudanum—you are to give her twenty drops, in a glass of warm water, as she requires it."

"But Eliza detests laudanum!" I cried. "I have known her dreams to be frightful under its influence."

"Her agony will be the more extreme without it." The surgeon doffed his hat to Edward and me, and stepped past us to the street.

"Mademoiselle Jane!" Mme. Bigeon's elderly voice quavered on the greeting; she gave way that we might enter the hall, her black eyes filled with tears. "At last you are come! I feared—but it is *not* too late. She sleeps much, yes, but she will wake for you, *mon Dieu!* Come to her at once!"

With unaccustomed familiarity—such is the strength of feeling in the face of Eternity—the old Frenchwoman grasped my hand and drew me swiftly up the stairs. I could not stay even to loose my bonnet strings; and that I should be aware of such a nothing on the point of seeing Eliza, must be an enduring reproach. I am ashamed to own it.

Mme. Bigeon hesitated before the bedchamber door; it was ajar, so that I could just glimpse the outline of the bedstead, my brother Henry dozing in a straight-backed chair set up against the wall; and the silhouette of Mme. Marie Perigord—the old woman's daughter and Eliza's dresser, her constant reminder of all the glories of France that are gone beyond recall. Manon, as she is called, was seated near the bed, her sharp-featured face thrown into relief by the flame of a single candle; in her hand was a small bowl.

And beyond—

Eliza.

Her eyes were closed, her breathing heavy; a few damp locks of hair escaped from her white cap. There was a peculiar odour on the air—a sweet, sickly smell that emanated from the open wound in her breast, and the great tumor lying malevolently there; no amount of warm compresses or fresh linen could blot out the taint.

I crept softly to the bedside, young Edward hesitating behind me.

Manon rose and drew back her chair. "Monsieur—mademoiselle . . . I cannot persuade her to take any of the broth. And it is Maman's best broth, made from a pullet. Five hours it has been simmering on the stove—"

"Hush," Henry muttered, as he jerked awake. My brother's dazed eyes met mine through the shuttered gloom. "Ah—*Jane!* You are come at last!"

He rose, and pulled me close; the stale odour of a closed room, and clothes too infrequently exchanged, clung about his person. *Henry*—who is the nearest example of a Dandy the Austens may claim—had been neglecting himself.

"Praise God you came in time," he whispered.

"Mademoiselle!" Manon tugged impatiently at my sleeve. "Perhaps you will try? Perhaps she will take some broth from you, *hein?*"

"What does it matter?" Henry burst out, worn beyond bearing.

"But she must keep up her strength!" the maid protested.

Pointless to observe that strength would avail her mistress nothing, now.

Manon's face crumpled into a terrible grimace and she began, painfully, to weep, turning away from the awkward crowd of Austens as though we had caught her at something shameful. Mme. Bigeon swept her daughter out of the room, murmuring softly in her native tongue, half-scolding. I had an idea of the maid's high pitch of nerves, waiting in that darkened chamber through all the hours of a night and day as her mistress's life slowly ebbed, ears pricked for the sound of a particular set of horses halting in the street below. How like Eliza to hold on to the last, as though she knew I was hastening towards her!

But was she even aware of my presence?

"Dearest," Henry whispered, bending over Eliza. "Here is Jane arrived from Chawton."

Her eyelids flickered; the clouded gaze fixed for an instant on my brother's face, unseeing. How great a change was come upon that sprite, that eager, winning countenance! And how helpless I felt, unable to save her, to forestall the dreaded end!

I took up the bowl of broth and the silver spoon still warm from Manon's hand, leaned close to my dying cousin, and whispered, "Come, my darling, and try a little—to please your Jane."

Young Edward returned in his father's chaise the next morning to Chawton. The rest of us watched with Eliza so long as our spirits would allow, although in truth Henry was never from the sick room. He dozed upright in a chair, regardless of whether the Frenchwomen or I were attending upon his wife. For my own part, I snatched at sleep whenever one of the others relieved me—curling fully clothed on the comfortable bed in the best bedchamber. We ate what we could at odd hours, taking cold meat and tea in the breakfast room; Mme. Bigeon had no heart to cook, or rather her cooking was all for Eliza: possets, puddings, coddled eggs that were returned, one by one, untouched on their plates. Through the hours Eliza shuddered, and turned, her mind beset by the demons brought forth in laudanum; and though Henry and I would have stinted her, she suffered too much when the draughts were denied.

What did she mutter, as I leaned over her in the depths of the night? *Regret . . . regret . . .* Her fingers claw-like at my wrist.

The upright and devout would urge me to believe in a deathbed conversion—some softening of her pagan heart, as the life sped out of her—but I am too well acquainted with the little Comtesse. *I regret nothing, Jane,* she would wish me to know. *Regret nothing.* Not the madcap days in Marie Antoinette's train, or the careless disregard for reputation and finances, the husband lost to the guillotine; not the dashing promenades in Hyde Park with a score of beaux dazzled by her wicked dark eyes. Her dead son she might yearn for—wasted from birth by too many ills—but even Hastings could never figure as cause for *regret.* Eliza cherished the boy, heedless of a world that declared him little better than an idiot.

She shall sleep beside him soon.

This morning, near dawn, there was a change. The poor roving spirit stilled and her body went slack, the eyes tightly closed. The sound of her laboured breathing mounted until it seemed to fill the whole room—the airless weight of that room, its single candle glowing. Henry's hand clasped hers, but she seemed insensible of it; and at the last, with barely a flutter of its wings, Death entered the room. She turned her head once on the pillow, towards the window—raised herself slightly—and then fell back, a shell.

I waited, breath suspended. And apprehended that her breathing, too, was done—the very walls listened for it, every window frame strained; no sigh murmured back.

Henry stared at his wife as if willing her eyes to open. Then he placed her limp hand gently on the coverlet, and rose from his chair.

I would have gone to him; but the look on his face was terrible. He walked without a word from the room, and after a final glance at the still figure at its centre, I fled in search of the maids.

30 APRIL 1813
SLOANE STREET

~

ALL WEEK THE CANDLES HAVE FLICKERED BY HER BIER IN the pretty little salon she loved so well, where her Musical Evenings collected a gay throng and her morning callers were wont to sit; tributes of spring flowers arrived daily from Henry's colleagues and Eliza's acquaintance both highborn and low. Lord Moira sent a massive wreath of lilies; but I think I liked best the posy of wildflowers offered at the kitchen door, by one unknown fellow Mme. Bigeon assures me was Eliza's favourite hackney coachman.

Mrs. Tilson—the wife of one of Henry's partners and a near neighbour—came to call, and sat with me a half-hour in Eliza's boudoir; I cannot love her, but she forbore to express her displeasure at my sister's frivolities quite so forcibly as in the past.

Eliza is to be buried at Hampstead tomorrow, beside her mother and son; Manon and I shall wait only for the train of black carriages to depart, before quitting Sloane Street ourselves.[2] The poor maid is quite worn down with nursing Eliza, and could do with a rest in the country—I am to carry her off to Chawton, until Henry comes to fetch her. It shall be

---

[2] Women generally did not attend funerals in Austen's day.—*Editor's note.*

a comfort to have the Frenchwoman beside me, merely to dull the edge of grief.

The rain and bitter fog descended upon us today; Spring, it seems, is quite fled. Eliza's death comes as a presentiment, a weight of dark cloud sitting over the house; we are all of us growing older, Henry and I and the two Frenchwomen.

The Autumn of my life is come—my hopes of happiness long since buried in an unmarked grave—and how long, pray, shall the sun endure, before Winter?

CHAPTER TWO

An Interval for Reflection

IF MY THOUGHT WAS TO PROVIDE MANON WITH SUCCOR IN her time of grief, my impulse was misplaced, however well-intentioned. It is virtually impossible for a woman of middle years, who has served others nearly all her life, to leave off doing so, be she ever so eager to attempt the exercise. No sooner was Manon settled in a chair, with a bit of needlework to pass the time, than she must be jumping up and shifting the pillows for my mother's back; or helping Mademoiselle Cassandra with the gathering of the new peas; or busying herself in the kitchen about the boiling of the tea. I spent our first Chawton morning following her anxiously about, and urging her to leave such cares to others, that she might take a refreshing turn in the garden, where the syringa is in bloom—but she would have none of it. I therefore set her to fashioning my mourning gowns—for I would not appear a dowd in respect of Eliza's loss. Of all the women I have known, my late sister's passion for dress was insatiable. The task suited Manon's needle so admirably, and animated her instincts as a

Frenchwoman so well, that nothing would serve but that I must carry her into Alton for the purchase of such trimmings and lengths of muslin and silk as a country village might provide. We were not many hours returned from our shopping, with the packages sent round by dogcart, before I was summoned to stand before the tiny looking glass that serves Cassandra and me for doing up our hair of a morning, while Manon pinned and trimmed to her heart's content.

I was arrayed in a sober dark grey, with rosettes of black silk cord about the bodice, the following morning—Manon having sat up with work candles the better part of the night so that the gown might be finished. Overcome by this evidence of her devotion to her mistress, I apprehended—amidst my profuse thanks—that the unfortunate creature could not get a wink of sleep in any case, for the utter silence of the country, and was desperately in want of her beloved London's racket. Her exhaustion failed utterly to diminish her energy, however—the maid *would* look mumchance at the prospect of taking up a book in the chair nearest the fire— and so my mother set her to baking bread, and later despatched her to Alton's butcher and poulterer—which errand occupied so many hours, and gave her such a sense of importance, as a Londoner and a Foreigner in a country town, that I am sure her grief for Eliza was momentarily forgot.

As day followed day, however, I found myself seeking comfort alone in the out-of-doors, where I might walk towards the Great House in the hope of seeing Fanny or another of my nieces; I made no progress at all in the thorny question of Mr. Henry Crawford, and his possible salvation through the love of a pure heart. It was impossible to write at my little table in the front parlour, with Manon endlessly sweeping the floors.

It was with a measure of thankfulness, therefore, that I saw a travelling chaise draw up before the Cottage door this

Wednesday evening, and my brother Henry alight from it. There is no doubt that Manon is eminently useful about the place—but we are all of us fatigued beyond what may be borne, in finding out tasks for her.

"Jane," Henry said as he took my hand, "you look entirely recovered from your recent exertions."

"From the exertion, perhaps—but not the loss."

He inclined his head; we neither of us said anything further; we should not be reviving Eliza, after all, in talking over her end. But I could not like the cast of Henry's countenance—whatever repose I had found, in regaining the country, he had failed to secure in Sloane Street.

When he had paid off the coachman and directed the man to the Crown at Alton, where he might find stabling for his team, I slipped my hand through Henry's arm. He had exchanged his usual bright waistcoat for apparel of a sombre hue; the picture he made being so unlike our Henry that I suffered a pang, as though my brother, too, had gone into the grave with Eliza.

"Come inside. We keep shockingly *country* hours, as you know, but you are only a little late for dinner—Mme. Perigord will certainly warm something for you."

"How is she?"

"Pining for Town, I'm afraid. She holds our ways very cheap, in Hampshire. Other than the quality of our peas, she can find nothing to admire." I leaned towards him conspiratorially. "I confess I shall be heartily glad to have her off my hands, Henry! So much for benevolent impulse!"

"Yes—one tires of nothing so quickly as benevolence; and it is never valued as highly by the object as the giver!" The smile he flashed was *almost* the Henry of old. "Very well; I shall carry off my good French maid tomorrow, as soon as she has cooked us breakfast. She is sorely wanted at home.

For you must know, Jane, that I have in mind a scheme of re-moval—I have set old Bigeon about it already. I intend to give up Sloane Street—"

"So soon!" I interjected.

"—and live quite neatly and comfortably above my offices. Only think what a saving in the lease!"

"Indeed," I managed, having a sudden, sharp vision of the neighbourhood round No. 10, Henrietta Street—the building that houses Henry's bank. Covent Garden, in all its noise and bustle, its theatre linkmen, its throng of carriages and torch-lit entryways; its gentlemen swaggering among the Impures who ply their trade in the shadow of opening nights—is hardly the locale for an Interval of Reflection, so appropriate to one But Lately Bereaved. No, for a Henry stricken in grief, something wilder and more severe was required; something like the fall of the rocky coast at Lyme, or the noble crags of Derbyshire! What a pity it was not November! There is no nursing a grief in May. . . .

"Henry," I said as he pulled open the Cottage door, "I have had a capital notion. Should you not like to repair to the sea-side for a period, in order to take the air, and recruit your strength?"

"The seaside, Jane?" He frowned at me. "I thought you were wishing Mme. Perigord at Bedlam!"

"Indeed," I assured him. "You might seek the seaside *after* you have restored Manon to her mother. While the good Frenchwomen effect the removal of your things to No. 10, you might be taking restorative walks along the Cobb."

"The Cobb?" he repeated, bewildered.

"In Lyme," I persisted. "You will recall that poor Father was forever taking Cassandra and me there, and at the very end of the Season, too, when the town was dreadfully thin of company and the Assemblies almost run. Or perhaps Wor-thing—"

"*Worthing?*" His tone of revulsion was not propitious. "Jane, only such relicts of the country gentry as are tottering on the edge of their graves, seek to be known in *Worthing.*"

"Very well. Ramsgate."

He took me firmly by the arm and propelled me within the Cottage. The most delicious odour of roasted fowl still hung upon the air, but I am afraid the better part of the bird had long since been consumed, and the excellent Manon would already be thrusting the carcass into a soup pot; it was her decided passion, this affair of bones and broth.

"Henry!" my mother cried, and rose from her chair—not without effort, but with at least the suggestion of alacrity; for, after all, she is four-and-seventy. "My dear boy! We have all been so grieved—so *shattered,* indeed, by the passing of Eliza! How such a hearty soul can be taken, when I linger here, a burden to you all—"

He kissed her cheek, and she smoothed his hair, and for a moment as I watched them we might all of us have been thirty years younger—and Henry a boy of fifteen, returned from school.

"There will never be another like her, Mamma," he said softly, "as Heaven is daily learning—to its chagrin!"

"Come and sit by the fire," she said fondly, "while that busy French scold warms your dinner. You look fagged to death!"

"It has been a long, weary, and mournful winter," he admitted with a sigh, "but that is all to be mended."

"Indeed?" Cassandra murmured, with an anxious glance for me; it has long been her assertion that Henry is incapable of living alone, and will throw himself at the first well-endowed widow who offers. "Mended, you say? And so soon?"

My brother smiled. "Our sister Jane has a decided inclination to visit the sea. She believes that a period of exposure to salt air is as essential as balm to a wounded heart. You know her devotion to Eliza; they were sisters as much as cousins; and I think, after all her signal exertion during the past few weeks—her devotion to my wife in her final hours—that it behooves me to offer this small gesture of thanks. I have consented to bear her company on an expedition to the seaside."

"Jane?" my mother repeated, aghast. "But she is only just returned from London! Who is to put up the strawberries, if not Jane? And there will be no dealing with the butcher if Jane is gone off again!"

It is painful, in such moments, to learn exactly *how* one is valued by one's parents. But I was too diverted by the expression of mischief in Henry's visage to pay my mother much heed.

Her face darkened. "Do not be thinking to leave that Perigord woman on our hands, Henry! We should none of us survive it! An excellent creature in her way, I am sure—but so dreadfully *active*."

"She is to be gone on the morrow, Mamma. Jane's plan—"

I could not suppress a gasp at this; but Henry was always adept at effrontery.

"—is that once we have seen Manon safely restored to Sloane Street, she and I shall pursue our interval of reflection. A period of long walks about the cliffs—the refreshment of our jaded spirits—deep draughts of restorative salt air." He surveyed the room with a satiric eye. "We are bound, you see, for the wilds of Brighton."

BRIGHTON.

The most glittering resort of the present age, the summer haunt of expensive Fashionables, the exile-of-choice for every member of the London *ton* possessed of the careless means of securing a lodging—Brighton, where the betting is high on the horses raced with spontaneous abandon over the hard-packed Downs; where the Assemblies at the Old Ship are a crush of the highborn and the low; where the Prince Regent and his cronies hold indecent revels beneath the Chinese lanterns of the Marine Pavilion.

I could not conceive of a less reclusive spot for Henry to chuse, but before I opened my lips in a torrent of protest, a single thought arrested me.

How Eliza would have loved it.

They were a different sort of animal, Henry and Eliza, from the general run of retiring Austens. Not for them the solitude of Nature, the steadying influence of contemplation or prayer. Henry would never survive his grief by embracing melancholy; he was not an one to drape himself in crape, and sigh over the grave of his beloved. Henry seized at Life, and it is probable that his final vigil by Eliza's bed—the sleepless-ness and darkness, the nightmares of laudanum—were the closest he should ever come to Death's abyss. He had leapt over it now, and the brightness of pleasure called to him. Brighton, in all its strumpet glory, was *exactly* what he re-quired.

"Brighton?" Cassandra repeated, in a tone of bewilder-ment. "But is it not a very *vulgar* place, Henry, of decided dis-sipation? Recollect that it was in Brighton that poor Lydia Bennet made her fatal choice to elope with Wickham, in dear Jane's diverting novel. I am sure *I* should never care to go there."

"And due to your goodness, our mother shall not be en-tirely abandoned! You have my gratitude, Cass, for the sacri-fice." Henry placed his hand over his heart, and bowed. "But as to your scruples—I have it on good authority that the 10th Hussars are grown so respectable now Napoleon has immolated himself among the Tatars, that you need not be in a fret regarding dear Jane's virtue. She shall not run off with a red coat, while she is under my protection."

"Unfortunate," my mother sighed, "but we cannot be having everything. It is enough, perhaps, that she has the opportunity to be *seen*. One may meet with so many Eligibles in Brighton, I am sure—and though Jane is long since on the shelf, you cannot deny that her complexion improves with exposure to salt air!"

On this happy thought, my mother retired to her bed-chamber, while I thanked Henry prettily, if somewhat archly, for the treat he meant to bestow.

"Save your breath for Manon," he advised. "If that woman is to be credited, there is only one right manner of folding and packing gowns—and she will be busy with your trunk and silver paper the better part of the night."

I left him to recruit his strength with the remains of a pie, while I hurried above-stairs, certain that nothing like silver paper was to be found in Chawton Cottage—to discover my bedchamber strewn with the stuff, and Manon up to her elbows in my meagre wardrobe.

CHAPTER THREE

An Incident on the Road

I WAS TO LEARN WITH MORTIFYING SWIFTNESS THAT I OWN nothing fashionable enough for the display of Brighton; indeed, in our dusky clothes, Henry and I appear little better than a pair of crows flapping about this expanse of frivolous and sunlit shingle—but more on the vexatious subject of *dress* later. Having arisen at the first cock-crow, with a mizzle on the air, we bundled ourselves into the hired chaise and made with all possible haste to London, sparing only half an hour for our nuncheon at the White Lion in Guildford. Manon was the most anxious of us all to get on—having put Hampshire to her back, she could not be quit of the country soon enough. It was with an exclamation of incomprehensible Gallic relief that she alighted at last from our chaise, a mere nine hours and five days since she had escaped the confines of her adoptive city; and swept without a backwards glance across the Sloane Street threshold. We did not see her again that evening.

She was present, however, to wish us well on our journey

south the following morning—for Henry is incapable, I find, of resting long in the house where Eliza breathed her last, and nothing would do but that we must press on for Brighton immediately after breakfast. The journey being to be achieved in a curricle and pair, the sensation of air about the face was so delightful when the top was put down, just past Westminster Bridge where we gained the New Road, that I declared I should never wish to travel again in any sort of closed conveyance.

"—Until you are bound for Godmersham one wretched, chill November, and ready to sell your soul for a pan of coals at your feet and a glass of hot lemonade," my brother unkindly observed.

We were to change horses thrice, at Croydon, Horley, and Cuckfield. The Chequers Inn at Horley saw us arrived a mere three hours after we had quitted London, and it was not above half-past two when our third flagging team was claimed by the ostlers at Cuckfield. The King's Head is an easy, genteel establishment accustomed to the crush of visitors descending upon the seaside in the month of May; the landlord, one Puffitt, was at the door in his white apron, ready to offer Henry a tankard and myself anything I should require, while our team was changed for the last time.

I quitted the curricle, glad of the opportunity to ease my limbs, and began to pick my way through the mud of the yard. I had worn stout boots for the road, and was glad of my foresight; it had rained in the night, and the ground was uneven. I reached out a hand to steady myself against the cream-coloured body of a magnificent travelling chaise, bearing a crest I could not recognise upon its door; the owner had quitted it for refreshment in the inn, and the traces were already free of its team. As I touched the chaise, it rocked slightly, and a faint moan emanated from within.

I paused, and looked about. The tone of voice was female,

and rather young; surely no one had abandoned a *child*, and possibly unwell at that, to the ostlers' indifferent care?

No one spared me a look; I leaned closer to the chaise, and said low and clear, "Are you all right? Do you require assistance?"

The moan was repeated, louder and more urgently than before—a stifled sound, as though the girl would speak volumes if only she might.

"Henry!" I called out. My brother had advanced halfway to the innkeeper's smiling form; he was nodding, and saying a word—the request for porter, perhaps. He turned and searched for my figure. I beckoned to him, and with a frowning look he made his way back across the churned expanse of yard.

"What is it, Jane? Surely you have not allowed a bit of mud to stop you!"

"There is a child trapped in this chaise," I declared.

His brows rose in surprize. "Are you certain?"

A third moan, more strident if possible than the last, and a thumping sound, as tho' a booted foot had been thrust against the door.

"Good God!" my brother said blankly. "We must enquire of the chaise's owner, I suppose. He will have gone into the inn."

"Are you *mad*?" I reached up for the door handle. "The owner is undoubtedly kidnapping an innocent girl! Would you deliver her completely into his power?"

The chaise sprang open as neatly as a jewel box.

"Jane," Henry objected. "Do you not think . . . ?"

"Nonsense." The steps were as yet let down; I mounted them, and peered within.

A girl of perhaps fifteen, dark-haired and doe-eyed, was sprawled on the forward seat in a state of considerable dishevelment. Her wrists were bound before her, with what appeared to be a gentleman's cravat. A second length of linen was folded and tied around her mouth in a manner painful to observe. She stared at me imploringly, and made the same pitiful moan.

"Help me, Henry," I demanded, and drew off my gloves, the better to untie the knots that bound her hands. I made swift work of it—I was always adept at untangling skeins— and chafed her reddened wrists. She was already struggling to her feet, bent upon exiting the chaise as quick as might be, regardless of the gag about her mouth. She spared no thought for the bonnet and gloves abandoned on the seat beside her— she moved as tho' all the imps of Hell were at her heels.

I helped her into Henry's arms, then gathered her reticule and discarded belongings. Henry eased the sodden cravat from her head; being Henry, he paid infinite care to her tangled curls, unwilling to incommode the poor child further.

"Oh, pray," she whispered hoarsely when once the offending gag was removed, "hide me! Hide me quickly, before he returns!"

I grasped her elbow and would have instantly conveyed her to the curricle, but that my brother impeded my path. "Before *who* returns, Miss . . . ?"

"Twining," she replied, a bit more strongly now. "Catherine Twining. I have been abducted all against my will, and should have ended in wretched ruin had you not intervened, kind sir. Pray, do not deliver me back again into his hands!"

"No one shall hurt you," I soothed, "only you must tell us how you came here. Only then may we know how best to help."

Henry's colder eye had sought my own while the girl spoke; and without a word being said, I apprehended his meaning—there were some who might convey a rebellious child, blessed with a petulant temper, to her relations in another town in just such a manner—or send her off to a hated

Seminary for Young Ladies in the care of a servant, now gone to fetch lemonade—with her hands bound. Much as we might abhor such methods, it was not within our province to interfere. We were nothing to Miss Twining, and her governance could not be our business.

She swayed as she stood, peering about the stable yard in apparent terror; nothing less like the picture of rebellion could one conceive. Her flounce was torn, and I observed her hands to tremble as she felt her swollen lips.

"Who has done this to you?" I asked.

But Miss Twining was no longer attending. Her palpitating gaze was fixed on the door to the inn, where a second figure had joined the innkeeper: a gentleman by his air and address, clothed all in black, his shoulders broad and his countenance pale under a mass of dark curls. He was a stranger to me—and yet, there was a something in his profile that tugged at memory, as tho' I *ought* to know his name.

"Oh, Lord," Henry muttered under his breath.

The gentleman had evidently seen us; his countenance altered. A storm of anger blew across his brow, and he made purposefully across the yard, violence in every jarring step. For despite his appearance of youthful vigour—his inordinate *beauty* of face and form—he walked with a painful limp; his right foot was the culprit, and marred every step he made.

Beside me, Miss Twining let out a squeak—then fell senseless to the mud.

"Henry," I gasped, as we both bent to assist her, "who *is* that man?"

"George Gordon," he returned grimly, "Lord Byron. And if I do not mistake, Jane, he is about to challenge me to a duel."

LORD BYRON. THREE SYLLABLES, THAT IN ANY OTHER case—were they, for example, as commonplace as *Mr. John-*

son—should excite not the slightest interest. Mr. Johnson may claim neither the ready curiosity of the literary-minded, nor the excited beat of the romantic heart. But Lord Byron! — Who broke upon the notice of the Fashionable World but a year since, with the publication of his epic poem, *Childe Harold's Pilgrimage*—the tale, in verse, of a wanderer through Attic climes, which has aroused the passions of more females between the ages of ten and seventy than any work of genius in the last century or this; *Childe Harold,* which has actually set a fashion in dressing ladies' hair *à la grecque,* and has made of its author a Darling of the *haut ton; Childe Harold,* which drove no less notorious a sprite than Lady Caroline Lamb to make a public spectacle of herself, mad with love and bent upon exposing her poor husband to all the ridicule of his dearest acquaintance; *Childe Harold,* both cantos of which, published in succession, my lamented Eliza was good enough to send me by carrier, direct from Hatchard's book shop, and which I found (to my disappointment) I liked only moderately well.

"You have interfered in my concerns, sir," Lord Byron declared as he reached our little party. "And I must demand to know the reason for it."

"Any gentleman should have done the same," Henry replied through compressed lips, "had he witnessed the outrage visited upon Miss Twining's person. Now I must beg you to stand aside; she requires immediate attention."

My brother had lifted the girl's inert form, and meant to bear her into a private parlour; but Lord Byron stood firmly in Henry's path.

"Outrage!" he repeated. "She came to me willingly enough. I call it an outrage when a stranger meddles in affairs not his own. You will oblige me by depositing the young lady back inside her conveyance, sir. If you do not—I shall know how to act."

"Lord Byron—it *is* Lord Byron, I collect?"

The gentleman glanced at me smoulderingly. "That is my name. All the world seems acquainted with it."

"And thus the more reason you should behave with care. Not *all* publicity can be to your liking. We are in a posting yard, my lord. Do you wish to invite enquiry? Miss Twining shall not support your assertions. Indeed, she may well bring down the Law upon your head."

He held my gaze an instant; then observed the ostlers, racing to meet another carriage—full of Fashionables, by its appearance—with a second approaching behind. The traffic of the day was constant; who knew when he might encounter a friend—or an enemy?

"It is not *I* who would excite comment. You might end all conjecture by depositing her within my chaise," he said evenly.

But Fate, in the form of Mr. Puffitt, intervened.

"Ah," the innkeeper wheezed as he lumbered towards us, "overcome by the heat, is she, pore young thing? Do you carry your daughter into the house, sir," he said with a beaming nod for Henry, "and Mrs. Puffitt shall see as she's attended to."

"Thank you," Henry answered brightly. "I am sure she shall revive in a moment; she was never a stout traveller, I am afraid—you are very good, Puffitt."

Bowing to Lord Byron, the innkeeper gestured for us to precede him. Henry stepped carefully with his insensible burden through the mud.

I made to follow, but halted as a strong hand grasped my arm.

"You have won this round," Lord Byron muttered in my ear, "but do not flatter yourself the matter is done. I *will have* your brother's name and direction."

I stared calmly into his glittering eyes. What countenance

he possessed! The features nobly drawn, firm in every outline; the lips full and sensual; the pallor of the skin akin to a god's beneath the dark sweep of hair. It was the face of an angel—but a fallen one. Lucifer's visage must have held just such heartrending beauty.

"You might have had name and direction both, my lord," I replied, "had you behaved in a more *gentleman-like* manner." And left him drawing his gloves furiously through his hands.

"I AM MISS AUSTEN," I SAID QUIETLY, TAKING UP A PLACE by the bow window of Mr. Puffitt's private parlour, "and that gentleman is my brother, Mr. Austen. You are perfectly safe, now, Miss Twining. Lord Byron has gone. Do not attempt to speak, I beg of you, until you are somewhat recovered."

She had revived enough to open her eyes and gaze wonderingly around her; then she lay back upon the sopha and drew a shuddering breath. "Papa," she said faintly, "shall be so very *angry*."

"Papa will be only too thankful to have you restored to him," I returned. I searched in my reticule for a handkerchief—I was in ample possession of them, Manon having hemmed several dozen in black—and knelt down beside the girl.

"You have a smear of mud on your cheek. Will you not allow me to wipe it clean?"

"You are very good," she said gratefully, "but oh, Miss Austen, I wish that I were *dead*!"

"Come, come," my brother muttered, in some discomfort.

"Henry—do you go in search of brandy," I suggested.

He quitted the parlour with alacrity.

I dabbed at Miss Twining's cheek. "Nothing, in my experience, is quite beyond remedy—*except* death. I must encourage you to determine to live, Miss Twining. You shall un-doubtedly discover that tomorrow is a far better day than the present one."

She had begun to weep; I pressed a second—and far cleaner—handkerchief in her hand, and awaited the return of my brother with restorative spirits.

He appeared within a few moments, bearing a tot of brandy on a tray. For myself, he had fetched a glass of ratafia and a plate of biscuits; in his free hand he clutched a tankard.

"Drink this," I urged Miss Twining as I offered her the glass. "You shall be much the better for it."

"But Papa is *most strict* in deploring strong spirits as an in-tervention of the Devil," the girl said doubtfully. On closer examination, she was excessively pretty, with a naïveté of manner that encouraged me to think she had played no part in her own abduction; here was a victim of depravity if ever I beheld one. The clarity of her vowels and the ingenuousness of her manner betrayed the gentlewoman, not to mention *Papa's* care—God be praised there *was* a Papa somewhere—for her upbringing.

"Regard it in the manner of a medicinal draught," I or-dered, "and swallow the dose all at once. I assure you, it is by far the best way of downing the stuff."

She did as she was told, her eyes flying wide at the strength of the cordial; hiccupped; *coughed;* and then stared at me in outrage. "That was nothing less than liquid fire!"

"Very true," I said with amusement. "You are beginning to be restored to yourself. Now tell me, if you will, how you came to be in Lord Byron's charge."

The girl flushed to the roots of her hair, and set aside her brandy glass. She could not meet my gaze, I found, as though I were a governess intent upon scolding her.

"I am only a little acquainted with his lordship," she said, "and must confess that I have never felt any particular partiality for him. But it is—*was*—otherwise with him; he appears to have formed an attachment, and has pressed his suit most ardently in recent weeks, whenever he is in Brighton—for Brighton is my home, Miss Austen."

"And being unable to return his lordship's affection, you have repulsed his advances?"

She lifted her eyes to mine. "At every turn! We have only met some once or twice, at the Assemblies—he is but rarely in Brighton, being much taken up with Lady Oxford and her set, who remain fixed in London."

Lady Oxford—the Countess of Oxford—was rumoured to be Byron's latest paramour. A very great lady of some forty years of age, and the mother of five hopeful children—possibly by as many fathers—she had taken up the young poet as her latest lover, and kept him the whole of the winter at Eywood, the Earl of Oxford's estate in Herefordshire. Or so I had gleaned, from the veiled hints of the *Morning Gazette*'s Society pages. Now it seemed Lady Oxford's protégé was determined to play her false—with a girl young enough to be her daughter.

"His lordship *will* descend upon Brighton without warning," Miss Twining persisted, "to indulge his passion for sailing; and on such occasions condescends to enter the Rooms at the Castle of a Monday evening, or even the Old Ship—which Assembly you will know is held on Thursdays—from time to time."

This flood of information conveying very little to me, being a stranger to the town and its delights, I contented myself with a mere, "I see."

"His lordship never dances, however," the girl hurried on, "being ashamed, so they say, of his lame foot. But he often skirts the edge of the Assembly with one of his intimates—Mr. Scrope Davies, or Mr. Rogers—to whom he alone will speak; and being forced to sit out several dances myself, I have had some once or twice the privilege of conversing with him. I never sought his attentions, I assure you—tho' all the town is *wild* about Lord Byron, and celebrates his verses, and swoons at his every entrance—I cannot *like* him, Miss Austen. Indeed, he frightens me."

This last was uttered in a whisper; I saw the threat of renewed tears, and said hurriedly, "But this morning there was a change?"

She swallowed convulsively. "I am afraid I have been *very* foolish."

I glanced at Henry.

"I was strolling with my maid along the Steyne, intending to exchange a book at Donaldson's, when Lord Byron's chaise came up alongside. Or rather—I should properly say *Lady Oxford's* chaise, for it bears her ladyship's crest, and is excessively well-sprung—the squabs are straw-coloured satin."

"Indeed—it was an admirable equipage," I stammered. Lord Byron had used *Lady Oxford's chaise* to abduct another woman? "And his lordship invited you to take a drive?"

"He was all politeness. He told me he was bound for London, and should be deprived of my society for at least the next fortnight; he added that my cruelty should be beyond everything, did I not consent to spare him a few moments. He pined already for my society, he said; could I not bear him company so far as Donaldson's, so that he might cherish my image the length of his journey to London?"

The gentleman was, after all, a poet, and the most celebrated Romantic of our age; what girl of fifteen should be proof against such ardent address? Miss Twining had dismissed her maid, and ascended into the carriage.

"But he did not stop at Donaldson's," she said wonderingly, "and indeed, he urged the coachman to all possible speed, so that we bowled out of town along the New Road at such a pace, I was forced to cling to the side-straps in sheer terror!"

She had attempted to flee the carriage when it slowed at Lewes; and it was then that Byron subdued her, his superior strength and the natural fear she bore him, combining to render her passive when he produced his cravats. His lordship was so good, at that juncture, as to inform Miss Twining of her intended fate: he travelled not to London but to the Border—a journey of several days' duration—with a Gretna Green marriage in view.

Apprehending that after several days in the gentleman's sole company, her reputation should be utterly ruined, Miss Twining cried—she pled for his lordship's mercy—assured him that she could not love him; but her shrinking only inflamed Byron further. He was unaccustomed, it seemed, to rejection; the adulation of all the Polite World having convinced him that Miss Twining must be hoping for just such an avowal of ardent love.

"Marriage?" Henry repeated, all astonishment. "I had not thought Lord Byron much taken with the married state—unless it be to persuade those ladies already shackled with it, to break their sacred vows! He did you a decided honour, Miss Twining, in thus singling you out; you should be the wonder of your acquaintance, did they know of it. To make a conquest of Lord Byron!"

"Do not be so tiresome, Henry," I retorted crossly. "You must know that she abhors the man!"

Outside Lewes, Byron overmastered her, and assured Miss Twining that she should not prove so *missish* within a very few hours—for her honour depended entirely upon marriage, as she should be brought to understand. She screamed for the coachman's aid, at which Byron laughed diabolically, and gagged her mouth.

"And if you had not heard me moan, Miss Austen," she

concluded, "I should be entirely ruined. How I am to face Papa, I know not! He is sure to blame me—to be most *frightfully* angry—for fast behaviour in a female is what he cannot condone, and try as I might, I cannot regard my behaviour today as anything other than *fast*."

"We shall engage to put the matter before Papa in the proper light," I told her. "He should do better to set the whole of the blame at Lord Byron's door—and I shall urge him most forcefully to do so. His lordship must be called to account for his insult, or no young female in Brighton shall be safe! Your father's interview must be absolutely discreet, however—the preservation of your reputation demands it. Is it known where Lord Byron lodges, when he is in Brighton?"

"He keeps a suite of rooms at the King's Arms, against those occasions when the whim overtakes him to sail. He has been staying at the King's Arms a good deal, of late. . . . Oh, pray that he never returns!" Miss Twining cried.

"Undoubtedly he shall not," I agreed, "—gentlemen being loath to admit their losses, you know; Lord Byron shall find other fish to fry in London."

"The blackguard," Henry commented coolly. "And now, Jane, the team is put to—if we make haste, we might be in Brighton within the hour. Miss Twining, you will of course accompany us?"

LADY OXFORD'S CHAISE, WITH ITS OUTRAGED OCCUPANT, was nowhere in sight when we ventured into the stable yard. But I could not help noting, as Henry's curricle bore us away, two lengths of soiled linen lying trampled in the mud.

⅜ CHAPTER FOUR ⅜

Pleasures of a Prince

7 May 1813, cont.
The Castle Inn, Brighton

I FIND PROXIMITY TO THE SEA A DELIGHT ABOVE ALL others—one that is especially dear, in being the more generally denied. Some two years' residence in Southampton, and the example of my Naval brother Frank, taught me a degree of comfort with quays and small boats, the bustle to be found on every sort of waterfront, and I sometimes yearn for the vigour of that life in my present, quieter abode at Chawton. The desire for fresh salt air and the constant tumult of the tides overwhelms me, some once or twice, of a hot Hampshire noon. My acquaintance with watering places, however, is not great—on two occasions I have been at Lyme, so sweet in its autumnal association with vanished romance, that I wish still for another glimpse of the Cobb and the bathing machines at Charmouth.[3] Of Teignmouth and Sidmouth I

---

[3] Jane probably refers, here, to her entanglement with a notorious Lyme smuggler known as The Reverend, previously related in *Jane and the Man of the Cloth* (Bantam Books, 1997).—*Editor's note.*

have seen a little, and Ramsgate in Kent, and Worthing but twelve miles west on this same Sussex coast. Yet I have never braved the mettle of Brighton, at once the most breathtaking and outrageous resort of the present age.

Breathtaking, indeed, from the moment our curricle began its descent from the sweep of untenanted Downs, a rolling country of grassland that affords a magnificent view of the well-ordered town at its foot, and the sea beyond, dotted with shipping and pleasure-craft. The sun, just past its zenith, glinted on the stately white buildings as we approached; on a welter of Corinthian columns and Adam-esque façades, and the classical purity of the Marine Pavilion, the Regent's residence.[4] The New Road swung directly past its western lawns, so that a splendid view of the edifice—all but dwarfed by its massive new stable block, constructed in the Indian stile— was obtained directly upon entering Brighton.

We turned into Church Street, and the direction of Miss Twining's home.

She was deathly pale as the curricle pulled to a halt, and had to be lifted to the paving by my brother. We each supported her up the steps, and waited for some response to Miss Twining's pull of the bell. During the short interval from Cuckfield, she had informed me that Lord Byron took her up in his chaise at a few minutes past eleven o'clock; it was now nearly half-past four. Her poor Papa must be frantic with worry.

The heavy oak was pulled back; a bent form in livery stared impassively out at us. "Miss Cathy," it said. "You have been wanted these two hours and more."

---

[4] The exotic reconstruction of the Royal Pavilion, as it is now called, with its fantastic spires, onion domes, and quasi-Indian style of architecture devised by John Nash, was not begun until 1815, two years after this account.—*Editor's note.*

"Oh, Suddley!" she cried, and stumbled across the threshold. "Indeed I did not mean to run away!"

"Miss Twining has met with a sad accident," I said as I followed my charge within doors, "and requires rest and refreshment. She was so good as to permit us to escort her home. My name is Austen; if Miss Twining's father should care for an explanation, we should be happy to offer it."

"That will do, Suddley," said a voice from the far end of the hall.

He was a soldierly-looking man, endowed with Miss Twining's dark hair, but scowling in a manner assured to quell a more ardent spirit than his daughter's. "Well, miss? And what have you to say for yourself? Gadding about in hoydenish pleasures—making a sport of my name throughout Brighton, I've no doubt, and not yet returned from school a month! I do not know what is to become of you—I declare that I do not! A disgrace to your name, and your sainted mother's memory—Good God, Catherine, have you no conduct? Have you no shame?"

"Sir—" Henry started forward, part anxiety and part indignation.

"Father, may I present Mr. Henry Austen, and his sister, Miss Austen, to your acquaintance? Mr. and Miss Austen, my father—General Twining."

"And who are *they*, pray?" this personage demanded, as tho' we were absent from the room entirely. "It is unusual, is it not, to force one's notice upon young ladies entirely unknown to one? And in mourning too! I cannot think it becoming."

"It was *I* who forced acquaintance upon the Austens, Papa," Miss Twining returned tremblingly. "Indeed, they have been my salvation this day, and are deserving of considerable gratitude—but I should prefer to tell you *all* in greater privacy. May we not go into the drawing-room?"

"Very well," he said grudgingly. "But I shall offer no re-freshment. It is not my policy to reward impudence. En-croaching manners! Town bronze!"

He eyed my brother dubiously as he swung past Henry towards the drawing-room; a tall, spare man of advancing years—perhaps in his middle fifties—but still powerfully built, with a breadth of shoulder and a strength of limb that suggested the seasoned campaigner. His forehead jutted over deeply-set eyes of an indeterminate brown; his thin lips ap-peared permanently compressed, and his chin protruded pug-naciously. A man of ill-managed temper, I concluded, and frequent periods of oppression; an uneasy man to endure. He was dressed in dusky black rather than regimentals, and swung an ebony walking cane.

"It is a pleasure, sir, to meet any member of Miss Twining's family," I managed, hoping to spare our acquaintance further mortification; but her father was not inclined to tact.

"—Having assumed, no doubt, that such a forward young woman had no relations at all." He eyed her with disfavour as he ushered us through the doorway. "I understand you were taken up in Lord Byron's carriage, miss—oh, yes, you need not look so startled, the maidservant has been your Judas! Thought to elope with the Rage of the Ton, did you? And when did you discover your mistake? When the fellow achieved his object—then wanted no part of you?"

I thought it probable Henry would so far forget himself as to strike the General; his fist was certainly clenching at his side. I placed a restraining hand upon his arm.

"Your daughter was abducted, sir, by his lordship. She was discovered by my brother and myself at the stable yard in Cuckfield—bound and gagged and imprisoned in his lord-ship's carriage against her will. It is to her credit that despite her pitiable state, she was capable of crying out for succor; which plea we heard, and came to her immediate assistance.

Miss Twining cannot be held to blame; she is entirely innocent of the affair; and we must all congratulate ourselves that
she escaped with no greater injury than a swoon, and considerable chafing to her wrists."

The General's eyes bulged in his head; his countenance
empurpled; and with a snort he reached roughly for Miss
Twining's right hand—staring at the red weals on her arm.

"Disgraceful." His head snapped up to meet his daughter's
shrinking gaze. "Did you connive in this outrage? Did you
hope to run like a harlot from your old father?"

"Never, sir," she whispered. Her pallor was so extreme, I
feared she might faint again—and observed my brother take
a step closer, in the event she slipped to the floor.

"Little liar," the General said through his teeth, and struck
Miss Twining with his open hand against her cheek.

She did not cry out, nor did she faint; she simply swayed as
she stood, her face averted and her hand shielding the spot
where her parent's hand had fallen.

"General!" Henry burst out. "You forget yourself!"

"No, damme, but I know who *does*. Get out of my house
this instant, sir, and never darken its door again!"

"Papa!" cried Miss Twining, all her outrage in her looks;
the General might treat her like the merest chattel, it seemed,
but she would not see her friends abused.

"We shall leave you now, Miss Twining," I said firmly,
with a curtsey for the trembling girl. "I am quite sure when
your father is restored to calm, he will better apprehend how
blameless you have been today. If he should require further
corroboration of your excellent conduct, I am happy to supply it at any time. But now I would urge you to seek your
room"— I gave her an expressive look—"and place yourself
in the hands of your maid; you will be wanting supper on a
tray, I am sure, and an interval of quiet. General, we must bid
you good day."

I dropped the old renegade another curtsey, and rose to find his snapping eyes fixed upon my face. "Very well," he said unexpectedly, "you have my thanks for my daughter's deliverance from Lord Byron—however much I may suspect the tale, and the motives of every member of this party! We shall not speak of this day again. I cannot like a Twining's disgrace to be known to complete strangers!"

"Be assured, General, that we shall dismiss *every* insult we have witnessed, from our minds as soon as may be," my brother said evenly.

And having bowed our farewells at the door, and seen Miss Twining hastening above-stairs—we had nothing more to do than seek our rooms at the Castle Inn.

THIS PROVED TO BE ONE OF TWO PRINCIPAL HOSTELRIES that Brighton affords, a modern building replete with every convenience, including an admirable Assembly Room some eighty feet long, of which the servant offered me a glimpse while conducting us to our bedchambers. The ceiling must be half again as high, and surrounded by a delightful frieze in the Classical manner. A ball is held at the Castle every Monday, as Catherine Twining had assured me, and thus Henry and I shall be treated to all the Fashionables the town at present affords—swirling animatedly in a crush of music, heat, and scent.

Our apartments overlook the Steyne, the Promenade Grove—a pleasant enough arrangement of poplars, flowers, and darting paths—and just beyond these, the sea. We are fortunate in having descended upon Brighton in advance of the true Season, which may be said to begin in June; and thus may command a commodious suite of rooms: two bedchambers with a private parlour between. Tho' the furnishings are nothing extraordinary, they are just bright and easy enough to suit a seaside holiday. The whole adventure, indeed, wants only *Eliza's* careless frivolity to make it quite perfect.

—And at that thought, to my surprise, I fancied I caught an echo of my late cousin's bell-like laughter. I turned enquiringly towards the door, but no quick step passed it; I shook my head impatiently, and answered some query of the chambermaid's regarding the disposition of my things.

"SHOULD YOU CARE TO WALK, JANE?" HENRY ENQUIRED perhaps a half-hour later as he thrust his head into my room, "or are you famished?"

"Walk," I said decidedly. "The sea air alone shall give me an appetite—and I have it on the best authority that even the Prince Regent dines *early* at Brighton."

"You have been gossiping with the serving-girl, I collect."

"Who better to impart the holy rituals of the place? Her name is Betsy; she is not above twenty years old, and is exceedingly wise; she is a native of Brighton, and she urges me to order our dinner for six o'clock, with no fear of being judged unpardonably vulgar."

Henry's face lit up; I do not think he has enjoyed a meal since Eliza slipped into her decline, some weeks ago. "I shall bespeak a green goose, Jane, and some turbot—for we cannot dine in Brighton without a nod to the sea."

"Lobster patties," I said dreamily, "and champagne."

My brother laughed aloud. "You shall have to walk a good two hours, my dear, to merit such indulgence! But do you know—I believe that is exactly the menu Eliza should have requested, were she our companion in dissipation."

"She is, Henry," I said seriously. "She is."

We set out across the Steyne, intending to seek the Marine Parade, and spent a good hour ambling west along the sea-front. The day being well advanced, the more notable denizens of the town could be discovered in the Promenade Grove, where an orchestra dispensed music from an elevated platform at its centre, and the Pinks of the *ton* might ogle the Beauties who effected to admire the profusion of May flowers in the neatly arranged beds. Thus Henry and I, in our funereal black, had the Parade entirely to ourselves. There is nothing so bracing as a brisk stride against the wind, with a lowering edge of cloud on the sea's horizon, and the waves churning whitely at a safe distance. I felt my spirits rise inevitably, and I thought from the glint in Henry's eye as he surveyed an elegant vessel, well hove-over on her keel with her sails full of wind, that he had left his grief behind him. He is wise to quit Sloane Street, with its memories that should not soon be forgot, and its loneliness that might never be altered; he is the sort of man who must be *doing* things, and I admire him for it.

"What is to be your programme for Brighton, Jane?" he carelessly asked. "Or do you intend to closet yourself in your room for hours on end, scribbling at your latest *oeuvre*?"

"I am hardly proof against the temptations of this town, Henry! How am I to write, when so much that is delightful is spread before my feet! Better to set down my pen until I am back at home, and the rain of June has descended with persistence, and there is nothing but mud and desolation to be had out-of-doors. *Then* I might give thought to Henry Crawford, and the salvation of his blackened soul."

"You admire Brighton, do you?"

"I have never seen such a place. There is not a beggar or a blight from one end to the other! The buildings, the plants, the horses, the *people*—all perfectly elegant, all seemingly immune to the decay of nature! How the equipages gleam, and the shop fronts beckon! I should call it unnatural, and the result of witchcraft, were I not aware that a vast sum of money is necessary to its achievement."

"Money, indeed—and most of it drawn from taxing the British subject," Henry returned drily. "It is the pleasure ground of a Prince, remember, and one who is no stranger to debt. Brighton is carried on the backs of the most impoverished denizens of London, and by the nabobs of India; by the canny traders of Chinese cantons and the millworkers of York. But I daresay if you asked the Regent, he would claim credit for the whole."

It was true, of course—trust a banker like my brother to advise me of it. Paradise is never granted for halfpence. The Regent had achieved more than fifty years of age without ever having been called to a reckoning of his accounts; a more expensive Royal never lived. Parliament itself had been forced to relieve his debts; he had married his hated cousin, Caroline of Brunswick, merely to obtain a handsome allowance; and was probably a million pounds to the red side of his ledger at present. The Regent remained as enthusiastic as ever in his schemes for the improvement of Carlton House, in London, and the Marine Pavilion here, without the scantest consideration of such an ugly word as *cost*.

"You ought to have seen Brighton as I first did, before the Prince discovered it," Henry murmured, his gaze still following the sailing vessel, on which two or three wind-whipped figures could just be discerned. "It was called Brighthelmston then, and was the simplest of fishing villages—the Pavilion a modest farmhouse Prinny leased for the enjoyment of Mrs. Fitzherbert. They were said to spend the majority of their evenings playing at cards, with their intimates, and retiring early from exhaustion at the salt air. One wag noted that there were more sheep than people on the Channel Coast in those days! An utterly wholesome and rather poignant interlude, in the Regent's shameful career."

Maria Fitzherbert. Unfortunate woman! I could not consider her without a lurch of the heart—for I had made the acquaintance of the Regent's true wife, the twice-widowed and Catholic beauty who, even in her twilight years, remained devoted to the memory of the Prince for whom she had sacrificed reputation, respectability, and the best years of her youth. I knew such truths of that lady—how she had borne the Prince a son, and been forced to give the child up; nay, how she had acquiesced in sending the boy *out of the Kingdom,* unacknowledged by his legitimate family, and given over to the kindness of strangers, across the Atlantic in America.

I had never spoken of these things to Henry; I had been sworn to secrecy; and besides, they formed a part of my own life too painful to contemplate. It was Maria Fitzherbert who had watched with me, as the one man I wholly loved—Lord Harold Trowbridge—drew his final, shuddering breath. It must be impossible to hear her name without the face of the Gentleman Rogue hovering just out of reach, in my mind's eye.[5]

How perfectly marvellous his lordship should appear against this backdrop of sea and Fashion, this playing-field of the Privileged, striding towards us in his impeccably tailored black coat, careless under the gaze of the most lofty—for he was a duke's son, after all, and no one conveyed such excellent *ton,* for all his dubious reputation, as Lord Harold.

I do not like to see you in mourning, Jane, the Rogue's voice murmured in my ear. *Black does not suit you. You should go forever dressed in silk the colour of wine.*

"Are you feeling faint, Jane? Is the wind too chill for your liking?" Henry asked in concern.

I shook my head, and rallied with an effort. "You have proved the perfect antidote," I told him. "When I exclaim at Brighton's perfection, you recall me to the rottenness at its

---

[5] Jane recalls events recorded earlier in the journal account subsequently published as *Jane and the Ghosts of Netley.*—*Editor's note.*

core. I cannot like the Regent; indeed, when I consider his lack of gallantry towards the fairer sex, I could almost hate him. The Prince is no model for his subjects, and I must assume that Brighton has taken its likeness from its patron—a glorious exterior, wrapped about a hollow shell!"

"Enjoyable enough for a fortnight, despite all that," Henry remarked comfortably. "Do not become *missish*, Jane, when you may command a suite of rooms at the Castle! Now—you have not answered my question. I am at your disposal for at least the next ten days. What do you crave, for your dissipation?"

"Nothing very scandalous. I should like to walk each morning, Henry, and fill my lungs with the tang of salt air, so that I might remember it in August when the drone of bees is soporific in Chawton. I should like to make a trial of the waters, by hiring a bathing machine and taking a dip in the sea. I should like you to drive me along the Lewes road, so that I might have a glimpse of the 10th Hussars at Brighton Camp—I am sure that Lydia Bennet would wish me to see a place of which I have invented so much! I desire to attend the Brighton Races. I should like to dance at the Assemblies— but such a thing is not to be thought of, in our state of mourning; visit this Pavilion, for which it seems we have all paid so much; and take out a subscription at Donaldson's Circulating Library."

"The Library we might manage," Henry said dubiously, "but as for an invitation to the Pavilion—I confess that may prove to be above even *my* touch, Jane."

"I do not expect you to secure it," I retorted indifferently. "I shall undertake to do so myself. Lord Moira is an intimate of the Regent's; and when his flowers arrived in respect of Eliza, the missive bore his direction at the Pavilion. He is even now in residence. He shall not forget us, I am sure."

Henry looked impressed.

"But should his lordship fail me," I continued, "I shall learn to be content with reading. The Circulating Library is certain to have the latest publications. Perhaps even Lord Byron has been scribbling something—provided Lady Oxford accords him sufficient liberty."

"Could not Miss Twining supply the intelligence?"

"I should never distress her by alluding to his lordship, Henry!" I scolded. "But Miss Twining assures me that all the most respectable persons in Brighton may be found at Donaldson's. The ladies display their gowns, and the gentlemen consult the London newspapers, and members of both sexes play cards there of an evening. It would not do to be a stranger to Donaldson's. Besides, I wish to see how often my book is in request. If the Fashionables of Brighton do not constantly solicit the privilege of reading *Pride and Prejudice,* I shall find no good in them at all—even if Lord Byron *is* the writer most commonly claimed by the town."

"Again, Lord Byron! That gentleman has certainly seized your fancy!"

"Gentleman?" I repeated, astonished. "—Merely because he claims a title? He is *no gentleman,* Henry, and well you know it! But I confess Lord Byron *has* seized my fancy. I should like to make his acquaintance, and tell him in the strongest possible language my opinion of his Turkish treatment of Catherine Twining!"

"The fellow is a common blackguard, for all he is a lord," my brother returned. "One has only to consult his past conduct. I do not regard his current *inamorata*—Lady Oxford is an established woman of the world, and entirely mistress of what she is about; but consider Lady Caroline Lamb! And her unfortunate husband! *There* one may justly say that hatred for the tender sex, as much as love, has animated Lord Byron."

My brother's intimacy with the Great, tho' it sprang from

his banking trade rather than privileged birth, had made me familiar with the names and histories of the gossiping *ton*. I had even seen Lady Caroline Lamb some once or twice during my sojourns in London; Eliza had been on nodding terms with her ladyship. Caroline Ponsonby was born the Earl of Bessborough's only daughter; her mother, Lady Bessborough, formed a vital part of the Devonshire House Set; her aunt, Georgiana, was Devonshire's first Duchess. I was once acquainted with the Cavendish family, during a precious interval in Derbyshire some years ago, when Lord Harold—an intimate of Chatsworth—introduced me to the family's notice. Caro, as she was called, had grown up in the chaotic and amorous atmosphere of that great Whig establishment, and had emerged as one of its chief eccentrics. Brilliant and charming in conversation, faerie-like in her figure, outrageous in her behaviour, Caro Ponsonby was apostrophised the Sprite by her gallant admirers and took London by storm in her first Season, when she was but seventeen. William Lamb, heir to Viscount Melbourne, married her two years later; and for nearly a decade now had endured her tantrums and scenes. Tho' Caro screamed hysterics at their wedding, tore her gown in a passion, and was carried fainting from the room, this was considered nothing out of the ordinary Devonshire way—and so William and his Caro determined to be happy. They read Great Works together all day, that Caro might complete her education, and went into Society all night; dressed their pages in a livery of crimson and chocolate; and once sent Caro to the dinner table, naked beneath a chafing dish, as amusement for her relations and friends. A notable Whig orator, William Lamb stood for Parliament and was rumoured for a Cabinet post—until George Gordon, Lord Byron, burst upon the scene with *Childe Harold* last year.

His lordship has said that he awoke upon the day of his

poem's publication to discover that he was famous. Certainly no one has shot from obscurity to fame as swiftly before. The street outside his lodgings was blocked with fashionable carriages delivering endless invitations; publick riots broke out whenever his lordship walked abroad. It was inevitable, in such a general fever of admiration, that Caro Lamb must pursue him. Byron's looks and verse alike were calculated to inflame her wild imagination; all decorum and propriety forgot, she committed every publick folly—riding openly with him in Hyde Park; entertaining him at Melbourne House, where he mounted to her rooms by a back stair; loitering outside the doors of gentlemen's clubs in the livery of a page. She was said to have entered his rooms by the upper-storey windows, a feat only a monkey might have performed. And like a monkey, she grew a dreaded nuisance on Lord Byron's back.

Once ardent and attached, he became, in a matter of mere months, indifferent and cold; met her protests and pleas, her hundreds of letters, with formal refusals; and in sum, cut the connexion dead.

It was as tho' he had studied the character of my Willoughby, confronted with an unreconciled Marianne, in his calculated cruelty.[6]

Caro, for her part, became nearly lunatic: stalking her Love by night or day; refusing food, refusing sleep; running out into the street, hatless, to pawn her jewels, with the intention of taking ship alone for God Knows Where, provided it were far from England and the desolation of her heart. Alternately disgusted and enthralled by her persistence, Byron played with the lady as a cat might with a mouse—and reduced her to a state of mental and emotional incapacity.

[6] Jane refers here to one of the principal thwarted romances in her first novel, *Sense and Sensibility*, published in 1811.—*Editor's note.*

William Lamb has stood by his wife, but declined to stand again for Parliament. His misery may be observed at any private gathering of the *haut ton,* by whom he is generally supported.

"Lord Byron *does* appear to confuse love and hatred," I admitted to my brother. "There was nothing very tender in his treatment of Miss Twining today—and yet he must be violently in love with her, to attempt a flight to the Border!"

"Perhaps he is simply mad," Henry replied. "A thread of misfortune dogs the Gordon family—and the men die young and violently, it is said."

Mad.

A poet touched by the insane.

A diabolical figure of licence and flame, armed with a pen.

Little as I could like him, I should wish to know more of Lord Byron. So few real writers ever come in my way. Perhaps, if I am *very* lucky, his lordship might yearn to sail again during my stay in Brighton.

CHAPTER FIVE

A Patron of Donaldson's

THE LOBSTER PATTIES WERE ALL THAT COULD BE DESIRED, the champagne beyond anything I had yet imbibed; and I fell into a dreamless sleep from the moment my head hit the pillow—despite the considerable degree of noise from both within and without the Castle Inn. A party of officers from the Brighton Camp had stormed the neighbouring King's Arms publick house, with a number of women from the Cyprian Corps—as the local members of the Muslin Company are known, in deference to their military service—and the echoes of rowdy laughter were the last I heard before insensibility claimed me.

I awoke to a sparkling sea under a brilliant blue sky; a freshening wind; and the chambermaid Betsy, who kindled a fire and placed a pot of tea on a silver tray directly next to my bedside—which unaccustomed luxury quite resigned me to the depravities of the Prince's chosen pleasure ground. Henry had been correct in turning to Brighton: where I should certainly have fallen into melancholy at Lyme, nursing my grief for Eliza amidst the desolate cliffs and ravines that mark that wilder coast, I could not help but be cheerful in such a place on such a morning—and hoped that the little Comtesse forgave, and somehow approved, my selfish happiness.

I informed my brother at breakfast that I meant to secure my subscription to Donaldson's without delay, having left Chawton so swiftly that I had brought little in the way of reading material—only my scribblings of *Mansfield Park,* in the small hand-sewn booklet of paper I construct for composition. I confess that the thought of sober Fanny Price held little attraction this morning, in the face of Brighton's charms. She is often a tiresome creature—very nearly as quelling as my sister, Cassandra, when she believes herself to be in the right, which is on almost *every* occasion; and did I open the composition book, I should be certain to hear Fanny's reproofs ringing in my ears each time I dawdled before a shopwindow. It was not to be borne. Therefore I tucked *Mansfield Park* into a bandbox for safekeeping. I do not expect to require that bandbox until I am forced to return to Hampshire.

"I shall accompany you, Jane," Henry said with alacrity, "that I might have a glance at the morning papers—and learn whether any of my acquaintance are in town."

Donaldson's being but a few steps across the Steyne, our object was very soon achieved. It was a handsome establishment, equal to any circulating library I had experienced in London, and far surpassing those of Bath—elegant, airy, and possessed of a large collection of books neatly bestowed on its shelves. The principal papers and important periodicals were arranged on broad tables, for the greater ease of perusal; and an extensive suite of rooms, becomingly draped and fitted out with occasional chairs, led to apartments at the rear, where card parties were held.

"We are pleased to offer musical recitals on certain evenings," Miss Jennings, the excessively genteel proprietress, informed me; "and I think you will find the company most select. Madame Valmy, late of Milan, is to sing airs in the Italian for us tonight."

"And the subscription?"

"Is five shillings the week," she returned—which dear sum I offered her with an indifference I should not have been equal to, a few years since. The return on my labour of love, however—my investment on the 'Change of *novel-writing*—permits me these little luxuries. I have been so happy in the publick's reception of *Pride and Prejudice,* which may actually run to a second edition, as to observe a set of the volumes prominently displayed among Miss Jennings's offerings.

When her clerk had pocketed my fee, and written my name in the subscribers' book, I enquired with affected carelessness, "I see that you have that interesting novel everyone is talking of—*Pride and Prejudice.* I wonder you may keep it on your shelves!"

"Indeed, I believe the story to be all that is charming," Miss Jennings said complacently, "—tho' there are some who will insist it is unpardonably vulgar. To be forever speculating on the matter of *fortune* in marriage is to appear unpleasantly mercenary—for even if the two *are* inseparable, it does not do to say so. I confess there is just *that indelicacy* in the notion of husband-hunting that argues against the work having sprung from a lady's pen, however boldly the papers may have advertized it as such."[7]

"And yet," I could not resist observing, "so many young ladies profess to enjoy it!"

[7] The first edition of *Pride and Prejudice,* published by Thomas Egerton in January 1813, was acknowledged as having been written "*by the Author of* Sense and Sensibility"—which had been written anonymously "by a Lady." Later newspaper advertisements transposed these words as: "by Lady A—.," which gave rise to much speculation regarding the identity of the supposedly noble authoress.—*Editor's note.*

Miss Jennings's delicate brows knitted in distress. "Indeed—indelicacy is all the rage! How else might one explain the success of Lord Byron? But it is true that *Pride and Prejudice* was greatly in request among the *ton* when it first appeared in January. I spend the better part of the winter in London, you must know, and was wont to hear of it everywhere. And so Donaldson's purchased several sets of the novel on the strength of my regard—but the volumes are less in request at present, the entire world having already looked into them."

"That must be sadly distressing for the author!"

"Fame is fleeting, Miss Austen—as even Lord Byron shall discover by and by, I daresay. Should you like to take the set on approval?"

I could not suppress a smile. "Unfortunately, I, too, have read rather more of Miss Eliza Bennet than is good for me."

Miss Jennings's eyes sharpened. "And what is your opinion, pray? Do you believe the tale to have been written by Mr. Walter Scott, as so many profess to do? No less an authority than Mr. Sheridan, the playwright, assured me it was one of the cleverest things he has ever read—and you know he must be considered a fine judge of words, however embarrassed his circumstances."

"Perhaps he wrote it himself," I suggested idly.

"That is *just* what I think," Miss Jennings returned warmly. "It has that lively flavour—that rapier wit—we may recall from Mr. Sheridan's early work. And he should never hesitate to comment on the rapacity of fortune-hunting mammas with daughters on the Marriage Mart, having been yearly witness to their triumphs! Indeed, I am sure the whole is *far* too clever for any lady of my acquaintance. We have not the brush for so broad a canvas."

"You are severe upon our sex!" I cried.

"Miss Jennings is severe upon the whole world," observed

an amused voice behind me. "Surrounded as she is by opin-ions—printed or voiced, wise or illiterate—she has fodder enough for a lifetime's contempt."

I turned. And beheld a visage I had not seen in many years: the lovely face of Desdemona, Countess of Swithin—the niece of my late, lamented, and never to be forgotten Lord Harold Trowbridge.

I FIRST MET LADY DESDEMONA NEARLY A DECADE AGO, when she was barely eighteen and at the height of her first Season. The years which intervened between that occasion and this, have greatly altered both our fortunes. She has be-come the wife of the man she would have fled, when first I knew her; and has grown in consequence as a formidable Whig hostess, presiding over one of London's most fashion-able salons. Allusions to her name, discreetly abbreviated in the accepted mode as *D., the C. of S———*, appear from time to time in all the principal papers; she moves (with an occa-sional hint of scandal—she *is* a Trowbridge, after all) among the most exalted in the land; her taste in dress is everywhere approved and generally copied; and her dashing perch phaeton with its team of blood chestnuts is a piquant sight in the Park of an afternoon—for she is an accomplished driver, and to be taken up beside the Countess is considered a great mark of favour.

All this I know purely as an interested observer: for Des-demona long since dropped my acquaintance. We met when I lived in Bath, at the behest of her uncle, the Rogue; she was a headstrong and willful young lady then, who learnt at her cost the value of respectability. The circumstances of Lord Harold's death—my apparent complicity in those events—and his lordship's bequest to me of a valuable cask of private papers, have alienated the interest and affection of the Trowbridge family. In short, I should not have been surprised had the Countess discovered my identity at a glance, and immediately cut me dead.

Instead, I was saved by the remarkable Miss Jennings.

"Your ladyship will give the world a very poor opinion of me," she said roundly, "and just when I had hoped to pass myself off with some credit! I was forming a new acquaintance. But Miss Austen will forgive me, I am sure, if I claim the press of business. There is always a crush at Donaldson's! How may I serve your ladyship?"

"Miss Austen," the Countess repeated, and studied my visage searchingly. "I should not have believed it possible!"

Am I, then, so wretchedly altered from 1804? It must be inevitable that the countenance of nine-and-twenty is fairer than that of seven-and-thirty; and I shall be eight-and-thirty this December. I am becoming an old woman, tho' I resist the knowledge.

"Miss Austen, in *Brighton,* of all places!" Desdemona continued. "No, I should not have believed it possible. I think of you perpetually in Bath, tho' why I should—It is a habit, I believe, or perhaps a failing in all of us, to fix our friends forever in the life we last knew of them. But how delightful to meet with you again!"

Delightful? She must have forgot the coolness of her parting letter, the implicit reproaches, the suggestion that I had been, perhaps, something disgraceful—her uncle's mistress, and had learnt to profit by it.

"I shall leave you now," Miss Jennings said briskly, "in the hope of seeing both of you often within Donaldson's. Do not forget, dear Countess, Mme. Valmy's concert this evening!" And she moved off in the direction of my brother—who was absorbed in conversing with a gentleman in buff pantaloons and a blue coat whom I did not recognise, and another I knew at once for Henry's banking client Lord Moira—Eliza's inveterate admirer.

"My lady," I said to Desdemona with tolerable composure, "you are well, I hope?"

"Very well, I thank you."

"And the Earl?" I could not enquire after her family; that must be taken as an impertinence—a reference to her father, the Duke of Wilborough—who had believed me a potential blackmailer, and very nearly threatened me with a court of Law.

"Oh, Swithin is in his usual roaring health," she said carelessly. "Nothing ever ails him, you know—he is disgustingly stout, unless one requires him to do what he does not like. But you, Miss Austen! How long has it been since we have met, I wonder?"

"Very nearly ten years."

"And you have not altered in the slightest," she said warmly, if untruthfully. "But I observe you are in mourning. May I offer my sympathy? A near relation, I collect?"

A lesser woman might have uttered unforgivable things at such a moment—*A paramour, perhaps? You are come into someone else's ill-gotten gains, I collect?* But she did not condescend to lash me. I do not think I should have been so benevolent, were our positions exchanged.

"My sister, Mrs. Henry Austen," I said with difficulty.

"The Comtesse de Feuillide?" The shock in her voice was audible as she gave Eliza her French title—how Eliza would have revelled in the notice! "I *am* sorry to hear it. I recollect her a little from our meeting in Bath—she was the gayest of creatures."

"Indeed."

"Well." Desdemona inclined her head, and held out her hand; for a fleeting instant, there was something of the Gentleman Rogue in her look, a flash of the satiric in her eye. She was as well aware as I, how magnanimous she was being.

I took her hand, and curtseyed.

"Now that we have scraped our disreputable acquaintance," she told me, "I hope we shall no longer be strangers— in Brighton, at least. It is a town for easy manners, you know. Do you make a long visit?"

"But a fortnight, I believe."

"And you are lodged . . . ?"

"At the Castle."

"Excellent! So perfectly to hand!" She reached into her reticule and offered me her card. "Swithin has taken a house for us on the Marine Parade, tho' he is hardly ever there. I shall hope to find you in my drawing-room one morning, Miss Austen."

And with that she passed on, to bespeak of Miss Jennings the latest verses of Lord Byron, the name of which she had forgot, but which her friend Lady Oxford assured her were most extraordinary.

CHAPTER SIX

Encounter at the Camp

"WHAT DO YOU THINK, JANE?" MY BROTHER EXCLAIMED as I perused the fashion plates of *La Belle Assemblée*, the latest edition of which was in considerable request among the patrons of Donaldson's. It was clear from the exquisite modes draped on the impossibly tall ladies represented by the artist's brush that I was fortunate in being obliged to wear black; not even the hundred and forty pounds I have earned from *Sense and Sensibility*—much less the hundred and ten Mr. Egerton gave for the copyright of *P&P*—should purchase a wardrobe suitable for Brighton. Spring fashions ran to jonquil crape, Nakara silk—a pearly shade ideally suited to a lady of my colouring, and which I guessed had been exactly the hue the Countess of Swithin was wearing—and apple green. Slippers were beaded and embroidered to match; pelisses of white jaconet, falling just to the knee, were buttoned over gowns; and a profusion of frills graced hemlines this season, which had risen above the ankle to reveal *patterned stockings*!

"Jane," Henry repeated, somewhat more stringently this time, and I set down *La Belle Assemblée,* only to see it immediately taken up by the lady on my left.

"What is it?" I asked with pardonable crossness.

"The Regent."

I glanced about me wildly. "In Donaldson's?"

"Good God, no. In *Brighton.* Lord Moira informs me that the Prince came down from London but two days ago, and already intends a Reception at the Pavilion this evening. We are both to go!"

"But would it be entirely proper? Recollect that we are in deepest mourning—"

"Piffle! I should not like to be seen dancing at an Assembly, Jane—but the crush of the Pavilion on Reception evenings is akin to that of Picadilly Circus; one may meet the world there, and be jostled about in the greatest discomfort, in an attempt to pay homage to the Crown."

"Little as I admire the Regent, I cannot think that Eliza would forgo such an opportunity," I admitted doubtfully.

"She should be wild to see the Pavilion—and all the quizzes who frequent it—and moreover, should already have secured the cards of invitation herself; for you know she was a little acquainted with Prince Florizel, as he was known in his elegant youth. But I have had our cards expressly from Colonel McMahon—he is the Regent's private secretary."

"The gentleman in buff and blue, I collect?"

"All of the Regent's intimates sport that livery. McMahon had only to hear my praise from Lord Moira's lips, to beg the honour of our presence. Do consider, Jane! The notice of the Regent! What a spur to my banking concerns!"

"—Or a possible run on them. That gentleman's pockets are perpetually to let; and you should be bankrupt in little more than a week, did his notice prove too great."

Impervious to caution, Henry merely grinned. "Our retiring Jane, amidst the Carlton House Set! How Mamma should stare!"

"She should suffer palpitations," I corrected, "and utter a vulgarity. She cannot help but do so—which is the spur, no doubt, to her daughter's deplorable novels."

"Who dares to say that your books are vulgar?" Henry demanded, momentarily diverted.

"The proprietress of Donaldson's," I returned dejectedly. "She abused *Pride and Prejudice* as mercenary, Henry, and not fit to spring from a lady's pen."

"As to that," he drawled, slipping my arm through his and leading me towards the door, "you should hate far worse to learn it was called *dull*, and that nobody of consequence could look into it without yawning. You must know by now, Jane, that your books are all the crack! You ought to be in high gig! I have half a mind to bring you into Fashion—see if you do not hear *P&P* spoken of, at the Pavilion this evening!"

"Henry," I said, in a voice heavy with suspicion, "you are not going to *puff off my consequence* before McMahon and his ilk, are you?"

"Puff off—! Where do you learn such cant expressions, Jane?"

"From my vulgar mother," I rejoined calmly, "and my fashionable brother. Promise you will not expose the secret of my authorship. I have a dread of its being generally known."

Henry cast up his eyes to Heaven. "I cannot think why. I should be proud as a peacock, had I done anything half so clever!"

"And I should as soon ride bareback at Astley's Amphitheatre as admit to publication! Were my identity known, I could not walk at liberty through the village of Chawton! I should be suspected as a spy at every dinner table, every Assembly—and I should never be so frank, Henry, in my expressions; or so faithful a depicter of the world and its follies. Anonymity accords me freedom to speak as I find—and I cherish freedom above all else!"

"Lord knows you have had little enough of it," he answered soberly. "Very well—I promise to guard your secret. Tho' it shall go hard with me! Do you not apprehend, Jane, that your whole family is bursting to boast of your accomplishments—that we are all devilish *proud* of you?"

"Then praise the novels rather than their wretched author," I told him roundly, "and inflate Mr. Egerton's sales! You cannot display your pride more profitably, or in a manner more suited to my taste; for I mean to have one of those gorgeous confections," I added with a nod towards *La Belle Assemblée*, "as soon as I have put off my blacks."

WE DAWDLED ALONG THE SHOPS OF NORTH STREET, stopping now and again to admire a particularly fine picture displayed in a window, or a daring hat, or a zephyr cloak such as might have driven Eliza wild; and after taking a cold collation in a parlour at the Old Ship, drove out in a hired gig along the coast. All manner of natural beauties may be found to the west of town—the fall of boulders known as The Rocks, at the mouth of a little inlet just brushed by the road near Southwick—and the natural wonder called Egypt, just shy of Shoreham, which looks to be the work of antique Pharaohs in its scattering of monoliths, standing upright amidst the sea. With the wind on my cheeks and my curls whipping from beneath my bonnet, I might almost have been nineteen again—and felt lighter of heart than I had in all the sad weeks since Eliza's decline.

On our return to Brighton, Henry elected to drive out a mile or two along the Lewes road to the encampment of the 10th Royal Hussars—being an inveterate Paymaster, my brother must needs renew acquaintance among the officers; he can never be entirely at his ease, even at a watering-place, but must be about the business of winning custom wherever it may offer. As his conversations could in no way include *me*, I was at leisure to walk about. I had alluded to Brighton Camp in *Pride and Prejudice*, without ever having seen it—and thought it should prove very good sport to learn how much the truth differed from my invention.[8]

There is much colour in the general scene, for the Prince of Wales Own, as they are called, are scrupulous as to the quality of their horses, their curricles, and their uniforms. They are among the most dashing set of men in England, and betray little sensibility of their losses in the Peninsula, at Corunna and Vittoria. Their manners, when in possession of their senses and not foxed from the bumpers of brandy they are known to take at all hours of the day, are elegant in the extreme; and so I suffered no impropriety or insult—on account of my black clothes, and matronly cap, and general appearance of outworn looks. There are silly girls enough for hanging on the sleeve of every red coat—and one of my advanced years must appear in the nature of deserted chaperon.

It was with a start, therefore, that I heard my name called in an excited accent. Turning, I observed Miss Catherine Twining, accompanied by her father. She was dressed with extreme propriety this morning, in dove-grey muslin drawn up to the neck and a dark blue spencer; a close bonnet concealed her glossy chestnut curls; her eyes, however, were sparkling with delight.

"Miss Austen! What good fortune! Is it not remarkable that we should meet again, within a day of our first acquain-

---

[8] Henry Austen began life as a banker when he was appointed regimental paymaster of the Oxfordshire Militia at the age of twenty-six—the year he married Eliza de Feuillide, his widowed cousin.—*Editor's note.*

tance? I must ascribe it to the workings of Fate!" Miss Twining cried.

"Providence, rather," the General corrected drily, "who
sees all and orders all. I wonder you have the courage to call
down His notice, unfortunate child."

Miss Twining's pink cheeks blanched; her imploring gaze
fixed on my countenance.

"General Twining," I said with a curtsey. "Miss Twining. I
hope I find you fully recovered from your ordeal of yesterday?"

"We were not to speak of it!" General Twining looked all
his rage. "I *wonder* at your insolence, ma'am! And your lack
of delicacy! Indeed, I must suspicion some dark purpose in
your deliberate allusion to events that cannot too soon be forgotten. Understand, Miss Austen, you shall never hope to
profit by your shameful knowledge."

"Profit?" I repeated, bewildered.

The obsidian gaze swept over my figure. "Was it *that hope*
that brought you to Brighton Camp? A handsome sum, perhaps, in exchange for the preservation of your silence—the
alternative being the publication of my daughter's wanton-
ness throughout the streets of Brighton?"

"Sir!" I gasped, outraged.

"Papa!" Miss Twining cried, at the same instant.

"How else am I to understand your pursuit of us here this
morning, madam? Disgraceful! On such a day of melancholy
importance to the Twining family! If it is not *advantage* you
seek—if it is not *interest* that has brought you hard on my
daughter's heels—then how may you account for your brazen
appearance here, in an encampment of soldiers, and entirely
without protection? I might almost assume you to have been
Byron's confederate, and posted in Cuckfield a-purpose, the
better to blackmail your victim!"

I stared at him, my body rigid with indignation. "I am

thankful that my brother, Mr. Austen, is unable to hear your insults, General—for he should not hesitate to answer them with a demand for justice. I have nothing further to say to you but *Good day.*"

I would have stepped past the repugnant fellow on the instant, and made my way blindly in any direction opposite the Twinings' own, had not Miss Twining impeded me. "Pray—I *implore* you, Miss Austen—do *not*—do not take my papa in bad part—it is only that he is suffering, you see, on account of dear Richard."

I stopped short. What courage the child possessed, to speak out against all caution, all portents in that black and furious face, wavering above her! Where had she learnt such courage? Or was it the broken voice of desperation that spoke—seeking a support of any kind that offered? I could not walk coldly from such a plea; my heart must hear it, and my temper cool. I felt my looks soften, and I forced a smile for the girl. She was so very young, after all—

"If I have offended you, Miss Austen, I beg leave to apologise," her father said stiffly. "Such words ought, I apprehend, to have been reserved for Byron himself. But he is unfortunately from Brighton at this present. When he returns, I shall know how to act."

"Papa!" In alarm, Miss Twining grasped his coat sleeve. "You cannot challenge a poet to a duel! Every feeling must be offended!"

He shook her hand away as tho' it had been a fly.

"It is difficult, Miss Austen, for a father to know what he should do for so wayward a daughter. How Catherine can have abandoned propriety yesterday, and entered the coach of a stranger—abandoning reputation and every claim to honour. . . . I know my duty—the girl *ought* to have been soundly whipped, and confined to her room—but circumstances prevented the natural consequence of sin."

This was heaping mortification upon mortification; Miss Twining looked weak with shame, and she could not lift up her eyes. I sincerely pitied her.

"I have an idea that your daughter repents of her impulsive folly," I said firmly, "and would be grateful for silence from us both on the subject. It is no deprivation to me, sir, I assure you, to talk of more cheerful matters."

"It would have been better for her, had she not been seen abroad this se'ennight," General Twining persisted heavily, "but our visit to the Camp could not be put off. I observe you are in mourning, ma'am—and that you will have noted, for your part, that I am in blacks as well. My son—my *only heir*—was killed on this day, a year since, under that disreputable fool Wellington's command in Spain. It is for that reason—for that solemn observance of our irremediable loss—that Catherine and I have visited the Hussars this morning."

"You have my deepest sympathy," I murmured.

"Mr. Hendred Smalls," the General said broodingly, "—a most respectable clergyman, with every distinction bestowed by the Regent himself—was so good as to offer a service of penance for the redemption of my poor son's soul. His brother officers took leave from their duties to attend—they have not entirely forgot my martyred Richard. You will apprehend that Catherine's absence should have excited comment, at a moment when comment was least desired. *Her* penance, therefore, has been forestalled a little." He unbent so far as to lean towards me, as if to confide. "I would not have Mr. Smalls think ill of her for the world. I should not wish *that gentleman* to have a horror of one who might, with a little push, be *all* to him in future."

I collected the General intended to make a match between his daughter and the loyal clergyman—was it for Mr. Smalls that Miss Twining had rebuffed so dramatic a *parti* as Byron?

Was it possible the clergyman had won her heart, to the exclusion of all other interests—even the most Romantic Lord to walk the streets of Brighton? And how had such an ardent attachment won the General's approval? The girl was, after all, but fifteen; Mr. Smalls, if he had advanced so far as to earn the Regent's notice and favour, must be somewhat older than a curate, and an unlikely companion for a child barely out of the schoolroom. I glanced at Miss Twining in sympathy—there is nothing as dreadful as the publication of one's love affairs—and found her disgusted gaze fixed upon some object behind me.

I turned, and espied a rotund gentleman of advanced years hastening towards our party. His face shone with perspiration, despite the mildness of the day; his hatless head betrayed a balding pate; and his general corpulence suggested a familiarity with the pleasures of the table that must supersede all other pursuits. A cheerful-looking gentleman enough; and however unlikely it seemed, on excellent terms with General Twining. He appeared determined, in his purposeful waddle, to pay his respects on the sad occasion.

"Ah," the General muttered uneasily. "How very unfortunate—Miss Austen, I must beg you to preserve the profoundest silence on the subject of my daughter's recent disgrace, before Mr. . . . . That is, I hope I may depend upon your discretion . . . Catherine, do not slouch so, and at least *attempt* to suggest the angelic in your looks!"

"You cannot mean, sir—"

"Indeed, Miss Austen," Miss Twining burst out. "Behold the aspirant to my hand! Am I not to be congratulated? Every girl in Brighton must envy me such a beau! I do not think he is above three years *older* than my father, indeed! May I present the extremely respectable Mr. Hendred Smalls to your acquaintance?"

CHAPTER SEVEN

The Regent's Reception

"A PLEASURE, TO BE SURE," MR. SMALLS PRONOUNCED AS he bent with effort over my hand; "for any young lady who is accounted a friend to our dear Miss Twining, must be a treasure indeed."

I murmured some pleasantry, acutely aware of Catherine Twining's discomfort; she had stepped back a pace, as though to put as much distance as possible between herself and this preposterous suitor, this puffing Romeo some four decades her senior, whose countenance shone with the exertion of making his bow and whose fingers clutched damply at my own. Hendred Smalls effected a smile—his teeth, as should not be unusual in a man of his span, were *very* bad—and then turned with a simper to his real object, Miss Twining. Having learnt, no doubt, from previous experience, she kept her hands firmly clutched on her reticule and merely bobbed a curtsey, her face all but obscured beneath the brim of her bonnet.

General Twining placed his hand in the small of his

daughter's back and thrust her ungently towards the clergy-man. "Pray show your gratitude to Mr. Smalls, my dear, for that most eloquent tribute to your brother. Mr. Smalls, for my part, I can conceive of nothing more fitting to the mar-tial nature of Richard's life—and the bitter waste of his end."

"Sacrifice," Mr. Smalls observed, with his small black eyes fixed upon Miss Twining's cheek, "is the highest purpose of man's existence on earth. You may be proud, General—if I may so express it—that Richard's life *was* wasted; for it is the death won without glory, the obscure and insignificant end-ing, that is most valued in the eyes of the Creator. We should not set ourselves up as rivals, I am sure, of that consummate sacrifice at Calvary."

I found this sentiment so revolting I had not a word to utter in response to it. Miss Twining's fixed regard for the paving-stones at her feet—she had ignored her father's in-junction to effuse her thanks—suggested that the poor child was as little moved. Mr. Smalls's eloquence may perhaps have been marred by his manner of speaking—he was given to richly rolling consonants, as affected as though he had been trained up in the theatre in his youth, rather than the pulpit; one might suspect him of prating *Hamlet* when he had no babes to baptise. I wondered if he spoke thusly even in the breakfast parlour, crying out for his bread and butter; or if he was liable to declaim from the nether end of the table, when desperately in want of soup.

"I am sure you have much to say to one another," I mur-mured, "and must beg to leave you in peace. General, my condolences on your sad loss; and Mr. Smalls, I shall hope to have the pleasure of listening to your sermon on the morrow."

His round face flushed darkly; his head inclined. "That is not likely to be possible, Miss Austen. You may not perfectly comprehend my position in life. You will know, I am sure, that there is but one church in Brighton—so charming a town should hardly need more—and that is the venerable St. Nicholas's, which dates from the fourteenth century, tho' certain of the tower stones are decidedly Norman in origin. It falls under the authority of the Bishop of Chichester, and his chosen vicar is the most Reverend Mr. Michel, an excellent man. We have argued points of great doctrinal significance from time to time. I myself am attached, however, to Brighton Camp; I am chaplain to the 10th Royal Hussars, whose Colonel-in-Chief is no less a personage than the Regent himself. I owe everything in life to His Royal Highness. Such benevolence! Such condescension!"

"Such unexpected wisdom," General Twining interposed warmly, "in a Royal of indifferent morals."

Hendred Smalls positively swelled with pleasure at this speech; his round shoulders thrust back, and the hidden stays that bound his torso creaked ominously. "I should like to offer your party some refreshment, General, before your return to Brighton—a glass of brandy, the hour being already advanced, with perhaps a lemonade for the ladies!—if such an indulgence should not be adjudged improper, on the melancholy occasion. There is something," he added, with a particularly offensive smile at Catherine Twining, "that I should like to say to Miss Twining."

I hastened to reply for myself in the negative, and with a final nod to Catherine—whose countenance was compounded of indignation and dread—hurried off down the High Street in the direction of Buckingham House, hopeful of encountering Henry. My pulse had quickened under the influence of recent events; I could not quite contain my wrath, indeed—and had General Twining not grasped his ebony walking-stick so firmly, I might have soundly thrashed him with it.

"IT WAS THE WORST SORT OF HUMILIATION, HENRY, to see that perfect flower of a girl bound over as chattel to an odious old man, who might easily have been her grandsire!" I fumed, as we mounted the stairs to our bedchambers at the Castle some hours later. We had contented ourselves with a moderate dinner in the publick coffee room, the better to restore ourselves and prepare for the Regent's reception, to which we were bid at eight o'clock. "Only conceive of the domestic picture! Little Catherine, huge with child at the tender age of sixteen, and her toothless husband laid up with the gout, from a constant overindulgence in Port! It should certainly drive the poor girl mad—or to publick ruin."

"She's not *quite* bound over to this fellow, however," my brother said thoughtfully. "There was no mention made of a formal engagement. Do not despair, Jane. Miss Twining, recollect, is not without alternatives. Byron may yet prevail!"

"Henry! Do not even joke of such a thing!"

He grinned at me heartlessly. "I should not put it past a girl of Miss Twining's mettle to escape her father's plots; she cannot be *entirely* without friends."

"She has no mettle at all!" I gasped. "I never knew a more shrinking child. It is clear she has been beaten into conformability from the time she could toddle. But perhaps we may contrive—perhaps the counsel of a friend . . ."

"Jane, do not involve yourself in the girl's affairs," my brother cautioned. "Recollect how her father meets opposition—with the back of his hand. You would not wish to *heighten* Miss Twining's misery."

"No," I agreed, "but I may yet stand her friend. If our intimacy should progress, I could perhaps invite her to accompany us to Chawton, for a visit of some weeks. She might then escape Lord Byron's notice—the General's wrath might cool—and his incomprehensible desire to shackle her to a dotard might dissipate. Excellent Henry! You have put me in mind of the very thing!" I seized his coat excitedly. "For you will not mind a third in the curricle, I am sure, when we quit this place at the end of a fortnight. It should not be so terribly uncomfortable. We are both of us slender ladies, after all—and you are remarkably fit for a widower of advancing years."

"Such a crush is not to be contemplated," Henry retorted firmly, "and if you think for a moment that I shall assist you in carrying off that girl, whose father has not the *least* inclination for our society, you've more hair than wit, Jane. I will undertake nothing of the sort. If your heroine is to escape the misery of her unnatural marriage, she shall have to shift for herself. I predict that an ardent young swain will soon appear, desperate to prove his honourable intentions. Allow *him* to rescue Miss Twining, I beg."

"Abominable!"

"But unanswerable," he concluded fondly. "Lie down a little while on your bed; take a glass of the excellent claret I have had sent up to your room; and be ready at my knock to storm the Marine Pavilion. I am sure its magnificence will put the Cheltenham tragedy of Miss Catherine Twining entirely out of your head."

THE PRINCE REGENT, IT IS SAID, FIRST VISITED THE SMALL village of Brighthelmston around the year '83, when he was a handsome youth of one-and-twenty. He was urged into Sussex by his doctors, who thought the sea water might ease the ominous swelling of certain organs in the Royal neck; being as yet unacquainted with the vastness of the Prince's appetites, they apparently mistook the thickening of his person for a more sinister disorder. Whether he dipped his head in the sea or not, remains a question for posterity; but certain it is he dipped his wick—as the Vulgar would say—in every unprotected maiden the surrounding country offered, until the reputation of Brighton, as it came to be known, was too black for any decent lady to contemplate. The Prince sampled every possible pleasure the watering place could offer, from horse racing to card playing to the wines of the King's Arms—and was led in dissolution by the example of his uncle, the notorious Duke of Cumberland. The Duke held the lease of Grove House, on the Steyne; his nephew enjoyed every freedom of the place, and its raffish circle; and within a few months of his coming of age, hired a modest farmhouse from the principal landowner in these parts—one Thomas Kemp.[9]

Mrs. Fitzherbert was swiftly installed at a neighbouring villa; and within a few years, the architect Mr. Henry Holland was tasked with transforming the farmhouse into a neoclassical Pavilion, complete with a domed rotunda and numerous columns. Christened the Marine Pavilion, it soon acquired two wings, clad in cream-glazed Hampshire tiles, and a conservatory jutting from the rear. Some eight years ago—so Henry informs me—the riding school and stables were begun, structures so vast as to dwarf the Pavilion itself, and constructed quite curiously in the Indian stile. The Prince was three years building these, and his debts mounting all the while. Happily for His Highness, however, he had by this time taken his detested cousin Caroline of Brunswick in marriage, got an heir to the throne, and been accorded a hand-

---

[9] Thomas Kemp owned most of the land in Brighton at the end of the eighteenth century; his son, Thomas Read Kemp (1782–1844), built Kemp Town in 1823, a significant Regency-style architectural neighborhood between the Royal Crescent and the racecourse on the Downs. The project eventually bankrupted him, and he died on the Continent, unable to meet his creditors' demands.—*Editor's note.*

some independence by Parliament; and could thus afford to be careless of money matters.[10]

"Sixty horses," Henry muttered as we crossed the short distance between the Castle and the Royal abode. "*Sixty horses* the Regent houses in that stupendous block of stalls, Jane. He has a passion for prime cattle—and for racing, of course. Yet they say he's grown so fat, he finds it difficult to spring into the saddle. Requires the assistance of *four grooms,* two at each Royal leg."

"More of a *heave* than a *spring,* I collect."

We were arrived at the gate, joining a throng of other finely dressed and coiffeured gentlemen and ladies; in any other town a line of carriages and teams, with shouting flambeaux-bearers, should have rolled up to the Pavilion doors; but in Brighton there are few who bother to drive the short distance between one house and the next—even when the house in question is royal. Most of the Regent's guests have only to step across the Steyne, like ourselves, in their slippers and shawls.

I could not allow myself to regard the finery all about me; I should suffer a pang of mortification at my own simple black silk, which appeared as incongruous amidst the paler colours of May as a vulture got among turtledoves. More than one of our fellow guests looked askance at Henry and me—as tho' we could not possibly be wanted here, and must be forcing ourselves on the Regent's notice. I knew none of them, and cared less for their opinion; and my brother's arm supported me the length of the gravel sweep. After an interval, we

[10] Although the Prince of Wales underwent a ceremony of marriage with the devoutly Roman Catholic commoner Maria Fitzherbert in 1786, he did so without the royal consent of his father, George III, and the marriage was thus regarded as illegal—by all but Maria Fitzherbert, presumably. The Prince's subsequent arranged marriage to his royal cousin, Caroline of Brunswick, was regarded as the legitimate union. The Prince's detractors continued to refer to him as a bigamist, however.—*Editor's note.*

achieved the front portico under its imposing dome; the massive doors were propped open to permit a flood of lanthorn-light to spill out upon the marble steps; and we joined the throng of the Select who trod slowly past the line of footmen arrayed in buff and blue.

Henry presented his cards of invitation coolly enough; an august personage took them in one gloved hand; and before I had time to entirely collect myself, "Mr. Henry Austen, Miss Jane Austen," were announced to the milling crowd.

What is there to say of the Marine Pavilion, that has not been said by others more intimate with its glories?

The interiors are very fine, in the classical manner, with much gilt and paint picked out à la Robert Adam; the furnishings, too, are of the latest mode—with winged gryphons and curving swans at the corner of every console table; and the walls of a certain gallery are remarkable for their hand-painted Chinese wallpaper, so intriguing and exotic in the boldness of its colours, and the strangeness of its figures, as to transport one to an Oriental clime. Here there are bamboo sophas, and japanned cabinets; Ming porcelain, and pagodas; and most startling of all—statues of fishermen dressed in Chinese silk, large as life and posed in niches built to purpose. The Regent, it is said, has a passion for the Exotic, and for the acquisition of fine things; for pictures in oils brought from every corner of Europe, and for snuffboxes, enamels, clock-work birds—for jewels of exquisite craftsmanship, which he bestows as the merest baubles on the ladies who excite his favour. The Pavilion, therefore, is less notable in its mere mortar and paint than for the objects placed in profusion on every surface: one could wander among them a se'ennight, and not be satisfied in their study.[11]

---

[11] Jane's description of the Marine Pavilion appears almost quaint to a present-day reader, reflecting as it does a simpler palace long since razed.

One *might* wander, I should say, if one did not swoon within a quarter-hour from the excessive heat of the Pavilion itself. The Regent abhors a chill; and requires his rooms to be as raging as a blast-furnace at every season of the year. There are fires in each of the principal rooms, and braziers of hot coals line the long passages; add to this a crowd of some two hundred of Brighton's Fashionables, and the resulting swelter is easily credited. I was soon wilting from the heat, the mixture of perfumes and pomades, the scents of warmed wine and of hothouse flowers, which were massed at every side; the odour of humanity in too close proximity; and the smells of food: pineapples and fish soup and the tiny, fragile figures of roasted ortolans—

"There is George Hanger," Henry murmured in my ear as he handed me a glass of champagne. "What an old villain, to be sure! You will know him by his hook of a nose, his lean frame, and his inveterate look of a satyr. They do say as it was *he* who arranged the illegal marriage of the Prince and Mrs. Fitzherbert seven-and-twenty years ago—procured the priest, and held the branch of candles at the midnight service!"

His was a raddled and dissipated face, much cragged and lined; he was famous for his patronage of the Fancy—the sport of boxing—for his military service during the late war in the American colonies; and for his general lack of sense. As I watched, one crabbed hand reached for the delicate pink silk of a lady whose rump was turned towards him, entirely ignorant of it; he pinched some portion of her flesh, and I observed the poor creature to jump out of her skin.

"Keep your distance, Jane," Henry chortled. "I doubt even

The Chinese wallpaper she mentions, however, is credited with having inspired the Regent's subsequent renovation of the Pavilion into the present exotic folly.—*Editor's note.*

the weeds of mourning would preserve you from such a roué!"

"Henry," I said faintly, "is there any purpose to this soirée beyond standing about and sampling the overwhelming expanse of food? Is there to be singing? I *had heard* the Prince was fond of playing the violincello with his orchestra. Or do we sit down to cards, perhaps? Is there to be an address by the Regent? Is His Highness anywhere within sight?"

"Not that I can observe," my brother replied. "I suppose we might make a push to see the other rooms—it *is* the Marine Pavilion, after all, and one ought to explore the length and breadth of it when such an opportunity offers—I cannot imagine we shall ever set foot within the place again!"

"You go," I urged him. The heat was proving more than my black silk or the beaded band of ribbon about my carefully dressed curls could support. I was certain I felt a drop of moisture working its way down one temple—and I would *not* be discovered by a member of the *ton* in a red-faced state of vulgarity. "I shall endeavour to find a cooler spot, perhaps by a window—tho' none of them appear to be open."

Henry surged off through the crowd, his champagne glass held high; and as my eyes followed his course, I thought I glimpsed Desdemona, Countess of Swithin—in animated conversation with a lady I did not recognise. She looked cool as September in transparent gauze, and I swear her underskirt was dampened so as to cling to her skin—her form might almost have been etched in marble for every eye—but I credited her for the canny preparation borne of past experience: in the heat of the Marine Pavilion, one might as well arrive already drenched. I debated approaching her, but a tide of humanity, swelling and lapping about the tables of food, separated us; I must hope to meet with the Countess at a more propitious hour.

"Miss Austen, this is a pleasure indeed!"

I turned with difficulty—being caught in a crush between a lady with three ostrich plumes waving on her head, and a corpulent gentleman whose broad stomach, expensively clad in white satin breeches and embroidered waistcoat, permitted him no movement at all—and discovered a beaming Lord Moira before me.

I had come to know the Earl in London, where he formed one of Eliza's court; and the mix of sympathy and delight in his notice at the present moment recalled her immediately to mind. I offered him my hand; he bowed over it and muttered some words regarding our dreadful loss—that no amount of time should reconcile us—that Heaven had acquired a hellion, or Hell its first real angel—and I found myself smiling back at him with a curious sensation of relief. The Marine Pavilion, and Brighton itself, could not be so awful when Lord Moira moved in their midst.

My brother enjoyed Lord Moira's patronage at his bank; but the Earl had also been an intimate of Lord Harold Trowbridge, during a period of high intrigue among the Whig Party, at whose centre Lord Harold always had been; and from this cause of friendship alone must remain an object of my regard.[12]

"And how do you do, my lord?" I enquired. "You are in excellent health, I hope? Does the sea air of Brighton agree with you?"

"Not at all, my pretty—not at all! I am never so bilious as when I am by the sea. But the Regent, you know, must have his household about him; and where His Royal Highness commands, I know my duty. I shall be playing whist for five-pound points until August at least, when the shooting season

---

[12] Francis Rawdon, then the second Earl Moira, had been appointed governor-general of Bengal in 1812, and left England later in 1813 without repaying the loans he had drawn on Henry Austen's bank.—*Editor's note.*

releases us all to the North. But enough of me! This is your first visit to Brighton, I collect? And have you been presented to the Regent?"

"Sir . . . I . . ." The words were stuttered in confusion. It was not enough that I was clad in dreary black, of which His Highness is said to have the greatest abhorrence; nor that I am well past my bloom, and could not excite admiration with the freshness of my looks; only add to all this, indeed, the profundity of my contempt for the man—who treats all women, particularly his wife, with a publick disrespect and callous conceit not to be borne—and you will understand the desperation of my desire to avoid the Regent's notice.

But Lord Moira was already searching beyond my head for the Royal figure, so vast and magnificent, with its dyed locks carefully arranged à la Brutus; its fobs and seals and various puffery orders displayed upon its vast expanse of bosom; its elaborately tied cravat and its ponderous thighs. And as I observed Lord Moira's countenance, it underwent a change; a suffusion of pleasure overcame the thickened cheeks.

"Mr. Austen!" the Earl cried. "My dear Henry! I have blockaded your sister here by the lobster patties, and must engage your support in overcoming her blushes! She protests she cannot meet the Regent! For shame! Why else is she come to the Marine Pavilion, indeed?"

"To gawk at all the *ton* in their summer pleasure ground, my lord. For you must know that Jane possesses as exquisite a taste as Beau Brummell—she holds the Regent in absolute abhorrence."

The Earl's expression of dismay was a visible reproach; poor Eliza should never have repaid his attentions so ill, and my conscience smote me. Henry's shot at levity had fallen too wide of its mark. We were both of us in danger of offending an old friend, and one who had every reason to expect our gratitude, in having procured the evening's tickets. There seemed no other recourse in such a *crise* but the lady's constant friend—the fainting fit—and so without hesitation I swayed dangerously where I stood, fluttered my eyelids helplessly, and said in a failing voice: "My lord—the *heat*—"

Immediately, Lord Moira's hand was at one elbow; Henry supported the other, and a path was cleared through the fashionable throng at the Earl's insistence. There is something to be said for buff and blue livery, when it may cut so swift a line through a crowd of gentlemen and ladies hell bent on pleasure. I was carried off to an airy, high-ceilinged structure filled with greenery: the Regent's Conservatory, I collect, where every manner of fragrant bloom, tropic palm, and sinuous vine trailed among the pillars. I could almost suspect a primordial snake to slither out at my feet, hissing its most seductive favours.

Tho' my eyes were half-closed, in pretence of swooning, and my head lolled like a doll's on my brother's shoulder, I was not so far lost in high drama as to ignore the presence of others, half-hidden amidst the serrated leaves of a verdant fig: the whipcord figure of a man, crushing like an inverted flower the delicate form of a girl, bent to ravishing point at his embrace. He had pinned her arms behind her narrow waist; his mouth was buried in her white throat; her head was tilted backwards. She looked for all the world like a doe caught in the slavering jaws of a hound.

"Henry!" I hissed, as Lord Moira halted in abrupt confusion.

The man swung round. George Hanger, intimate of the Regent and more than sixty if he was a day; and the girl—crumpling to the floor as he released her—

Was none other than Catherine Twining.

CHAPTER EIGHT

The Girl in Boy's Clothing

"Colonel Hanger!" Lord Moira cried. The Earl's heavy jowls trembled with emotion—outrage or uneasiness, I could not tell. "The young lady—I trust she has not been overcome by the heat—Miss Austen, you perceive, is in a similar case—"

"Miss Austen," Catherine Twining repeated faintly; her eyelids fluttered as tho' she roused from a dream. "Again you are my salvation!"

"Shhhh," I murmured, kneeling down beside her and shaking my head once, sternly, in mute admonition. It would not do to make a scene—any hint of scandal in such a place should damage Colonel Hanger not at all, but should leave Miss Twining's reputation in shreds.

"Allow me," Henry said gently, extending his hand to assist the girl. "Are you all right?"

The lace ruff at the edge of Catherine's bodice was torn and dangling; observing this, her cheeks were suffused with scarlet. Her fingers fluttered at the scrap ineffectually.

"Perhaps a pin," I suggested hastily, and searched in my reticule for one I kept there against just such a need.

My brother turned coldly on Colonel Hanger. "Sir, I have not the honour of your acquaintance, and must leave it to others more closely connected with Miss Twining to question your conduct—"

Hanger grinned, displaying a lamentable set of wooden teeth. "The General, d'ye mean? He's not likely to cross a brother officer over a bit of muslin, even if she *is* his daughter. From what I remember of her ma, there's not much virtue in the female line."

"Sir! You forget yourself!" Henry said fiercely.

Hanger's eyes narrowed. "Think you're entitled to teach me conduct, do you?" He stepped pugnaciously towards my brother. "And what if I slapped your face with my glove, you damnable mushroom? Would you accept the honour of my acquaintance then? The girl encouraged my attentions, if you must know—and led the way to this secluded spot!"

Henry stiffened, and I feared for the issue. "Sir, your imputations are insupportable! Pray step outside, where we may discuss this in greater privacy!"

Hanger strode like a bantam cock towards a pair of great iron doors that let out from the Conservatory onto the Pavilion's grounds. "Lead on, my fine fellow! I should be happy to draw your cork for you!"

I looked in desperation to Lord Moira, who shouldered his way between my brother and his unusual adversary. "George, if you do not take care, you will bring all of Brighton down upon us—and I cannot think you wish that! You have too many creditors among the townsfolk, ha! ha! And in any case—His Highness sent me in search of you. He desires you to attend him in the Blue Saloon."

"Does he, indeed?" Hanger eyed poor Catherine, huddled under my wing, with hungry chagrin. "I had forgot what I was about. It was the Regent who was wild to make your acquaintance, my dove, only I tarried too long in presenting you. But don't cry—we shall have other opportunities—and the Prince was never one for little girls, nor dark-haired ones, neither. He prefers them billowy and blond. I should know—I was ever Prinny's procurer."

"George," Lord Moira breathed warningly. "Have a care!"

Hanger smirked. "You're a diplomat born, Francis, for all you're so hopeless at cards. You'll do very well among the savages and Nabobs—you shall indeed. I wish you at Bengal right now, truth be told; or at the Devil—whichever you will. It's all one to me."

"I dare swear you're foxed, George," Lord Moira returned despairingly.

Hanger bowed in Catherine's direction. "Pleasure, Miss Twining—one I hope to have often repeated."

Henry surged forward, but I placed a restraining hand on his arm; we could not endure a meeting at dawn with such an opponent. Hanger might very well be foxed—his whole person reeked of brandy—and Henry might have the advantage of him in years; but the Colonel was known for an excellent shot. Catherine Twining's honour was not my brother's to defend.

As Hanger swung out of the Conservatory with the arrogant stride of a man half his age, Lord Moira, without requiring to be told, had the good sense to draw Henry aside and speak to him very sensibly on the subject of our late Eliza. I busied myself with tucking up Miss Twining's torn lace, using the least number of pins.

"How came you to be in such a sad case?" I enquired in a lowered tone. "Where is your father? Why are you all unprotected?"

"I am here at the invitation of a neighbour," she murmured, "Mrs. Silchester. I do not think she knows where I am. It was she who introduced me to the Colonel, at his particular request. He said he wished to present me to the Regent. I am sure Mrs. Silchester thought there could be no objection. Only that *odious* man carried me directly here, where I am sure the Regent has not been at all!"

"You ought not to have walked off with a strange gentleman alone, Miss Twining. That is considered to be very *fast,* you know. Let us hope it has not excited comment."

I glanced up, and discovered tears on the poor girl's face. I added firmly, "Tho' in such a crush, how could the movements of any one person be remarked upon? I am sure we need not refine too much upon events. Dry your eyes, lest Mrs. Silchester be in a quake, and escort you home too soon to your papa! You would not wish him to receive you in moping looks! But I am glad to know he allowed you to come this evening—he was so very stern when we met at the Camp, with his talk of beatings and locked doors. Shall I restore you to your party?"

"Oh, yes," the child said gratefully. She slipped her hand through my arm. Her thin shoulders, bare in her evening dress, heaved as with a sudden chill. "Is this not a *dreadful* place, Miss Austen? And yet the World would have it the Pavilion is everything great! I shall not recall it with anything but disgust. So hot and so crowded—and the people one meets are not at all kind, except for you! I confess I have the headache. I *wish* I might go home—"

"And so you shall, as soon as we achieve Mrs. Silchester," I soothed.

NOT LONG AFTER THE INCIDENT IN THE CONSERVATORY, Henry and I quitted the Regent's pleasure dome—having at last submitted to Lord Moira's persistent desire to present us to his crony. The man who would one day be King of England took my hand, patted it earnestly if absentmindedly, and remarked to the Earl that he could not abide to see a woman go in mourning—it made him feel quite low, in thinking of all the good friends lost in recent years. His Royal Highness took my brother's blacks in better part—as a banker and thus a possible source of funds, Henry should be an invaluable friend did the Regent's luck at faro turn sour. Henry treated the great man's notice with surprising circumspection, betraying a caution I had not thought him equal to; and so we parted without regret from the Royal Presence, feeling we had attained every sensation of body and spirit the Pavilion could offer.

I did not see Desdemona, Lady Swithin again—a disappointment—but was permitted a brief glimpse of Catherine Twining, departing in the train of a frail woman dressed in lavender silk with many flowing veils; Mrs. Silchester, no doubt.

"I rather wonder about your protégée, Jane," Henry observed as we crossed the Steyne once more towards the Castle Inn, and our longed-for beds. "That chit has a positive genius for landing in scandal with some of the most notorious men in England; and yet I swear there's not the slightest calculation behind it!"

"She is too much of a goosecap for *calculation*, Henry."

"Even the unintelligent may seek the world's notice. Perhaps Miss Twining craves flattery—excitement—the sensations of a broader world. Perhaps she dreams of treading the boards on the London stage, and Brighton is her apprenticeplay!"

"Surely not!"

"You persist in believing her a wide-eyed innocent?"

"She suggests nothing else!" I protested.

"—Tho' we found her on the verge of ravishment for the second time in two days? I wonder," he repeated. "Is Miss

Twining a mere fawn—or a cunning puss, as shrewd as she can hold together?"

I stopped short before the Castle door. "What *has* the poor girl done, to inspire such enmity?"

"Required me to defend her honour, at the risk of several duels, among a party of fellows with whom I am not the least acquainted!"

I could not subdue a smile. "Henry! Such Corinthian airs!"

"Be serious, Jane—I am uneasy at something Hanger said: that he had ever acted as the Prince's procurer, and was charged with presenting Miss Twining to the Regent. . . . Can it be so? Or was it invention, designed to shirk responsibility? How has such a meek little mouse drawn such a riot of notice?"

"For all she is so young and unformed, she will be a Beauty, Henry," I quietly replied. "Have you not observed it? Her skin, like porcelain; her features, all excellent—and the depth of innocence in those wide, dark eyes—her artless wonder at the Great World—Miss Twining is all that is enchanting! How else should she have ensnared both the greatest Prince and the greatest Poet of our age?"

SUNDAY MORNING BROUGHT FITFUL SUNSHINE, AND OUR dutiful attendance at St. Nicholas's Church. There was such a squeeze to obtain seats among the congregation that Henry chose to stand at the rear, and thus had a prime view of the Regent and his brother, the Duke of Clarence, as they made their ponderous way up the main aisle and took their places in the Royal pew. I was better employed over my prayer book, and in listening to the sermon of the Reverend Mr. Michel, who taught the Marquis of Wellington his letters as an ignorant schoolboy—or attempted to do so, for there are those, including the Marquis's mother, who insist the soldier's understanding was never powerful. Mr. Michel spoke on vanity and the Way of All Flesh, which brought the old roué Hanger uncomfortably to mind; these seemed to be pertinent topics for the collected *ton*, tho' from the expressions of virtue on every countenance, the clergyman's words fell on deaf ears. I gave up attending to poor Mr. Michel, whose voice is decidedly thin, and studied my neighbours' fashions instead.

At the close of Divine Service, Henry proclaimed himself anxious to seize the sea air in a stroll along the Marine Parade, a pleasant promenade that borders the shingle and the sea; and as little other amusement offered on the Sabbath for two raised by such observant parents, I readily agreed.

We had progressed some distance along the sea-front, in the direction of a local wonder known as Black Rock, when my name was called in a cheerful accent, and I confronted once more Lady Swithin. Beside her, elegant in figure and dress, was her lord: visibly older than when we last met eight years since, when the Earl of Swithin was a buck of the first stare, a celebrated *parti* on the Marriage Mart, and Desdemona's infuriated slave. As he doffed his silk hat, I saw that Swithin's forehead was a little lined, his hair beginning to thin; such are the wages of a vigourous career among the Opposition.

"My lord, my lady—how delightful to meet again." I dropped a curtsey. "May I recall my brother, Mr. Henry Austen, to your acquaintance?"

Henry had been presented to Lady Swithin when she was but a girl in Bath and the object of our sedulous researches, on the occasion of her brother's being taken up for murder; but he was unlikely to pursue the acquaintance once she exchanged the station of Duke's daughter for that of Countess.

Her husband, Henry knew not at all. But he bowed; the Earl returned the courtesy; and at Lady Swithin's suggestion, Henry and I retraced our steps towards the Steyne.

"And what did you make of the Marine Pavilion, Miss Austen?" the Countess enquired, drawing a fine Paisley shawl about her shoulders against the brisk sea wind. "You will shock Swithin, I am sure, for I know your pert opinions of old."

"I thought the place very grand, and befitting the honour of the Regent," I returned sedately; "but the heat and crush were intolerable."

"Not to mention the better part of the company," Swithin observed carelessly. "The Carlton House Set are never good *ton* in London, to be sure, but by the seaside the freedom of their manners is shocking. I've a mind to take a house in Worthing, Mona, for the rest of the summer; the children should be happier there, without all this bustle, and I should never fear my wife's receiving an insult. That blackguard Hanger was mincing about the passages last night like an unholy imp, itching to snatch at any passing female. I very nearly tossed him out on his ear."

Lady Swithin smiled, and rapped her husband's arm with one gloved hand. "Pay Swithin no mind, Miss Austen. You will recall he has a shocking temper. It would not do to be absent from Brighton when all the world is present—that excites comment, you know, and speculation, which should fuel the Tories' vile projects: they should say that Swithin was ailing in the country, and that the moment was ripe to strike against the Whigs. We cannot have that on any account. But I think I should like to remove to Italy in June, as Lady Oxford intends: a change of scene entire should suit me, and the children may by all means go to Worthing, with Nurse."

She glanced sidelong at the Earl from under her lashes, a ploy I remembered from her girlhood. "You, Charles, may do as you please—accompany me or stay behind; but I should find June sadly flat without you."

Her husband smiled wistfully; his plans did not include Italy, I suspected; but he remained as enchanted by his Mona's wiles as ever. "I do not like Lady Oxford."

"I am well aware of it." Desdemona dimpled.

"She is a pernicious influence."

"Piffle. You are simply jealous, Charles. She's far more clever than any man in London."

"A powerful understanding, I grant you, well supported by judicious study—but I cannot like her morals, Mona," Swithin said warningly.

"Oh, pooh—such stuff! She conducts her *affaires* quite discreetly; and were I chained to such a dead bore as old Harley, I should be forced to similar expedients—tho' fortunately I am *not*," she amended hastily.

I was amused to observe that eight years of marriage had not dulled the wits of either husband or wife; prone to argue vociferously as young people, they remained as testy in their affection as ever.

"What part of Italy does Lady Oxford intend?" Swithin demanded.

"Sardinia. Or was it Sicily? I am forever confusing the two."

"Then we shall be forced to descend upon the Lakes," he replied. "Have you yet been on the Continent since Napoleon retired to Paris, Miss Austen?"

It was like his good manners to recollect his acquaintance, and turn the conversation.

"I have not," I answered, with some dignity—never having been on the Continent at all.

"My late wife," Henry interjected, "was so unhappy as to be deprived of extensive estates in France, bequeathed to her by her murdered husband—the Comte de Feuillide, guillotined by the mob at the height of the Terror—and it has been in my mind for some years to attempt their recovery; indeed, we once ventured together to France to push our claim, during the Peace of Amiens—but now that my wife is gone, all such efforts must be futile."

The two men walked ahead a little, discussing Kutusov's rout of Buonaparte; and I seized the opportunity to mine the Countess for intelligence. Lord Byron had tossed Catherine Twining out of Lady Oxford's chaise; and Desdemona was intimate with Lady Oxford. I know nothing of the woman at all—except for her scandalous reputation, which I liked as little as did the Earl.[13]

"You have known the Countess of Oxford some years, I apprehend?"

"Indeed. We have been friends this age—tho' she is considerably my elder. I believe she may be as old as forty," Desdemona observed.

I winced, but forbore to announce my own decrepitude. "I did not see the Countess at the Pavilion last evening."

"No—she cannot abide the Regent, you know; she is all for the Princess's party, and remains in London to support her."[14]

"I commend Lady Oxford's loyalty," I said warmly. "I pity the Princess exceedingly; and must believe that however imperfect her conduct *has been,* had her husband's been above reproach, she should not have erred. His was the poor exam-

---

[13] Jane confirms here an opinion of Lady Oxford already expressed to her friend Martha Lloyd in a letter dated 16 February 1813. *See* Jane Austen, *Jane Austen's Letters,* Deirdre Le Faye, ed. (Oxford: Oxford University Press, 1995), Letter No. 82.

[14] By this, the Countess of Swithin refers to Princess Caroline, the Regent's estranged wife, who maintained a separate residence and household. Such a degree of hatred subsisted between the two royals that one could not be a friend to both.—*Editor's note.*

ple; his the duty to guide; and his negligence the more to be deplored, in exposing his wife to contempt and ridicule."

"I am entirely of your opinion, Miss Austen!" her ladyship cried, and slipped her arm through mine. "But the gentlemen will not see it; they abuse the Princess as a jade and a joke. Can any woman stand mutely by, and allow such indignities to go unanswered?"

We conversed a little longer in this vein; and I could not help but be forcibly put in mind of Lord Harold Trowbridge, as I listened to his niece's sentiments. She marshalled her arguments with logic and care, as Lord Harold had been wont to do; and I thought it very likely her husband's success in Parliament owed much to the cold judgement of his primary auditor—his wife.

"And Lady Oxford is just such another," Desdemona concluded as we achieved the far end of the Marine Parade, and halted to observe some boats putting into the waves. "Swithin is in the right—he is *always* in the right: her conduct goes beyond what is pleasing, even in so great a lady, in the constant parade of her *amours*. But she should not have behaved so ill, I am sure, had her husband not been so weak. He practically *abandoned* her to Sir Francis Burdett, her first lover, and when one is left entirely alone in the house for a week with so eloquent a man, I am sure one cannot be blamed for the consequences."

The consequences, as even I was aware, ran to several children—members of what were unkindly called the "Harleian Miscellany," in a nod to their uncertain parentage. Desdemona lost me here; only friendship could excuse her support of Lady Oxford, and I had no such tender feelings to persuade me from what was right. Mona's frankness, however, absolved my conscience of any pang; I might be as inquisitive as I chose.

"Her ladyship is a great admirer of Lord Byron, I collect?"

Desdemona smiled. "That young man has been practically living in her pocket all winter, if you will credit it! And he is barely of age, Miss Austen! And she is old enough to be his mother—or very nearly! It is one of the *on-dits* of Town; and we are forced to treat the liaison as the merest commonplace, tho' he has been staying at Eywood—the Earl's estate in Herefordshire, you know—since before Christmas, and has only exchanged it for London once the Countess quitted the place. He has settled in lodgings in St. James's, but hardly dares show himself out-of-doors, for fear of meeting Caro Lamb."

"I had hoped that lady might have learnt resignation," I said. "But still she pursues Lord Byron?"

"For a wonder! I should not be capable of enduring such ridicule as she wins—for all the world is talking of it, you know. Lady Melbourne, Caro's mother-in-law, is no friend to her; she has taken up with Byron herself, and serves as the poet's maternal counselor—all from vanity, of course, at succeeding where her daughter-in-law has failed! I wonder that William Lamb can bear it—to have both wife and mother enthralled by the same swaggering boy, nearly ten years his junior, and admitted on terms of cordiality in his own home!"

"Lady Melbourne, the intimate friend of her son's rival," I gasped. "How does Lady Caroline bear it?"

"Seethingly," Desdemona said. "She communicates with her mother-in-law solely by writing. They inhabit separate floors of Melbourne House; and such scenes as must occur upon the stairs I do not like to think! But I feel some pity for Caro Lamb, tho' she has brought her ruin upon herself; she is become the most tragic sort of spectacle—hardly anyone receives her now. One cannot predict what she is capable of— one cannot know what she may do. *Violence,* perhaps, to herself or others. Emotion has carried her beyond the bourne of reason."

"And yet," I observed, reverting to our earlier subject of conversation, "Lady Oxford is Byron's current *inamorata*—and Lady Oxford is welcome everywhere."

Desdemona smiled. "Not *quite* everywhere. The Regent will not receive her, on account of her support for the Princess; and so Byron, too, is given the cut direct when he descends upon Brighton."

"I am glad to know that man has suffered *some* rejection, at least!"

But the Countess was no longer attending. Her eyes had narrowed, in gazing at a particular boat just then thrusting out to sea. It was a sailing vessel, not at all large as such things go: but a single mast and sail, and what my Naval brothers should have called a jib—I might almost have ventured abroad in it myself. It had been some years since I had rowed my nephews in a little boat about Southampton Water. But Desdemona was not lost in contemplation of the boat, pretty tho' it was, with its gay sails and dark red paint.

"And so the Devil is come to Brighton," she murmured softly. "And I *do mean* Devil, Miss Austen. That is Byron himself—just there, springing into the boat with a quickness surprising in one who is lame—George, Lord Byron, about to set sail. Is there not something poetic about the scene?"

She spoke a simple truth. There was the boat: bright-hulled, bucking on the waves like a horse impatient for a gallop; and the broad-shouldered, lithe young man with the windswept black locks, his deft fingers working at the ropes. A timeless image; beautiful in its clean lines and brilliant colours, its implicit promise of freedom—

"My dear," called the Earl of Swithin, from where he stood a little advanced from us in company with Henry, "I believe we should beg our friends' pardon for detaining them so long, and enquire whether they might dine with us, before the Assembly tomorrow?"

But Desdemona was deaf to her lord.

I was scarcely more attentive myself. For a young boy had raced, barefoot, across the sand directly for Lord Byron's boat. His blond hair was cropped short, in curling waves over nape and forehead; his nankeen breeches were so loose on his wiry frame that they were lashed to his waist with a stout leather belt; and his shirt—a rough linen one with flowing ruffles and sleeves, that put me strongly in mind of a Gypsy's—was so blowsy as to suggest it might better have fitted Byron himself. A local urchin, I thought, whose intent was to earn a copper or two by helping his lordship heave his vessel into the sea.

But the lad was too late—his lordship was already afloat—and in desperation, the boy surged out into the waves, hailing the vessel in a high, excited accent, the linen shirt ripping free of his breeches in the brisk wind.

Byron turned and fixed his gaze upon his pursuer's countenance—and his own visibly darkened. As Desdemona and I observed the scene, his lordship's beautiful mouth curled in contempt and hatred. "Little Mania!" he shouted. "You may go to the bottom and welcome, for all I care!"

And he let out his sail with an impatient twitch of line, willing the little boat to surge forward, away from the boy.

"How cold the water must be," I murmured. "I have only assayed it once, in Charmouth—and that, from a bathing machine—I am sure it is far colder in the midst of the ocean, against one's sodden clothing. Poor lad—what *can* be his purpose?"

Desdemona's gloved hand gripped my wrist with painful urgency. "Turn away, Miss Austen. Turn away this instant! We must not look, or I shall not be answerable for the consequences—Oh, Lord, that I had not seen what I have! That I should not feel myself *compelled* to inform Lady Oxford—"

I stared at her in wonderment. "Whatever are you speaking of? It is only a boy. Observe! His lordship is waving him off! He is letting out more sail, and the wind has taken it! The water is too deep for the lad—he cannot reach the boat, and indeed, indeed, Lady Swithin, I believe the poor fellow is drowning!"

The Countess whirled on the instant, her eyes seeking the fair head as it bobbed, sank, and disappeared beneath the waves. Byron was staring resolutely in the opposite direction, out to sea; at least fifty yards now separated him from the desperate boy.

"Good God!" Mona cried. "Swithin—Swithin, *do something*, for all our sakes! Do you not see? There, in the wake of that vessel? It is Lady Caroline Lamb who is perishing in the sea!"

CHAPTER NINE

A Remedy for Drowning

9 MAY 1813
BRIGHTON, CONT.

MY BROTHER HENRY, I KNEW, COULD NOT SWIM.

The Earl of Swithin's fingers were already working at the buttons of his dark blue coat, however, and his hat was tossed on the paving at his feet. "Hullo the boat!" he cried towards Lord Byron's diminishing vessel. "Byron! Lord Byron!"

I saw what he was about in an instant; Byron should be more likely to reach the drowning woman, did he abandon his vessel in an attempt to save her; but the wind carried Swithin's words back into his throat.

Henry leapt from the Parade to the shingle below, and began to halloo in company with Swithin; but it was of little use. The only notice he secured was that of the fishwives who gutted the local catch on trestles set up near the sea, their skirts kirtled high about their waists and their heads wrapped in bright scarves. Several stilled their knives and stared up at us in wonderment, as tho' we were drunken or mad.

"She surfaces!" Desdemona cried.

Her husband, boots discarded and clad only in pantaloons

and linen shirt, pelted over the stony sand with the speed of a schoolboy; and as he plunged into the sea, fighting against the waves that dragged at his thighs, I saw the dark gold head of Lady Caroline Lamb—was it truly she?—rise like a seal's and then disappear, almost instantly overwhelmed. Beside me, Desdemona was dancing with anxiety and fear, muttering imprecations and encouragement, her eyes narrowed in a desperate attempt to locate Lady Caroline once more. I, too, was searching the serrated water frantically with my gaze; but the sodden curls did not reappear.

Lord Byron's yacht, taken by the wind, had moved far from our party; he had tacked, I thought, and was visible as a gull-winged shape against the bright horizon. Had he known Caro Lamb could not swim? Had he wished her to die while he sailed onwards, indifferent? Could any man—however tormented by a discarded lover—be so callous as *this*?

But of course he could, I recollected. This was the same Lord Byron—the *poet*—who had abducted Catherine Twining in his carriage.

Desdemona had quitted the Parade to hasten after the gentlemen; she was straining towards her husband, just shy of the tide's reach. I hastened to join Henry, who said, "I believe Lady Caroline has been submerged some minutes. Swithin will have to dive. Let us pray he has sufficient strength—*I* should never be equal to it. The force of the waves! I am all admiration for such a man."

It was as Henry said: Swithin was drawing great breaths, then plunging fully under the sea. I had an idea of his eyes, blinded by salt water, searching the murky depths in frantic haste for the slim figure of the boy-girl. I found I was clutching at Henry's arm with my gloved fingers in a manner that he might generally have regarded as painful, but appeared not to notice at this present; I heaved a shuddering sigh of dread, as tho' my breath might supply the swimmers'.

Desdemona had begun to pace the sand, tossing anxious half looks towards the sea, and I sensed her mounting anxiety—where was Swithin? He had not resurfaced from his last dive. Had his strength flagged? His senses been suddenly overpowered?

"Henry," I attempted—

But at that moment, Swithin's head surged out of the waves and he shook it, like a dog. Under his left arm there was a white and limp shape—a neck, a dark blot of head; with his right arm he began the painful crawl back towards us.

"Pray God he is not too tired," I breathed.

"Pray God that is not a corpse," Henry returned. His lips were set in a thin line. "Damned foolish, Jane. Damned foolish. What can she have been thinking?"

I did not answer, but hurried towards Desdemona, who was now urging her husband on with every call of encouragement she could think of, entirely oblivious to the crowd of Fashionables that had gathered, slowly but inevitably, on the Marine Parade behind us. They could have no notion whose drama was played in the waves below them; they were drawn, rather, by the spectacle—and by the clear interest of our own anxiety, the fact that Henry and I were dressed in mourning, as tho' the outcome of events were already certain. Some few of them would certainly recognise the Countess of Swithin.

"My lady," I said, "we are the object of all Brighton. No one must be allowed to penetrate Lady Caroline's disguise. Are we not agreed?"

She gave me a swift glance, then drew her fine Paisley shawl from her shoulders. "We shall wrap her in this. And carry her to our house—it is but a few steps off the Marine Parade. Only how are we to convey her?"

Swithin was standing in the shallows, now, his burden lifted in his arms; his lungs gasped for air and his stumbling legs sought a secure foothold. Soon, he would deposit Lady Caroline on the sand—and the moment of danger would be arrived.

"Henry!" I cried. "Fetch a chair! Surely there will be one standing before the Castle! A *chair*, and make haste!"

He dashed off on the instant, heedless of explanation. A stout pair of chairmen must suffice; hackney chaises were difficult to secure in Brighton. Time enough to fetch a doctor once we knew whether Caroline Lamb still breathed.

Desdemona went to her husband; he set down the frail figure and fell to his knees beside it. "Rub her limbs," he urged. "Your vinaigrette, Mona—do you have it?"

She shook her head, mutely chafing Caro's wrists; Desdemona had never been one for die-away airs, nor the remedies employed to defeat them. Hartshorn would be absent from her reticule as well. Burnt feathers might serve to bring Lady Caroline round—but where to procure them? I glanced about. The fishwives burnt charcoal near their trestles; perhaps the smoke from this would do? I hastened to beg a bit of coals, and as my half-boots trod the shingle, I caught sight of a veritable gull's feather among the rocks. I snatched at it, lit the tip in the fishwives' fire, and hurried back to my friends, my palm cupping the flame against the sea wind.

Swithin had turned Caro Lamb on her side, and was supporting her insensible form as she retched; he had been careful, I saw, to face his charge *away* from the curious who were massed on the Marine Parade. A few of these—gentlemen all—had ventured down onto the shingle; and one, in catching my eye, loudly enquired, "May one do anything? May one be of service?"

"It is only a local lad," I returned as I handed my burnt feather to Desdemona, who waved it vigourously beneath Caro's nose. "A cabin boy, off a fishing vessel. He ventured out too deep."

The gentleman nodded, indifferent now, and turned back. I saw him convey the quelling news to others in his party, who swiftly related it to the rest; and of a sudden, the crowd began to disperse in as leisurely a fashion as it had gathered. There was nothing in the life or death of a cabin boy to excite the interest of the Great.

"She breathes," Desdemona whispered.

And indeed, the small chest rose slightly and fell; some life remained unextinguished.

My brother's figure appeared on the low wall that separated Parade from sand; he lifted his arm in salute.

"The chair is come," I murmured in a low voice.

"Excellent," Swithin said. "Your shawl, now, Mona, if you please. I shall carry her; the weight is no more than our son's."

The frail face—like a faerie's or a sleeping child's—was still insensible as the Earl conveyed Lady Caroline across the sand. I had read of her looks in every newspaper in the land— how she was called the Sprite, in respect of her ethereal grace and a certain fey quality to her character. But in her looks I saw desolation, rather—as tho' some great flame had passed through her being and burnt away all substance, leaving but a husk.

The chair stood waiting between its stout fellows, under Henry's anxious eye. The Earl shifted Lady Caroline gently within, and stepped back, that Desdemona might have the arranging of the Paisley shawl. As the Countess's hands secured the folds, Lady Caroline's eyelids fluttered.

"Am I drowned?" she muttered.

"No, my dear. You are saved. Hush, now."

"*He* saved me?" The eyes, clear as agates, searched Desdemona's face. "Mona Swithin—what are *you* doing here?"

"It was my husband who brought you out of the sea."

The eyes closed; a tear seeped from one. Caro Lamb shuddered the length of her body as tho' suffering an intolerable pain. "And so he sailed on! I should rather have died, Mona, than have it so."

"Hush," the Countess said again, and closed the chair door. "Number 21, Marine Parade," she told the chairmen.

"My pantaloons are ruined," Swithin said conversationally as the Irish carriers moved off. "And it is the first time I have worn them. I shall have Byron's neck for this."

WE PARTED FROM THE EARL AND HIS LADY BEFORE THEIR door, having secured from them a promise of swift news of Lady Caroline's health—and our assurances, in return, that we should be delighted to dine with them on the morrow. We should not be attending the Assembly at the Castle, of course—for two such figures as ourselves, deep in the throes of mourning, it could not be seemly to dance. But a private dinner among friends, and an early evening of retirement while the music drifted up from the floors below—there could be nothing objectionable in *this*.

"Besides, Jane," Henry said as we achieved our inn, ravenous for our well-earned nuncheon, "I shall not be deprived of every detail the Swithins learn of Lady Caroline's exploits—whether she comes down to dinner, or keeps to her room as solitary as a nun! I feel I have won such intelligence by my exertions today. I was in a quake the whole time, in the belief that if Swithin failed, I must be hurled into the breach next—and you know how many victims the fishwives should have had to rescue *then*!"

"Only think how dull our days would be, Henry, had we chosen Lyme over Brighton," I said thoughtfully. "There is a deceptive mildness about this place—and yet so much passion beneath the surface!"

I meant the words in jest; but they bore a prophetic quality I learnt to regret.

CHAPTER TEN

Friends in High Places

MONDAY DAWNED IN LOWERING CLOUDS AND RAIN.

The bed in this chamber is hung with heavy curtains—very grand, to be sure, but nothing I am accustomed to at home; I do not draw them when I sleep, and thus was afforded a glimpse of heaving grey seas beyond my window from the moment I awoke. It was a desolate sight, and made plain the truth that few enjoyed the pleasures of Brighton in winter; it should prove a dreary clime. I was happier when my gaze fell on Betsy, kneeling at the hearth with her kindling and tinder-box in full employ; there was a damp chill to the room that a cheerful fire should soon dispel. I raised myself up on my pillows, and at this slight sound the chambermaid turned, dusted off her hands, and rose with a hesitant smile.

"Would you be wanting your tea, then, ma'am?"

"That would be delightful," I said.

I recall a time when I was perennially addressed as *Miss;* but those days are sadly fled.

She rubbed her hands on her apron and disappeared into

the passage, returning seconds later with the silver tray; I humped up my knees under the bedclothes, held the delicate porcelain cup to my lips, and allowed the scent of China Black to drift gratefully to my nostrils. There is such a luxury in being waited upon of a morning, that I shall hardly know how to endure the return to Chawton, where Cassandra is abroad at the first cock-crow, tending to her poultry and her little dogs, and it is my office to walk down the village lane to procure the day's bread. I am content with such a life, of course—the gentle habits of the country entirely suit my need for quiet reflection, and provide endless studies of character, in the subtle turns of Fate that are visited upon the village's inhabitants—but an interval of harmless dissipation, of gazing upon the rain without the slightest need of going out, safe in the knowledge that no one should make a claim upon my attention until the dinner hour at least—was bliss to savour.

"It rains so hard this morning, the Lord must be looking for Noah," Betsy observed, as she halted with her hand on the door latch. " 'Twill go hard with them as serve the Assembly tonight; such a mess of wet wraps and dirty shoes as shall have to be looked after! And I'll have the cleaning of the floors, I don't doubt, on the morrow!"

I had never considered the inconvenience of rain to the servants at an inn; and the thoughts uppermost in my own mind—that the delicate silk sandals of the ladies intent upon dancing should never survive such weather, without the ladies themselves being carried by gentlemen of their acquaintance from their carriages to the Castle's threshold, which should serve as a delicious intimacy to every girl who had yet to be clasped in a gentleman's strong arms—unless that gentleman disappointingly proved to be her brother. And how was such a feat to be accomplished, in a town where almost *nobody drove*? Would the gentlemen walk staidly under their umbrellas beside the chairs procured for the ladies? How *did* the poor chairmen manage in such a deluge, when all the world was mad for chairs? Did the cost of such a conveyance *rise* as the mercury fell? —None of these questions appeared compatible with the more practical sentiments of a Betsy; but they were perfect for the delights of hot tea, sipped in bed, with a view of the stormy sea.

"I am sure you shall have much to do," I managed to say to the chambermaid sympathetically.

"Aye, and there's nothing new in that," the girl returned. "You'll not be attending the Assembly yourself, ma'am, on account of your loss?"

"I shall not."

"—Because I should have been happy to dress you, had you the need."

"Thank you, Betsy—I may in fact require your services, around six o'clock. Mr. Austen and I dine out this evening, with a small party of friends." I was conscious of vanity, and added, "We are expected at the home of the Earl of Swithin, on the Marine Parade. I should be very happy to have your help in dressing my hair, if you feel equal to it."

She eyed me doubtfully, being almost half my age, and uncertain whether the fashions of twenty should suit a lady so stricken in years as myself—but the desire for advancement overcame all hesitation, and she bobbed a curtsey. "Six o'clock, ma'am, without fail."

I poured myself a second cup of tea as the door closed behind her, and allowed myself to drift happily into the world of Henry Crawford—who waited in suspense for the decision of his insipid Fanny, his Creator being otherwise engaged by the frivolities of Brighton. I cannot *like* my poor Fanny, tho' her scruples are such as must command respect; I believe I shall spare the darling Henry such a cross, and bestow the lady upon her cousin Edmund—who has earned her as penance, for his utter lack of humour. Edmund has taken

Holy Orders, after all; and a clergyman requires a certain daily disappointment in earthly life, as confirmation of his spiritual worth.

BETSY WAS AS GOOD AS HER WORD, AND ARRIVED A FULL ten minutes in advance of six o'clock, in order to dress my hair. She brought with her—God knows where she found them—a set of curling tongs, which she proceeded to heat by the bedchamber fire. This had died down during the course of the day, which I had spent in dutifully writing such news as obtained to Cassandra, and in scribbling bits of dialogue as came to my mind—truly delightful badinage, if I do say so myself, on the subject of the *ha-ha,* as both landscape feature and metaphor of female bondage. *I cannot get out,* Maria Bertram cries, as she rattles the iron gate in frustration. At which Henry Crawford must smile knowingly—such delightful creatures being *always* possessed of the instruments of licence, when ladies desperate for freedom appeal to them—and show the foolish girl how to escape her betrothed.

My own Henry had spent an unobjectionable day in perusing the sporting papers at Donaldson's; met with me for a hearty nuncheon; declared himself determined to attend both tomorrow's cricket match and race-meeting, weather permitting; and, having rubbed up against Lord Moira during his interval at the library, was carried off by the Earl to Raggett's Club, for a debauch of silver-loo during the afternoon.[15]

I did not enquire whether Henry's luck was in; it mattered

[15] Raggett's was a gentleman's club opened by the proprietor of the exclusive (and Tory-affiliated) White's Club in London. At Raggett's the aristocratic Regency gentleman might secure all the comforts of Pall Mall while exiled in Brighton—gaming, privacy, and a neat dinner free of women. —*Editor's note.*

more whether Lord Moira's was out—for as the Earl's banker, Henry was doubly his surety for anything in the gambling line.

"Aye, ma'am, and you *do* look fine," Betsy offered in a kindly tone; she was patronising me, I am sure, for there was nothing very extraordinary in my black silk, it being the same gown I had worn Saturday evening. I had clipped my topaz cross on its fine gold chain around my neck, however—no gift from such a brother as Charles should ever disgrace me— and I was determined to leave off my matronly cap. My chestnut hair, tho' shot with grey, is nearly long enough to stand upon. I had already brushed it, and plaited it into four tight braids, which I suggested Betsy should arrange about my head in a becoming fashion. This she managed to do with surprising aplomb, looping two strands first into a chignon at the crown of my head, and the remaining two at the nape, with a profusion of short curls about my ears and brow. Through all this, she wove a gold ribbon—just the touch required to relieve my inky black, and pick out the note of the topaz cross. I was quite pleased with the result; and tho' my looks are no longer blooming, I believe my appearance would do justice to the Earl of Swithin's table.

"They do say, ma'am, as you were on the shingle when the poor lady from London was saved of the sea yesterday," Betsy observed as she plied her curling tongs. "Blue as Death they do say she was, until the Earl tore off her clothes, and rubbed her body all over. A sight it was to make a Christian blush! But perhaps you know better, being intimate with the Earl and his lady."

I was astounded to learn that Caro Lamb's disguise had already been penetrated, and turned—the tongs searing my scalp—to stare at Betsy. "I assure you the victim was a local cabin boy! A fisherman's lad!"

She suppressed a smile. "Aye, and I'm your grandma's old tabby! The Earl's scullery maid—she's a Brighton girl, Lucy is, and goes with the house whoever takes it of a season—is my cousin. She said as how the lady was brought in, wearing a boy's breeches and all of a swoon, and carried directly upstairs. Hot milk and bread she was given, tho' precious little she ate. Lucy says the trays all came back, and the sops went to the house cat."

"Lucy is likely to lose her place, if her taste for gossip outstrips her good sense," I said calmly. "The Earl should not like his servants to spread his business to the world; and as I am dining on the Marine Parade this evening, I may feel it my duty to inform his lordship how his confidence is betrayed."

"Oh, no, ma'am, please to say you wouldn't do *that*!" Betsy's hands were suspended over my head, her horror writ upon her simple countenance. "I won't breathe a word of Lucy's tales to anyone, I promise. She's forever telling 'em—it goes with her place, you see, she's privy to monstrous goings-on, every season, for the house is let only to those as is that high in the instep—"

"Naturally. But she shall never be more than a scullery maid if she does not guard her employer's secrets. You, Betsy, I know, are anxious for advancement."

"I am that, ma'am," the chambermaid said, her tone subdued.

"I am very pleased with the dressing of my hair," I told her. "And I thank you. Now, be a good girl—and do not spread this malicious gossip among the Castle's servants. The poor creature the Earl saved from drowning shall no doubt be despatched to London tomorrow, and once gone, there is nothing more need be said. It will be as tho' the incident never occurred."

"I beg your pardon, ma'am," Betsy countered, "but the

lady's *not* bound for London. Lucy says as how she took herself off this morning to the Pavilion, her being a special friend of the Regent's. Perhaps it was in longing for Prinny that she threw herself into the sea! Only fancy! One of the Regent's light-o'-loves, naked on the shingle, with the Earl of Swithin caressing her body—and everybody certain it 'twere a boy! There's been nothing like it since Maria Fitzherbert turned respectable!"

"IT IS TRUE," DESDEMONA TOLD ME AS WE STOOD IN HER drawing-room before a great pier glass, sipping ratafia, "Caro *would* be gone—and has begged a room in the Pavilion itself. Her mother, Lady Bessborough, is forever staying there, you know—having been an intimate of the Prince these thirty years at least—but I had not thought Caro capable of such effrontery as to invite herself to become one of the Royal party. The Lambs are Whigs, as are all the Bessboroughs—as indeed we are ourselves, not to put too fine a point upon it—and the Regent is heartily turned against his old Whig cronies, now he has the reins of power in his hands. Such ingratitude! When it was we alone who championed his cause, when the King was run mad!"

I chose to sidestep this swamp of politics, being country-bred and of Tory stock myself; I should leave the navigation of Whig waters to Henry, who was adept at playing every side to advantage. "But what can be Lady Caroline's purpose in remaining in Brighton?"

"She intends to plague poor Byron—so much is certain. He will not meet her in London if he can help it—deliberately avoids every rout or ball that Caro is pleased to attend—and is forever in Lady Oxford's keeping. Caro employs an army of pages deployed upon the streets, expressly for divining other people's business; from one she learnt that Byron quitted London on horseback late Saturday, intending to do a bit of sailing in Brighton. He has come down from Town some once or twice in recent weeks, drawn by the lure of the sea, and keeps a room at the King's Arms, I believe, against just such whimsical excursions."

Or drawn, I thought, *by the ingenuous charms of Catherine Twining, of whom neither Lady Oxford nor Caro Lamb has yet an inkling of.*

"Learning of his departure," Mona persisted, "nothing must suit Caro *then* but that she should rattle down the New Road in her perch phaeton, with only her tyger up behind her, on *Sunday*! There has never been a propriety she feared to flaunt; and this is the result of it. She must have set out while it was yet dark, to achieve the shingle at the hour she did. But that is Caro Lamb all over—careless of opinion and sense."

"—And mad as Bedlam into the bargain," added Lord Swithin. "I confess I was not sorry to see her quit our house almost as soon as she entered it—having gained a foothold, she might have stayed all summer."

"—Forcing us to flee delightfully to the Lakes," his wife murmured, with one of her sidelong glances. "But no matter. Having seen Caro plunge after him into the sea, Byron will wish nothing more to do with boats or sailing for a time, and has probably already bolted back to St. James's."

"You believe that he *knew* her ladyship, then?" Henry demanded. "—That Lord Byron did not *mistake* her clothing and appearance for that of a boy, and sailed on in ignorance as tho' the merest stranger had hailed him?"

"Certainly he knew his pursuer for Caroline Lamb," Swithin replied, "and was willing to let her try her strength against the sea. Lord Byron knows her ladyship to be indestructible. *Little Mania,* he calls her; and claims she haunts his very dreams, like a virago. One can hardly blame him for coldness; anything else should be read by Caro as encouragement."

"But I cannot forgive his lordship's total indifference," I protested. "To push resolutely forward, while the poor creature was o'erwhelmed by the waves—suggests a coldheartedness of which no *poet* ought to be capable."

"You would have Byron stand by the spirit of what he writes?" Mona enquired, as the bell was rung for dinner.

"A poet *ought* to be all sensibility—else he should better engage in political speeches, which nobody bothers to believe. Lord Byron's verse offers every range of emotion—ardour, violence, the bitterest loss—but his behaviour yesterday betrays a coldness of inhuman proportions."

"Caro Lamb is inhuman in her proportions," Swithin corrected. "No girl can be so thin, and yet survive; I am with Byron—and believe her to be a walking Wraith."

"Charles!" his wife cried. "Confess that you admired her, in her first Season! Indeed, I understood you nearly offered for her!"

"A pitiable ploy, my darling, to pique your interest. You were decidedly averse to my suit in those days."

Desdemona pursed her lips to prevent herself from laughing; for indeed, she had treated poor Swithin abominably when she was but eighteen.

"Caro Lamb's persistence should drive any man mad," the Earl concluded. "Moreover, it suggests a passion for self-abasement—and that cannot be admired. She is like a dog that craves to be whipped, and is forever kicked instead. Had George saved her from drowning, as I did, he should never be rid of her!"

"Then let us hope Caro does not transfer her affections to *you*," Desdemona said teasingly, "out of bottomless gratitude."

"If she does, my darling, you have my hearty consent to toss her back into the sea!"

"Charles, you are the greatest beast in nature. Is he not, Mr. Austen?"

The Countess, despite her words, was gazing at her husband with immense good humour. She slipped her arm through Henry's. "I think I shall allow *you* to escort me into dinner!"

CHAPTER ELEVEN

Cut Dead

STRAINS OF MUSIC DRIFTED FROM THE ASSEMBLY ROOMS as we mounted the Castle's stairs, and the entry was crowded with young ladies in white muslin, gentlemen in satin knee breeches, and duennas of imposing gravity determined to protect the virtue of their charges. We were to part from the Earl and his lady at the Assembly Room doors, where the Swithins intended to form a part of the glittering throng; and as Henry and I turned from the brightly-lit room—hundreds of candles being illuminated in chandeliers suspended from the lofty ceiling—I was greeted in a barely audible accent by my young acquaintance, Miss Catherine Twining.

She looked all the youthfulness of her fifteen years, a slight figure beside the imposing height and breadth of her father, the General; the white muslin she wore made her skin appear sallow; but her dark hair and eyes were as lovely as ever. Only a natural flush to her cheeks and an appearance of joy common to one of the Season's first Assemblies, were utterly lacking—Catherine, I perceived, was not in spirits this evening.

I begged the honour of making her known to our friends—performed the introduction of Earl and Countess, to Catherine's pleased confusion; and joined my thanks to Lady Swithin for our delightful evening, with my brother Henry's.

"I shall call upon you first thing, my dear Miss Austen, to give you an account of the ball," Desdemona promised, twinkling; and then her lord swept her into the Rooms, which were as full as they could hold.

"How very fashionable the Countess is, and how very kind the Earl," Catherine Twining breathed. "He looks most *truly* the gentleman."

She may have compared him to the unfavourable memory of Lord Byron; or perhaps to that of her more determined suitor—for a second glance at the crowd mounting the stairs behind General Twining revealed Mr. Hendred Smalls. He formed a third in the Twining party, and had no doubt already claimed several of Catherine's dances.

She made so bold, however, as to renew our acquaintance; pressed her father to acknowledge my brother Henry; extended the honour to Mr. Hendred Smalls, who bared his unfortunate teeth; and concluded breathlessly, in a lowered voice meant for my ears alone, "Oh, Miss Austen, are you indeed attending? Might I hope to speak with you in the interval between dances? For you must know, I am all of a quake!"

"My state of mourning prevents me entirely from joining the Assembly; but I shall sadly miss your society, Miss Twining." And I confess I *did* regret retiring to my bedchamber; the music was infectious, my foot was tapping out a reel. "What has occurred, my dear, to discompose you so?"

"*He* is here!" she breathed. "Do but glance through the doors, and you shall espy him leaning against a column, for all the world as tho' he were not in the habit of abducting unwilling females! I had thought him returned for good to London! Am I never to be free of his society?"

"Lord Byron shall hardly attempt to seduce you in the middle of a ball." I was amused despite myself. But Miss Twining was too agitated for ill-applied humour.

"Oh, Miss Austen, do you think it possible he has published my shame to all of Brighton? Am I entirely exposed? Is it likely I shall enter the Assembly, only to be cut *dead* by all my acquaintance?"

"Hush, my child!" I glanced with a casual air through the doorway. As the sumptuously-dressed throng shifted and parted before my dazzled eyes, I caught a glimpse of a classic profile, a sweep of dark curls, a snowy cravat carelessly tied. Lord Byron leaned negligently against the wall, his lame right foot crossed over his left, one hand tucked into the breast of his coat. A branch of candles, flickering in the great room's draughts, threw his face half in shadow—as romantical a picture as any poet could desire. As I watched, he leaned to whisper in the ear of another gentleman—a tall, thin exquisite with receding hair. Both men smiled.

"His lordship is engrossed in conversation, and it does not appear that anyone has cut *him* dead," I observed.

"That is only Mr. Scrope Davies, who has been intimate with Byron for ages," Catherine retorted. "I am sure he is already in possession of every detail—indeed, it was probably *his* cravat I choked on in my misery; Mr. Davies is a *dandy,* you know, and ruins a score of freshly-ironed cravats each morning, before his valet declares the last to be perfection."

I suppressed a smile. "Recollect that Lord Byron cannot publish an iota of your unfortunate encounter without bringing the whole world's indignation on his own head. You may rest easy, Miss Twining—indeed you may. Do but remain by your father's side, and all shall be well. You are certainly safe from *dancing* with his lordship."

"True, he never dances," Catherine said despairingly. "Not even with Lady Caroline Lamb."

I gazed at her in astonishment. "You are acquainted with Lady Caroline?"

"Not at all," Catherine admitted. "All the world is aware of her connexion with Lord Byron. It is said that he forbade her to *waltz at Almack's*, because he could not bear to see her in the arms of another; and that she submitted to the prohibition!"

"We may assume Lady Caroline is waltzing again," I said drily, "Lord Byron having formed a rival attachment."

Catherine flushed. "I think her a very *dashing* female," she said wistfully. "Quite out of the common way. I should like to have a glimpse of her. Did you know that she is come to Brighton?"

"I had heard as much, yes."

"But oh, Miss Austen—" this was becoming a refrain with Miss Twining, rather as tho' she had learnt it from a novel— "I am ready to sink! Papa shall retire to the card room as soon as the first dance is struck up; and I shall be consigned to the care of Mrs. Silchester. She is Papa's chosen chaperon on every occasion, having been at school with dear Mamma; but she shrinks from offending the gentlemen. You saw how little her protection availed me with Colonel Hanger—and this is *Byron*! Could I not accompany you to your rooms, and sit with you for a little while?"

I studied the hectic looks of my young friend—the wide, startled eyes—and saw that she had worked herself into a nervous passion. "You are looking far too pretty to give up an Assembly, Miss Twining, and should be wasted on the closed air of my rooms!"

"Catherine!" the General's voice called peremptorily from behind his daughter.

"Could you not stay a little?" she pressed in an urgent whisper.

"Even were I of a mind to sit down throughout, I am told

that the Master of Ceremonies—Mr. Forth, is it not?—is very strict in observing the proprieties. I should not wish to excite his censure."

"No—that is, I quite understand—"

"Catherine!" the General barked. "You are not attending! Make your excuses to your friend—Mr. Smalls awaits your pleasure!"

"Coming, Papa." Catherine made her curtsey. "May I call upon you tomorrow, Miss Austen?"

"—And relate every detail of your Success. I shall be in the Castle's writing room at one o'clock. I absolutely forbid you to be abroad any earlier—after the fatigues of the Assembly, you shall require a late morning."

"I shall depend upon finding you." And with one last, speaking look, Catherine Twining hurried off to place her flower-like hand in the crabbed paw of Mr. Hendred Smalls.

"WHY IS THE GENERAL DETERMINED TO THROW AWAY HIS daughter upon that aging cleric?" I demanded of my brother as we mounted the stairs to our rooms. "Were she a lady of *my* age—long since upon the shelf, and every prospect of romance blasted—I should understand his grasping at the most grotesque fellow who offered; but to thrust poor Catherine— who has everything to recommend her: youth, birth, and beauty—at a man who has none of these, is beyond my comprehension!"

"Do not be offering her a place in our curricle, Jane," Henry warned as he paused before my door.

"I shall be as firm as you desire."

"Our journey home shall be sadly flat," he sighed, "without the prospect of duels or abduction to lend it spice."

———

THE MUSIC AND BUSTLE THROUGHOUT THE CASTLE BEING likely to keep me awake some hours, I settled down to pen this account in my journal; and as my candle guttered low, and the cessation of the instruments suggested supper was being served, I stirred up Betsy's excellent fire, replenished my candlestick, and got into bed to read by the dim light. The improving nature of the text—I had selected a volume of sermons in deference to Recent Events of a Melancholy Turn—was unequal to the fatigue of so advanced an hour; my mind was prone to wander. Laughter and hubbub drifted up from the Assembly Rooms, and I had an idea of the overheated girls, catching a chill as they moved from ballroom to supper, picking at their ices and smoked salmon. Catherine should yet be among them; I hoped for her sake that Lord Byron had quitted the rooms at an early hour, and that Mr. Smalls had retired, as the elderly must, to the card room—leaving the object of his fancy to more suitable partners. Poor Catherine! To be caught between the rage of the poet, and the simpering of the clergyman!

What she required, I thought, was a simple, bracing sportsman like my brother Edward had been. Henry, indeed, was confident that just such a suitor *must* appear. But what if the Unknown came too late? *Jane, Jane,* I scolded myself as I snuffed out my candle near two o'clock, when at last the sounds of revelry had died from the rooms and streets below—*You ought to have nothing to do with the child's troubles.* But Lord Byron had decided that; it was his abduction that had ensnared me.

TUESDAY, 11 MAY 1813

~

"SUCH A SCENE, MY DEAR MISS AUSTEN, YOU CAN *NEVER* have witnessed!"

Lady Swithin threw back her head—which bore a pert little jockey bonnet this morning, worn with a spencer of French twill—and crowed with laughter. "Caro Lamb, with a circlet on her brow, a robe fit for a Greek chorus, sandals, and her *toenails painted with gold leaf.* She stopped all conversation dead when she appeared in the Assembly Rooms; and I am certain one of the violinists snapped a string, from the resounding *twang!* that greeted her arrival."

"But she was known to be a guest of the Regent's," I observed reasonably. "I suppose she may attend the local ball, if she chuses."

"It was not *Caro,* so much as her appearance! I do not think she could have aroused greater comment had she paraded through the Assembly naked. She was determined to figure as Lord Byron's Attic Muse—the breathing heart of *Childe Harold.* When instead, as poor Swithin observed, she succeeded merely in suggesting a Cyprian Goddess."

By this, of course, Lady Swithin meant a harlot.

"And Lord Byron?" I enquired.

"—Was a veritable picture of Persecuted Genius. His brow darkened stormily; he threw off all restraining hands; he muttered imprecations in Caro's general direction; and departed without speaking so much as a word to her."

"Very ungentlemanly. He thus exposed Lady Caroline to the ridicule of her world; and I cannot admire him for it."

"No; but you shall be glad of one thing—Caro's arrival freed your little friend, Miss Twining, from Byron's pursuit at least! He was *most* determined last evening. She had only to quit the floor at the close of a dance, and loose the hand of her partner—who might be gone in search of lemonade, or pineapple ice—to be set upon by his lordship, blind to all else, and quoting impassioned words over her shrinking form. Poor goosecap, I quite pitied her; Swithin was just such an one, you know, when in the throes of passion for *me.*"

I had seen Lord Swithin in disappointed Love; he had never approached the diabolical figure who struck terror in Catherine's heart.

"Then Miss Twining has cause to be grateful to Lady Caroline," I observed.

"Yes, indeed! And I observed the two ladies conversing, if you will credit it, later that evening—so perhaps your friend found occasion to convey her thanks, however awkward Lord Byron might regard such a conversation, did he know of it. And now I must be off—Swithin has a horse running in the race, you know, and I dare not stay away. I wish you would make another of our party!"

I begged off, having formed a prior engagement; and looked forward to hearing an account of Catherine's interesting evening from her own lips—but she did not appear in the Castle's writing room at one o'clock.

I could not wonder at her absence; she must have been abroad very late, and no doubt slept until noon. I had crossed full two sheets to Cassandra with a report of our dinner in Marine Parade, and the hour was advanced, when my brother Henry burst into the panelled chamber. His looks were agitated and his face dreadfully pale.

"Henry!" I cried, starting up. "Are you unwell?"

He glanced around him wildly; I was not the sole occupant of the writing room, and whatever his news might be, it was not intended for a stranger's ears. I collected my papers swiftly and joined him in the doorway.

"You have not heard," he murmured, grasping me by the elbow and propelling me towards the Castle's front door.

"You bear some dreadful news?"

"Catherine Twining. Your acquaintance. It is all over Raggett's."

"What scrape has the foolish girl fallen into now? She did not keep her appointment this afternoon."

"Nor shall she keep any in future, Jane."

I stopped short and studied his face. "She has quitted Brighton?"

"For good and all." He drew me inexorably out into the fresh air of the Steyne, where I saw that a crowd had gathered near the old publick house called the King's Arms—the place so roundly patronised by the officers of Brighton Camp and their devoted followers. But Henry avoided the publick house, and turned hurriedly into the Promenade Grove. He led me to a seat in a neat square of shrubbery.

"You must prepare yourself, Jane." His grey eyes were flat with despair.

"Tell me what you must, Henry—I beg of you."

"Miss Twining's body was discovered in Lord Byron's bed at the King's Arms this morning."

"No!" I cried.

Catherine as I had last seen her—the agitation in all her looks, her dread of that man—sprang vividly to mind.

She had been right to fear him.

He had killed her.

In a fit of passion—whether rage, love, madness, who could say?—Lord Byron had torn out the life of that delicate flower. But how had he lured her from the General's side? What possible mischance had delivered the girl into Byron's hands?

And what profound indifference to his own security had led him to murder her in his very bedchamber?

"Was she . . . had he . . ."

Of course he had; but the word *rape* was one I found difficult to utter.

But Henry was hardly attending, his gaze fixed on his gloved hands.

"It is the oddest thing, Jane," he said. "She was wrapped in a sailor's hammock, sewn tight; and when the thing was slit open, it was discovered that she had *drowned*."

CHAPTER TWELVE

Canvassing a Murder

HENRY'S SMALL FUND OF INTELLIGENCE WAS IMPARTED IN a matter of moments as we sat in the sheltered privacy of the Promenade Grove.

"It was the chambermaid who found her. The girl thought it odd that Lord Byron's door should be slightly ajar, and yet no sound of movement be audible within," he said. "The maid hesitated to disturb his lordship, because of course it is well known the man is a poet, and has been engaged in writing out cantos of his latest work—"

"He is writing here in Brighton?" I said numbly.

"Apparently so. At all events, neither Byron nor his traps were to be found in the bedchamber; but the unfortunate Miss Twining—"

It was whispered at Raggett's that the girl was still clothed in the white muslin gown she had worn at the Assembly. There were marks of brutality at her throat, as tho' she had been forcibly held under water—and she had died in the sea, for the dried stains of salt water were everywhere upon her person.

"The chambermaid put it about that her eyes were wide open," Henry said in a subdued tone, "and that such a look of terror as lingered in them, she hoped never to witness again."

"But the hammock, Henry?" I knew of such things from my Naval brothers; when a sailor died, his sleeping hammock served as shroud—sewn up around him, before burial at sea. "Was Miss Twining forced into it alive—*trapped* inside?"

The image of the girl, fighting like a blind kitten tossed with its brethren into the mill pond at birth, was too hideous to contemplate. How terrified she must have been—the darkness of the night, and the blacker dark of the water as it flooded around her—

"No," my brother said. "The marks on her neck suggest otherwise. The hammock may have been intended to hide the deed—or dispose of the body—but somehow or other it ended in Byron's rooms. Miss Twining was probably already dead when she was placed into it, and carried to Byron's bedchamber by her murderer."

"Can its owner be identified?"

"The word *Giaour* is embroidered on its edge."

"Giaour?" I repeated blankly. "What sort of word is that, Henry?"

"I have no idea. But presumably Miss Twining's murderer knows; it will perhaps be the name of his boat—or one readily to hand, at the moment he . . ."

"Forced her head under the waves." I stared at my brother, a scene from two days previous recurring to mind: the crimson-hulled yacht, surging out to sea, and the dark-haired sailor at her helm, ignoring the foundering woman in his wake. "Why must you persist in referring to *her murderer*, Henry, as tho' we had not an idea who it was? Are we both not certain in our minds? It will be *Lord Byron's* boat that is found to be called *Giaour*."

And in the most intense irritation at the entire race of men,

I swung away from him abruptly, striding down the Marine Parade in the direction of Black Rock.

I COULD NOT BE EASY IN MY CONSCIENCE. I WAS BESET with the demons of regret. Nothing could be clearer than that the poet, spurned, had exacted a hideous revenge upon young Catherine Twining—and we had been the agents of her release from his chaise. But how had she died? What fateful events had determined the hours after I parted from poor Catherine at the door of the Assembly Rooms—and why, oh why, had I refused to *stay*? It seemed, in retrospect, so little that the girl had asked; and I had prated about *propriety*. But for me, Catherine Twining might yet be alive.

When Henry caught up with me, far down the Marine Parade, I was more mistress of myself. But he paced beside me wordlessly, both of us buffeted by the wind. The rain of the previous day had given way to a cloudless sky, the sun brilliant and hard-cut as a diamond; sea wrack lay everywhere strewn about the shingle.

"Have they arrested the poet?" I demanded at last.

"They cannot find him, Jane."

I looked swiftly round.

"The publican at the King's Arms would have it his lordship settled his accounts and quitted his rooms late last night after the Assembly—having encountered Lady Caroline Lamb at the ball, to his apparent rage."

"Lady Caroline! Good God, I had forgot—so Lady Swithin told me this morning. Your intelligence had put such trivialities entirely out of my head," I exclaimed.

"Directly Byron espied her ladyship—she appeared about midnight, so they said in Raggett's, and you must know that Byron's good friend Scrope Davies is a member whose word may be relied upon—his lordship left the Assembly, packed up his traps at the King's Arms, and repaired to Davies's lodgings for the night."

"And Miss Twining remained, as yet," I said slowly, "if Lady Swithin is to be believed. The Countess *saw* Miss Twining in conversation with Caro Lamb, of all people—we laughed about it this morning. The lady obsessed with Lord Byron—and the lady with whom Lord Byron is obsessed—trading pleasantries before the eyes of all Brighton."

"Scrope Davies insists that Byron slept under his roof, and quitted Brighton on horseback at eight o'clock this morning—well before the . . . well before Miss Twining was discovered at the King's Arms."

I frowned. "But then how did poor Catherine—"

"Exactly. Is Davies lying to protect his friend? Or did Byron slip out of Davies's house and meet with Catherine elsewhere—drown her on the shingle—pack her into the hammock—carry her to the King's Arms, enter his old rooms to deposit her there . . . and then repair once more to Scrope Davies's for an appearance at breakfast?"

"It strains belief, Henry," I muttered. "His lordship should have to be mad."

"Well, Jane . . ." my brother began dubiously.

But I shook my head. "Why shroud the girl in a hammock at all? Why not leave her as she lay, drowned on the shingle, so that the tide might take her? No possible connexion could then be made between his lordship and Miss Twining."

"I *had thought*, Jane, that perhaps *some other*, with designs upon the girl's life, might avail himself of Lord Byron's empty rooms. None can say. I understand, however, that the local magistrate has sent his constables post-haste up the New Road towards London—in the hope of overtaking Byron on his way, or meeting with him at his lodgings in St. James's. His lordship must appear at the inquest—for there will have to be an inquest, naturally."

We were now perhaps a mile and a half from the Promenade Grove; and the day being fine, we were treated to such scenes of quotidian Brighton life as must grace each fleeting May: the fishwives about their endless gutting; children, half-clad and barefoot, scampering upon the sands; and the bathing machines with their dippers, drawn down to the shoreline by a team of horses.[16]

"I cannot accept what you are telling me, Henry," I said, as my gaze drifted over the happy scene. "Miss Twining was in the company of her father last evening. She was escorted by that repugnant clergyman. How, then, did she go missing long enough to meet her end—and the General never sound the alarm?"

"All excellent questions, to which I may return no answers."

I clasped my hands in frustration. "How I *wish* it might have been possible for us to attend that ball!"

Henry placed his hands over mine. "Do not berate yourself, my dear. You *cannot* regard yourself as responsible for Miss Twining's death. I will not allow it. You could have had no notion—"

"You do not perfectly understand," I managed. "The last words Catherine Twining uttered to me were a plea that I re-

---

[16] Part of Brighton's attraction was the belief that sea-bathing was a healthful practice; and for those who could not swim, wooden bathhouses on wheels—drawn to the water by horses—were employed, particularly by women, who were deemed too modest to be seen in wet clothing. The dippers were persons of the serving class who helped bathers descend a ladder into the safe enclosure of the bathhouse once it was immersed in the sea. Having bathed, the lady would once more ascend the ladder with her muslin shift clinging to her body. It was said to be a common practice for idle gentlemen to train telescopes upon the bathing houses, in the hope of seeing various women of their acquaintance in the Regency equivalent of a wet T-shirt contest.—*Editor's note.*

main. She *feared* him, Henry—so much I knew; but I thought her a goosecap for doing so, in the midst of an Assembly. I actually *laughed* at her a little. When in fact she went in fear for her life. Oh, God, I am to blame! I am to blame for the loss of that innocent creature!"

The picture of Catherine as she had been—flower-like in her white muslin gown, the thin bones of her shoulders as subtly molded as porcelain—and the image of what she must *now* be, were too melancholy to contemplate. My eyes filled with tears.

Henry grasped my arm and turned me firmly back along the way we had come. "Jane," he said bracingly, "we require a revival of your formidable spirit—one I have not seen in nearly two years. You must take up the rôle of Divine Fury. You must penetrate this killer's motives, and expose him to the world!"

"It should be a form of penance, I suppose."

"Penance! It should be nothing less than justice for Miss Twining's sake!"

"There are so many persons, Henry, far more adept than I—the magistrate, the coroner . . ."

"Neither of whom knew Miss Twining in the least."

I glanced at him in grudging acknowledgement.

"But what if the man you ruin is indeed *Lord Byron?*" my brother suggested. "Would you hesitate, when guilt falls upon a poet—one the Polite World acclaims as a genius?"

I did not bother to reply, but strode only more swiftly towards the Steyne.

"I tremble for the poet." Henry sighed.

AS WE DINED QUIETLY IN ONE OF THE CASTLE'S PARLOURS that evening, a serving-man appeared with a note for me, presented on a silver tray. Desdemona, Lady Swithin, had scrawled it so swiftly as to blot her words, on an elegant scrap of hot-pressed paper. Struck afresh by the Swithin crest, a tiger rampant, I broke the seal—and begged permission of Henry to peruse the communication.

21 Marine Parade
11th May 1813

My dear Miss Austen,

If you do not take pity upon Charles and me, and come round directly after dinner to discuss this miserable affair of Byron's, there will be no living with either of us. We may promise you tea and an excellent Rhenish cream in return; Swithin is most anxious for Mr. Austen to sample his Port. Two dozen of his finest bottles sent down from London, wrapped in cotton wool and supported by goose feather pillows, so as not to disturb the sediment! But I digress. I would not have you believe we are mere gluttons for gossip—that not an hour may pass, but we must surfeit on the latest whiff of local scandal—but my interest has been sought in the present tragedy, by one I hold in friendship. I shall say no more. We shall expect you at eight o'clock—but if you are otherwise engaged, pray send your reply by the footman; he awaits your pleasure.

I remain, etc.,
Desdemona, Countess of Swithin

"We are invited to take tea on the Marine Parade," I informed my brother.

"Nonsense," he replied, reading over Mona's note without

so much as a by-your-leave. "We are invited to canvass a murder. There is no end to the dissipations of Brighton! I never thought to enjoy myself so much!"

I drank down my glass of claret, knowing I required the fortification; there could be only one *friend* of Desdemona's interested in the death of Catherine Twining—Lord Byron's lover, Jane Elizabeth, Countess of Oxford.

CHAPTER THIRTEEN

The Passions of Lord Byron

TUESDAY, 11 MAY 1813
BRIGHTON, CONT.

IF I EXPECTED TO FIND LADY OXFORD ALREADY ESTAB-
lished in the Marine Parade, I was disappointed; but upon reflection, too little time had intervened between the discovery
of the murder, and the arrival of such news in London; even
were she in constant communication with Lord Byron, it
must be impossible for the mistress of so considerable an establishment to fly south on a whim, as Caro Lamb had done.
The Swithins were not quite alone, however: a dozen guests
were arranged in the pretty drawing-room of No. 21, Marine
Parade, a fact which caused me to hesitate on the threshold. I
was suitably dressed for dinner *à deux* in the Castle's private
parlour, but not for an intimate soiree of the *haut ton*. It was
impossible to draw back, however, or to wish that Betsy had
had the dressing of my hair—and so, with Henry's arm guid-
ing me gently forward, I braved the tiger's den.

"Miss Austen." It was the Earl who greeted me, elegant as
ever in evening dress. His smile was so warm that I wondered
how I had ever thought him haughty, upon first acquain-

tance, in the Bath of our youth; perhaps nearly ten years of marriage had softened the ruthless opium trader he had once been. "It is very good of you to join us. Desdemona, I know, is most anxious to speak with you. Mr. Austen! As you see, the gentlemen—some of whom I believe are known to you— have by now rejoined the ladies; but pray allow me to fetch you a glass of Port!"

With merely a look, the Earl summoned a footman; Henry bowed to a tall, lean fellow with very little hair, and murmured, "Pleasure, Sir John—had thought you tied to Hertfordshire at this time of year—" and I was claimed by Lady Swithin.

"Miss Austen," she said as she curtseyed. "I am in your debt, dear creature. And I said nothing of this crush in my note to you! I feared you would not come, did you know we were encumbered with acquaintance this evening. Now, in penance for my sins, I shall make you known to only a few of these ladies—Miss Kemp, who is quite musical, and shall presently repair to the instrument, thereby allowing us to converse under cover of its noise; Mrs. Alleyn, who is so animated that no one may avoid her notice; and Mrs. Silchester, who acted as duenna to your unfortunate friend, Miss Twining."

Mrs. Silchester! Here was a treasure, indeed!

I fixed a smile to my countenance; moved sedately under Desdemona's guidance through the gauntlet of eyes, and found that Miss Kemp was of that uncertain age, when one does not know whether to hope for salvation in the form of an eligible *parti;* or accept the inevitable degradations of spinsterhood with private relief. She was, in short, approaching the age of danger, and should soon be at her last prayers. Her interest, therefore, was fixed upon such single gentlemen as the room afforded—a cousin of Swithin's called Mr. Stanhope, and a dark-haired rake in his late thirties who went by the name of Hodge. If he possessed any other, I never learnt it. He was absorbed in casting dice, his right hand against his left—which, tho' hardly the most genteel occupation for a drawing-room, appeared to be regarded as the merest commonplace by his intimates.

"So pleased," Miss Kemp fluttered; "I hope you shall find Brighton to your liking." Her gaze drifted continually over my shoulder, to follow the course of one gentleman or another through the crowd of her rivals.

"Augusta," Desdemona said, "we are expiring for want of music. Would you be so good as to play an air or two upon the harp?"

"But if Miss Austen should care to exhibit—?" she demurred.

"I know nothing of the harp," I assured her. Of the pianoforte prominently positioned at one end of the room, I chose to say nothing. Miss Kemp fluttered over to her instrument, which was conveniently placed next to Hodge and his dice—fluttered a bit in composing herself to play—and allowed her fingers to flutter over the strings. At the first note, Hodge frowned—collected his dice in one sweeping movement—and repaired to the pianoforte, where he lounged in heated debate of tomorrow's horse race with Mr. Stanhope.

Poor Miss Kemp.

Mrs. Alleyn, next in the gauntlet, was a vivacious widow who formed a principal part of Brighton's charms, I was made to understand; her children being not yet out of the schoolroom, her fortune secured, and her taste for Society as rich as in her first girlhood, she was at liberty to accept as many invitations as the Season afforded—and in her case, these were many. She was the decided object of Sir John Stevenson's gallantry—which, as Henry observed later, had much to do with her fortune of thirty thousand pounds, and explained why that gentleman was *not* tied to his estates in Hertfordshire at present.

"And so you are come down from London," Mrs. Alleyn said. "How long a stay do you make in Brighton?"

"But a fortnight." I glanced at Henry. "My brother, Mr. Austen, has been so unfortunate as to recently lose his wife; and we are here in an attempt to raise his spirits."

"A widower!" She surveyed Henry with an appraising eye. "And in what part of the country are Mr. Austen's estates?"

I stifled a smile. "My brother is a banker, ma'am, and thus fixed in London."

Her interest waned.

"Mr. Austen is endlessly useful to Swithin," Desdemona supplied, "and Lord Moira quite *dotes* upon him, I believe. But *Miss* Austen is an intimate friend of my girlhood, and knew my dear late grandmamma in Bath. I was so pleased to brush against her in Donaldson's, and discover that she had come to Brighton for a bathing-cure."

"Do you mean to try the machines?" Mrs. Alleyn asked, her eyes widening a little; "I should not attempt it before July, at the earliest—the water is far too cold for my taste in May. But perhaps that is part of the cure; the nerves are shocked into order by the frigidity of the plunge."

"No doubt. Have you long been resident in Brighton?"

"Above five years. I removed here when my husband died—I was but a child, as you may conceive," she added, self-consciously, tho' I should never accuse her of being mutton dressed as lamb; she retained the bloom of youth, and *looked* several years my junior. "There is nothing like Brighton for banishing melancholy!"

"I had begun to wonder," I suggested doubtfully. "The distressing news of Miss Twining's death last evening—the probability of its being *murder*—very nearly convinced me to return to London! Such a town *cannot* be safe for unattached females! Poor Catherine, I said to my brother—To end in such a way!"

"You were acquainted with Miss Twining?" Mrs. Alleyn's countenance was all interest.

"A little."

"Ah," she said with satisfaction. "Then you will be wishing to condole with Louisa Silchester. She is quite cut up, poor lady—tho' not so melancholy as to avoid *all* society at present. Were she to hide in her rooms, the malicious might suspect her of negligence with regard to Miss Twining; and Louisa should never wish to forfeit the good opinion of Brighton. *She* cannot be held responsible for the girl's death,—or not before the inquest, at least. Of the coroner's opinion, we can as yet know nothing."

"—Or of General Twining's, I presume? If he held Mrs. Silchester in trust—placed his daughter in that lady's care—"

"General Twining! Do not *speak* to me of that odious fellow!" Mrs. Alleyn cried. "He had the presumption to *dangle* after me, Miss Austen, a full twelvemonth, when first I came to Brighton; and his persistence could hardly be endured! I was forced to speak quite plainly to the gentleman, and assure him in the strongest language that we should not suit. I've long since cut my Wisdoms, my dear—and saw in an instant that fortune was the General's first object! Female society is as nothing to *him*."[17]

"And has he proved inconsolable? Has any other lady excited his notice? Mrs. Silchester, perhaps?"

"My dear," Mrs. Alleyn returned, "she has no money—and the General is entirely about *interest*. I am sure Louisa Silchester would have got him if she could—she was bosombows with his late wife from girlhood, I understand. The

---

[17] "To cut Wisdoms" refers to the emergence of wisdom teeth—a phrase suggesting age, experience, and knowledge of the world.—*Editor's note.*

General is very sly—content to give his *daughter* into Mrs. Silchester's charge—but nothing in the matrimonial line has come of it!"

"If General Twining must be mercenary, I wonder that he did not promote his daughter's prospects," I observed. "Miss Twining felt herself doomed to a marriage she could not like—with a clergyman, greatly her elder. But perhaps there was a fortune in the case."

"You cannot mean Mr. Smalls?" Mrs. Alleyn laughed. "No fortune whatsoever, my dear. Such a match is in every way inexplicable; unless one assumes that the father was determined to destroy every hope in the female breast. So grim and humourless as he is! I make it my business to avoid any meeting with the General—and can only pity what his daughter's life must have been. Perhaps she drowned herself in despair! I can believe such a thing more readily than that Lord Byron killed her. But I detain you—Mrs. Silchester is at liberty, Sir John having quitted her; you will observe her by the bow window—the frail-looking lady, in the dove-grey. Louisa!"

Drowned herself in despair. It was a thought, indeed; and had Catherine Twining been discovered cast up on the shingle, and not sewn into a hammock in Lord Byron's bed, I might have accorded Mrs. Alleyn's views more weight. But Henry had said there were marks of brutality at the girl's throat; she was no victim of self-murder. Someone had deliberately held her head beneath the waves.

Lady Swithin having been claimed by the fellow named Hodge, who was determined to teach her how to cast the bones, Mrs. Alleyn presented me to the tiny Mrs. Silchester, adding with an attempt at carelessness, "Miss Austen was a little acquainted with that unfortunate child, Miss Twining, you know."

Mrs. Silchester started and her eyes widened, as tho' I

sported a Gorgon's head. She pressed one hand to her breast; both breast and hand were bony; and I concluded that the lady suffered from a nervous complaint, excited by the least novelty. "You *knew* poor Catherine?" she whispered. "But *how*? I thought you quite a stranger to Brighton, and all our little concerns!"

I should hardly describe murder as a *little concern*, but having no desire to frighten the lady further, I merely said: "I met Miss Twining in Cuckfield, on my journey hither. Indeed, we met under rather unusual circumstances."

That Mrs. Silchester understood my allusion, I readily perceived by her repressive look at Mrs. Alleyn. That far-too-penetrating lady, her object achieved, merely said, "You will have much to talk over, I suspect," and left me to my quarry with a nod and a smile.

"So it was you, I collect, who tore her from the Fiend's clutches in the stable yard? You, who delivered her from that unhappy state of bondage?" Mrs Silchester whispered.

"I and my brother. We were happy to be of service to Miss Twining."

"But, alas, her enemy proved too strong for us all." Mrs. Silchester's eyes closed, and her face blenched; she groped for support, and found only the bow window.

"I am sure you are unwell. Will you not sit down? On this sopha, perhaps?"

I led the frail being to a settee placed at an angle to the window, where she leaned back against the cushions a moment. Her countenance was dreadful. "If you could search out my vinaigrette," she said faintly, thrusting her reticule into my hands. "When I consider of that poor child—so young, so innocent, a mere dove among wolves—"

I loosed the strings and felt in the depths of the fabric bag; the vinaigrette was there, of course—no lady of Mrs. Silchester's demeanour could travel far without it. I removed the cap and wafted the bottle under my companion's nostrils. She gasped, pressed her fingers to her lips, and stared at me with welling eyes.

"You are unmarried, Miss Austen, but I am sure you cannot be entirely ignorant of the world."

"No indeed."

"Then you apprehend what *beasts* men are."

"In every person, I believe, there is the potential for bestiality—as well as for good."

"Not in Lord Byron," she said heavily. "He is entirely evil. The sort of evil Lucifer knows, that walks with an angelic face. I say so, Miss Austen, tho' the world acclaims him as a god; I want nothing of such idolatry. He killed poor Catherine because she saw him for what he was; she feared rather than loved him; and he could not endure to be repulsed."

"You are very sure in your accusations, ma'am, but it would appear not all the facts are yet known. Lord Byron may be innocent."

"Innocent! A false word could never apply!" She struggled upright on the sopha, and seized her vinaigrette. "Since that Fiend came to Brighton, my poor Miss Twining has known not a moment's peace. Those who are little acquainted with that man's character like to say it is *sailing,* and the promise of good Society, that drew him here in defiance of Lady Oxford's wiles—but I know better! It was poor Catherine he sought, and Catherine upon whose frail body he slaked his vile lusts!"

Such language from so fragile a creature could not but be shocking; and had I been ignorant of Miss Twining's history—known nothing of the attempted abduction at Cuckfield—I might have judged Louisa Silchester a prey to fancies of the most lurid type, a creature enslaved to novel-reading and Gothick romance. But I had seen the cravat knotted around Miss Twining's wrists, had seen Lord Byron's countenance alter to something just short of demonic, upon the discovery of her liberation. I could not dismiss Louisa Silchester, however excessive her language.

"When did his lordship first meet Miss Twining?" I asked her.

"Some three weeks since, when she was sent home from her seminary in Bath." Mrs. Silchester dabbed at her eyes with a square of lawn. "Poor, dear child. Such an innocent, always. She had conceived a passion for a well-born young officer whose estates were in that part of the country—and dismissal was the result!"

"Indeed!" This was news of primary importance; Henry's Unknown made a tentative appearance. There had been a rival to Mr. Hendred Smalls—and a prior claimant to the heart Byron had so boldly besieged.

"Miss Twining in love!" I exclaimed. "She said nothing of this to me."

"She kept the matter very close, in terror of the General. I confess *I* do not even know the young gentleman's name, for she would never tell it to me. But I have thought of him often, in the hours following her death—and wondered how the intelligence was to reach him. . . ."

"The General did not look with favour on a brother officer—and one in possession of estates?" I asked in some puzzlement.

Mrs. Silchester shook her head. "When Catherine's childish infatuation was penetrated by her headmistress, a letter to the General was the unfortunate result. The General sent for his daughter immediately, and threatened to keep her so close she might never see the light of day again—but that I persuaded him to let me try what a little judicious chaperonage might do. I thought it very likely that the Brighton Season should put all thought of officers out of her head. And the General agreed! He trusted me to put all right! I do not know *how* I am to meet with him now. His reproaches—"

"And Lord Byron?" I persisted. "That affair began some few weeks ago?"

"—He glimpsed her, as I understand, in the Promenade Grove. He fell instantly in love—sent round a tribute of flowers to Church Street that very afternoon—begged to be introduced to the General, which favour was immediately repulsed; and left again for London in flat despair. We congratulated ourselves that he had been defeated—for it would never do, you know, Miss Austen, to encourage the pretensions of such a person; his reputation for vice is so *very bad*. And he has no fortune to speak of—only debts, which intelligence the General naturally procured, before repulsing his lordship entirely."

There it was again: General Twining *must* be mercenary. That Louisa Silchester saw nothing to object to in this was hardly to be remarked upon; her understanding did not appear to be powerful.

"Lord Byron returned to Brighton, I collect?"

"And to his pursuit of Catherine," the lady said ominously. "A direct approach having failed, he began to haunt Church Street—he has acquaintance in the vicinity—and barely a day went by that we were not forced to meet with his pleas. Entire cantos of poetry were left with Lord Byron's card, which verses the General immediately confiscated and threw on the fire; a sad waste of talent, I daresay. It was as tho' Lord Byron was *mad with love*, and I might have pitied him—but for the turn his passion took. You know too well the episode at Cuckfield; that he returned to Brighton at all, in defiance of a parent's natural indignation, is to be wondered at—and that he should prove so bold as to appear at the *Assembly*, as tho' nothing untoward had happened—"

Mrs. Silchester was correct: Such behaviour must provoke wonder. Either Lord Byron was too firmly in the grip of passion to retain his reason, despite the claims of propriety; or he cared nothing for propriety at all. Either attitude, for a gentleman of his consequence, argued a disregard for the bounds of society that bordered on the mad. But when one had already so far overstepped convention, it was not, I reflected, so very far a stretch to *murder*.

"Having been discovered in an attempted abduction, I had assumed that his lordship would never descend upon Brighton again," Louisa Silchester muttered. "But I failed to consider that nobody but ourselves was aware of the event; it could not be generally published; the town remained in ignorance, and welcomed Lord Byron's return; the General observed the strictest silence, for Catherine's sake. He had lately formed the idea of uniting her in marriage to a respectable clergyman—Mr. Hendred Smalls—from a desire to preserve the child's good name. Questionable young officers and poets proved too much for the General's patience; he wished to see Catherine safely bestowed in matrimony before another month was out. No reproach could attach to the virtue of Mr. Smalls's wife, the General believed; no blemish could darken the Twining name. The General is very jealous of his dignity," she added, by way of explanation.

"So I have been made to understand."

"Lord Byron saw his advantage in our silence. Not content with destroying the poor child's peace, he pursued her the length and breadth of the Assembly last night, calling Catherine by a heathen name—*Leila,* some Attic language of which I know nothing—glowering at her through every dance; thrusting his way, on that hideous leg, into her slightest conversation, to demand a private word she could not grant—his face by turns burning with passion, and dead white with rage. I could have kissed the painted feet of that Caro Lamb, when she entered the ballroom and put flight to the Fiend—I was never so pleased to see anybody in my life!"

Startled, I asked, "You are acquainted with her ladyship?"

"I knew her mother, the Countess, a little in my salad days," Mrs. Silchester said dismissively. "Her daughter I confess I know not at all—but only fancy! *She* sought an introduction to Catherine and me! And nothing would do but that she must carry Catherine away for a private tête-à-tête at the Pavilion—such an honour, I am sure—promising faithfully to see the child home in one of the Regent's carriages, when at last they were done."

I felt myself go swiftly cold. "Miss Twining left the Assembly in Lady Caroline's company? And the General made no objection?" This was hardly being jealous of his dignity, or his daughter's reputation; only the ignorant encouraged the attentions of the scandalous Caro Lamb.

"The General was no longer present; he could not be appealed to. I saw no harm in Lady Caroline's condescension. Catherine wished to go."

Catherine had wished to return to a place she despised upon first acquaintance—a place where no less a roué than George Hanger had forced his attentions upon her—and the woman entrusted with her safety had sent her off with a complete stranger. The whole narrative defied comprehension.

"You blame me," Louisa Silchester said. "I am *sure* you blame me, Miss Austen. But after all, what was I to do? The Pavilion, you know! It was very nearly a Royal summons! I could not gainsay so obliging and august a personage. Indeed I could not. And so of course I granted my permission. But the General is so dreadfully angry! He would not admit me this afternoon, when I attempted to pay a call of condolence! If the General abandons me, Miss Austen, so shall all of Brighton—and then I do not know *what* I shall do!"

CHAPTER FOURTEEN

A Call to Justice

TUESDAY, 11 MAY 1813
BRIGHTON, CONT.

"WHAT HAVE YOU BEEN SAYING TO POOR LOUISA SIL-chester?" Lady Swithin demanded as she led me to the fire, where a pair of chairs were at liberty, owing to the general warmth of the night. "She looks as if she had received a sentence of death—tho' I suppose that is very natural, given the loss of her protégée."

"I did not rebuke her; tho' I confess I was tempted. She is an excessively silly woman, my lady—and ought never to have been entrusted with Miss Twining. She tells me she allowed the child to go off to the Pavilion last night with Caro Lamb!"

"Did she?" Desdemona enquired, all interest. "I had not an idea of it. I stayed only to observe Byron's outrage at Caro's entrance—to judge the effect her costume made upon the room—and then Swithin pled boredom, and we made good our escape. What did Caro mean by carrying that child off to the Pavilion? They were not acquainted before last night, I am sure—and there must be more than a decade between them in age. It is a singular condescension."

"I cannot say what her ladyship was about, but I must endeavour to learn," I replied. "Lady Caroline should have been one of the last to see Catherine Twining alive. It may be in her power to disclose something vital of the child's movements. At what hour did you quit the Assembly, my lady?"

Desdemona shrugged. "Far too early for Fashion. It was not above one o'clock, I am sure—Lady Caroline having put in her appearance just after midnight. But do sit down, Miss Austen"—the Countess was already arranging the folds of her silk gown—"so that we may be comfortable. No one shall teaze us; your blacks will keep them all at a distance, you know."

I sat. My mind, I confess, was worrying at the problem of Lady Caroline—and my thoughts ranged so far abroad as to render me almost uncivil. I drew my attention back to my hostess; she had, after all, summoned me to her home that evening with the object of conversation.

"You must have formed your own opinion of Catherine Twining," she began. "For my part, I knew her not at all. But any lady capable of engaging Byron's entire interest, must have been a paragon. And when one considers her youth—it is in every way extraordinary. He has been in the habit of pursuing *married* ladies of a certain age—not virgins of fifteen."

"Our acquaintance was so slight, and of such recent formation—we met in a stable yard in Cuckfield, on the journey south," I said. I hesitated at disclosing the nature of our meeting—but the silence so fervently embraced by the General and Mrs. Silchester had already done damage enough; I could not regard myself as bound by it. "I rescued Miss Twining from Lord Byron's clutches, in fact. He had formed the intention of abducting her—to what end, a Gretna marriage or a swift ruin, I know not. Certainly he had bound her wrists and gagged her; she made her presence known by beating on the side panels of Lady Oxford's chaise, which his lordship had borrowed for the purpose."

"Good God!" Desdemona said blankly. "And he chose *Jane's* chaise for his seductions? The man's insolence knows no bounds! I shall have to suppress the fact—tho' it may already be all over Brighton."

The fact of the abduction did not appear to outrage her ladyship nearly as much as the bad *ton* his lordship betrayed; there was little that could shock Lord Harold's niece.

"I do not think anyone but the Twining family, and ourselves, is aware of it," I assured her. "Lady Oxford may remain in ignorance—but I cannot think it wise. There may be worse shocks in store, if Lord Byron is charged with murder."

She looked at me speculatively. "What sort of girl was Miss Twining?"

"I should have said that she was no different from every other young lady of respectable birth and gentle rearing. She was diffident, shy, easily imposed upon—" I might, at this juncture, have disclosed my encounter with George Hanger in the Pavilion Saturday, but doubt as to what I had actually seen, stopped my mouth. "Her appearance of goodness, I thought, was entirely genuine. And she was afraid of Byron—she dreaded a meeting with him. Indeed, only last evening, she begged me to remain with her."

"And now you berate yourself for having failed to do so." Desdemona reached impulsively for my hand. "My dear Miss Austen—*you* were not her parent. *You* were not her chaperon. Having saved her once from a predator's clutches, you cannot always have been her protector. What of the girl's family?"

"There is a General Twining—Mrs. Alleyn had much that

was ill to say of his character—and a brother in the 10th Hussars, lost in the Peninsula." I hesitated. "My lady, to what end do these questions tend?"

She chose her words with care. "You are aware, I think, that Lady Oxford is my friend—Swithin would not have me call her so, to be sure, as she is regarded askance by almost everyone of consequence in the *ton,* on account of her sad tendency to seek consolation outside her marriage."

"And yet you brave the Earl's displeasure?" I interjected, curiously. "This is being a loyal friend indeed!"

"The Countess is a clever woman, and unafraid to appear the bluestocking before her friends; it is for this reason so many gentlemen seek her company—she possesses a well-informed mind. Have you any notion, Miss Austen, how rare a powerful understanding is, among women of Fashion? It is insupportably dull, I assure you, to spend all one's days among creatures who talk of nothing but dress, and children, and the gifts their husbands have lately showered upon their mistresses! I prize Lady Oxford for her courage in living life as she chuses, without entirely affronting the Polite World, as Caro Lamb must perpetually do; and if Swithin fears her ladyship's example—so much the better for me," she added with a droll glint in her eye. "Anxiety keeps the Earl attentive; and that is saying a good deal."

We had wandered from the subject of Catherine Twining, and the Countess recognised it. She took up the reins of conversation with a brisk twitch. "I do not need to tell you that Lady Oxford is in love with Lord Byron. Indeed, a degree of affection subsists between them that would make any risk to his life or reputation a matter of extreme anxiety to the Countess."

A degree of affection subsists between them . . . and yet he had been obsessed with Catherine to the point of madness.

How to explain it? Was Lady Oxford deceived, or was Byron the sort who must seduce every creature he encountered?

"That can be nothing to me," I said, tho' the words felt thick and ungracious on my tongue. "I am acquainted with neither the Countess nor the poet; my bond, slight as it was, lay with the unfortunate victim, and my sympathies must be entirely devoted to her cause."

"I *do* understand," Desdemona said with swift warmth. She squeezed my hand. "Indeed, I expected no less—and honour you for your sentiments. Which is why I craved your society this evening; I cannot help recalling, Miss Austen, how brilliantly you acted in the matter of my brother Kinsfell's being mistakenly taken up for murder—and how deftly you *then* penetrated the motives of those who would have seen him unjustly hanged."[18]

"It was your uncle's brilliance that prevailed on that occasion, not mine."

A bold statement and a painful one in such a house, with all that remained of the past lying unspoken between us; and for an instant, Desdemona stiffened. "We will not speak of *my uncle,* I beg."

She had loved Lord Harold like a daughter—or perhaps, their natures being so alike, more as a companion in adventure. When he was killed, I must believe she blamed me—for tho' present, I was entirely unable to avert the deed, or save him from the mortal effect of his wounds. I had fully expected to be petitioned for the details of the Rogue's final hour; but thus far, her ladyship had not asked for them. I guessed it was a form of Wilborough pride—and the fear of

[18] The Countess refers here to events set down in Austen's third journal of her detective adventures, *Jane and the Wandering Eye.—Editor's note.*

opening old wounds. I waited all the same for the moment when Desdemona's desire should overcome her dignity.

"Are you suggesting that I ought to exert my energies to clear *Lord Byron's* name?" I demanded. "—Given that gentleman's extraordinary history, I doubt any woman could do so."

Desdemona's countenance eased. "You are annihilatingly frank, are you not? I care nothing for Byron myself; it is merely the fashion, you know, to swoon over his verses. I find him boorish and ungentlemanly; which is to say that he has never made the slightest push to engage my attention. Naturally I must regard him as my enemy! But with Lady Oxford it is otherwise; and I should not be most *truly* the friend I profess, did I not endeavour to help where help was wanted."

"What is your honest opinion of Lord Byron's mind?" I asked. "I spoke to him only once—in Cuckfield—and he was not then master enough of himself to know what he said. But you, who have seen him a good deal . . . would you regard him as entirely sound?"

"Are you asking whether he is mad?"

I made a diffident gesture with my hand. "I had wondered, indeed, whether he was perfectly sane. His behaviour of late has been most unsteady. Even in his writings there is much that is violent. It is of a piece, you know, with Romantical poetry, to be driven to the brink of murder—by thwarted love."

"Caro Lamb would certainly think so! I am sure she is wishing it were *she,* and not poor Miss Twining, who was dropped like a sacrifice in Byron's bed last night."

The words, however farcical, were too close to truth for comfort. Her ladyship seemed to feel it; there was the briefest uneasiness between us; and then Desdemona attempted a recovery.

"Such stuff may be *exotic,* and feed the rage for all things Oriental that the Regent himself is so wild about—but it is not to *my* taste at all! I vastly prefer a good novel, about people such as one knows, and circumstances one may comprehend—something delightful and brimming with excellent conversation! I adored *Pride and Prejudice*—has it come in your way, by the by?"

"It *has*, yes—*indeed*, I was so happy as to look into it this winter," I stuttered, feeling my countenance flush as tho' her ladyship had let slip an indecency; and then, reverting to safer subjects, "But if you do not care for Byron, how can you be so solicitous for his welfare—?"

"It is all Lady Oxford. She sent me *such* a letter by Express this evening—the courier drew rein at our door just as the dinner bell was rung. I do not scruple to say, Miss Austen, that her ladyship is wild with fear that Byron will be *hanged*."

My senses sharpened. "Has he been taken, then?"

"You did not know?" Desdemona sat up alertly in her chair, the fire in the hearth edging her profile in gold. "He was met at the door of his lodgings—he has rooms in Bennet Street, St. James's—by the Brighton constabulary. Lady Oxford—her Christian name, like yours, is Jane—says Byron listened to them patiently, but when told he must return for the inquest, he kicked up a dust. One of the constables had his cork drawn, and another was tossed on his ear into the street, whereupon Byron remounted and rode directly to Mortimer House, the Oxford residence in Town. The constables followed, and it was the Earl of Oxford in the end who urged Byron to do their bidding—fearing, no doubt, a hideous scene at his very door. Adultery may be one thing—Oxford is accustomed to *that*—but murder is quite another."

"And Lady Oxford?"

"—prepares to follow her heart. She wrote to beg a room here on the Marine Parade, and tho' Swithin dislikes it, he has given way to my wishes." She glanced affectionately at her husband, who was deep in conversation with Sir John and my brother. "He is an excellent husband, is he not? I never dreamt, during those distant days in Bath when Charles was disposed to be excessively disagreeable, intent upon winning every battle and making myself the object of his conquest—that I should be so content with my surrender!"

"I am glad to hear it," I said; and meant it. Tho' the Earl and his Countess had rarely met without quarreling in their salad days, it had been obvious to all who observed them that they were formed for each other. I envied them completely.

"Jane—I hope I *may* call you Jane?"

"Of course."

"And you shall call me Mona. Everyone does." She leaned towards me confidingly. "I shall not tax you to save Byron's neck—he will come to a bad end regardless. No one can pursue so ruinous a course, in love and debt, without he ends in a sponging house or flight to the Continent. I *will* urge you, however, to pursue justice. Someone drowned Catherine Twining like a helpless kitten; and I cannot bear to think that such a horror should go unpunished. Even if it *was* Byron who killed her. We should be doing the world a service, in publishing the murderer's ill fame—whoever he proves to be."

"We?" I repeated dubiously. Justice was a far higher plane of talking for the Countess of Swithin, who had begun with mere ties of friendship to a woman whose morals I could not like.

"Well, naturally, I shall do my *all* to help you," Mona said indignantly. "I may open any door in Brighton on your behalf; nothing is more easily done; and I should think it very good sport, to be frank, to be privileged to hear of your researches. Uncle used to tell me *everything,* you know."

There; she had referred to him, despite herself.

"He even told me," she said distinctly, "that he intended to marry you one day."

My breath stopped in my throat; my face, I felt, was blazing. I wished of a sudden that I might run from the room, heedless of the Alleyns and Silchesters and Hodges who might stare after me, astonished and babbling; I wished only for darkness, and a soothing bout of tears.

"I wish that he had," Mona persisted. "I wish that he had lived. I might have called you Aunt."

"Pray, say no more," I whispered.

"Will you do it? Will you find Catherine Twining's murderer?"

"I cannot simply thrust myself in the way of an investigation, Mona." I sighed in exasperation. "There are *men* charged with finding the truth. The magistrate, for one—and the coroner, for another."

"The magistrate is Sir Harding Cross, who is intimate with the Regent—hence his token office," Mona said shrewdly. "Sir Harding lives for the next race-meeting, considers himself a dashing blade, for all his stays creak when he attempts to bow; and is disinclined to bother himself very much in anybody's death. He is a three-bottle-a-day man, too intent upon draining the last drop to attend to trifling affairs like a drowning. Rather than untangle this web, he would vastly prefer to charge Lord Byron with the deed—and have an end to it."

"Then the truth will out at his lordship's trial."

"—Do you believe it? So do *not* I." The Countess's voice had sharpened. "Once Miss Twining is in her grave, any proofs that might have pointed to the culprit will have been neatly swept into the rubbish."

"It is for her family to pursue justice, not a stranger."

"The Jane Austen so valued by Lord Harold should *never* have hesitated to learn the whole!"

Her voice had risen, on this last; a few curious eyes turned in our direction; I observed Henry to set down his glass of Port with an audible clink. He looked as if he would approach; I shook my head slightly.

It was unfair of Mona to invoke, again, the Gentleman Rogue. I looked at her ladyship, whose grey eyes were as cool and satiric as Lord Harold's own, and whose wits were certainly as sharp, and said, "But what if it was indeed Lord Byron who held Catherine Twining's head beneath the waves? What shall you tell your friend Lady Oxford?"

"The truth," Desdemona replied without hesitation. "It should, after all, be the salvation of her."

CHAPTER FIFTEEN

Evidence of an Undergroom

WEDNESDAY, 12 MAY 1813
BRIGHTON

~

THE CONSTABLES BROUGHT LORD BYRON BACK TO Brighton under cover of darkness last night, hoping, no doubt, to escape the notice of the general populace—but they reckoned without the avidity of the lower orders in all matters having to do with murder, and found to their discomfiture that the way into town was lined with torches and a gallery of faces four deep along the roadside. I observed some part of the chilling progress from my window at the Castle, for it was to this inn that his lordship was bound. He has not, it seems, been charged with murder or placed under arrest— merely summoned to appear at the coroner's inquest—and thus could not be housed in Brighton's gaol. The King's Arms, it seemed, would not have his lordship back again— Mr. Scrope Davies, tho' sympathetic, could not assure Byron's safety in his private lodgings—and so his lordship was consigned to the comforts of our own temporary abode.

"Once the verdict is brought in at the inquest," Henry mused as he stood beside me in the window, "he shall have to be placed under the 10th Hussars' guard at Brighton Camp. No other place will hold him."

We had a brief glimpse of the poet—dark head, dark clothes, and a face whose pallor was dreadful—as he limped from coach to Castle entry; and it required the combined efforts of four constables and a burly individual I took to be a Bow Street Runner, who brandished a pair of pistols and met the crowd jeer for jeer, for his lordship to achieve the door.

Who, I wondered, had hired the Runner as Byron's guard—Lady Oxford, perhaps?

"When is the inquest to be?" I asked my brother.

"Tomorrow," he replied. "They were waiting only for Byron."

He left me then to my bed and my thoughts, which were so numerous and tangled as to keep me awake, long into the night.

HAVING FORMED NO PART IN THE DISCOVERY OF CATHERINE Twining's body, I was not permitted to attend the inquest this morning; that was for the select company of the coroner, his chosen panel of local fellows, and the magistrate, Sir Harding Cross. The King's Arms' publican should be present, indeed; and the chambermaid who found poor Catherine; and Lord Byron, whose bed she had lain in; and General Twining, whose office it must be to confirm the identity of Deceased. Even Mr. Scrope Davies should be there—to swear on his oath that Byron had spent Monday night in his lodgings, and quitted them for London early Tuesday morning. All the oaths should avail Byron nothing; if Lady Swithin was to be credited, Sir Harding would make swift work of the business, and a verdict of willful murder should be returned against the poet. There was no very great loss in being barred from the inquest; Henry should have an account of it almost as soon as it was done, from the knowledgeable at Raggett's Club.

"Betsy," I said to the chambermaid as she tidied the ashes from my grate, "are you at all acquainted with the servants at the King's Arms?"

Her eyes grew round. "That I am, ma'am, but if it's the murder you're wanting to talk of, I must beg to be excused. Not a word I've heard of anything else, since yesterday noon, and not a wink of sleep I've had, for brooding over all I've heard, and dreading to find a similar case each time I open a bedchamber door! —For if there's a madman throwing young ladies into beds at the Arms, what's to keep him from doing the same at the Castle? There's little to chuse between them, except we've more beds to hide a body in! And now they've lodged that Lord Byron here! I declare, it's enough to make every man, woman, and child pack up their traps and quit the place, for all he's so handsome. Mr. Anson, the head steward, allows as how our patrons is too high in the instep for the use of hammocks, besides needing a servant to do the sewing for 'em, but I never pay no mind to Mr. Anson. He's from Liverpool," she added, as tho' such an origin could hardly be trusted.

"I was a little acquainted with the young lady who died," I said.

Betsy sat back on her haunches, her dustpan slack on her knees. "Were you now? No wonder you look so peaked this morning. Probably never caught a mite's sleep all night. But wasn't she fearful young?"

"I should judge her to have been no more than fifteen."

Betsy bit her lip. "Then she'd no cause to be walking abroad alone at night. Foolish, I call it, and *fast*, tho' the poor thing *was* murdered. Got what she asked for, didn't she?"

"Nobody asks to be drowned," I said sharply, "much less

sewn into a hammock. But why do you say Miss Twining walked alone?"

"Jem saw her."

"And who is Jem?"

"Undergroom at the Pavilion," she said immediately. "He's by way of being a cousin."

"I see." Betsy's relations were extensive enough to cover most of Britain. I set down my teacup. "And this fellow *saw* Miss Twining before her death? Well enough to recognise her?"

"Not so as to know her name. Jem's not the sort to be acquainted with young ladies. Asleep, he ought to have been, at such an hour—but one of the Regent's mares was dropping a foal that night, and Jem was up in the loose box a-helping of her. The mare's first, it was, and having a hard time of it. Jem stepped out with a lanthorn to fetch hot water from the kitchen, and that's when he saw her—a girl with dark hair, dressed in white, hurrying away from the Pavilion. Headed towards the Steyne, she was, but powerful late Jem thought it, to be abroad alone."

"He did not chuse to speak to her?"

Betsy shook her head. "Wasn't his place, ma'am, to take notice of young ladies leaving the Pavilion in the middle of the night. The Regent'd have had his head, like. Young ladies've been slipping in an' out of the Regent's quarters for years, and nobody the wiser. Besides, there was the mare to think of."

"Did he say what time this was?"

"No, ma'am."

"I should like to talk to Jem," I said thoughtfully.

"If you're wishful to have a word, I can always send for him." The maid coloured painfully. "Jem is always ready to oblige me."

"You would do better to send him to the magistrate. The

coroner's panel assembles this morning, and they would give much to know what your cousin saw."

"A reward, like?" Betsy eyed me curiously; ladies who were knowledgeable of the workings of inquests had probably never come in her way. I slid out of bed and went to my reticule. Within it, I kept a few coins. I withdrew a shilling.

"Please give this to Jem," I said, "and urge him to seek out Sir Harding Cross. The Regent, I am sure, shall not reproach him for speaking publickly in a matter of murder."

If I surprized her, Betsy made no comment—but pocketed the coin and promised to do as I urged.

BEFORE THE EVENTS OF YESTERDAY, I HAD MADE A thousand plans with Henry for the balance of the week. We were to take in today's race-meeting, on the course established by the late Duke of Queensberry just outside of town; we were to drive past Hove, to the ruins of St. Aldrington's Church; we were to hire a pair of dippers, and *bathe* in the frigid seas, first obtaining a respectable costume for the purpose; we were to attend a concert at the Pavilion, at the express invitation of Colonel McMahon, who had taken an inexplicable liking to my brother, or perhaps to the depth of his pockets. But some part at least of these frivolous pursuits must be set aside. The race-meeting was not to be thought of. I took breakfast in my room, being certain that Henry was already at Raggett's, awaiting the issue of Miss Twining's inquest—and as I sipped my coffee, and fiddled with my bread, I compiled a list of questions that *must* be answered, if the truth were to be known.

1. With whom did Catherine Twining dance at the Assembly, besides Mr. Smalls?
2. When did Catherine arrive at the Pavilion in Caro Lamb's care?

3. What was the purport of the ladies' tête-à-tête?
4. When did Catherine quit the Pavilion?
5. If the undergroom observed her walking towards the Steyne, how did she come by her death in the sea?
6. Where was Lord Byron at the time?
7. Colonel George Hanger?
8. General Twining? Mr. Hendred Smalls?
9. What did Lady Caroline Lamb do after Catherine left her?
10. When did the General discover that his daughter never returned home Monday night—and did he sound an alarum?
11. How could a body be carried into the King's Arms in the dead of night without being seen?
12. Did anyone at the Arms hear a disturbance in Byron's rooms? Query: Who was lodged next to Byron?

I should have to speak with the principals on my list, of course—tho' some might bar their doors against me. The endeavour should demand considerable address. I considered of the prospects: the General, whom I knew already for a formidable man, and whose plans for his daughter I had reason to suspect; Mr. Smalls, from whose interview I should derive little but platitudes and no pleasure; Caro Lamb, who should be unlikely to disclose her schemes to anyone. Desdemona might better assist me *there*.

And Byron himself: a slight shudder coursed through my body at the thought of the man—so much a prey to his passions, so entirely a complex of contempt and ardour. Would he recall my visage from the Cuckfield Inn, and regard me as his enemy? How had the murder of Catherine Twining worked upon his lordship's emotions?

Amidst such a company, my enquiries were likely to be fruitless.

In the course of my mature life—dating, indeed, from my first acquaintance with the Gentleman Rogue, more than ten years ago—I have been so circumstanced as to meet with a variety of murderers, some very clever and some merely cold. Avarice has been their motive, or revenge, or a passionate love turned to hate. There were aspects of this case—the sewing of the hammock, the delivery of the corpse to Byron's bed—that argued a deliberation of mind; and other aspects— the forcible drowning of a young girl, her head held violently under the water as she struggled—that bespoke a destructive passion. It was almost as tho' *two different persons had been involved*. Had they worked in concert, or in ignorance of each other? Had Byron done murder—and another delivered the proofs of it?

The only possible motivation for such an act must be to see the poet tormented, upon the discovery of his beloved's corpse; or to see his lordship hang.

If Byron were innocent of Catherine's death, then he, as well as the unfortunate girl, was the victim of a merciless intelligence. There was cruelty and forethought in the execution of the whole; someone had derived *pleasure* from dropping that sodden package in his lordship's bed.

It smacked of hatred. Or a desire for vengeance. And in all this, the life of a young girl had been snuffed out as nothing.

And so, after a pause, I penned the last of my queries on the Castle's sheet of paper:

13. Who, among the respectable and the highborn of Brighton, hates Lord Byron to the point of madness?

CHAPTER SIXTEEN

Conflicting Testimony

MY PERIOD OF REFLECTION WAS BROKEN BY A KNOCK AT the bedchamber door. A footman stood in the passage, with the intelligence that my brother awaited me downstairs— with a party of friends.

"Has the inquest adjourned?"

"Not a quarter-hour ago, ma'am."

I hastened below, and discovered Henry established in a little side-parlour with the Earl and Countess of Swithin; all three were taking glasses of something fortifying—brandy, in the case of the gentlemen, and ratafia, in the person of Desdemona.

"What is the coroner's verdict?" I enquired, as I accepted a glass of wine.

"Oh, murder, of course," Swithin said grimly; "but to everyone's surprize, it was brought back against *a person or persons unknown*. There is much talk as to the motives in such a judgement; it was said at first that the Regent must have intervened, to preserve the freedom of a celebrated poet and nobleman; but those acquainted with the two gentlemen are well aware that no love is lost between them, the Regent detesting the very sight of George Gordon. His Royal Highness finds the poet's club foot distasteful, and cannot forgive him for forming a part of Princess Caroline's court. So there is astonishment in many quarters. Old Sir Harding Cross cannot be to blame, as he owes his position to the Regent; it was hardly he who taught the jury mercy. Perhaps it was Frogmore, the coroner, who urged caution."

"For a wonder," I observed, "a coroner's panel has drawn a conclusion independent of the magistrate—and declined to hang a man who insists he was elsewhere when murder was done! What is likely to happen now?"

"Byron shall have to go to ground, somehow," Henry said. "There are any number of folk in Brighton out for his blood, chief among them the poor young lady's father."

"General Twining was in attendance, I apprehend?"

"He testified as to the remains being his daughter's, at which point the panel was required to view the corpse. Several went quite green, I understand. The General said only that he had entrusted his daughter to the chaperonage of Mrs. Silchester, who had failed in her duties; that he had quitted the Assembly Rooms at the decent hour of eleven o'clock; ordered Miss Twining's maid to wait up for her; and was roused at five o'clock in the morning with the intelligence that his daughter had never returned. He suspected, he claimed, a further abduction on the part of Lord Byron—and informed the Brighton constables of the fact."

"Abduction? So the tale of Cuckfield came out—and still the jury did not find against his lordship?"

"It was viewed, rather, as a point in Lord Byron's favour; a man who wished so ardently for a Flight to the Border can hardly be suspected of murdering his lady."

"General Twining cannot have regarded the matter thus."

"No, indeed," Henry agreed. "Having given his evidence—and heard Mrs. Silchester, amidst much tears and lamentation, assure the panel that Lady Caroline Lamb had been most insistent upon carrying Miss Twining away to the Pavilion—the General retired into his handkerchief. His face emerged from it only at the announcement of the panel's verdict—at which, in a rage, he slapped Lord Byron's face with said handkerchief, and vowed to see him dead at twenty paces if he were to escape hanging."

"Lord!" Desdemona breathed. "And Byron?"

"—Merely looked contemptuous; and said he should be only too happy to meet the General, his honour and reputation having suffered injuries enough already at his hands. Scrope Davies—who provided my intelligence—said Byron has long hated the fellow, and might more readily have drowned the father than the daughter." Henry rubbed his nose in speculation. "I daresay poor Byron's life is not worth a farthing in Brighton at this present. Your Lady Oxford might take him back to London, Countess—but for the magistrate's demand that Byron remain in town for the nonce."

"Are further researches to be undertaken? Does the magistrate mean to learn the *truth* of Miss Twining's death?" I enquired.

"Not at all," Mona scoffed. "It is as I predicted; Sir Harding shall be content to say that *persons unknown* killed the girl, and have done."

"I cannot agree, my love," Swithin objected. "Indeed, I think Old HardCross intends to charge Byron regardless of the inquest's judgement. It is within his office, you know, provided he can recruit his proofs, and present them along with Byron at the next Assizes."

"The magistrate is a fool if he believes Byron should be witless enough to leave Miss Twining's body in his own rooms. Good God," Desdemona said bitterly, "had he indeed drowned the poor child, as all of Brighton supposes, he had merely to leave her lying on the shingle! For what possible purpose should he have taken a hammock from his own yacht, and sewn her into it like a lost seaman, in order to carry her to his bed?"

"The hammock was indeed Byron's?" I repeated, startled.

"Yes," Henry supplied. "The word *Giaour*, you will recall, was embroidered on the canvas—and as you correctly divined, that is the name of Byron's boat. It is a Turkish word, apparently, meaning infidel, or heathen . . . or . . . some such. Sir Harding would have it the hammock alone indicts his lordship."

"Nonsense!" Desdemona cried. "Does any murderer leave his calling-card on the body?"

"Sir Harding can think of nobody else to blame, my dear," her husband soothed. "This adjournment is a lull in the battle merely, with further salvos to come."

"But what did Lord Byron say, that so persuaded the jury of his innocence?" I demanded.

"It was his valet, rather than Byron himself, who moved them," Henry supplied. "The man is Brighton born and bred. Byron employs him only when he chances to descend upon the town for a bit of sailing; and with little in the nature of loyalty due to such an indifferent master, the valet—one Chaunce by name—was readily credited by his fellows on the panel. He declared that Byron returned to the Arms at a quarter to one in the morning, well before Miss Twining is known to have quitted the Assembly with Lady Caroline Lamb, which may be put at one o'clock; and that his lordship demanded that his bags be packed. He paid his shot with the innkeeper while Chaunce collected his traps. Chaunce and Byron then quitted the Arms for Mr. Scrope Davies's house, Davies affirming that he had waited in the publick rooms and escorted Byron and his man to his own lodgings. At no point was Byron out of sight of either of his fellows—he cannot *then* have effected murder."

"Did Mr. Davies say when they achieved his lodgings?" I asked swiftly.

"He would put it at perhaps a quarter to two in the morning. He and Byron sat up drinking Port, and talking over the regrettable behaviour of Lady Caroline Lamb. I'm told that Byron declared he fled the King's Arms in order to avoid Lady Caro—he was certain she would attempt to breach his rooms that night, as she is forever doing. The two gentlemen sought their beds at three o'clock. Byron was up again at eight, mounted and riding north for London. All this he told the coroner, under oath."

"I suppose he might have killed Miss Twining between three and eight, with no one the wiser," I said thoughtfully, "but how was the deed effected? Is Mr. Davies to be relied upon?"

"I daresay Davies would sell his own mother to get Byron off," Swithin confided. "They've been friends for ages."

"Would he, indeed?" Desdemona turned on her husband swiftly. "Even in a matter of murder? This is not a debt of honour Davies stands security for, Charles! —None of your vowels offered over the faro table at White's! Even so frippery a fellow as Scrope must apprehend the gravity of the case."

"More reason to stand buff, if his friend is in danger of hanging—"

"I do not understand," Mona said petulantly, "why Byron should be suspected *at all*. It is distinctly tiresome! Simply because the corpse lay in a room he once inhabited!"

"The mere fact of Miss Twining having been killed *outside* that room must materially lessen Byron's security," I said. "His lordship's assertion that he quitted the Arms at such-and-such an hour, and Mr. Davies's statement that his friend spent the whole of the night in his lodgings, are worth little, given that Miss Twining did not die in Byron's room at the Arms—*she was only found there, much later*. It might as well have been Lord Byron, as anybody, who drowned her and left her body in his bed for safekeeping."

"But it is all absurd, from beginning to end!" Desdemona protested. "Why should Byron kill Catherine Twining? He was passionately attached to her! Moreover, how could he possibly have carried that dripping hammock upstairs, under the eyes of the whole publick house, in the middle of the night? Do you not think it appears as tho' the *murderer*—whoever he might be—hated Lord Byron, and *meant* for suspicion to turn upon him?"

"That is what the jury believed," Henry said.

"But not the magistrate," Swithin countered. "Absent Byron, all of *Brighton* is subject to suspicion—and when presented with such a bewildering array, Old HardCross is sure to take comfort in the obvious. He shall prefer to arrest the one man he may name."

Being too well acquainted with the limited understanding and general indolence of the magistracy, who are appointed more for their connexions than their zeal, I could not find it in me to argue with the Earl. Moreover, I saw a certain cunning in the very implausibility of Byron's guilt—a cunning of which I suspected him perfectly capable.

"By ostentatiously paying his shot and quitting the King's Arms at an unlikely hour," I mused, "his lordship may have deliberately established his absence in the eyes of all observers, *precisely* to avail himself of those same rooms only hours later. He may depend upon the world exclaiming: 'Byron was long gone when the girl was killed! Byron should never place his victim in his own bed!' He may be clever enough to incriminate himself, if I may so express it, in order to convince us all of his innocence."

There was a pause as the whole party digested this bit of reasoning. Then Mona said, "What a terrible and penetrating mind you own, my dear Jane. I should not like to live too long with such thoughts as yours; they cannot be comfortable. But you have not heard the most diverting thing of all— I have had it from almost every lip in town, tho' none were present at the panel—how swiftly a delicious *on-dit* does fly about, to be sure! You will never guess who forced an entry to the inquest!"

"Lady Oxford?"

"She is not yet arrived, else I am certain she should be impatient to meet with you—I have assured her of your good offices on Byron's behalf."

"But, Mona—!" I cried, shocked; never had I said my slightest office was devoted to his lordship.

"You have agreed to discover the truth," she said, shrugging; "and while *we* may be aware that the truth could run counter to Byron's interests—Lady Oxford need not know it. It was *Caro Lamb* who descended upon Mr. Frogmore and Sir Harding! —Dressed in cloth-of-gold, for all the world like Lady Macbeth, excepting only a bloody blade raised high above her head. I am sure she may have been walking in her sleep, or in the grip of a fit at the very least—by all accounts, her looks bordered on the deranged."

"I had it from Scrope Davies himself," Henry said with a grin, "at Raggett's Club not an hour since, that Byron nearly tore his hair when her ladyship invaded the inquest—thrusting back the door with an audible clang, pacing ceremoniously down the aisle between the chairs, calling out in agitation to Mr. Frogmore that *she must be heard, for tho' he would not stay even to save her from the sea, she would not wish Genius to perish under the heel of the rabble.*"

"Good God," I murmured.

"Byron, I'm told, called her ladyship a carrion bird not

content with hounding him to death, but that she must come and feast upon his bones. He was on the point of quitting the inquest entirely, which should have been most improper and prejudicial to the jury's judgement, had friend Scrope not constrained him."

"And Lady Caroline?" I asked eagerly. "Did she explain her excessive interest in Catherine Twining?"

Mona's eyes narrowed, and she leaned towards us all conspiratorially. "Caro would have it she wished to warn the dear child against Lord Byron—that his lordship was *mad, bad, and dangerous to know,* as she put it. You may imagine the sensation her words produced!"

"I wonder he was not taken in charge immediately!" I observed. "But did Lady Caroline state at what hour Miss Twining arrived at the Pavilion?"

"She could not be certain—never looks at clocks—does not keep a timepiece by her—thought it was close to one o'clock, but should never swear to the hour—and in general, suggested such *ennui* at the question that one wonders how she kept from falling into a doze—or so my sources assure me. As to the manner of Miss Twining's departure—I am told that Lady Caroline was shockingly vague. She *supposed* the girl was shown out by a footman. She *supposed* a chair was found for her. At that juncture a lackey from the stables stood up to claim that he had seen a young lady, dark-haired and dressed in white muslin, hastening towards the Steyne alone, in the middle of the night. He could not immediately swear to the time, but when urged by the coroner to consider the matter, thought it was perhaps a few minutes after the Regent's great stable clock chimed the three-quarter-hour."

"And Byron reached his friend Davies's house, in the company of two witnesses—the self-same friend and a valet—at a quarter to two," I observed. "They must have just missed Catherine Twining on the paving!"

"But you forget, Miss Austen," the Earl interjected. "Whatever may have been her intention of crossing the Steyne, she did not meet her death there. Something—or *someone*—persuaded her to turn back towards the shingle, where she was undoubtedly drowned."

I had a sudden idea of Catherine in the night—weary, bewildered, and quite alone—catching sight of the gentleman she most feared, Lord Byron, striding along the paving opposite the Steyne. And cowering back into the shadows of the Marine Pavilion's grounds, from a dread of meeting him at such an hour . . .

"What do you make of Lady Caroline's behaviour?" Henry asked curiously.

Mona shrugged. "Not even the murder of an acquaintance, it would seem, may penetrate her absorption in *herself*. She is the most selfish creature ever born, you know; the entire world might suffer violent death, and she should go on existing in one of her fevered dreams."

"Does she *wish* Lord Byron to hang? —Her words suggest calumny, at the very least, if not a desire to sway the jury against him," I said.

"Her object was perjury." Lord Swithin stretched his long legs before him, one beautifully polished boot crossed over the other. "Having disposed of Miss Twining by the happy expedients of imaginary footmen and chairs, Caro would insist, in an elevated accent, that Lord Byron was in her rooms at the Pavilion for the remainder of the night in question—and that she would die rather than alter a word of her testimony, tho' the sacrifice to her reputation must be complete."

I raised my brows. "Then either she or Mr. Davies is lying. Let us hope, for Byron's sake, that Lady Caroline may not be believed. Did the magistrate credit the idea of his lordship passing Miss Twining on her way out the Pavilion door, he might certainly find an opportunity to prove Byron drowned the child, as a sort of Attic sacrifice to Lady Caro!"

"I do not think Sir Harding Cross credited her ladyship's assertions. He thanked her for her testimony, then quietly ordered her withdrawn from the room. She went, I am told, rather as Anne Boleyn went to the axe, with her head high and her arms grasped by two bashful constables."

"It is all a sort of play to Caro," Desdemona said; "it comes from growing up among the Devonshire House Set; they could none of them be serious. But tell me, Jane: What do you propose to do in this matter? How shall you set about your researches? How may Swithin and I be of service?"

"Lady Oxford is even now on her road to Brighton?" I asked.

"We expect her by four o'clock. Should you like to dine with us?"

"Far better, before she is arrived in Brighton, to speak to Byron himself." I glanced at the Earl of Swithin. "Can it be managed, sir, do you think?"

He threw me an engaging smile. "Nothing could be easier, my dear Miss Austen. If I know Byron, he went directly from the inquest to Scrope Davies's rooms, to drown his sorrows in brandy! Davies has long been an acquaintance of mine—we may certainly pay him a call!"

CHAPTER SEVENTEEN

The Poet

MR. SCROPE DAVIES, I AM TOLD, IS POSSESSED OF A complex character. Indeed, if I may believe the Earl of Swithin, who knows Davies best, he is singularly equipped to serve as Lord Byron's intimate, being possessed of a mind brilliant enough to win him a scholarship at King's College, Cambridge—but too indolent to long remain there. It was at Cambridge he formed his acquaintance with Byron; and being, like Byron, of impoverished background, the two were continually borrowing money of each other. Davies is a gambler, and a familiar among the denizens of Crockford's and White's; a dandy who counts Mr. Beau Brummell among his friends, he is known for his immaculate dress and his existence on a pecuniary knife's-edge.

"I *had heard,* from sources I should judge unimpeachable," said our own particular banker, Henry, as we quitted the Castle, "that Davies stood surety for a significant loan—nearly five thousand pounds—when Byron was but a minor; which sum was not repaid for *nearly six years.* The duns so hounded Davies he was said to contemplate suicide; he was subject to arrest, and petitioned for the arrears in interest; and all the while, his lordship was abroad—enjoying the exotic climes that should inspire him to write *Childe Harold*. In this we find the measure of the gentleman's loyalty—poor Davies has every reason to hate Lord Byron; and yet the two remain friends."

There it was again; the word *hate*. If one were intent upon exonerating the poet, one might well begin by examining those who should wish to see him hanged. Cuckolded husbands, ladies spurned, and friends upon whom he presumed too much. "Mr. Davies was *not* arrested for debt, however?"

It was the Earl who answered me. "Byron mortgaged his birthright—Newstead Abbey in Nottinghamshire—last year; perhaps *then* he discharged his debt to poor Davies. The gentleman has been patience itself; not even the destruction of his peace may diminish his regard for Byron. He is even named as one of the Executors of his lordship's Estate."

It was not until we were arrived at Mr. Davies's door that I understood he lived in Church Street—and, moreover, had taken a house directly opposite General Twining's, where we had let down Catherine only a few days previous. The sudden knowledge of Byron's proximity to his alleged victim brought me up short—any sort of meeting, in the dead of night, should have been possible. The poet might have been watching Catherine for weeks past, under the cover of his friendship for Mr. Davies! He might have stood, in the wee hours of Tuesday morning, at an upper-storey window and observed the poor girl's solitary progress towards her home. *He might have intercepted her*. Avowals of time and place, the witness of friends, were as nothing, once the position of both households was observed. I must pay a call of condolence soon on General Twining—and learn what I could of that fatal night.

Henry, I am certain, was alive to the possibilities in

Mr. Davies chusing to live in Church Street; he gave me a significant look as the Earl pulled his friend's bell.

Davies's man opened the door, and would have denied his master to our party, but that Swithin commanded the fellow to convey his card within. A few moments of uneasiness followed; and then the man reappeared, to usher us blandly upstairs.

We found a mingled party of gentlemen: Mr. Scrope Davies, tall and lean and impeccably dressed, his cravat a marvel of neat complexity; his forehead broad, his hairline receding, and his countenance mottled as befitted a hard drinker. I judged him to be in his late twenties, older than Byron but younger than some of the company that had repaired to his house. The gentleman named Hodge—last met at the Countess of Swithin's the previous evening—was bent over a table with his inevitable pair of dice; but on this occasion he cast against an actual partner, a harsh-featured and sandy-haired fellow in his fifth decade, I should judge, who stared at Desdemona and me with pugnacious contempt. In him I recognised the Bow Street Runner glimpsed on the box of the constables' carriage; Byron's personal guard. A fourth fellow leaned against a bookshelf, tenderly tuning the strings of a violin; he did not so much as glance at us as we entered the room, but persisted in humming a scrap of Beethoven to himself.

Sprawled on the sopha, his dark locks disarranged, his waistcoat loosened, and his cravat untied—was George Gordon, Lord Byron.

I suppose I ought to pause at this moment to record my impressions of so celebrated a man; and so I have paused, and lifted my pen from the page of this journal as I sit writing tonight in my bedchamber at the Castle. I have allowed my eyes to stare at the candle-flame, wavering in the draughts from the sea. I stared so long that my vision blurred, and cast phantasms on the walls; I shook my head to clear it. I would prefer to be able to dismiss Lord Byron as an ill-mannered and disreputable pup, a spoiled boy possessed of more arrogance than wit, an insolent darling of the *haut ton* unworthy of any respectable woman's notice. But I cannot. Our tête-à-tête worked upon me strangely, and I have yet to reconcile my warring opinions of him. Perhaps the interval of reflection—a thorough consideration of my interview with the poet—will bring welcome clarity. The mere summoning of his person to mind is enough to cause tumult in the breast—an inward clamour, tho' the Castle is peaceful enough this evening.

Most of the inn's occupants are abed; being a Wednesday, the town was not very lively this evening, given over to card parties and boxes at the theatre in New Road—tho' I have an idea that the better part of the populace was gathered privately, in a multitude of salons, to talk over the scandalous news of murder. But to return to the scene in Scrope Davies's drawing-room—

Lord Byron was drinking claret as he lay on the sopha, nursing a bottle to himself. His bloodshot eyes moved dully over our party, but at his friend Davies coming forward to bow to the Earl and Countess—clearly astounded that Swithin had not come alone, as his card had suggested, but had actually brought his *wife,* not to mention a pair of strangers—Byron forced himself upright, and set the bottle between his feet.

I tried not to stare at these; one, his right, was perceptibly deformed. His lordship is said to be morbidly anxious on the subject of lameness.

"Our intimate friends," the Earl said to Scrope Davies carelessly, "Mr. and Miss Austen."

"Pleasure," Davies murmured, looking about him with a wild air, as tho' we four had stumbled upon an orgy. "Countess, I had no notion—beg you will forgive the general air of disorder—I live as a bachelor, as you no doubt know—believe you are acquainted with Mr. Hodge. . . ."

Upon hearing his name, this gentleman shot our uncertain group a sharp look and said, "Mona, your servant. Miss Austen," and went back to throwing his dice. The sandy-haired Runner who cast against him swore loudly and fluently, without a thought for ourselves, and slammed his free hand upon the table. "That's seven pounds you've stolen from me!" he cried. "I shall have to sell me pistols."

"I would not have you do so for the world," Hodge replied in a bored tone, "for then Byron should be killed; and there would be no end to the women laying blame at my door. Let's throw again—Luck's the very Devil, but it changes as swift as affection."

The Earl of Swithin, meanwhile, had bowed to the dissipated figure on the sopha. "My felicitations, George. You came out of the morning's affair rather well. Have you any notion of when you may be released from your obligations to the Law, and return to London?"

"None," the gentleman said curtly. "The magistrate is a fool. Mona, have you had a letter from Lady Oxford?"

"We expect her every hour," the Countess said. "Pray dine with us this evening; there shall be no one but yourselves."

"She means to stay with you, then?"

"So I understand."

"Bloody hell," Byron said heavily. "I wish she had not got it into her head to come here. She shall be subject to every sort of insult—and from *that* I would preserve her at any cost. The rabble of Brighton are nothing, you know, to its *haut ton*. They may freeze the blood of Satan's imp at a single glance; and my poor Jane shall be held in abhorrence, being known for an enemy of the Regent's. The office of *maîtresse* to a murderer is as nothing to it. Well, we have given them something to chatter about, at least! *Society is now one polished horde / Formed of two mighty tribes, the Bores and / Bored.*"

"Byron, I believe you're foxed," Swithin observed.

"*What's drinking, quoth he? A mere pause from thinking. And why should I not be drunk?*" his lordship demanded belligerently. "It is of a piece with all the rest. Do you not know me for a hellhound? Is that Miss Austen, did'ye say? Miss *Jane* Austen?"

"That is my Christian name," I returned calmly, "but how you are in possession of it, I know not."

"I am by way of being a collector of Janes," Byron replied coolly. He reached for his bottle and drank deeply of claret. "Augustas, Annabelles, Ara . . . Ara . . . bellas; such a multitude of vowels as women employ! Give me plain *Jane* any day."

"Or . . . Catherine, perhaps?"

The poet lifted sodden eyes to mine. "She declined to be collected. As you yourself observed. We last met, I believe, in a stable yard in Cuckfield—tho' I should not call it so much as a bowing acquaintance."

"And yet, you know my name."

He smiled secretly to himself, the leer of a successful Cupid. "I can get anything from the mouths of ladies, my sweet; they fall over themselves to offer me confidences. Eliza was one of those."

Startled, I stared at him narrowly. Could it be possible he spoke of my late sister?

"Did they not inform you I've a taste for older women? Married, where possible, but I have been known to violate my principles. Indeed, I only hold principles that they *might* be violated."

"Sir!" Henry said through his teeth. "Consider what you say!"

Byron allowed his glittering gaze to drift over my brother.

"I do not like your face," he said. "It suggests stupidity, without the redemptive air of Fashion. Indeed, Mr. Austen, in you I smell the *shop*. With your wife it was otherwise. Stiled herself a *comtesse*, did she not? I wonder what Mona has to say to *that*."

Henry stiffened, but the Earl grasped his sleeve with a strong hand. "Do not regard him," he said in a lowered tone. "He is far too *well to live*, at present. I shall urge Davies to wrest the bottle from him presently, and put him to bed."

"Miss Austen," Byron sang out from his sopha-throne, "I should like to speak with you, for all you look so melancholy. Do you go in mourning for your life—all its hope of love long since lost—or for some nearer being? Come, sit beside me. I do not reek of spirits yet; I promise I shall not *drown* you."

I had a strong impulse to slap him, man of five-and-twenty tho' he was; yet a burning spark in his eye and a dangerous throb of feeling beneath the rude words piqued my interest. *This* was the man who had bound Catherine Twining with a cravat; this the man who had sailed on, regardless, as Caro Lamb foundered in the sea. What impulse of destruction rode him like a monkey? What would he *not* risk, of the lives of others—and why did danger draw him like strong drink? Was he capable of seeking the final proof of his violent impulses—capable, even, of murder?

"Let us go, Jane," Henry urged in a lowered tone. "I do not like this fellow. I do not like him at all."

"You should do me the greatest service, my dear," I murmured, "if you would but cultivate Scrope Davies. He is too plausible a foil for his lordship by half. Learn what you can of him. And leave Byron to me."

Before he could protest, I gathered my skirts and glided towards the listing figure of the poet, whose delicate fingers—quite beautiful—caressed the neck of his wine bottle.

"Tell me how you know my name," I demanded quietly as I adopted a position beside him on the sopha.

"The ambitious must always know their rivals." It might have been a cherished aphorism, so swiftly did the phrase fall from his lips; and then he glanced up, to hold my gaze with his own. The dark intensity of that look, the unnerving penetration—the impression immediately received, that I alone existed for this man, that he breathed for me and me entirely—was almost overpowering. It was as tho' a swift magnetic bond had formed between us, dragging me within his orbit, a bond I was incapable of breaking. The room and its several occupants slid effortlessly away; I heard the distant chatter as through a roaring in my ears; I might have been falling into the dark pools of those eyes, and all they promised of passionate annihilation. I was aware, as I had not been a few moments previous, of the rapidity of my pulse, the wave of heat rising in my frame, the sudden parting of my lips to protest or plead—all involuntary, all ungovernable. It was impossible that my body should thus betray me—should throw me into the power of one I *despised,* indeed! And yet, each fibre of my rebellious being strained towards that pale countenance, that burning gaze.

I apprehended in an instant how a Caro Lamb might crave such thralldom; how to enter a room Byron owned was to breathe a more electric air. *How,* my reeling mind stuttered, *had Catherine Twining been proof against such a man? What better angel had sustained her? Impossible to ignore Byron's will!*

A faint smile formed at his lips; he was waiting for my reply. What was it he had said? —That the ambitious always knew their rivals?

"I do not understand you," I gasped.

The smile widened. "Was there ever so fickle a tongue as

that of woman? You understand me too well, I suspect. Nothing has been so praised or sought as *Pride and Prejudice* since Scott last cast his wretched verses upon the adoring public; and therefore it was imperative in me to pierce the veil of *A Lady.* —Is that not your captious name, my Jane? For shame, for shame, to disavow it! How could you deny your own child, and at *birth*? I call it *missish,* a sort of prudery and deceit that will not be borne! If you will write, then proclaim your words to the World! Let the avid ghouls of Bond Street and Pall Mall know to whom they owe the mirror of Mrs. Bennet, in all her mercenary glory!"

My eyes dropped; I drew a shuddering breath, and regained some shred of composure. "How can you know this?" I demanded. "Whom have I trusted, that ought rather to be suspected?"

"Do not make yourself anxious—I am sure dear Eliza carried your secret to the grave," he said. "—But for the one exception all women must make, soon or late—*myself.*" Of course. She would have felt it immediately: that quivering, seductive bond—that cord impossible to break. In her dying state it would have been as life-blood to Eliza, to brave a rout party where Byron lounged, merely to have his gaze meet hers and feel, for an instant at least, more alive and ardent than she should ever feel again.

"My relations with the frailer sex rarely conform to rules, you know," he said, "and they have next to nothing to do with *vows.* I am sure she meant to keep her promises most faithfully—but poor Eliza was a butterfly creature, susceptible to flattery and the influence of fashion; I was all the rage in her final months. *Childe Harold* having lately broken upon an astonished *ton,* she *must* use her knowledge to attract me."

"Her knowledge?" I repeated.

Those eyes raked over me once more. "It was as gold in

Eliza's hands. She possessed something no other lady possessed: the name of a greater writer than I."

My gloved hands formed tight claws where they lay in my lap. My second novel, sped by the success of my first, had appeared in January; and in April Eliza had expired. When had she shared her secret?

Of a sudden, I was visited in memory by her dying words. *Regret . . . regret.* Had this been meant for me?

"You should rather thank than blame her," Byron said in a lowered tone, meant for my ears alone. "I have not thought to publish your secret to the world. There is no value to anything once it is known everywhere. But do, Miss Austen, confess to your next work— It ought to be your policy, as it is mine, to proclaim your every sin. The publick will devour you alive—but it will also devour your books, which is all to the good." He took another draught of his claret, and for an instant, I was freed of the consuming gaze. "Sins are the writer's stock-in-trade, however vicious. Incest, rape, idolatry, sodomy—nothing is too violent for my appetites; all these have I known, and you may find their ghosts reanimated in my verse."

I believed it now, when I might have scoffed earlier, but it was time to summon control, and place a quelling distance between myself and the poet. Intimacy must be unsafe, when one fenced with Byron.

"I have only looked into *Childe Harold*," I remarked mildly, "but enjoyed what little I read of it."

Those eyes glittering with drink or fury narrowed at my tepid praise; then he bestowed upon me the most seraphic of smiles. Instantly, the hectic brow was revealed as a child's; the vicious tendencies, as mere play-acting. Another woman might have felt swift sympathy; my cooling brain was the more active, in perceiving a warning.

"You chuse to invoke our first meeting, Lord Byron, at

Cuckfield," I persisted. "I am emboldened, therefore, to ask a home question. What drove you *then* to take up and bind a respectable young lady of only fifteen—one known, moreover, to enjoy the protection of a father?"

"Snapping my fingers beneath the General's nose was half the attraction." His eyelids drooped, brooding. "But Catherine herself incited me to it, that morning, as my coach came alongside her—so fresh as she was, so delicate, her look half-shy, half-inviting, as tho' she had begun to trust me at last. She gave me her hand, and I lifted her into the chaise—ready to cherish her, ready to ravish her if she would but swoon in my arms a little—Pure innocence! Can you have an idea of it, Miss Austen?"

The piercing gaze held mine again and I drew an unsteady breath.

"—How o'erwhelming the throes of passion for an unaccustomed purity might be?" he muttered. "All the complicity of that closed carriage! Her face, her figure, her soft voice were incitement to anything you may imagine—and I should never be proof against their charms!"

A groan broke from somewhere in the room—I looked away, and saw Scrope Davies with his hands pressed against his face, as tho' his skull throbbed with acutest pain. Henry, who had been conversing with the gentleman, paused in perplexity and placed a hand on Davies's arm. Byron, however, heard nothing of his friend's distress—being too intent upon reliving his thwarted passion.

"Catherine did *not* trust me, however. She did *not* swoon. When presented with the soul and heart of a poet—she first screamed, and then shrank, as tho' from a leper. It is my lameness—I know it is my lameness; she saw the blighting mark as the Devil's touch. His token of ownership." Byron sneered, but the hateful look was entirely for himself. "The beautiful Catherine was as repulsed by me as by a reptile, slimed and dank; as by a relic dug too soon from a foetid grave. In her disgust, I knew my worth. Perhaps it was *this* that formed the chief part of her fascination—the girl despised me almost as much as I despise myself."

Ah! Sudden comprehension flooded my mind. Not self-hatred, but self-love, was Byron's consuming demon. He was incapable of apprehending a fellow creature's outline, however ardent his object might feel in his presence; the world entire must be viewed solely as it related to *Byron*.

"Being the victim, as I see you mean to stile yourself," I observed in a lowered tone, "why stop at abduction? If Catherine could not love you—could never endure to be yours—why not end the agony of her refusal, with her life?"

"Ah, but that should be a *poem*, Miss Austen—not the sequel to a dull evening's entertainment at the Brighton Assembly," he said abruptly. "I might write such a poem; but I should never form the elaborate intention of quitting a ball, deserting my rooms, and employing my friend Davies as surety for my reputation, in actual life. I was too drunk to hunt the girl through the entire town at the dead of night, for one thing; and for another, too sick of Caro Lamb. Besides, I must confess my ardour for young Catherine had already begun to wane; one cannot always be proclaiming deathless love to a chit who colours, avoids one's eye, and ducks behind a pillar rather than surrender her heart. It verges on the ridiculous; and I avoid the ridiculous at all costs—in life, as in poetry."

I glanced about the elegant little drawing-room: the Earl was tossing the bones with Hodge and the Bow Street Runner; Lady Swithin was tuning the strings of the violinist's instrument; and my brother was once more trading pleasant nothings with Mr. Scrope Davies, who appeared to have recovered from the head-ache. Our host was remarkably pallid, however; sweat stood out on his brow; and he determinedly avoided glancing in his friend Byron's direction. All was not perfect cordiality between the two, I supposed; tho' Byron should probably fail to observe it.

"My lord," I said, "that child's body was wrapped in a hammock taken from your yacht. It was placed in the bedchamber thought to be yours. If we regard as credible your assertion that you did *not* drown her—"

He bared his teeth and I was reminded, inevitably, of the wolf. "The coroner has proclaimed it!"

"—then someone has gone to great lengths to see you hang. Who hates you so much?"

He drained his bottle to the dregs. "The better part of England, my poor darling."

The voice was a caress I forced myself to ignore. "That will not do. You must confine yourself to those who hate you, *and* knew of your passion for Miss Twining. A much more select gathering, I'll be bound."

His eyes roved over my form, as tho' my gown were transparent, and I revealed in all my nakedness. I raised my chin and stared back at him.

"You are decidedly imperturbable," he observed. "Our Jane is not *missish*. Neither an ape-leader nor an old maid; nor yet a simpering dowd, for all she *does* go in black."

Perversely, I blushed—the words and the intensity of his tone having their predictable effect. Indeed, the man should not be allowed to roam unfettered in polite Society!

"Shall I draw up a list of my enemies for your private perusal?" he jested. "Do I understand you undertake to *name* Miss Twining's murderer?"

"She was by way of being a friend," I retorted. "And indeed, I should relish any list you could summon. You might send it to my direction at the Castle Inn."

"Then start," he said bitterly, "with Caro Lamb—she lives for the amusement of spinning webs, and is entirely capable of drowning a rival. There is a Lucretia Borgia quality to the act that should undoubtedly appeal to her more lurid phantasies. And now, Miss Austen—I *beg* your pardon—but I feel an overwhelming need to relieve myself. You *will*, I know, excuse me." —With which churlish frankness, he quitted my side—and I felt myself to have been released from a disturbing influence, powerful and heady.

All of us in that room, so carelessly crowded, fell silent as we observed his limping progress towards the door—the club foot swinging with clumsy violence. It was as tho' a spirit beloved of the gods—given every gift of beauty and conceit by a benevolent Olympus—had been deliberately blighted. Lord Byron was a warning against the human quest for Perfection; it could not be attained in *all* things.

I doubt I am the first to make this judgement of his lordship—and I am certain I shall not be the last.

CHAPTER EIGHTEEN

The Rivals

WE PARTED FROM THE EARL AND COUNTESS ON SCROPE Davies's doorstep. It had been agreed that Henry should accompany Swithin to the day's race-meeting—"for murder or no," he said, "I have a horse running at four o'clock, and must not fail to appear, or the betting shall be all against me. Wyncourt—old Gravetye's heir, you know, and as sound a judge of horseflesh as any ever born—is my only competition."

"I have seen Lord Wyncourt's gelding," Henry observed coolly, "and thought it a trifle too short in the back—" At which the Earl clapped my brother delightedly, and the two set off in search of a hackney carriage bound for the Downs east of town.

Lady Swithin was to return to the Marine Parade, in expectation of her friend Lady Oxford's arrival; and she invited me cordially to accompany her—but a nearer duty obtruded. Directly opposite our position was General Twining's house, its doorknocker muffled and its windows hung with crape.

"I must pay a call upon a bereaved parent," I said, "however much I should prefer a few hours of sun and excitement on the racing-ground."

The Countess's face lit up. "But I have a capital scheme! I shall call round in my perch phaeton, with or without my London friend, in half an hour's time—to save you from the General's clutches, and carry you off to the races. All the world shall be there, you know, and it *must* prove an excellent opportunity for your researches."

"I can have no objection, and should be delighted to accept of your ladyship's invitation," I replied.

Lady Swithin unfurled her sunshade with a look brimful of mischief and said, "I almost hope Lady Oxford is delayed. We might enjoy a most delicious tête-à-tête in the phaeton— for I mean to hear *every word* Byron spoke to you this morning. Never have I seen him so little bored by a lady's conversation—even Caro Lamb's!"

I coloured, and deflected suspicion with the novelist's chief tool—a facility for timely invention. "That is because I was impertinent. Lord Byron cannot often meet with a woman so little inclined to captivate him."

"I wonder it did not send him into strong hysterics," Desdemona said, "but you must school your tongue a little, my dear, before entering the opposite abode—it should never do to carry pugnacity to the General!"

She was correct, of course; the encounter with Byron had perhaps been *too* invigourating. I ordered my emotions into a confirmed serenity, bade her ladyship *adieu,* and crossed to the far paving with a step that was the very picture of meek womanhood.

It seemed, at the first, as tho' my efforts were for naught— Suddley the butler being little inclined to admit me this morning, whether he recognised my countenance from my previous visit, or no.

"The General is not at home to visitors," he said austerely; and I could well imagine that the General was loath to parade his grief before the stream of the curious and the hypocritical who had left their cards upon the foyer's table. Suddley's elderly face was marked with the ravages of grief; and I recalled how Catherine had greeted him as one might an old nurse, a friend of the schoolroom. How little right the serving class was accorded to mourn for those they loved, of whatever station—duty must always intervene. *Someone* must lay the fire each morning; *someone* must answer the door.

"I quite understand." My voice was firm and a trifle overloud; behind Suddley's stooped form was the hushed length of the Twining hall, and if there was to be any hope of the General's overlistening our conversation, I must condescend to bray a little. "If you would be so good as to convey Miss Jane Austen's deepest sympathy to General Twining. Tho' I knew his daughter only briefly, I could not help but regard her with admiration and respect—and know how severe his loss must be."

"You are very good, ma'am," the butler said in a quavering voice, and his gaze—which had been correctly fixed at an indeterminate point over my right shoulder—met my own. "It is an affliction we never looked for, in plain terms. Such a sweet and biddable child as she was—hardly one of these harum-scarum misses, wild for a red coat and no thought to her family name. I wish that Lord Byron had never been born! Her death, that Devil's imp was, from the moment his evil foot crossed her path."

I murmured encouraging nothings.

"Right there on the paving he bowed to Miss Catherine, being arm in arm with our friend Mr. Davies. I may say, meaning no disrespect to the gentleman, that I was surprized at Mr. Davies's judgement—knowing Lord Byron's vicious tendencies as he does, he should *not* have encouraged the acquaintance, in my opinion. But, however, Mr. Davies may have felt he had no choice but to accede to his friend's wishes, in all politeness."

Scrope Davies, on intimate terms with the Twining family? I had not had an idea of it—and felt a ripple of excitement twist my entrails. I *must* speak to Henry. Surely my piquant brother would have learnt much from his brief conversation with the gentleman.

"Not a moment's peace did any of us know, from that day to this," Suddley went on. "His lordship was fair took with a passion for Miss Catherine. It wasn't like the usual courting of a gentleman and a young lady. Quite dotty he was—mooning about below her windows of a midnight, and calling her by some foreign name."

"Leila?" I suggested.

"That was it! Spanish, I thought it," the butler confided, "or maybe French. It was as tho' his lordship had been took with a sickness, of the heart and head. Miss Catherine went in fear of him—her poor little self all of a tremble when the bell was pulled, lest it be his lordship calling—and the General could not abide him! *A wolf*, he said, *come to ravish my white lamb*. And look where it's ended! With that Devil's white hands round the sweet child's throat!"

"You believe, then, that he drowned her? —Tho' so respectable a friend as Mr. Scrope Davies vouches for Lord Byron's movements?"

"Suddley!"

The General's voice, as harsh and bellicose as tho' he commanded the heights of a battlefield, rang out from the far end of the passage. "Cease your prattle at once and send that woman away! She calls only to feed upon our misery, like all the rest!"

"Very good, sir," Suddley said woodenly; then added in an undertone, as he made to close the door in my face, "May I beg leave to apologise—"

"Pray do not regard it. You have all my sympathy." I turned away.

"Miss Austen, is it?"

The General's form was just visible behind his man's as Suddley hesitated, his hand on the door.

"I am come to condole, sir—but have no wish to intrude upon so profound an affliction."

"Then be off with ye," he snarled, thrusting his head round the jamb, "and do not presume to return! I have nothing to say to you, madam! Nor to any woman of my acquaintance; you are all jades, whores, and vultures—not a pure soul among you. Not even," he added, his voice breaking down entirely, "my poor Catherine, tho' her winding sheet be white! Oh, God, that I should live to see the sins of the mother visited upon the child—"

There is no uglier sound, to my mind, than that of a grown man weeping; its utter desolation strikes the heart to stone.

"Forgive him, ma'am," Suddley whispered as he drew his master inside. "He does not know what he says."

But I wondered very much, as I walked towards Marine Parade, whether Suddley lied. A new train of thought had been opened to me: I must speak to Mrs. Silchester once more.

LADY OXFORD HAD *NOT* BEEN DELAYED, HAVING FLOWN south that morning with the lightest of traps and a team of four high-steppers to speed her journey. She declared herself an excellent traveller, who suffered not at all from the headache, requiring only a simple nuncheon to restore her jangled nerves—was only too happy to encounter all her acquaintance at the race-meeting that afternoon—was sure that Byron would venture out to lay a wager on Swithin's horse—and would be charmed to further her acquaintance with *any* of dear Mona's intimate friends.

I had progressed, in a matter of days, from a lady briefly recollected from Mona's Bath girlhood, to an *intimate friend,* and was hardly likely to quarrel with the change.

Jane Elizabeth Harley, Countess of Oxford, was nothing that I expected. From her reputation as a captivator of powerful men—her liaisons with such Whig potentates as Sir Francis Burdett, Lord Granville, and the reformer Lord Archibald Hamilton being everywhere known—I had predicted a heavy-lidded seductress, with expansive bosom and swaying hips, her indolence suggestive of the boudoir. But here was a trim and adorable creature some years my senior, whose pert nose and rosebud mouth belonged to an ingénue. Brisk and merry in her attitudes, she was nonetheless as sharp as she could stare—pronouncing some blistering insight upon her fellows with every second sentence. She kept a lorgnette in her reticule, the better to examine any fragment of leaf or fossil that might fall in her way, and was forever losing herself in a book. At present, she informed Desdemona, she was engrossed in fourteen volumes of a history of Ancient Rome, and had brought Volume the Seventh with her to peruse in the phaeton on the way to the race-meeting.

There could be no one less akin to Caro Lamb on the face of the earth—and that the same man could find The Sprite captivating, as swam in Lady Oxford's orbit, defied comprehension. Still further did Byron's passion for Catherine Twining strain belief, when presented with the worldly and erudite Countess. I began to think that my judgement of his lordship's character was correct—any lady must be mere window-dressing to his fundamental love of *self*, each affair representing an attitude he tried on as another man might study various ways of tying a cravat.

Or his lordship was mad.

Lady Oxford's excellent spirits on the present occasion were explained by the intelligence she had received at Cuckfield but an hour earlier, on her road from London.

"Even the ostlers were talking over the news," she observed boisterously as we were handed into Mona's phaeton, "that the inquest was done, and no judgement returned against Byron! There remains, then, some sense in the minds of men! I despaired of it when in my twenties; but with the gravity of age—or perhaps second childhood—have lately found my innocence returning."

"Impossible," Mona said drily. "That will do, Hinch—I shall take the reins. Stand away from their heads!"

She had undertaken to drive a team in the perilously sprung high-perch phaeton, the sort of sporting vehicle rarely adopted by ladies, and only then in Hyde Park of a summer's afternoon. Had the team been Swithin's breakdowns, turned off to his wife for the remainder of their useful years, I should have felt greater security; but in fact they were beautiful goers, with velvet mouths that responded to a feather touch on the reins.

"Poor things," Mona observed as one bucked and reared in the traces, "they have not been out of their stable since Hinch brought them down from London three days ago. I fear they will be a trifle fresh!"

I was reminded of nothing so much as her uncle, Lord Harold, as the blood chestnuts sprang from before No. 21, Marine Parade, and nearly ran away with their mistress in the direction of the Downs, scattering sedan chairs, promenaders, and errand boys to the kerb. Desdemona was magnificent, in complete command of her team and herself, responding to the surging animals as tho' to a delightful gambit in courtship—she had only to tug a little, and the rampant course was contained. Lord Harold had taught her well; no other could have instructed her ladyship how to feather a turn, or catch the thong of her whip with a flick of her wrist; she was masterful—and fearless.

For my part, I clung to the sides of the phaeton as it swayed, and found that I had neglected to breathe for the first dreadful seconds. Lady Oxford quite abandoned her history-book, being engaged in keeping a firm hand on the crown of her jockey bonnet.

The race course set out by the late Duke of Queensberry and various Royals mad for horseflesh—the Regent chief among them—traverses a rolling saddle of Down-land. There is a neat little stand erected for the use of spectators, but the majority of those present—gentlemen, in the main—preferred to sit their mounts or stand in ranks along the turns of the course, which is irregular and demanding as it cuts through the hills.[19]

Desdemona pulled up her phaeton alongside a curricle, which I observed to contain Mr. Hodge and a companion— the redoubtable Mrs. Alleyn, who was looking very pert in a deep rose spencer and green sunshade. She hailed us smartly and complimented Mona on her courage, in sporting so dashing an equipage.

"I am accustomed to drive myself everywhere, you know," Mona returned indifferently; "and Swithin is too wise to oppose me. Mrs. Alleyn, may I have the honour of presenting the Countess of Oxford?"

The lady's brown eyes widened at being made the familiar

[19] Jane would appear to be describing what we should term a steeplechase; a race derived from the gentlemanly habit of riding to hounds at a punishing pace, rather than a flat course designed solely for speed.—*Editor's note.*

of so notorious a personage; but she accepted the honour with good grace, inclined her head sweetly; and recovered herself a little in gazing out at the general scene. I smiled to myself as I watched: the jaunty Mrs. Alleyn might stile herself a prize in Brighton; but she had not yet encountered a ship of Lady Oxford's draught.

"How do the odds run at present, Hodge?" Mona enquired.

If any gentleman were likely to know the state of the betting, it should be Hodge; he embarked on a fluent discourse regarding the points of the various horses and the weight of their riders; the variability of one animal's response to dry turf, versus another's liking for mud; the possibility of Lord Wyncourt's gelding being a trifle touched in the wind; and the excellent action of Lord Swithin's horse, which was called by the lovely name of China Trade. From which we concluded that the Earl's entry was a high favourite.

"Then put it all on the nag for me, Hodge," Lady Oxford said gaily, tossing him a silken purse that clinked delightfully with coins. "You know I cannot approach the bookmen."

"Your servant," Hodge said with a bow, and sprang down from his curricle, quite deserting Mrs. Alleyn. I might have shifted my place to supply her want of a companion—but that I observed her eagle eye already fixed on an elegant sporting figure making its way on horseback to the curricle's side: Sir John Stevenson. He tipped his hat, acknowledged his old acquaintance Lady Oxford, and soon made Mrs. Alleyn the grateful recipient of his exclusive attentions.

"Did Byron say whether he intended the race-meeting?" Lady Oxford asked carelessly of Desdemona.

There was a pregnant silence, both Mona and I being well aware that Byron's determined drinking must make all exertion impossible; but then some imp in the Countess's soul encouraged her to declare, "I do not recollect. Jane—Miss

Austen—may have heard him mention it, however . . . they were much in conversation. . . ."

"I cannot say," I stuttered, as some memory of that engrossing tête-à-tête obtruded. He had penetrated the secret of my authorship. Stripped me naked with a single look. And called me a writer greater than himself. . . . "Indeed, we spoke so briefly—the merest nothings . . . but were I pressed, I should imagine his lordship too greatly fatigued by the labours of his morning, to venture out-of-doors so soon after the inquest. And then, too, there is the undesirability of drawing notice—"

"Whatever do you mean?" Lady Oxford retorted coolly. "Byron *adores* drawing notice. It is as life-blood to the man."

"But I do not think his Bow Street Runner should advise it."

Lady Oxford turned her head to frown at me a little. "Are you suggesting he means to skulk *within doors,* from fear of the rabble? His innocence has been declared!"

"I beg your pardon—say rather that his *guilt* has been *doubted.* Until *some other* is charged with the murder of Catherine Twining, the general feeling against his lordship remains high."

Her ladyship emitted a brittle little laugh. "I collect you are entirely unacquainted with Lord Byron's character, Miss Austen; and it is as well that I have remembered the fact, else I should resent your picture of the gentleman—for it is the picture of a *coward.* Good God! He can hardly have known the chit who drowned—a brazen piece who thought nothing of wandering the shingle at the dead of night, and got herself tossed like a sack of flour into a stranger's bed—"

Understanding shot through my brain with the clarity of a lightning-bolt. I glanced swiftly at Desdemona, whose countenance was alive with anxiety. She gave the barest shake of the head in my direction; it was true, then: Lady Oxford had no notion of her lover's passion for another.

"I *had understood*," Mona said breathlessly, "that the two *had met* some once or twice."

An exclamation of annoyance escaped Lady Oxford's lips. "Very probably! The better part of the known world has thrown itself at poor George's head! If you only *knew*, Miss Austen, the throngs of ladies desperate for his lordship's notice! —The stratagems and schemes to which they resort, without the slightest regard for their own dignity! Did I not possess a keen delight in the *absurd*, I should be reduced to *tears* by the folly of their display! But his lordship remains insensible to all!"

"Not *quite* all," came a whisper from somewhere beside us.

A shiver ran up my spine, as tho' an incorporeal spirit and not a human form had spoken.

Lady Caroline Lamb had condescended to join the race-meeting.

CHAPTER NINETEEN

Incident on the Downs

SHE WAS MOUNTED ON A LEGGY BLACK COLT, PERHAPS three years of age, with a strong Arab nose and a venomous look—culled from the Regent's stables, no doubt. I may say that she had an excellent seat, and became it to admiration in her Prussian blue riding habit, cut as severely as tho' Weston had fashioned it for the Marquis of Wellington, with a stiff, high collar and narrow sleeves. The colt was restive, snorting and tossing its head, but she paid it no heed, her tiny hands in their doeskin gloves grasping the reins with ease.

"Lady Caroline," Desdemona murmured. "How delightful. I hope you are entirely recovered from your misadventure on the shingle?"

But Caro Lamb ignored her. Her queer, light eyes were fixed entirely on Lady Oxford, and as I watched, a smile quirked at her mouth—not with malice, but with the threat of uncontrollable laughter.

"Poor Aspasia! Did you *believe* his lies? Did you truly think he never met that wretched girl?"

"Go away, Caroline," her ladyship spat. "I have nothing at all to say to you."

The smile widened. "What fools we women are! I have an idea of the two of you, in your Herefordshire idyll; your complacent and stupid husband absent for weeks at a time; the fireside in January, the hectic conversation over books—laughing until you *died* at how easily you had rid yourselves of me, wretched little Caro Lamb, with her broken heart and hysteric looks—How nobly poor William stands by her! And *you*, believing all his lies, believing when he claimed he had never had a lover quite as *rich* as you, content to think a callow youth of four-and-twenty fascinated by your worldliness . . . for he, who is older in his bitterness than *recorded time*, is too adept at playing the callow youth. . . . Telling yourself that it was right and just he should worship a woman whose teeth are almost all dropt out! —A woman, moreover, taken in love by so many others that she has long since given up reckoning the countless pokes she's suffered in the night—"

"Lady Caroline!" Desdemona cried.

The severe figure on horseback, as tho' backed with military steel, tossed her head defiantly. "*Pathetic* Aspasia. You are quite in the autumn of your reign, are you not? You *require* the lies. You beg for them, with your tit in his mouth. You wish to think them purest Truth! Whereas I hear the golden words that drip from his blessèd lips and love them for their sheer deceit. I *cherish* them for their mockery, their trickster's toils. I am quite otherwise from you, *dearest Jane*—at whose knee I once sat, to learn the wisdom of the World. You require his lies, the better to hide from yourself—whereas I hear them in order to know *exactly* how degraded I am become."

"*Shut up*, Caroline," Lady Oxford muttered; but there was violence in her words.

Lady Caroline had begun to sob: dry, wracking sobs that lifted her frail breast as tho' a vast bellows filled it.

"Make him *tell* you!" she shrieked. "Make him tell you how he loved the Twining girl to the point of *madness*! He could not bear to keep away—flying south from your arms to haunt the lanes and rooms she frequented. He could not endure her unsullied innocence—the childlike purity of her tender frame—he wished for nothing more than to ravish her, and break that innocence on a stone!"

I saw Lady Oxford wince. Then she stiffened, as tho' some barbed point had found its home in her flesh. "I do not believe it," she whispered, groping for her friend's hand like a palsied ancient. "Mona—Tell me she lies."

The black colt jibbed, and backed; the little hands must have clenched on the reins.

"Did you know," Lady Caroline queried in the mildest amusement, "when you pressed your chaise upon him for the ease of his travels—poor boy, he worked so long into the night, scrawling verses for his Leila, he *ought* to take refreshment, he *ought* to steal a day or two in sailing o'er the seas— Did you know that it was to *her* he coursed, in your golden carriage? *Her,* he bound by wrist and mouth, to carry off to Gretna, for a Border wedding? She would not have him, Aspasia, by fair means or foul. Innocence is innocence still, that can reckon up the lies and find them short in weight. She threw all his passion in his face—and still she was his *Leila*! Not you!"

All around us, a hush had fallen over carriage and horse alike, every fashionable head averted, but nonetheless in thrall to the slight figure who sat her mount as brutally as any Cassandra, crying doom to Agamemnon's house. There had been nothing to equal the charm of this Season in Brighton for a decade, at least!

A tall figure thrust its way through the crowd; the Earl of

Swithin, come to claim his lady at last. I saw his broad frame, his unbowed head, with profound relief; but even Swithin's face was white at the scene he had been forced to witness. He paid no heed to Caro Lamb, merely slapping the flank of her colt from his path, his eyes fixed on Desdemona's phaeton.

"Have we not a race to run?" he cried. "The gun is about to fire!"

All heads swung as one towards the far end of the course, past the spectator stand, some fifty yards distant from our position, where a ragged line of seven horses fretted and sidled at the starter's mark; and then, an indeterminate figure raised its arm and triggered a duelling pistol.

The thunderous pack shot forward.

I had no idea which was China Trade. For an instant—or even an hour, perhaps, so thoroughly is one's sense of time suspended in contemplating a race—the horses seemed barely to move at all as they advanced upon us; we could not easily gauge their speed or distance in staring directly at them. Once they had swept past our position, however, in a surge of pounding flanks and striving forelegs, their jockeys crouched at their necks, whips flying, the sensation of speed was immediate. And suddenly one horse had leapt a stile, and another, and a third—

"That is China Trade," Mona murmured for my benefit; "the neat little bay with the small head and long neck. She is not so powerful as a stout hunter, mind, but she is built for speed—and leaps every obstacle like a gazelle, Swithin says."

I strained my gaze to distinguish the mare, flying away from us towards the far end of the course; it seemed to my eye that she was gaining. I had quite forgot Lady Caroline Lamb in all the excitement of the turf—but she obtruded suddenly and emphatically on my notice.

"Hola, Sir!" she cried.

The black colt surged powerfully forward, past our phaeton and into the mounted crowd before us; I thought with thankfulness that her ladyship had done hounding the Countess of Oxford for a moment.

"Dear God," Mona muttered. "What queer start will she next attempt?"

And it was true: Caro Lamb did not merely seek a better position from which to view the race. With a slackening of her hold on the reins and a kick to her mount's belly, she shot through the assembled viewers and dashed headlong out onto the course.

The pack was long since gone, but Caro paid no heed—throwing herself flat along the black colt's neck, the reins loosed as tho' she wished to be run away with, she gave the horse its head—and galloped straight at the first stile.

"She'll break her neck," Lady Oxford said grimly; and I was surprized to find no hint of satisfaction in her voice.

"Not Caro," Mona replied. "She has hunted her whole life with the Duke of Devonshire—I am sure there is nothing she will not throw her heart over."

And indeed, the black colt had carried her safely beyond the first three obstacles in the course; to my amazement, the gap between Caro and the rest of the field was shortening.

"That's a devilish fine horse," I heard Sir John call out from beside Mrs. Alleyn's curricle; "what do you say, Hodge, to a side bet on the black colt?"

"Ten pounds on Lady Caroline to place!" Hodge replied.

And all around us, a feverish spate of betting commenced, with gentlemen hastening towards the little knot of men whose employment it was to record such wagers, and tally the winnings.

Fragments of intelligence drifted over our heads . . . one horse was down on the far side of the course, beyond our view; Lord Wyncourt's had refused a hedge. There was no word of China Trade.

"How much to see the lady thrown?" a random voice called from the crowd; and a guffaw went up amidst the more vulgar members.

Three horses were rounding the final curve in the course. A last fence remained, with a broken trunk beyond it—as deadly and as frightening a jump as any I had ever witnessed. One head rose up, shoulders bunched and forelegs dangling—the neat little mare with the long neck. Her mount was clinging like a monkey to her back, a diminutive fellow in the Earl of Swithin's colours. As I watched, her body seemed to extend—to soar—and both fence and twisted mesh of fallen tree branches were behind her. A cheer went up as the mare laid back her ears, extended her head, and flew for home.

And behind her—

The black colt, with Lady Caroline's Prussian blue train lying like a flag along its back.

She was perfectly positioned as her mount took the final fence, her frail figure aligned with the horse's as it leapt; and there was no doubt of the heedless courage in every fibre of both creatures' beings. I had no doubt they moved, in that instant, as one; which made the horrendous destruction that followed almost incomprehensible. The colt cleared the fence, but sailed just short of the vicious trunk; his hind legs caught in a tree limb; the horse staggered, fell forward on its knees, and somersaulted—with Caro Lamb going straight over its neck.

A moan of horror went up from our assembled crowd; and for an instant, all breath and movement was suspended. I saw, as in a dream, China Trade swirl across the finish; saw her jockey pull up his heaving mount in expectation of universal acclaim—and watched, as horror freed its grip, the first of the gentlemen bolt past the victorious mare in the direction of the insensible lady lying prone on the ground.

"As I observed," Lady Oxford said drily, "the wretched fool has broken her neck. How in God's name are we to explain it to William Lamb?"

Desdemona made as if to descend from her carriage, but her husband's hand on her wrist stopped her.

"Stay," he said. "I shall go. You can do nothing there."

The black colt had scrambled to its feet but stood all of a huddle, head hanging, one back leg pulled up as tho' in agony. Several gentlemen had reached Lady Caroline, and knelt about her; one of them called, in an agitated accent, "She breathes!"

"Praise God," Lady Oxford murmured; and again, I was startled at her charity.

A crack, as of a pistol shot, rang out—and I saw to my horror the beautiful black colt crumple to the ground, with a shudder as profound as thunder—a ruin to Lady Caroline's whims. It was the starter's pistol that had done it; and a gentleman stood a moment over the pitiable creature, staring at its noble head, pistol dangling, before turning away.

"I suppose the hind leg was broken in the tree," Lady Oxford said with a slight catch in her voice. "I cannot bear to see it—a hunter of mine went in just such a way, some years since, when I rode with the Quorn.[20] God forgive us for the way we use our beasts."

"I hope He may find it in His heart to forgive Lady Caro-

---

[20] The Quorn Hunt, founded in 1696 by Mr. Thomas Boothby of Tooley Park, Leicestershire, is still in existence today. It was considered one of the most rigorous, demanding, and exciting of the hunts of Jane Austen's time, and to be invited to ride with its members conferred considerable prestige. It takes its name from the village of Quorn, where the pack was kenneled from 1753 to 1904.—*Editor's note.*

line, at least," I murmured. "She drove that colt to its destruction."

Lady Oxford was silent a moment. "I have often thought it is *herself* she wishes to destroy. But until that day—Caro will be content to smash everything near her," she said.

CHAPTER TWENTY

The Green-Eyed Monster

WEDNESDAY, 12 MAY 1813
BRIGHTON, CONT.

I MAY BE FORGIVEN IF I CONFESS THAT AFTER SO EX-hausting a day, replete with inquests, seductive poets, du-elling *inamoratas,* and suicidal races, I looked for nothing more engaging than an early dinner and an inviting bed. First, however, I was required to witness Lady Caroline Lamb's re-tirement from the field—sensible at last, and carried aloft on a hurdle, with her riding habit trailing to the ground like a heroine out of Shakespeare.

I must observe, as an aside, that I am forever put in mind of the *stage* when I am treated to one of Caro Lamb's scenes; and I am hardly alone in this. Her life is lived on so dramatic a plane that the theatre cannot be far from one's thoughts. This reflection leads me inevitably to another: Does the air of High Tragedy persist, even when the lady is entirely alone, and playing only to her mirror?

I should like a private interview with Lady Caroline—she betrayed herself as so completely in possession of the history of Catherine Twining, when she chose to spar with Lady

Oxford, that I imagine she gained rather more of the child's confidence than she admitted at the inquest. It is even possible she might say more of her *parting* from Catherine—the exact hour and circumstance that left the poor girl without escort home to Church Street—if properly managed.

And what, I wonder, is the significance of the name *Leila*? We two shall have much to discuss, once Caro's shattered frame is on the mend.

I say shattered, but in truth she broke no bones, being but shaken to her core. The ground dealt a shocking blow to the head; she took leave of her senses; and was less than coherent for several hours after, according to general report. Lord Wyncourt—whose horse had come to grief without the necessity of being shot—was kind enough to bear Caro Lamb back to the Pavilion in his laudaulet; and it was from his words the intelligence soon emanated the length and breadth of Brighton, which had seen nothing to equal her ladyship's display since the Regent had grown too fat to gallop over the Downs.

I shudder to think what must have been Caro's reception, once the news of the black colt's end was received at the Pavilion. The Regent's love for his horses is everywhere known—and is said to exceed even his love of women. His Royal Highness cannot, in good conscience, despatch an injured lady post-haste back to London, even were the magistrate to allow it; but it is certain that Caro Lamb is in disgrace, and shall be barred from the stables so long as she remains in the town.

"What a race, eh, Jane?" my brother crowed as Mona backed and turned her phaeton in preparation for quitting the meeting-ground. Henry was standing with deceptive insouciance beside China Trade, as tho' he had been an intimate of Lord Swithin's this age, a privileged friend and sporting companion.

How Eliza should have loved the picturesque! I thought with a pang. And almost forgave her betrayal.

The sprightly mare's bay coat was darkened with sweat, but she appeared to regard the exertion so little, as to be ready to try a second round of the course. The Earl's countenance had regained its colour, and he met a hail of felicitations from the gentlemen whose wagers he had justified, with becoming relish.

The ladies of the party, I may disclose, accomplished the return to Brighton in subdued spirits. Desdemona was disposed to exclaim about Caro Lamb and her mad behaviour, and I might have seconded her observations with praise of the Earl's game little jumper, had not Lady Oxford's demeanour silenced us both. Her ladyship was lost in distraction, and that the tendency of her thoughts ran to Lord Byron, and all that Lady Caroline had disclosed, was revealed by her asking abruptly, "Does George *truly* mean to dine with you tonight, Mona, or is that but a falsehood as well?"

Desdemona shot me a sidelong look—I was wedged between the two Countesses—and said diffidently, "I depend upon his appearance, as he accepted the invitation with alacrity only this afternoon. He was most solicitous for your welfare, Jane, I assure you—being well aware that the Regent is no great favourite of yours, and that it is His Royal Highness who sets the tone of Society in Brighton. Byron had no wish to see you come to hammer-and-tongs with Prinny over Princess Caroline."

"—He did not wish to see me *snubbed,* you mean," Lady Oxford returned. "It would never do for the acknowledged *maîtresse* of so celebrated a poet, to receive the cut direct from all Brighton. Pray speak plainly, Mona. Does he dread my coming?"

"*What?*" her ladyship exclaimed, as tho' outraged.

"George, *dread* to see the lady nearest his heart? Do not be a goosecap, my dear! You cut your Wisdoms too long ago!"

It was perhaps unfortunate that Mona should have invoked Lady Oxford's *age,* at such a moment, when her friend required only reassurance; it was done entirely without malice, however, as the unfortunate adoption of cant expressions usually is—with frequent disastrous effect.

"Yes, I'm rather more than seven," her ladyship observed acidly; and to my horror, she began to weep. Mona, on my left hand, was entirely unaware of the distress she had caused. Tears streamed silently down Lady Oxford's cheeks, trailing through the powder and rouge her ladyship employed—which can only have served as salt in her wounds. I drew a clean handkerchief from my reticule and wordlessly offered it. Lady Oxford mopped delicately at her face.

"I have known Caroline Lamb long enough to declare that while she is an accomplished little liar, she rarely tries it on in publick," she told us. "Every word she uttered today, whether in a whisper or a screech, was potently true, was it not, Mona?"

"I could not undertake to say," stammered the Countess of Swithin. "Certainly as regards the more *intimate* of her barbs, I cannot be allowed to have an opinion."

Lady Oxford made a dismissive gesture with her hand; my black-hemmed square of lawn fluttered away behind the dashing phaeton. "But the gist of it, Mona: Byron was in love with the girl? —This Twining chit? And has been deceiving me liberally the whole spring long? When I believed him *besotted*—"

The Countess of Swithin was silent an instant, as tho' marshalling her arguments. I may say that despite the necessity of preserving her wits and temper in the face of her friend's turbulent spirits, she continued to drive her demanding team to the very *inch,* for which I was no end grateful.

"Who can tell what George Gordon truly feels in that place he claims for a heart?" she declared at last. "Never having penetrated it, my dear, I should not attempt to say. Certainly he conceived a passion for Catherine Twining—but whether as a *man,* or a poet inspired by a particular *muse,* who knows? The girl was the merest child! And he has *always* been enslaved by ladies of more . . . experience . . . and . . . and *maturity* . . . as you know. Such innocence as Catherine displayed could not have captivated him long."

Lady Oxford drew a shuddering breath and closed her eyes. She ought to have been reassured by her friend's words, but her face was become a mask, distracted and anxious; Desdemona had only increased her misery.

"With those of Byron's stamp," her ladyship persisted, "it must be enough to figure in his imagination; one can never hope to possess it solely, as one might with a lesser Genius. You have been Aspasia, your little daughter has been Ianthe—must you strive to be his Leila too?"

There it was, again: that haunting name, so evocative of climes far from England's shores. Caro Lamb had caught it; from Byron himself—or Catherine Twining?

"It was Caro who named me thus, not Byron," Lady Oxford said, reverting to the first part of Mona's sentence. "Aspasia—for Socrates' wise mistress. We used to meet so often, in past years, to talk over the latest radical ideas—there is a wild Genius, when all is said, to Caro's understanding. Mad she may be, untamed her heart shall always be—but there is nothing deficient in her intellect. Indeed, there are few women I should prefer to meet, had this unfortunate break not come between us."

She spoke as tho' the break had not been of her making—and yet, I thought with amazement bordering on revulsion, there had been a *choice* when she succumbed to Byron's ardour. Lady Oxford had certainly known of Caro Lamb's amorous history—that lady had made a gift of every detail to her entire world. But Jane Harley had deliberately taken as her lover the man who had discarded her dear friend. That both ladies were married already was of the slightest consequence, it seemed.

Aspasia, indeed!

I should never become accustomed to the casual betrayals that served as bread-and-butter to the *haut ton.*

THE COUNTESS OF SWITHIN SEEMED LESS INCLINED TO AN intimate dinner with Lady Oxford, now that her friend was decidedly blue-deviled, and was most pressing in her invitation to both Henry and me to swell their family party. But I pled weariness, and remained firm in declining all frivolity. As I stepped down from the phaeton before the Castle's door, and walked round to Mona's side to curtsey my thanks, she leaned from her seat and muttered, "I shall urge the Countess to trust you *entirely,* dearest Jane, with references to my brother Kinsfell, and your perspicacity on numerous occasions—indeed, it should be enough to mention my uncle Trowbridge's regard, for they were as intimate as two peas in a pod, you know. I shall write to you on the morrow— provided my friend is not taken up for the murder of Lord Byron in the interval—"

With a roguish smile and a flick of her whip, she left me to turn slowly into the comparative peace of the inn, in search of my comfortable dinner—which was fated to be discomposed by fruitless pondering of the terms *intimate* and *peas in a pod.*

Had Lord Harold, too, been Lady Oxford's slave? What had *he* called her—Aspasia, Ianthe, or simply *Jane?*

I was unaccountably brusque with Henry throughout the evening.

"BY THE BY, JANE," HE SAID AS THE GUINEA FOWL, TURBOT, radishes, and shrimps were removed, and a dish of pears in jellied wine and a syllabub were set before us, along with half a local cheese—"you have not asked me one *word* about my conversation with Scrope Davies. I thought you intended for me to pump the fellow!"

As the better part of Henry's conversation had concerned horses during dinner—the various points of those in the field, and those capable of completely outshining it, that had scratched at the last moment due to strained hocks, or other vagaries of Fortune; the obscure genealogy of Lord Wyncourt's colt, which was said to require a *fomenting of the knees* as a result of its fall; the practices pursued by the Earl of Swithin on his estates in Ireland, where the bay mare had been bred; and the general outcome of the betting—I found this declaration self-serving, if not openly unjust.

I stabbed the cheese with a spoon. "I should like to hear what you thought of the gentleman."

"Oh! As to that—he's an excellent fellow! Highly intelligent, with an air of Fashion, and unfailingly good *ton*. I could wish him rather more plump in the pocket—he ought to bag an heiress one of these days, but the mammas are all against him, smelling the fortune-hunter. It is a sad thing when a man of no particular profession sets up as a Dandy—without he carries a title, or the expectation of an inheritance, the Polite World is apt to look askance. However, there is nothing to quarrel with in the tying of Davies's cravat, or the set of his coat; he moves in the first circles, and if he *does* play too deep at basset, I am sure it is no affair of mine. He banks with Coutts."

"Henry," I said with a commendable effort at controlling

my temper, "did Eliza never tell you that you are the most in-furiating *Henry* in all the world?"

"Eliza doted on me, as well she ought." He tossed a grape in the air and caught it between his teeth, as tho' he had been yet a boy; and it occurred to me that he must have placed a good deal of money on the bay mare, for his spirits verged on the giddy.

"Out with it," I commanded. "How much did you win?"

"Seven hundred guineas."

I sat back in my chair, astounded. Such a princely sum should never have entered my head—and the betting surely had not argued such massive winnings—the bay mare was the clear favourite stepping out of the post—

"You bet *against* Caro Lamb," I said. "Didn't you?"

"Having seen that lady come to grief on the shingle, did you expect me to back her on the turf?" he retorted drily. "For all I could judge, her ladyship was likely to *ride* as poorly as she *swam*. It was a close-run thing, of course—the colt very *nearly* cleared that final jump, and had Lady Caroline placed, it should have been bellows to mend with me. . . . May I offer you a grape, Jane?"

I will never underestimate the reckless disregard of bankers.

I shook my head, and concentrated on consuming a bite of cheese.

"Very well," I said. "On the strength of seven hundred guineas, I have no compunction in demanding that you sing for your supper—*and* frank me in a new gown I shall order tomorrow at a modiste's I fancy in North Street. I regard my-self as entirely responsible for Caro's queer freaks, merely from having overlistened her speeches to Lady Oxford. With-out myself as audience, she should hardly have performed to such a height—or been moved to plunge into the field, from a fevered desire for further applause."

"Done," my brother said. "What would you have me sing?"

"Your opinion of Scrope Davies. And I do not mean of his *cravat*," I added. "The Twinings' butler would have it that Davies was acquainted with the family—that it was he, in fact, who made his friend Byron known to Miss Twining."

"Did he, tho'?" Henry returned, with an air of surprize. "That is devilish *odd*, Jane. I'd have sworn he carried a *tendre* for the young lady himself."

I studied my brother. The elation natural to a gentleman who has raped Fortune of so grand a sum as *seven hundred guineas* had been heightened by the liberal resort to an excellent French claret, which had been followed with applications of a mellow Port; and it was obvious that my brother was rather *well to live,* as the saying goes. I had not seen him so jubilant since Eliza's illness first clenched its talons all too palpably in her breast, some ten months ago. I love Henry so well—he is, not even excepting Frank, the *dearest* of my brothers, as being the most aligned in temperament to myself—that I revelled in this resurgence of his native jubilance; and indeed, found that my own megrims were entirely banished, at the sight of Henry's high colour and dancing looks.

"Go on," I said.

Henry threw down his napkin and rocked backwards on his chair, the picture of happy surfeit.

"It was obvious you required an interval to examine his drunken lordship," he began, "so I made it my business to entertain Mr. Davies. I commenced with the usual gambit—felicitations all round on the happy outcome of the inquest, and the undoubted part Mr. Davies's own evidence had played—but I found him unreceptive. Throughout the quarter-hour in which we spoke—or *I spoke,* rather, for the exertion was almost entirely on my side—the gentleman was decidedly ill-at-ease."

My interest sharpened. "From what cause?"

"Divided attention. He was engrossed in overlistening *your* conversation with Lord Byron, and at first I assumed he did so from an anxiety to protect his inebriated friend. However, I swiftly concluded he was consumed with a desire to know the *gentleman's* sentiments, not your own, and was more nearly attending to Byron's words than mine. Indeed, I was forced to enquire *thrice* whether he meant to visit the racing-ground this afternoon, before receiving less than a distracted answer."

"He groaned, I recollect, and clutched his face with his hands, at something Byron said."

"Quite right," Henry replied. "But I have no notion of the subject; my ears are less acute, it would seem, than Davies's."

"The poet was describing his intention, once happily in possession of Miss Twining's notice in that closed carriage he employed for abduction," I said drily. "He was attempting to frame the spur to his passion, as I recall. *Her face, her figure, her soft voice were incitement to anything you might imagine—and I should never be proof against their charms!—* Or that was the burden of his periods; he's much given to windy declarations, fairly besotted with his own words. He might as well have said: *I wanted to tear her clothes from her body and have her right there against the squabs,* and be done with it. I wonder why he did not? —Have her, I mean, not *talk* about it?"

If the image of Byron in the throes of passion caused my skin to tingle, I did not share the fact with Henry.

"I should imagine Mr. Davies is asking himself the same thing. As well as why he wastes his friendship on such a blackguard as Byron—the fellow's tendencies are vile." Henry leaned across the table conspiratorially. "I suspect that the idea of Miss Twining's embarrassment has weighed heavily on Davies's mind ever since the attempt at abduction was made. Perceiving his distress, I made so bold as to offer my condolences on the sad loss of his young neighbour. Davies stared at me in starkest misery. 'Neighbour?' quoth he. 'You may call her such, if you wish; for it is true I took this house for the Season merely to observe her beauty. To meet with Miss Twining in the street by chance was unlooked-for happiness; to hear her voice, a benediction. To know that such a perfect flower is cut down, in the midst of her blooming . . .' and then he was overcome, and could not go on."

"You fascinate me, Henry."

My brother's countenance turned sombre. "Consider of it, Jane. How the man must be *tortured*. If indeed Davies *loved* Catherine Twining—took a house in Church Street on purpose to meet with her at every opportunity—"

"Only to have Byron descend upon him within days of Catherine's return from her Bath seminary, and demand an introduction—"

"—and watch, powerless, as the greatest rake in England pursued his *perfect flower*—"

"—and presumed so much upon friendship, as to make Davies his *accomplice* in Catherine's ruin—"

"—used Davies's lodgings as a base for his amorous interludes, and made him privy to his lewdest schemes, not excepting the foiled attempt at abduction—"

"And capped all, by naming his *friend* as chief witness to his movements and character, on the night Davies's love was murdered!"

I sat back, all animation fled. "What a dreadfully *sordid* little tale it is, Henry."

"Yes," my brother agreed, "and all the more pitiable, from Davies's apparent devotion to the girl. The fellow is suffering all the torments of grief, Jane—I'd *swear* to the fact, from having known that abyss myself."

There was a little pause; I had not expected Henry to invoke his loss—indeed, I had been watching him determinedly *outrun* it these several days past. At length, my brother resumed, with suppressed violence: "Whether he believes his friend to be innocent or no, I wonder Davies can bear to admit Byron into his drawing-room—or tolerate a word the fellow says!"

Unlike Henry, I could comprehend how impossible it might be to thwart Byron's will. But I was revolving the curious code of friendship and honour that obtained among gentlemen who had known one another since their schooldays. Scrope Davies had served as witness to Byron's movements— but so, too, had Byron served as *Davies's*. We had no independent witness to attest that Davies cooled his heels in the publick room at the Arms, while the valet packed Byron's traps and his lordship settled accounts with the publican. What if Davies, that Tulip of Fashion, had required a restorative breath of air after the heat of the Assembly Rooms—and taken a turn upon the shingle?—And there met the adored object of all his phantasies, Byron's Leila, Catherine Twining?

I had an idea of a drowned sylph, with the marks of violence about her neck—whose only crime was to have been *too well loved*. At what point did passion for a woman prove weaker than a murderous jealousy, of the kind Othello had known?

CHAPTER TWENTY-ONE

Mrs. Silchester's Confidence

THURSDAY, 13 MAY 1813
BRIGHTON

~

THE RAIN THIS MORNING WAS TORRENTIAL, FORESTALLING all ventures out-of-doors; there would be no drives along the sea, no visits to picturesque ruins, no picnics on the Downs—and to my secret relief, no assaults upon *bathing machines*. Henry should spend the better part of the morning at Raggett's Club, talking airily of his keen sense of the turf; I might do as I chose—whether my whims tended towards the patronage of a favoured linen-draper's on North Street, or several hours' indulgence of reading in my rooms. I debated the former: Of what use was the purchase of a gown that *must* be black? And should I be justified in securing a *different* colour at Henry's expence, against a future freed of mourning? What, I asked myself, would Eliza do?

And therein had my answer.

Eliza should buy the most *outré* gown to be had in Brighton, in a shocking colour of silk that became her extremely, and complete the toilette with gloves, reticule, diaphanous shawl,

and bonnet. Furthermore, she should sport the ensemble at the
first opportunity—and the Regent's invitation—and set the
whole town on its ears.

La comtesse est morte. Vive la comtesse.

I drank the scalding tea that Betsy supplied, and smiled a
little wryly at my vanished sister. I was *not* Eliza de Feuillide,
and however much her unquenchable spirits had inspired my
admiration in the past, the present demanded a less frivolous
duty.

Tucked beneath the journal on my bedside table was a
scrap of paper; the list of questions regarding Catherine's
death I had penned only yesterday. I glanced at it, then threw
back the bedclothes, donned my wrapper—one of the few
things I presently wear, along with my nightdress, that is
thankfully *not* black—and settled into an armchair close to
Betsy's fire.

1. *With whom did Catherine Twining dance at the
    Assembly, besides Mr. Smalls?*

    —I had yet to ascertain. Mrs. Silchester might
    supply the intelligence; but the most dependable
    source should be the Master of Ceremonies, a
    quelling gentleman by the name of Forth, who
    held the social world of Brighton in his thrall; and
    as today was Thursday—when, murder or no
    murder, the *second* Assembly of the week should
    be held, at the Old Ship—I knew where he might
    be found. Surely even a lady in mourning might be
    admitted to the ballroom, if her object is to
    interrogate the Master? I should have to secure
    my introduction to Mr. Forth from the Countess
    of Swithin. In Mona's presence, even he *must*
    unbend.

2. *When did Catherine arrive at the Pavilion in Caro Lamb's care?*

    —I noted down the approximate time of one o'clock.

3. *What was the purport of the ladies' tête-à-tête?*

    —According to Caro Lamb, so that she might warn Miss Twining against Byron; but Catherine required no warning—she went in fear of the poet already. I scribbled, rather: *so that Caro Lamb might learn every detail of her former lover's passion for Miss Twining, and then toss her out into the street in a fury of jealousy.* I could readily imagine her ladyship committing such an unpardonable act of rudeness; it explained her vagueness as to the time and manner of Catherine's departure. But had she been jealous enough to observe the girl's movements . . . lure her back into the grounds of the Pavilion . . . lead her down to the shingle, and force her head beneath the waves? Caro Lamb looked frail; but I had watched those supple hands on the reins of her flying horse, and guessed she commanded a wiry strength.

    I could not, however, imagine her ladyship trussing the body into a hammock stolen from Byron's boat—which must be moored at a distance from the shingle, necessitating a midnight swim from a woman who had nearly drowned in those waters the day previous—much less carrying the shrouded body into the King's Arms in the middle of the night.

Could Caro have bought the aid and silence of
Another?

4. *When did Catherine quit the Pavilion?*

—I might trust the undergroom's testimony by the
stable clock; she had been seen at three-quarters
past one. But did she truly leave the grounds at
that hour?

5. *If the undergroom observed her walking towards
the Steyne, how did she come by her death in
the sea?*

—It seemed certain Catherine had tarried in the
shadow of the Pavilion long enough to be seized—
or lured—down to the water. But by whom?

6. *Where was Lord Byron at the time?*

—Walking with his friend Scrope Davies and his
valet towards Church Street, along the very route
Miss Twining should have adopted on her way
home. Were the three men conspirators? Had one
killed her, and the others observed it—agreeing,
out of loyalty or avarice, to lie on each other's
behalf? Of Davies I could believe mendacity
possible; but the valet owed Byron no particular
loyalty—he must live among his fellows in
Brighton for years to come, long after Byron
should be forgot; he might hang for his lies, were
they discovered; in sum, the man named Chaunce
had too much to lose and too little to gain. I could
not think conspiracy likely.

7. *Colonel George Hanger?*

He was the Regent's guest, and might have
observed Catherine Twining's arrival with Caro
Lamb—and her solitary departure. Did he think to
finish his attempted rape by the water line, and
grow too violent when Catherine screamed?

Did Catherine scream—and if so, did anyone
hear it?

I sighed. There were a number of enquiries to be made at
the Marine Pavilion—and I could wish them to have been
made anywhere else. One does not easily put pointed questions to Royalty and its circle. Henry would have to work a
miracle with his acquaintance, Lord Moira or Colonel
McMahon, to secure an interview on that exalted ground.

8. *General Twining? Mr. Hendred Smalls?*

—The General claimed to have left the Assembly
at eleven o'clock Monday evening, leaving his
daughter to the care of Mrs. Silchester. One could
assume Hendred Smalls quitted the place at the
same hour—perhaps even letting down his friend
in Church Street before proceeding in a hack
chaise to his lodgings at Brighton Camp; but what
if the cleric had lingered? I had an absurd idea of
the moist-handed gentleman conceiving a jealous
passion against Lord Byron; of lurking in sight of
the Assembly Rooms; observing the departure of
Miss Twining for the Pavilion; and at a quarter to
two in the morning, halting the young lady in her
path with a confused declaration of suspicious
love. Even an absurd fellow may have feelings;

even a bald and aging cleric may be moved to violent passion. I must endeavour to learn the movements of Mr. Smalls on the night in question.

9. *What did Lady Caroline Lamb do after Catherine left her?*

—Bathe; sleep; stay up until dawn writing a screed to Byron . . . or pursue her rival down to the water's edge? Would any of the Pavilion's servants be likely to know? Had Caro Lamb brought her personal maid?

10. *When did the General discover that his daughter never returned home Monday night—and did he sound an alarum?*

—The General claimed to have learnt the news at five o'clock in the morning, from his daughter's maid, who had every reason to be truthful; he then stated he had alerted the Brighton constabulary that Catherine had very probably been abducted again by Lord Byron.

While the General may be pardoned for leaping to such a conclusion, he appears *not* to have considered asking first at Mrs. Silchester's for Catherine, who might easily have spent the night with her chaperon. A mere omission in his testimony, or something else?

11. *How could a body be carried into the King's Arms in the dead of night without being seen?*

—There was absolutely nothing I could put down

beneath this question. I had no idea how to answer it. Neither, it would seem, did the magistrate nor coroner—for not a single point of information had touched upon the subject at the inquest. The body had been found in Byron's bed, therefore it had been brought into the Arms; but everyone connected with the enquiry appeared content to ignore the question of HOW.

12. *Did anyone at the Arms hear a disturbance in Byron's rooms? Query: Who was lodged next to Byron?*

—I glanced towards my streaming windows; it would certainly rain all day. Perhaps dear Henry would consent to escort me to a nuncheon at the King's Arms; he should have little else to do.

And finally:

13. *Who, among the respectable and the highborn of Brighton, hates Lord Byron to the point of madness?*

—The poet himself had promised to supply me with a list; but I doubted, once restored to sobriety, he should recollect the offer. I need not wait for it. The tendency of the question was this: Who hated Byron enough to make him *look guilty of murder,* solely in order to see him hang? In this framing of Catherine's death, she might have been anybody— a mere convenience, as victim.

General Twining, of course, had every reason to hate Lord Byron; but that should hardly urge him to murder his daughter. Mr. Hendred Smalls was capable, perhaps, of a jealous rage—but of the subsequent black joke, the hammock from the *Giaour,* and the sodden gift of his cherished bride in Byron's bed? I could not think him capable; I judged him to lack the necessary subtlety of mind. Lady Oxford was brilliant enough to fashion the scheme, but had known nothing of her lover's unfaithfulness, and was in London at the time. Caro Lamb . . . I had already judged Caro entirely equal to such devious ploys, and heedless enough to execute them. But if she drowned her rival, *how had the body been deposited in the King's Arms?*

My tea was cold, my fingers cramped, and my mind disordered. I thrust aside my pen in frustration, and put on my blacks for breakfast.

"IF YOU WISH TO SAUNTER DOWN TO NORTH STREET," Henry urged over the last of his toast, "I am happy to procure a chair for your use, Jane, and even walk alongside it until the modiste is achieved. That was an excellent notion of yours, that I should frank you in a new gown; for without your kind solicitude for my health, I should never have come to Brighton at all—or engaged in so advantageous a wager."

"It is remarkable, is it not, how unforeseen are the consequences of benevolence?" I returned. "I shall be urging you to adopt my slightest whim in future, Henry, from a desire to see you rich. But you need not accompany me to the modiste; I have been dressing myself for donkey's years, you know."

"Not in Brighton. Do you expect Madame La Fanchette to extend credit to a complete stranger?" He drew his purse from within his coat. "Here is a draught on my bank, Jane—

if you require anything over, I daresay the woman should consent to send the bill to the Castle with her compliments."

Fifty pounds. When Henry said *my bank,* he meant his bank—and the signature of the proprietor of Austen & Tilson over the draught should be all I required to win Madame La Fanchette's confidence. But *fifty pounds?* I had existed an entire twelvemonth on as much. I stared at my brother in awe; whatever one might say of the evils born of gambling, stinginess was not one of them.

"Henry—are you *entirely* sure—"

He gestured me away, his colour heightened. "This is nothing, Jane. Recollect that I shall not be dressing Eliza in future—who cost me four times *that* whenever she entered a modiste."

We were both of us silent an instant; my throat constricted. Trust Henry to suggest that I did him a *kindness* by accepting of his winnings.

"Is there anything else you require of me, Jane?"

"Only to meet me at the King's Arms for a nuncheon," I replied recovering. "Perhaps one o'clock?"

"I should be delighted. I don't know how it is—but even so elegant a table as the Castle's begins to grow tiresome after several days. And you will be wanting, of course, to put your questions to the publican."

Wise Henry.

"Or his bootboys."

"Just so. One o'clock it is."

He threw down his napkin and left me quite happily to my own devices—the sort of freedom that is almost never afforded me in the more crowded household at Chawton. I think I should be content to travel with Henry forever, did his luck hold out.

THERE WAS ALREADY A KNOT OF FASHIONABLE LADIES AT Madame La Fanchette's, in North Street, all of them a little breathless from having walked hurriedly along the paving in the rain, umbrellas held high. Three of them were young matrons, consumed with talk of children and measles; one was a mamma with a young, fair-haired daughter, just out, from her looks, which were compounded of hesitancy and exuberant conceit; and the last was Mrs. Silchester.

"I cannot be so presumptuous as to go into *full mourning*," she murmured from among her floating veils, when I had greeted her, "for that is most truly the province of *family*, and however I may have cherished dear Catherine as another daughter—tho' I attempted to supply her dear mother's place—I cannot claim so near a connexion. I thought it not unpardonable, however, to put on some *grey*. The funeral, you know, is to be tomorrow at ten o'clock—Mr. Hendred Smalls is to lead the service—and tho' as a lady I shall not, of course, be in attendance, I should not like to be remiss in any mark of respect on the occasion. What is your opinion, Miss Austen?"

I assured her most earnestly that grey—whether charcoal or dove—must always be unexceptionable.

"I am *most partial* to lavender," Mrs. Silchester pursued doubtfully, "and cloth of silver for evening—you do not think either would *offend*?"

On no account could so conservative a choice *offend*, I insisted—but would Mrs. Silchester prefer that I review the gowns in question?

This was officiousness in the extreme from a relative stranger; but the lady appeared to require reassurance. Her reference to Catherine Twining's mother had recalled certain phrases of the General's I should dearly wish explained. I determined to profit from the happy chance that had thrown us together this morning, and put my questions to Mrs. Silchester while half her mind was distracted by millinery.

Presently we were joined by Madame La Fanchette herself, a strong-featured, rail-thin woman with a pronounced Yorkshire accent who had certainly never seen Paris; her toilette, however, was the last word in elegant severity, and I imagined I should be happy in anything her workrooms might fashion for Henry's fifty pounds. At the snap of her fingers, a bevy of young women appeared to exhibit the latest modes, all of them nicely suited to a lady of Mrs. Silchester's station in life; Madame was familiar with her clients' tastes.

"You will not have visited any of the warehouses," the modiste mused, "but I may be able to supply you with a lavender silk—only observe, Miss Austen," she said with polite acknowledgement as an assistant brought forth the bolt for my inspection, "as the weave is that fine, and the colour not too sharp."

"It might almost be grey, in a certain light," I admitted. "I cannot think this to be objectionable. One so dislikes to go in darker shades during the summer months—which are nearly upon us."

"I take it you've recently lost a close relation," she said, with an assessing glance at my black gown. "The workmanship is not without merit."

"A Frenchwoman who resides in London made it for me," I said carelessly. "Have you a clear dove sarcenet or perhaps a slate-blue twill, for Mrs. Silchester's walking dress?"

Indeed Madame La Fanchette had; and while she discussed necklines and sleeves, and ordered her assistant to measure Mrs. Silchester's waist, I looked on as tho' granting opinions to an acquaintance was all the joy I required. Mrs. Silchester's countenance, which had been suffused with anxiety, gradually relaxed under the combined ministrations of Madame and myself—there is nothing like ordering one's clothes to lift a lady's spirits, after all—and when at last we had arrived at the coveted cloth of silver, with a beaded hem and matching headdress, her spirits were entirely restored.

Madame promised faithfully to send round the lavender silk on the morrow, with the rest of the gowns to follow; then turned her blunt features upon me. Was there anything Miss Austen required?

I saw, to my regret, that the hour was now too advanced to permit of my own frivolity *and* a nuncheon with Henry, and informed Madame of the unfortunate fact of a previous engagement—promised to return at the first opportunity—and accompanied Mrs. Silchester as she quitted the establishment.

"I must assume that tho' we cannot attend the funeral itself," I observed as we walked back along North Street in the direction of the Steyne, "that we ought, in good conscience, to pay a call of condolence upon the General at the conclusion of the service. Surely there will be any number of Brighton's notables who shall do the same?"

Mrs. Silchester hesitated. "In truth, the General lives so quietly—and tho' commanding respect, has never sought a broad acquaintance among the first families in the town—I cannot undertake to say whether he shall be receiving or not. However,"—and she squared her shoulders a little—"that shall not prevent *me* from paying a call. I hope that I know what is due to that poor lost darling, tho' her father may not. I hope I am conscious of what her *mother* should have wished, on the occasion."

Here was my opening. "She died some years since, I collect?"

"When Catherine was but three years old, and her brother seven. Richard had already been sent away to school, of course, and Catherine was in the care of her nurse when

Lydia . . . but that is ancient history, my dear Miss Austen, and cannot be of interest to yourself."

"I hope you will not think me inquisitive," I returned with an air of apology, "but the General was so indiscreet as to speak of his late wife in a manner I found rather shocking. I attempted to pay a call on him only yesterday, to offer my sympathy at the loss of his daughter; but he refused to admit me, and so far forgot himself as to declare that *the sins of the mother had been visited upon the child*. Naturally, I could not know what to think. I ascribed it to the excesses of grief."

"Ye-es," Mrs. Silchester said hesitantly, "tho' with my knowledge of the General, I should be inclined to call it spite rather than sorrow. You will forgive me for speaking frankly, Miss Austen—the General is *not* an amiable man. Dear Lydia was quite otherwise—possessed of perhaps *too* much sensibility, indeed—and a more ill-sorted pair I never hope to encounter again."

"The marriage was unhappy?"

"She fell in love with a red coat, I fear—and never gave a thought to the nature of the gentleman who wore it."

"Many ladies might say the same, to their infinite misfortune," I offered piously.

"But few with poor Lydia's result."

Poor Lydia. It might be a veritable quotation from my own pen.

And as we walked towards the King's Arms and my expected nuncheon, Mrs. Silchester shared her friend's sad history.

CHAPTER TWENTY-TWO

A Passion for Publick Houses

"IT IS QUITE A DISMAL TALE, HENRY," I WARNED AS THE potboy set a tankard of ale, half a cold ham, some new-baked bread, and a Stilton cheese before us. I was drinking lemonade. We were seated in the King's Arms' coffee room among perhaps half-a-dozen other parties, with the horde of more common folk collected in the Ordinary beyond the communicating passage, and the cheerful din made the perfect foil for intimate conversation. The Arms was a handsome-enough old publick house, broad-beamed and low-ceilinged, with smoke-darkened walls and ample hearths. Henry had already informed me that the Regent had been frequently revelling here in his salad days—before Mrs. Fitzherbert or the unfortunate marriage to his cousin Princess Caroline—and that the carousing of the 10th Hussars, whose preferred publick house it was, could be as nothing to the example His Royal Highness had once set.

"No local maiden was safe from his party," Henry observed. "And the gallons of wine and ale that were drunk!

The publican, Mr. Tolliver—who has lived in the Arms, man and boy, his father being publican before him—says there was nothing to equal Prinny's lust for life, in his youth. The reputation of the house grew so tarnished among the gentry, indeed, that Mr. Tolliver's father very nearly barred the Prince from the premises—but for the uncomfortable fact of his *being* the Prince. But you were speaking of General Twining: Pray forgive my interruption."

"I fear that what I have to relate is less amusing." I allowed my brother to serve me a cut of ham. "General Twining was once himself a member of the 10th Hussars, as should not be unusual; and while in London a quarter-century ago, met and married a beautiful young heiress named Lydia Montescue—only then in her first Season. He was thirty; she was but seventeen, and wild for a red coat, as Mrs. Silchester would have it—the two ladies were together at school, and remained friends ever after. As is so often the case, poor Lydia discovered that she had married a stranger on the strength of three weeks' acquaintance, several balls, and a drive or two in Hyde Park—who proved, as a life partner, harsh and incomprehensible: so strict a disciplinarian, that her frivolous pleasures were at an end; so parsimonious a master, that her ample purse was hers no longer; and so jealous a husband, that she might not stand up with one of his fellow officers at a garrison ball, without earning a blow from his hand. In short, she left the General—who was but Major Twining then—when her son was five and her daughter an infant still in arms."

"Eloped with another?" Henry suggested.

"One of her husband's cavalry officers—Captain the Honourable Philip Barrett, Mrs. Silchester persisted in calling him, as tho' his courtesy title lent greater glamour to his memory. Captain Barrett was the second son of the Earl of Derwentwater, she tells me, and exquisitely expensive—being addicted to gambling. Poor Lydia appears to have possessed appalling taste in men."

"Fellow ditched her?"

"I am sure his family would have preferred him to have done so. In the event, Twining pursued them, challenged the Honourable to a duel—and killed him at twenty paces."

"Good Lord!" Henry almost choked on his ham. "And having put his rival below ground, Twining did not feel obliged to flee to the Continent?"

"He stood his trial, and was acquitted the crime of murder on the plea of having defended his honour—the first duty of any soldier or gentleman. Mrs. Silchester, however, could not quite condone such violence. I believe she was as smitten as all the rest with the dashing Captain. A *tragedy*, she called it."

"And Lydia?—She was hauled back to do penance, I suppose?"

I shook my head. "Having killed her lover, Twining cast off his wife without a penny, Mrs. Silchester says. Lydia died in extreme poverty in a back slum of London when Catherine was but three years old, and lies in an unmarked pauper's grave. Mrs. Silchester knows this to be true, because she received a letter from the vicar of St. Martin-in-the-Fields, which parish had the burying of Mrs. Twining; Mrs. Silchester's direction was found among the unfortunate lady's effects, when she had died."

"And the Montescues? They made no effort to support her? They allowed their Lydia to end in misery?"

"She was an orphan, I understand—which accounts for her considerable fortune, which fell entirely to General Twining's use."

"Melancholy," Henry observed. "And do but consider, Jane, how little his course in life has availed him—only son killed in the Peninsula, and now his daughter snuffed out in violence."

"Yes. One might almost call it a judgement—if one were possessed of a vindictive turn, in matters divine."

"I am *glad* I disliked that fellow upon first meeting," my brother persisted. "I can only wonder that little Catherine did not fly to London with Byron when he asked—so eagerly must she have yearned for liberty."

"But that is exactly what she would *not* do, Henry," I countered. "Recollect her sheer terror at being returned to her home in disgrace—the reliance she placed upon us bearing her company—and the blow she received for her courage in having outwitted Lord Byron! I had heard before this that the General is most anxious on the subject of his name, and family dignity; and now we may know the cause. He perceives the world to be laughing at him, for having a shameful wife—and therefore no taint of a similar disease should be allowed to mar Catherine. *She* must be perceived as purer than the driven snow. What a curse for the poor child, that she should draw so rakish an eye as Lord Byron's!"

"It explains the General's determination to marry her off so early to Mr. Smalls," Henry added. "What better safeguard against calumny than an aged clergyman?"

"What better inducement to a second elopement!" I cried. "No, Henry—the General understands nothing of women, and has been at every turn a fool. Did I not dislike him so thoroughly, I should be inclined to pity the man—so hamfisted as he is. He even finds *shame* in Catherine's murder—as tho' she deserved it, through some moral lapse of her own. Could anything be more unjust?"

"For my part," my brother replied, "I should like to *strike* General Twining."

"And such are our ungenerous sentiments, on the very eve of his daughter's funeral!" I mused. "Which puts me in mind of something—you must attend, as a representative of the family."

Henry's brows rose. "Indeed, Jane? I have this comfort: there can be no difficulty in procuring mourning."

"I should not ask it of you," I pleaded, "but that I cannot attend myself; you know it to be most improper. And I should dearly like an observant pair of eyes upon Mr. Hendred Smalls—he is to conduct the service."

"Ah," Henry said knowledgeably. "And at the cold colla-tion that is certain to follow—not even the General could be so remiss in what is due to his daughter as to forgo the cold collation!—you would wish me to enquire as to the clergy-man's movements in the small hours of Tuesday morning. Say, between one and three o'clock?"

"Henry," I sighed as I took a bite of cheese, "you are in every way a most *excellent* brother."

THE PUBLICAN, MR. TOLLIVER, PRESUMING SO FAR ON HIS earlier conversation with Henry to approach our table, and beam in a kindly way at me—enquiring whether the ham was cured to my liking, and whether I should not wish for a glass of ratafia, as an aid to my digestion—I seized upon chance and professed myself entirely delighted with every aspect of the meal and the establishment. However *modern* the Castle's conveniences, I assured him, it could offer nothing so com-fortable or sound as the King's Arms.

"Well, and it's a home-like place enough, which I allus think the traveller appreciates," Tolliver observed, gratified. "The lady has an appreciation, I take it, for fine old publick houses?"

"And posting-inns," I added ingeniously. "I have made a little habit, I confess, of looking into every one I find, upon the various roads of England. The White Hart in Bath, for ex-ample, is the very *soul* of a posting-inn; and my brother and I were recently treated to a fine example in Guildford."

"That'd be the White Lion, mebbe, or the Crown?"

"The Crown," I agreed. "Mr. Spraggs, the proprietor, was most generous in showing us about the place."

Tolliver took the hint, and despite a swell of custom—the hour being close on two o'clock—invited Henry and me to follow him through the principal rooms of the place, so that we might admire a quantity of ancient iron pots, pewter tankards, copper taps, oak settles, and stout barrels—all but the last, dating from Elizabeth's time.

"For the Arms—it were called the Ship and Bottle then, before the Royals descended on Brighthelmston and we were forced, in deference, to make the change—in my old dad's time, that were—has been the place for comfort and cheer, particularly along of the winter months, for time out of mind."

"And you let rooms, I understand?"

Tolliver's countenance lost a little in animation. "That we do—tho' I'm considering whether I shall in future. Only the four bedchambers have we above-stairs, most of the gentry preferring the Old Ship or the Castle, if they're not already in lodgings; and I don't mind to say that with the goings-on of late, it's hurt my reputation as an honest publican. You'd think, from what has been said, that the Arms was no better than a bawdy house! I thought we'd recovered from that indignity once the Regent grew too fat to stir out-of-doors—but there, you can never hope to serve the publick without suffering an injustice now and again. But Mrs. Tolliver feels it most acutely, I don't mind saying—took to her bed these two days past, from a dislike of the gossip as is going around the town."

"I am sure no impropriety can attach to your management of the house," I said with sympathy, "or Mrs. Tolliver's arrangements, either. It is not as tho' you *invited* a brigand to carry that poor child's body upstairs! And having seen Lord

Byron quit the place—at such an unseasonable hour, too—you must have thought all business at an end for the evening."

"Now, it's odd you should mention it, ma'am," Tolliver said, with one hand on the stair-rail. "For wracking my brains I have been, as to how that poor drowned girl was put in his lordship's bed."

A thrill of exultation stirred along my spine; at *last* we were coming to it!

"I allus keeps the doors unlocked and set a lad to wait up for folk, on Assembly nights—meaning Mondays and Thursdays—for the dancing *will* go on until all hours, and there's no telling as when a lodger will want to seek his bed, nor an officer wish to wet his whistle, as the saying goes. So certain it is the doors was unbarred and the Ordinary rollicking with a number of hearties. But I'd turned in at eleven o'clock myself—and Mrs. Tolliver was that put out when his lordship decided, in the dead of night, that nothing would do but he must settle his accounts—and sent the boy to rouse me out of bed! *He's not to have a room from us again, Tolliver,* she said, being fed to the brim with Lord Byron's whimsical ways."

"And, of course, the noise of packing would disturb the rest of your guests," Henry said sympathetically, "who cannot have spoken kindly of it in the morning."

"Jest the one other fellow upstairs there was," Tolliver said. "Mr. Laidlaw, a gentleman down from Oxford, most interested in those bits of rock and sich you may find along the shore—here for his health and a spot of rock-hunting, he is, and not the sort to burn the oil of a midnight. A most quiet and respectable gentleman is Mr. Laidlaw. His bedchamber gives onto the stairs at the head of the passage—quite near the water closet, for he's an elderly gentleman, is Mr. Laidlaw. Lord Byron being most insistent in the matter of *quiet*, for all he's scribbling at his verses when he's here, chose the room at the very end of the hall—quite pertickular when he first set eyes on the Arms. In April, that'd be, when he hired that yacht of old Benbow's down't the shingle. He's kept it ever since, to be certain of having it whenever the notion to sail oversets him—a most whimsical gentleman, his lordship, as I said."

Whimsical indeed, to demand *quiet* in a publick house, and chuse the haunt of cavalry officers for his writing-room. However, in Byron's world the hubbub of the Arms—so different from the genteel drawing-rooms of his usual circle— might seem to promise anonymity. Until Caro Lamb appeared on the scene, and forced him to fly.

"Mr. Laidlaw, I suppose, did not mention a disturbance in the night—as tho' a heavy load of baggage was carried past his door?"

"Mr. Laidlaw takes laudanum," Tolliver replied heavily, "and sleeps with a green eyeshade, and his ears plugged up with beeswax. A dreadful light sleeper, Mr. Laidlaw is, and a martyr to it, in publick places—and so he never retires but with his *precautions,* as he calls 'em. It was the first thing I asked him, after poor Mary carried in the coffee to Lord Byron's rooms—her meaning to lay the fire, not knowing as his lordship had quitted the place, her sleeping out at her mother's. It was Mary found that unfortunate lady sewn up in the hammock, and she screamed so loud not even Mr. Laidlaw's beeswax could preserve him. But he declared as he'd heard nothing—not even Lord Byron's valet, packing up of his traps."

"When does Mary lay the fires?"

"Around eight o'clock, on the mornings after Assemblies—the patrons preferring a bit of a lie-in, from being out so late."

And Lord Byron, at eight o'clock, had been waving farewell to Scrope Davies in Church Street. It was probable, however, that Catherine's body had arrived at its resting place hours earlier. There were still five hours, between Byron's seeking his bed and mounting his horse, when his lordship might have been anywhere—but was the publick house open to his use all that time?

"After his lordship quitted the place, with his dunnage, I am sure nothing would do for Mrs. Tolliver but to bar all the doors!" I told the landlord in amusement. "I should never risk a second disturbance to my sleep, having the considerable cares of a publick house to manage on the morrow."

"That she did, ma'am, and was that full of wrath she even cleared the Ordinary—tho' there was some as were disposed to give her lip about it. But, there, we've been and owned the Arms for donkey's years—and nothing no officer of the 10th can say will ever discompose Mrs. Tolliver. She's turned the Regent himself out of the premises, when he was but a stripling prince, and if Royalty must give way to Mrs. Tolliver, there's not much else that shan't."

"Very proper," Henry opined. "I admire her pluck. And so the doors were barred from the moment his lordship left— around half-past one, I think it was said at the Inquest. And you opened the house . . . at what hour?"

"Cock-crow," Tolliver said promptly, "which is round about five o'clock in May; tho' nobody'd come knocking at the back door—meaning such of the servants as sleeps *out* of the house, which is most of 'em—until six o'clock. I'm a fair man, for all I'm so pressed with custom, and don't ask even them as works for me to be abroad afore daylight."

"And yet," I persisted, with an air of feminine bewilderment, "poor Miss Twining's body materialised upstairs sometime between the hours of two and . . . let us say eight, despite the fact that the outer doors were barred! —For she was certainly seen alive in the grounds of the Pavilion at a quarter to two, and cannot have met her death any earlier.

You did not detect a *forcing* of your doors, Mr. Tolliver, I presume?"

"No, ma'am."

If my questions were beginning to appear too pointed, the good publican failed to take umbrage. He appeared as genuinely puzzled as I, regarding the murdered body in the bed.

"Might the kitchen doors have been left ajar?" I wondered. "A very daring and reckless murderer might be moved to take his chance—and carry Miss Twining's shrouded form up the servants' back stairs."

"But Nance, the scullery maid, sleeps on a pallet next to the hearth," Tolliver countered, "and the rogue should be forced to step over the girl to reach the stairs, even if she *did* neglect to bar the back door, which I doubt. Nobody could've mounted those stairs, without Nance screaming fit to bust, of ghosts and demons in the night. No, I'm afraid there's only one way possible that corpse found its way into Lord Byron's bed—and that's from the use of the tunnel, what my old dad, God rest his soul, swore was filled in when the Prince established Mrs. Fitzherbert in her villa, and left off his rakehell ways."

I stood rooted to the spot, unable even to risk a glance at my brother Henry. A *tunnel*? Good God!

"A tunnel," Henry said flatly. "There is a tunnel leading into the Arms?"

"Long since filled in, as I thought, and never used in thirty year or more," Tolliver rejoined. "It was Miss Austen's word as made me think on it—*materialised,* she said, as if that unfortunate young lady's remains jest floated up like a ghost! Many's the time my brother and me used to frighten the folk upstairs, when we were young, with a clanging bit o' chain and a sheet over our heads—jumping through the panel in the dead of night and howling so's to turn the blood cold. Our dad had our hides for it, of course, but that never stopped Sam—he's my brother, and saw worse every day in the Peninsula. A rifleman he is, now."

"A panel," I repeated, as tho' possessed of a weak understanding.

Tolliver nodded. "Comes right out beside the chimney stack in the middle bedchamber, as is unused at present. You are welcome to look at it, if you like—having an interest in old publick houses, as you do, ma'am."

He led my stupefied brother and myself immediately upstairs, Henry ducking to avoid collision with the low ceiling of the staircase. At the far end of the upper passage was a closed door—which must give on to Lord Byron's old bedchamber. I should dearly love to have a look round it; but Tolliver turned immediately into a doorway on our left: one of the middle bedchambers, its fellow being across the hall.

A pleasant-enough room, low-ceilinged like the rest, coated in plain white plaster with two small windows offering a view of the Marine Pavilion. The wainscoting was oak, and reached halfway up the walls, with a frieze of sporting dolphins carved along its upper edge. In the middle of the wall to our left sat the hearth—which was narrower than those in the publick rooms below; the stack, however, must serve both storeys, and run from the cellars to the attics.

Tolliver winked at us, crossed to the panelling on the right-hand side of the chimney, and pressed one of the carved dolphins. An entire section of panelling swung outwards, like a servant's door; narrow and not above four and a half feet in height—but an opening nonetheless.

"There," he said. "The Regent'd never fit through it, now."

"It was made for him?" Henry said.

"Aye, so he could come and go without the world observing him, whenever the need for a lightskirt or a dozen bottles of claret should take him and his disreputable friends. There was never anything like 'em for raking the night away—those Barrys—Cripplegate, Hellgate, and Newgate as they called 'em! *And* Sir John Lade, what married a Covent Garden doxy! *And* that George Hanger! —He's the only one the Regent will keep by him, now."

I stepped forward and gazed down; a winding stair descended into darkness.

"Is the whole of the publick house familiar with its existence?"

Tolliver slapped his thigh. "Not even my wife is aware! Have a fit of hysterics on the subject of burglars, Mrs. Tolliver would, if she knew there was a secret way inside the Arms. And as I said—my old dad insisted it'd been filled in long since. I haven't given it a thought since I was a boy, and Sam ran off to take the King's shilling."

"You made no mention of it at the inquest," I observed.

"Nobody asked," Tolliver said simply.

It was true; not a word had been said about the *means* of placing a dead girl in a bed at the Arms. Both coroner and magistrate appeared indifferent to the matter.

Henry met my gaze. "Where does the tunnel lead, Tolliver?"

"Why, to the Pavilion, of course!" He beamed.[21]

---

[21] In 1822, the Regent had a tunnel dug from the Pavilion to his riding school and stables, which is still in existence today. He had long been rumored, however, to possess a similar tunnel leading to Mrs. Fitzherbert's villa, as well as this one leading to the King's Arms. As the original pub no longer exists, the existence of a tunnel leading from it to the Pavilion is impossible to verify.—*Editor's note.*

CHAPTER TWENTY-THREE

Where the Tunnel Led

"Tolliver," my brother said, "you have been most generous with your time already, and I am loath to demand any more of it; but I do believe, in the interests of justice, that we ought to explore this tunnel—to ascertain, if nothing else, that it is indeed as yet unblocked for its entire length. The magistrate's pursuit of Miss Twining's murderer may depend upon it."

I could have wished Henry had left Sir Harding Cross well out of our prospective adventure, for at the mention of *the magistrate,* the publican's countenance underwent a change.

"I don't know as the Regent will like to have all his little arrangements laid before the publick, like," he said doubtfully. "It should not be seemly, to publish all that old business to the world."

"Then say nothing of His Royal Highness's use of the tunnel," I suggested, "and make out that it was for the purpose of providing the publick house with access to the shingle . . .

for . . . the ready unloading of goods brought round by the sea. Fish or . . ." I did not like to say *smuggled brandy and claret*, although that is what I was certainly thinking, having encountered such tunnels in coastal villages before. "The Pavilion was once a simple farmhouse, was it not?"

"Aye—belonged to Mr. Thomas Kemp, as is a great landowner hereabouts. But the tunnel was built well after his time."

"That is a point that need not arise."

"I don't know," Tolliver temporised. "I'm all of a flutter—the gentleman and lady having taken me by surprize, as it were, and caught me up in the spirit of the hunt; but I did ought to consult with Mrs. Tolliver, perhaps, and consider what should be done."

The result, I little doubted, should be the suppression of all evidence, from a desire to avoid any dispute with the Regent. Very well—if I must pay a call upon Sir Harding Cross and lay the information before him myself, I should do so—but nothing could induce me to turn my back on that tunnel, unexplored, while it yawned so tantalisingly before me now.

There was a quantity of tapers standing ready in a spill box on the mantel; I reached for several, and said to the publican, in as commanding a tone as I could muster, "Pray fetch a light, Mr. Tolliver, if you would be so good. I *must* and *shall* explore the cunning little tunnel—it shall add immeasurably to my collection of ancient publick houses!"

"To be sure!" Henry cried, all decided animation; and before two such ardent hearts, Tolliver's better sense gave way. He fetched a candle from the hall, lit our tapers, and then took a step backwards. "I'll ask you to wait for Young Bob," he said firmly. "Dear as I'd love to trot down those steps along of you both, I hear the missus calling, and we're that full to the gills with custom, on account of the race-meeting *and* the murder, that I'm wanted in the Ordinary. Bob'll see you come to no harm; he's a good fellow, and a rare one for rats."

With which obscure and daunting remark, he went to the head of the main stairs and halloed, "You there! Young Bob! Up with ye this instant! Aye, Polly, I'm just coming—"

Young Bob appeared within moments, and having received his duty, glanced at the pair of us doubtfully, as if to say that there was no end to the oddities of London folk. He was anything but the boy I had expected—being grizzled and bent with years of labour in the publick house, hauling barrels and cans of hot water to the bath; he was called Young Bob, he explained, "on account of my grandfer, Old Bob, who's that spritely at ninety-two, and may be found having his pint on the Steyne any morning in fair weather or foul."

Having received this confidence, we prepared to follow Young Bob into the black depths of the tunnel—which was, at the outset, a winding staircase fashioned of stone. I swept my skirts close about my legs, thanked Heaven I had seen fit to wear stout boots against the morning's rain, and lit my taper at Young Bob's candle.

Tolliver bowed his way to the door and left us, no doubt relieved to be rid of so persistent a charge.

"I say, Jane," Henry put in as we hunched our backs and squeezed after Young Bob through the opening in the panel, "you don't think this ends in the Regent's *bedchamber,* or . . . anywhere else, actually, *inside* the Pavilion?"

"I cannot think it likely. Recollect that Tolliver and his brother, Sam, were wont to don sheets and chains, and startle the unfortunate guests—and they cannot have done so if the far entrance to the tunnel was within the Regent's dwelling," I said with more confidence than I felt. Given the Regent's predilection for constant renovation of his residence—the expansion of the original farmhouse, and the repeated pulling down and setting up of new walls—Tolliver's tunnel might have undergone a decided change; but I had no wish to further alarm my companions. "I am sure this debouches within the grounds—but in a manner that must preclude its being obvious to the general eye."

Henry appeared mollified, but Young Bob merely grunted. This may have been because he had stepped without warning from the last stair to hard-packed earth; but in any case he said, "Never thought to live this day."

"I beg your pardon?"

"—When I should see the Prince's tunnel with my own eyes! Fair pother of rumours there was, year out of mind, but none as paid no real heed to 'em—thought it was the wine-fed tales of maids no better than they should be. There was Sal Norton, who claimed she was carried off to the Pavilion by night and ravished there three days; and old Jenny Featherbright, who put on such airs when Sir John Lade gave her a bauble as a token of esteem—not but what she came to a bad end on the streets of Lunnon not long after. Ended in Covent Garden, she did, walking the lobby of an evening."

"Ah," Henry said wisely. "Many's the girl as has found her ruin in the lobbies of Covent Garden."[22]

"I daresay, sir, but never having been to foreign parts, I couldn't speak to it."

We were walking steadily along a hardened passage, quite sandy underfoot and lined in stone, that was remarkably fresh in its air tho' *not* free of damp. So close to the sea, moisture is constant; and I reminded myself that above ground, it must still be raining.

"This tunnel's existence, then, is generally known?" I per-

---

[22] In Austen's day, prostitutes strolled through the crowds of theatergoers during intermission at Covent Garden, plying their trade.—*Editor's note.*

sisted. "Mr. Tolliver seemed to think it was a great secret, shared only among his family."

"Not *known*, if you're meaning *known*," Young Bob said. "My old grandfer recollected the digging of it, years since; but most folk thought as it was just a bit o' nonsense. So much ill was said of the Prince, ye ken, in his salad days—it were just another faradiddle, him spiriting away the maids with a passage underground. But Lord! Here am I, a-pacing of it!"

The passage had commenced with a gradual descent, then leveled off—somewhere, I should judge, beneath the Steyne—and had now begun to steadily incline. Our tapers were almost burnt down; and their flames began to flicker in a gentle air that came from above.

"Presently we shall see where it ends, Jane," Henry said with barely suppressed excitement.

The combined light of our dying flames revealed, of a sudden, a blank wall—made not of stone, but of wood planking. I glanced about, hoping to espy another staircase, twin to the one at the King's Arms—but there was none to be seen. And at that instant, my taper went out.

Henry's suffered a similar death within seconds.

The unfortunate thought of *rats* sprang unbidden to my mind, and I found that I had wrapped my skirts quite narrowly round my ankles once more, as a paltry defence against rodent teeth.

Fortunately, however, Young Bob's candle—being made of good, honest, smoking tallow—was as yet in strength; and his spirits remained phlegmatic despite the featureless height of plank wall.

"This'll be back of the New Stables, I'm thinking," he said with confidence. "The Regent'll have ordered the tunnel end walled up, when the Riding School and stalls was built; a few years ago the workings was done, and that's why Tolliver was so sure as the tunnel was filled in."

"But that cannot serve at all," I replied in consternation.

Henry reached for my hand through the darkness and squeezed it in warning. There was no need, in truth, to share our suspicion that Miss Twining's body had been carried into the Arms from the Pavilion. We were but visitors from London, after all, with a passion for publick-house oddities.

"You were not treated to Mr. Tolliver's demonstration at the Arms," I said, as conversationally as my fear of rats would allow, "and so did not witness the cunning shift in the panelling. There was a device—a carved dolphin—and when Mr. Tolliver pressed it, the tunnel opening sprang back. Perhaps there is a similar door *here*. If you would be so good as to raise your candle—"

Young Bob did so without demur.

Henry and I stepped forward, to push and press at every wormhole and whorl in the panelling; the publican's man obligingly moved his candlelight some five feet one way, and a yard the other; our fingertips grew sore with excited vigour; and still the wall remained immoveable.

"You do not think, ma'am, as that track in the dirt bespeaks a *sliding* door?" Young Bob at length suggested doubtfully.

I glanced down. The candlelight, being raised almost to ceiling height, had left our feet in welling darkness. But it was as Young Bob said: when one studied the ground, one espied a grooved board laid beneath the panelled wall—as tho' the entire thing was meant to slide back. Suppressing a most unladylike oath, I turned to Henry.

"Shine the light on the far corner," he instructed.

Young Bob did so.

Henry ran his gloved fingers along the seam where planking met the perpendicular stone wall. "There is a peg, Jane—almost indistinguishable."

He pulled it back; and the panel slid away from us, into a recess.

"Coo," Young Bob observed with respect.

We were faced with row upon row of bottles, laid on racks a bare two feet from our noses. The tunnel came out into the Regent's wine cellar.

"YOU APPREHEND," I SAID TO MY BROTHER ONCE WE HAD returned the way we'd come, pressed a shilling into Young Bob's work-hardened palm, and thanked the harassed Tolliver most prettily for our treat, "that only an intimate of the Regent's could have used that passage Tuesday morning. Someone who knew that the tunnel existed—where it commenced, and where it led. There cannot be above five people in the Kingdom with such knowledge, and only two or three at present installed at the Pavilion."

"Do not be hasty, Jane," my brother said. "Consider of the fact that the Regent is a great talker—one who delights in conducting tours of the oddities of his home—and that there are any number of guests in years past—ladies as well as gentlemen—whom His Royal Highness might have made aware of the novelty of his secret sliding door."

"George Hanger certainly knows of it," I said grimly.

"But so, too, might Lord Moira, or Colonel McMahon—he has served the Prince for years, and as a trusted secretary, must be intimate with every corner of the Pavilion. A lifelong friend such as the Countess of Bessborough—Lady Caroline's mother—who has been staying here forever, might well have glimpsed it. And then there are the servants—particularly the footmen charged with fetching the wine. For a fellow of the Regent's appetites, and his vast generosity as a host, there cannot be too constant a replenishment of the wine stores. I should imagine those shelves are emptied once a month, at the very least—however immense the wine cellars may prove—and that in the course of stacking new bottles, the panel has been shifted."

"Very well, Henry," I said dubiously, "you have succeeded in turning me from the idea of exclusivity. The tunnel alone cannot *entirely* narrow our hunt for the murderer. But do admit that it goes a long way. We may *suggest* how Catherine Twining's body was conveyed into the Arms, despite its doors being barred; and we may *suggest*, as well, that an intimate of the Pavilion—whether servant or guest—was vital to that body's conveyance. Surely you will not quarrel with me *there*?"

Henry considered of my logic for a moment. "I fear I cannot, Jane. But what is to be done?"

"*You*," I said firmly, "must pay a call upon the magistrate—Sir Harding Cross—and inform him of what you know. From what I have observed of the gentleman, he is likely to take the word of a reputable banker—and an intimate of the Earl of Swithin—far more seriously than he should a mere spinster Jane Austen."

Henry sighed. "There are moments when I find myself wishing for a solitary ramble along the Cobb at Lyme, Jane, as balm to a widower's grief. Whatever made you so mad for Brighton this Season?"

CHAPTER TWENTY-FOUR

Ode to a Drowned Girl

THURSDAY, 13 MAY 1813
BRIGHTON, CONT.

THE RAIN HAD TAPERED TO A MIZZLE BY THE TIME WE quitted the King's Arms. Henry and I were agreed upon the necessity of paying a call at No. 21, Marine Parade—he to solicit an introduction to Sir Harding Cross from the Earl of Swithin, and I to beg Desdemona for her intercession that evening with Brighton's Master of Ceremonies, Mr. Forth. We hastened along the damp paving beneath Henry's fortuitous umbrella, and were gratified in discovering the Swithins at home.

It was a fine family party that presented itself to our eyes: the Earl in his book room, surrounded by mellow bindings of calf, and a good fire against the chill; Desdemona at her tambour work, with her children—a son of five, and a daughter of seven—playing at spillikins on the drawing-room rug. Lady Oxford was seated at a writing desk, embarked on correspondence; and I was sorry to see all five rise up, and set aside their several pursuits, at our unexpected arrival. The children, indeed, were swept away by their nurse for hot milk and bread in their quarters; and I should imagine them fulminating darkly at the tiresomeness of unwanted callers, on a rainy afternoon.

Desdemona, however, was charming; declared that Henry and I had saved them all from insufferable boredom; and confided, in a whisper, as Lady Oxford tidied her writing things, that her friend had been longing to see me—had sent round to the Castle begging for just such a visit, only to discover we were gone out.

"Such an adventure as we have had!" Henry declared, as the Earl offered him a glass of sherry. "But Jane had better relate the whole; it is her story, in truth."

In as brief a fashion as possible, I related the particulars of the Regent's tunnel, to the astonished exclamations of the other three.

"I cannot pretend to shock," Lady Oxford declared, "for Prinny was always very wild as a boy. Maria Fitzherbert did a great deal to settle him, I believe—but of course, I was the merest *child* when that alliance was established."

"But you apprehend what this signifies," Swithin said with a troubled look. "If the Regent's undergroom last saw the girl alive, and her body was carried to the Arms through the Regent's tunnel . . ."

"It would appear more than likely that somebody at the Pavilion killed her," I concluded baldly. "Henry and I have been canvassing the same point. While there are some, wholly unconnected with the place, who may have *known* of the tunnel's existence—"

"The man Tolliver!" Desdemona broke in excitedly.

"—it must be extraordinary for murder to be done at such an hour, and the Regent's wine cellar penetrated, by a total stranger."

"As is true of Miss Twining, a stranger should have been remarked," the Earl agreed. "What do you intend to do with your dangerous information, Henry?"

"Set it before the magistrate, of course!"

"Are you sure that is wise?"

"What has wisdom to do with it, when a murderer is to be found?"

Swithin merely shrugged, his gaze drifting quizzically to his wife's. "You are correct, naturally. But I fear a frontal assault upon the Law may achieve more harm than good."

"I cannot very well suppress the intelligence," Henry said in perplexity.

"As you say." Swithin bowed. "You are acquainted with Sir Harding Cross?"

My brother flushed. "I regret that I have not that pleasure."

"Then I shall carry you off to Raggett's Club. Old Hard-Cross is certain to be established at the betting tables of a rainy afternoon, and I have a yearning to play at whist myself—the boredom of a grey sky in Brighton being insupportable."

"You are very good," Henry said haltingly. An impression of the Earl's vast condescension, in lending his name to an effort he found both unwise and distasteful, had clearly struck my insouciant brother. But not even Swithin was immune to gratitude; he unbent enough to clap Henry on the back.

"Do not neglect to throw me a line," he murmured as the two quitted the drawing-room for the front hall, "should you sink up to your neck in this."

"NOW, MISS AUSTEN," MONA BEGAN WITH A FORMALITY I must believe was due to the oddity of having *two* Janes in the room—"tell us what *else* you have learnt from your researches."

What ought I to disclose?—That Scrope Davies, upon whose friendship Byron had *always* presumed, was in love with the object of Byron's obsession—and might at last have grown tired of sacrificing for his friend? That General Twining was a brutal husband and a jealous father? Two such Fashionables as the Countess of Swithin and the Countess of Oxford might enjoy turning over the sad misfortunes of the late Lydia Montescue—might even, indeed, have been acquainted with the lady in her youth—but I lacked sufficient time to indulge in a comfortable coze of gossip.

I settled on the one fact sure to afford Lady Oxford some comfort: "It is now quite certain that the doors of the King's Arms were barred against all comers, once Lord Byron had quitted the place about half-past one o'clock on Tuesday morning. According to the publican Tolliver's own information, nobody—including his lordship—could have reentered the place before five o'clock that morning."

"And Davies shall certainly swear that George was asleep at the hour, breakfasting by seven, and mounted for London by eight," Lady Oxford mused absently. I noted that she did not say whether she *believed* these things, or that they were indisputable facts; merely that Davies should swear to them.

"But, Lady Swithin," I said briskly, "having penetrated so much of the King's Arms—I should like to know more of Catherine's enjoyment of the Assembly. I mean to approach the Master of Ceremonies, and learn whether he observed her dancing partners."

"There is nothing Mr. Forth does not observe, my dear—or comment upon, should the spirit move him. A most *fastidious* and *exacting* fellow, hideously high in the instep—which comes, of course, from a dearth of breeding. Only those unaccustomed to the most excellent Society from birth, should chuse to ape its snobbery rather than its easiness."

If I winced inwardly for poor Mr. Forth's sake, I did not betray it. "I *had heard* that he should not look with favour on a lady in mourning attending tonight's Assembly," I said calmly, "but I should like to brave Mr. Forth's displeasure—

with your support, of course. Would you consent to carry me into the Old Ship, Lady Swithin, in defiance of all propriety, and make me known to the redoubtable Master?"

"With pleasure," she answered, a glint in her eye.

"And with so notorious a lady as the Countess of Oxford on your *other* arm," her friend interjected, "our dear Miss Austen is unlikely to arouse comment."

"Exactly!" Mona cried in gay amusement; but I do not think Lady Oxford meant it for a joke. There was a bleakness to her looks that suggested some dire reckoning had commenced in her brain and heart. I wondered very much how the previous night's dinner had gone off—whether his lordship had indeed put in his promised appearance, and how the lovers had met or parted—but could not find the courage to enquire. Even *my* boldness must find its limit.

Lady Swithin sprang to her feet. "I must pay a visit to the nursery, for a report on little Charles's cold; and then I believe I shall recruit my strength with a nap in my boudoir, before dressing for dinner. Miss Austen, I shall not bore you with a tedious dinner when your day has already been so full of incident—but if you and your brother would be good enough to join us for coffee, we may then set out in a grand complement to the Old Ship. Shall we say—nine o'clock?"

I gratefully accepted the Countess's invitation, as well as her dispensation from the necessity of dining—for one so stricken in years as myself, a period of repose is *vital* before any attendance at a ball—and gathered my reticule in preparation for leaving. But as I rose from my chair, Lady Oxford astonished me by saying, "I should be grateful, Miss Austen, if you might spare me the benefit of your excellent understanding a few moments—if there is no other claim upon your time, naturally."

Mona being already out of the room, it was evident she had contrived to leave the two Janes in possession of it; and so I resumed my seat. Lady Oxford, however, paced a little restlessly before the fire, as tho' in an effort to order her thoughts.

"I need not inform you, I know, of the nature of my sentiments towards Lord Byron," she began. "Nor must I beg you to hold anything I might say in complete confidence. Mona assures me that I may trust in your discretion—and tho' Mona may act the goosecap at times, she owns an excellent heart, and should never betray a friend."

"I honour her esteem, and shall endeavour to deserve it," I said quietly.

Her ladyship paced some once or twice, her ringed hands braced upon her hips; it was a regal pose, and entirely unconscious, as was the forbidding look upon her countenance. "I should begin, I suppose, by allowing you to read *this*," she said abruptly. She drew from an inner pocket a piece of closely-penned paper.

I must have shrunk back a little, because she said hurriedly, "It is no private correspondence, I assure you. Only some verses of Lord Byron's he left behind last evening. He has been working on a long narrative poem some months— during the winter at Eywood, my estate in Herefordshire— and this spring, both in London and Brighton. As he certainly means to publish, I can see no harm in showing the verses to you. The poem is called *The Giaour*."

I glanced up. "As is his yacht?"

"Yes—a word his lordship picked up in Turkish, during his wanderings—it means infidel, or foreigner, or perhaps simply Christian Englishman. I suppose it most truly refers to *himself*: the lone traveller in distant lands. A pretty enough name for a seagoing craft, certainly.... But this latest fragment..." Her voice trailed away. "I find it disturbing. And suggestive. Please read it, Miss Austen, and lend me your thoughts."

I accepted the piece of paper, and studied Byron's hand—
which was fair copperplate, entirely legible, and not the impassioned scrawl I might have expected from a Romantic.

> *Yes, Leila sleeps beneath the wave,*
> *But his shall be a ~~colder~~ redder grave;*
> *Her spirit ~~charged~~ pointed well the steel*
> *Which taught that felon heart to feel.*
> *He called ~~on Heaven~~ the Prophet, but his power*
> *Was vain against the vengeful Giaour:*
> *~~Thou Paynim heart~~*
> *I watched my time, I leagued with these,*
> *The ~~blackguard~~ traitor in his turn to seize;*
> *My wrath is wreaked, the deed is done,*
> *And now I go,—but go alone.*

And further down, at the bottom of the page, another few
couplets, as tho' scrawled at random:

> *Much in his visions mutters he*
> *Of maiden ~~drowned~~ whelmed beneath the sea;*

> *On ~~jagged~~ cliff he has been known to stand*
> *And rave as to some bloody hand*

> *Her treachery was truth to me;*
> *To me she gave her heart, that all*
> *Which Tyranny can ne'er enthrall*
> *And I, alas! Too late to save!*
> *~~Yet all I then~~*
> *~~Something, something,~~ our foe a grave*

> *But for the thought of Leila slain*

Give me the pleasure with the pain,
So would I live and love again

???

'Tis all too late—thou wert, thou art
The cherished madness of my heart!

"Poor Lord Byron," I said soberly. "He grieves, certainly."

"I must conclude he truly loved the girl."

Lady Oxford's voice was tight with pain; to have believed that smouldering passion hers to command—and then know it to have been incited by Another—

"And you have read the earlier verses?" I said by way of distraction. "Are they all a paean to Miss . . . to Leila?"

Lady Oxford shook her head. "It seemed, at first, rather a dashing tale of battle between Infidel and Christian, as told by an old campaigner to his priest." She sank at last into a chair by the fire, her eyes bent upon the flames. "But this. . . . It is as tho' the narrative turned to something other—a *revenge* tale, Miss Austen. There is grief in it, to be sure—but also bloodlust, a desire to see violence given where violence has taken away."

Her understanding—of both her lover and his verse—was certainly acute; hers was a formidable mind. Byron had claimed, during our interview the previous day, that his passion for Catherine had already been waning. But what if that were merely a pose, adopted to veil his vengeful heart? A chill swept over me. "Countess—what is it that you fear?"

She met my gaze bleakly. "That George means to have a private justice. Miss Austen, he knows *exactly* who killed Catherine Twining."

CHAPTER TWENTY-FIVE

Dancing Partners

THURSDAY, 13 MAY 1813
BRIGHTON, CONT.

HENRY'S INTERVIEW WITH THE MAGISTRATE, HE ASSURED me over dinner this evening, went quite well. He found Old HardCross as the Earl had predicted: playing at faro for pound points before a comfortable fire at Raggett's, while the rain lashed the windows outside. Sir Harding's mellow mood may be attributable to the quality of Raggett's cellars, or perhaps to his luck at cards; in any case, he quitted the faro table for the privacy of a side parlour, and listened while Swithin's odd banking fellow told his tale of sliding panels and stone tunnels.

"Good Lord!" he snorted with something between shock and amusement. "Always said the Prince was mad for pleasure in his youth. Confess I see no point in a tunnel—subterfuge should be entirely unnecessary in His Highness's case—never made any bones about his penchant for carousing—should wonder why he concerned himself with publick opinion a'tall!"

Henry had mentioned something about an *allowance*—the Prince's funds being managed by his father, George III; the

King's open displeasure with his son's reckless spirits; the power of the purse being used to curb a wild temperament; deceit therefore being the natural recourse to defray paternal ire, etc.

"But a *tunnel*," Old HardCross replied. "He'd have had to hire labourers! Put down his blunt on pallets of stone! Must've cost him a fortune, first and last!"

Henry referred to the Regent's comfort with indebtedness, and known passion for building.

"The fellow never *has* had a particle of sense, where bricks and mortar are concerned," the magistrate agreed gloomily.

Henry suggested, as delicately as possible, that the tunnel's being let out into the King's Arms might prove of material interest to the Twining murder.

Old HardCross's eyes narrowed a little at this, and he appeared to take thought on the subject. There was a silence of several moments, painful to Henry's ease.

"Something shall have to be done about it, of course," the magistrate said at last. "You did quite right in coming to me so quietly, Austen—we may hope now to keep the facts from being too widely known. Much obliged, indeed."

And he clapped Henry on the shoulder before returning to his cards.

"But what does Sir Harding intend?" I demanded. "Does he mean to interrogate the Regent's guests? Interview the footmen charged with fetching wine from the cellars? Discover whether Lady Caroline Lamb brought her maid—or has become the surrogate employer of someone else, fully capable of carrying the corpse of a young girl from the shingle to the Arms?"

"I could not undertake to say, Jane."

I frowned at my brother. "It is high time you begged Lord Moira or Colonel McMahon for a private tour of the Pavilion—on behalf of your grieving sister! Without we make a

thorough canvass of the intimates and servants, I begin to
think the truth shall *never* be learnt!"

WE PRESENTED OURSELVES IN MARINE PARADE AT NINE
o'clock, and after a desultory cup of coffee—desultory, perhaps, because Lord Byron was absent, and the Countess of
Oxford decidedly flat—set out through the mizzle for the Old
Ship. The Assembly Rooms in this comfortable inn, which
are much picked out with gilt and satin, are regarded by
Brighton's notables as having slightly the preference over the
Castle's. I looked into the suite as we arrived—saw much the
usual arrangement of ballroom, supper room, and card
room—and felt that the length and breadth of Britain, there
was nothing new under the sun.

I was arrayed in dark blue silk—one of my older gowns,
last worn at Eliza's musical party during the spring of 1811—
but less quelling to the sensibilities of the Master of Ceremonies, I thought, than dusky black should be. If I did
violence to what was required of one in mourning, my conscience was assuaged by Henry's saying nothing in reproach;
as we met in the passage, he merely assured me I was in excellent looks, as any wise brother ought. It was without much
trepidation, therefore, that I followed Lady Swithin into the
gaiety of the Assembly Rooms—and after a little interval of
greetings and introductions among her varied acquaintance—Lady Oxford having to be exclaimed over by all those
of the *ton* as yet ignorant of her arrival—Mona took me aside
and said: "The Master of Ceremonies, Mr. Forth, is over
there—by the French window letting out onto the balcony."

He was a tall, broad, and exceedingly corpulent fellow,
dressed in satin knee breeches, silk stockings, and shining
black slippers with large gold buckles. His coat was dark blue
superfine; his cravat was snowy, and so intricately tied as to

support several of his chins. The top of his head was quite bald, but he compensated for the lack by wearing what remained of his hair luxuriantly long—a fall of curls, as gold as a newborn's. He was so like an illustration from a ladies' magazine of what a Master *ought* to be, that I nearly laughed outright; but Mona had seized my hand and begun to thread her way through the throngs of Fashionables and red-coated cavalry officers, all milling about the floor in expectation of the first dance. I had time enough to glimpse a touseled dark figure limp towards Lady Oxford—saw the Countess turn as though under the force of a spell, her countenance transformed by the intoxicating presence of Byron—and Mona had achieved the French windows.

"Good evening, Mr. Forth," she said. "You have a sad crush this evening! I think we may declare the Brighton Season launched!"

"Countess," the Master responded in a tone of profound gratitude; and swept Desdemona a low bow. For a large fellow, he was surprisingly nimble. "Our poor hamlet is made infinitely finer by your presence, and that of your excellent Earl—his Hessians undoubtedly by Hoby, his coats by Weston, his collars *exactly* the correct height, neither so low as to suggest a despicable carelessness, nor so high as to trumpet the Dandy—"

"Yes, yes," Mona said impatiently, "but you must attend, Mr. Forth! I have been wanting to present my dear friend Miss Austen, lately of London and Hampshire, to your acquaintance—for this is her *first* visit to Brighton, you know, and there is no one but *you* who may put her in the correct way of things!"

"Charmed," said Mr. Forth, taking my hand and bowing over it—but not before his gaze had run the length of my blue gown, and calculated its worth and probable age to a nicety. "London *modiste,* but not one of the greatest talents; beaded trim no longer fashionable this year—ought to have changed it for grosgrain; colour suits her, however, but I should recommend next time she chuse claret-colored sarcenet," he murmured *almost* inaudibly under his breath.

"Do not regard him for the world, Jane," Mona hissed in my ear as the Master recovered from his bows, mopping his bald pate with a handkerchief; "it is said he was born the son of a tailor, and cannot leave off the instincts of his trade however glorious his present station. Mr. Forth!" she cried. "You were present, I know, at Monday's Assembly at the Castle. Miss Austen unfortunately was not—but her particular friend, Miss Catherine Twining, danced several dances to my certain knowledge."

"Ah! Our lamented Miss Twining!" the Master cried; and his brown eyes—lugubrious and reminiscent of a hound's—filled with sadness. "Diaphanous white muslin, circlet of rosebuds and pearls, satin slippers with shoe-roses to match. Irreproachable taste, of course, for Mrs. Silchester had the dressing of the girl—and tho' the woman *will* be feather-brained, she remains good *ton*. I recall the toilette well. Miss Twining was everything that was charming. And a particular friend of Miss Austen's, you would say? You have my sympathy, ma'am. Such an unaccountable death—nothing in her stile to suggest it—I fear the world is a very *wicked* place. Even in our poor hamlet!"

"I have been attempting to make sense of the senseless myself, sir," I managed in a hollow tone. "And I have been endeavouring to record all the details of Miss Twining's final evening—her last on earth!—no matter how small. I wished to convey a *picture* of her in a letter to my family, which shall be amazed to learn of her death"— as how could they not be, knowing nothing of Miss Twining at all—"and felt that in justice I ought to remember the gaieties she enjoyed, as only

Catherine could, before her young life was so brutally cut short. The Countess"— I felt Mona's title offered excellent value on the present occasion—"thought immediately of *yourself,* and said there should be no one in Brighton better able to recall the evening—which dances poor Catherine stood up for, and who were her partners. I should be infinitely happy if you should be so good as to search your memory . . ."

Mr. Forth closed his eyes an instant. "We opened, naturally, with a minuet, and closed the ball with another. Now, I recall Miss Twining had Mr. Hendred Smalls—nothing to remark in either stile or person, being entirely unworldly in his aspect, except as pertains to the Regent, whom he toadies unbearably—as partner for the first dance; also to the second, poor child, which was a contredanse. Mr. Smalls could not keep his mind on the figures, and was constantly giving offence with his stupidity in the dance. Now, who was her partner for the third? That would be the cotillion with Allemande; I believe it was young Holsten, the baronet's heir just down from Oxford—excessive padding to shoulders and calves, coat by Hearn, white waistcoat and satin breeches— good *ton,* of course, but no shoulders, no air or address, and apt to stutter. Poor Holsten was greatly incommoded by Lord Byron—most careless in his cravat, patterned waistcoat not at all the thing, and that lamentable right foot—who persisted in interrupting the dance to importune Miss Twining for an interview, which she steadily refused. At the close of the cotillion, General Twining quitted the Assembly and left his daughter in Mrs. Silchester's care.

"The fourth was a Scots reel; Miss Twining had young Captain Viscount Morley of the 10th to that one—very dashing fellow, excellent figure, excessively charming, cravat *à la Napoleon,* the new patent leather pumps. Captain Morley was *most* attentive, frowned down Lord Byron, whom he appeared to regard not at all, and carried Miss Twining into the supper room after the reel; they partook of smoked salmon, pistache cream, and champagne. Lord Byron again approached Captain Morley, and words were exchanged, at which point I intervened, so that peace might be restored. Lord Byron retired to the card room; and after this little interval, the Captain would, I believe, have partnered Miss Twining again—but she very rightly declined, so as not to appear *too particular.* The Captain, as I recall, watched the next dance—another cotillion—but solicited no other partner; none could please him after Miss Twining, it would seem. *She* acceded to Mr. Scrope Davies's request—one of our *most* distinguished gentlemen. Such refinement of person! Such elegance in his watch chain and fobs! And tho' his hair may suffer a trifle from thinning at the top—one cannot reproach a *true* gentleman for the vagaries of nature."

My gaze inevitably strayed to Mr. Forth's own gleaming scalp. He went on, imperturbably: "Miss Twining appeared greatly fatigued after the cotillion, as should not be remarkable in one so young. Mr. Davies, as I recall, endeavoured to lead her apart; he appeared most anxious to speak with her in private—pleading his friend Byron's case, perhaps. He carried Miss Twining off to one of the chairs drawn up against the wall, and went in search of lemonade, for indeed his fair partner looked as tho' she might faint—and I observed, in his absence, Lord Byron approach her. Miss Twining immediately started up, and would have quitted her place, but at that moment—it was perhaps midnight—Lady Caroline Lamb appeared at the entrance to the Assembly Rooms, and Lord Byron's temper changed. Ah! Lady Caroline—remarkable air, extraordinarily *outré* looks, not at all what one wishes to emulate with the Brighton crowd, yet undeniably compelling.

The Sprite, as Greek Muse! What one should call a *leader of Fashion,* if one could but find a lady brave enough to *follow* her. Sad, to see such talent enslaved to a mercurial temperament—"

"Did you happen to observe, sir," I interjected, "how Lady Caroline came to make Miss Twining's acquaintance?"

"Went bang up to her, barely a few moments later. That would be once Lady Caroline had crossed the entire ballroom to meet Lord Byron, who appears not to have valued the honour as he ought. He left the Assembly in considerable dudgeon not long thereafter. Miss Twining, however, appeared most gratified by her ladyship's attention, and declined to dance again, tho' Captain Viscount Morley attempted to lure her back to the floor for the waltz. I rather wondered the Silchester did not throw her charge in the Captain's way—for he is a most charming young officer, and is Derwentwater's heir, to boot. But perhaps she guessed he is addicted to gambling, like all the rest of the family, and did not like to put Miss Twining forward."

Derwentwater. Where had I heard the title before? And not so long since? My thoughts raced backwards. Not at Mona's, nor yet in Lady Oxford's conversation; it was Mrs. Silchester herself who had uttered the name.

"Derwentwater?" I repeated. "Do I collect you to refer to the Earl?"

"Indeed. Grown sadly ramshackle since his wife's death, and spends too much time hunting with the Quorn to keep his good looks; but a gentleman to the teeth. One wonders at him exposing his son to all the dangers of a cavalry regiment in the present age—he has only the one, and the Captain, they say, was very gallant at Talavera—but soldiering is a passion in the Barrett family, you know, and young Philip would not be denied his colours. Barrett, of course, is the Earl's family name; Derwentwater being the Earl's title, and Viscount Morley the Captain's honourific, until such melancholy time as he is forced to sell out, and accede to his father's duties."

It was just such a fussy point of pedantry as a Master of Ceremonies might be expected to convey. Lady Swithin sighed impatiently beside me; but she could not know how Mr. Forth's words had electrified me.

"Did you say . . . Philip?" I stammered. "Was there not . . . *another* Barrett of that name?"

The Master of Ceremonies's rich murmur dropped even lower. "The Viscount's *uncle*, I believe. Present Earl's younger brother, killed in an affair of honour. Derwentwater never speaks of him, I understand."

"Of course," I murmured. Because the Earl's brother had eloped with Catherine Twining's mother.

Could it be possible the dashing young Captain had unknowingly courted the daughter of General Twining—whose pistols had put paid to his uncle's life? Or, as seemed more probable, had he *deliberately cultivated* the connexion under the General's very nose? And had the General *observed* it, and known the Captain for his persecutor? Was it for *this* reason—one he might hesitate to disclose to his daughter— he had quitted the Assembly early? But if fearful of the Captain's knowledge and influence—why had General Twining not carried his daughter home with him? It was a decided puzzle.

And then a more sinister thought entered my head, conjured by Lady Oxford's ominous phrase. *A revenge tragedy.* Good God—what if the Captain had merely bided his time, until the child of his family's enemy had been alone and defenceless? What if he had followed Catherine from the Assembly that night, and awaited her release from the Pavilion, only to spirit her off to her watery death? He was, after all, a soldier—accustomed to killing through years of hard campaigning. Was that the same, however, as deliberately drowning a young girl?

And could he have known of the tunnel from the Pavilion? Having known of it, and determining to use it, was but a simple step; to throw all suspicion on Lord Byron, whom the Captain apparently held cheap, should make a lark of murder.

"Jane," Mona said to me, "are you quite well? You look faint."

"It is nothing, I assure you. Merely that Mr. Forth's descriptions—so exact in every detail—bring the whole of Monday evening before my mind; and I confess the impressions *must* make any friend of Miss Twining's rather low. Do not regard it, I beg. Mr. Forth has been everything that is patient and kind, and has been wishing me at the far end of the earth this quarter-hour, I am sure. I shall not trespass longer upon your time, sir."

"It was a pleasure, ma'am," he said with regal condescension; and offered me a final bow.

Mona and I curtseyed; I observed a mamma and daughter hovering near the French doors in the hope of being noticed by the Master and put in the way of introductions for the dance; and made good my escape. I should dearly have loved to have heard Mr. Forth's assessment of their dress, however—for his calculation of the cost of their trimmings should, I am sure, have been entirely exact.

Italian lace, twelve shillings the yard, purchased on the cheap at Pantheon Bazaar . . .

"If you should like a glimpse of the fascinating Captain," Mona muttered in my ear, "I believe he is even now in the card room—playing at whist with Lord Byron."

"Mona," I said, "General Twining killed the Captain's uncle in a duel."

"I know," she calmly replied. "I have been acquainted

with Derwentwater from my cradle; he very nearly offered for me when his first wife, Lady Sarah as was, went off in childbirth—but I have never believed in second attachments. And a wise decision it was—the Master is correct in saying he hunts too much."

"But were you at all acquainted with the younger brother?"

"Philip? Naturally. He was a rakehell if ever I knew one. But an *elopement*—I cannot think why he thought it necessary! Such *affaires* never end well."

"But do you not think it exceedingly odd that his nephew should be dancing with General Twining's daughter?"

"Well—she *was* excessively pretty," Mona said blandly. "Recollect that I was present at the ball, Jane; I observed the Captain and Miss Twining dance; but I did not find anything particular to remark in it. Else I should have told you the whole."

I could have shaken the Countess for her imperturbability. "Nothing *particular*—even when the Assembly was concluded with Catherine's murder? And I suppose you see nothing untoward in the Captain's playing at whist with a man he despises?"

She gazed at me, bewildered. "But men are always gambling with those they despise! It lends spice to the winnings!"

"Exactly," I returned, in my driest manner. "Lead me to the Captain, Mona, if you please."

CHAPTER TWENTY-SIX

Damning Testimony

THE OVERWHELMING FIRST IMPRESSION OF CAPTAIN VIS-count Morley was his remarkable beauty; the second, must be of his relative youth. The former I had expected; the latter took me by surprize.

He was a golden lad, with eyes of cornflower blue; a slim and sinewy figure, whose whipcord body suggested the hunting field—or the cavalry ring. The social excesses of the 10th Hussars were made much of, owing to their patronage by the Prince and the breathless breeding of their officers; but the 10th was also a disciplined, honed, and formidable fighting machine tempered by hard campaigning in the Peninsula—where this *boy* had conducted himself with "gallantry." I knew full well what that meant—he had cut his way with a sabre, on horseback, through rank upon rank of the French; and he had come out unscathed at the other side. Seen from the rear in his regimentals, the Captain appeared compact, spare, and efficient—one glance at his face, however, which was suggestive of the angel, and any girl of fifteen should be lost.

He rose from the card table as Mona approached; bowed with charm and correctness as she forced my acquaintance upon him; and remained standing, to Lord Byron's impatience, until we should have passed on. I met those limpid blue eyes only once, before demanding of myself how I could possibly have imagined such a boy capable of *murder*. He could not be above four-and-twenty years of age. That he should find Catherine's face and form alluring must be natural; that he should then ruthlessly force her head beneath the waves, impossible.

But the questions must be asked—and I alone should ask them. How to effect a tête-à-tête?

"My luck is out, Mona," Lord Byron said with a scowl, throwing down his cards. His pale countenance bore a restless, feverish look, and his fingers played with the stem of his wineglass, which was only half-full. "Morley's a deep one; he has had the best of me tonight. I must summon my Runner and make for home."

The Captain gathered up the cards—coolly pocketed the winnings—and said, "I imagine your mind is engaged on greater matters than whist, Byron. You are writing a poem, are you not? To the memory of your *Leila*? But then—you are always writing a poem to *someone*. The ladies who have figured in your verse are legion. Only one, however, has suffered mortally from the honour."

Byron's countenance flushed, as tho' all the wine in his veins had roared angrily to the surface, and his glittering look fixed upon the Captain. I felt, with a sense of shock, all the violence of passion that emanated from the man; it attracted far more powerfully than it repelled.

"She shall live long in my verse, Morley," he growled, "when you are already rotted in your grave!"

"No doubt," the Captain returned, "—if you are permitted time enough to finish your poem. I thought you exceedingly brave to show your face at the Assembly tonight—and should have feared for your very life on your return home. But you relieve my mind; I had forgot the fact of the Runner."

Did I detect a menace in these words, so carelessly spoken? But Byron was no longer attending to the Captain; his ire was fleeting. He rose unsteadily to his feet and demanded of Mona, like a weary child, "Where is Davies? And where has *Jane* got to?"

I flushed as he uttered my name, but he referred, of course, to Lady Oxford. I did not exist for Lord Byron this evening, and was woman enough to feel a pang. The greater writer than he, however, overcame it.

"I believe she is in the ballroom, observing the dancing," Desdemona faltered. "George—are you unwell? Shall I summon Swithin?"

But Lord Byron's smouldering gaze had fixed on three men who were advancing across the card room towards our party. They were not dressed for a ball, and their countenances were stolid and unreadable. Constables at the beck and call of Sir Harding Cross, and I did not mistake.

"George Gordon, Lord Byron?" the chief of the three intoned.

"That is my name," his lordship replied; "but I did not give you leave to make free with it." And he snapped his fingers beneath the constable's nose.

The fellow's countenance did not alter; he might have been confronting a mad dog, run loose on the shingle. "It is my duty," he said, "to arrest you, sir, on the charge of murder."

At which his lordship knocked the poor fellow down.

THE ASSEMBLY ROOMS FELL SILENT AS BYRON WAS dragged away—all of Brighton horrified, as it seemed, by the

sudden plummet of its favoured comet. The moment his lordship's black head disappeared from the main staircase, however, the orchestra struck up a tune—the old chestnut, "Lady
o' the Timmer Lands." A few couples moved hesitantly to the
floor, and soon the scene was one of gaiety; Lady Oxford did
not faint, but continued talking with deliberate animation to
Sir John and the man named Hodge; and I found my brother
Henry hastening towards me from the supper room. The Earl
of Swithin was hard on his heels.

Mona pulled at Swithin's sleeve with urgency. "Do something, Charles! They cannot simply throw Byron in gaol!"

"It may be the safest place for him, Mona," her husband
replied grimly.

"Is the whole town so opposed to the notion of innocence?"

"The Regent is—and that must be enough for the magistrate. I have been talking with Old HardCross." The Earl's
eyes flicked dispassionately towards my brother. "The intelligence the magistrate received this afternoon, of a tunnel leading from the Marine Pavilion to the King's Arms—or, not to
put too fine a point upon it, from the *Regent's home* to a
place of *murder*—has animated His Royal Highness as nothing else should. He is demanding a swift period to the Twining business. Sir Harding assures me that nothing shall equal
his efforts to set the Prince's mind at ease; and therefore, it is
to be hoped Byron will hang for the corpse found in his
rooms, and there is to be an end of it."

"But that is unjust!" Mona cried. "That is . . . that is *crim-
inal*, Charles!"

"I am mortified," Henry said in a low voice. "To think that
Byron's liberty is denied him—that his very *life* might be laid
at my door—when my only object in speaking with the magistrate was the achievement of justice!"

"I believe we should collect our party and return home," the Earl said gently. "We can do nothing more here."

"Where have they taken him?" I asked.

"To Brighton Camp. He is to be held under the armed guard of the Regent's own—the 10th Hussars."

My eyes drifted across the room, and observed Captain Viscount Morley, his military helmet hiding his golden curls, slipping neatly out of the room.

I could not think a barracks the safest gaol for Byron.

Friday, 14 May 1813
Brighton

I HAD BEEN DRESSED ONLY A QUARTER-HOUR THIS MORNING, and was taking tea and toast in the private parlour set aside for Henry's and my use, when the Countess of Swithin sent up her card—followed hard on its heels by the Countess herself.

"We must corner her," Desdemona cried as she sailed into the room, a perfect picture in straw-coloured linen trimmed in dull rose, "and make her tell us what she knows."

"Who?"

"Caro Lamb, of course!" She drew off her bonnet and gloves, and set about prosaically pouring herself a cup of tea. "You cannot *think* how low poor Jane Harley is become. She is certain Byron will hang, and is torn between a jealous desire to see him do so—born of her discovery of his passion for Miss Twining—and outright despair at the World's Loss. She persists in believing him a genius, tho' the rest of us are inclined to consider him out of his wits." Mona took a sip of scalding tea, and grimaced.

"Swithin went this morning to appeal to Old HardCross

for the setting of bail, and the release of his lordship into our own household—bail to be paid by Swithin, of course—but Sir Harding refused. He had the sheer effrontery to say that he regards Byron as excessively dangerous, on account of his knocking down that constable last evening; and in the next breath, told Swithin that he now *believes* Caro Lamb's testimony at the inquest! —For you will recall she claimed Byron spent the remainder of the night at the Pavilion, in her arms, and *not* at Scrope Davies's at all. Anybody in Brighton might know her for a liar—except, it would seem, Sir Harding Cross."

"I am sure she offered her testimony *then* with the intention of protecting Lord Byron—by swearing to his presence, and offering an alibi, when he might have been anywhere," I said thoughtfully. "The discovery of the tunnel leading out of the Pavilion, however, has secured the noose around his lordship's neck. Sir Harding need look no further. Miss Twining's body is believed to have found its way to Byron's rooms at the Arms through the cunning tunnel that commences in the Regent's wine cellars; Lady Caroline swears Byron was at the Pavilion during the critical hours of the murder and disposal of Miss Twining's body—and therefore, Lord Byron shall be found guilty of having drowned the girl he passionately loved. Nobody seems to give a ha'porth of interest in *why* he should be moved to do so, however."

"What I chiefly wish to know," Mona retorted, "is what *Caroline* was doing Monday night—or Tuesday morning, whichever you will—when she claims to have been making passionate love to his lordship! She has never said *why* she parted from Miss Twining in that churlish way. Even a Ponsonby born and bred should never behave so ill as to send a child of fifteen alone out into the night. I believe the lady prevaricates. I smell deceit in Caro Lamb at fifty paces, and I am determined to know the whole."

"You intend to summon her to Marine Parade?"

"Not at all!" Mona set her cup on its saucer with an audible ring. "We shall beard her ladyship in her bower! Do you not believe the answer to the entire affair lies within the Pavilion itself?"

"I do. It is the last place Miss Twining was seen, and whence her body was certainly conveyed to the Arms. *That* cannot have happened without someone—guest or servant— noting a disturbance. I have been working upon my brother to use his influence with Lord Moira, in order to gain some entry there. For myself, I should dearly like to meet with George Hanger again."

Mona look startled. "I cannot think why! Odious man. And his teeth are wooden. But you need no other *entrée* when I am with you, my dear—let us go at once, if you have quite finished your breakfast!"

I had quite finished my breakfast. It remained only to scrawl a hurried note to Henry, who had—at my behest— presented himself in full mourning dress at Catherine Twining's funeral. The service was even now commencing, at the small chapel belonging to the 10th Hussars, so beloved of the Twining family; and Mr. Hendred Smalls should be presiding. It was not the service he had *anticipated* enjoying with young Catherine—and I wondered how he should get through it without breaking down entirely. But I must await Henry's account. I put on my bonnet—and was away with Mona on the instant.

"I wish that I were *dead*," Lady Caroline offered in a thread-like whisper.

The sentiment should not be unexpected in one who has tumbled from a powerful young horse to the hard ground of the Downs, and sustained a considerable bruising, if not a cracked rib or two; but Lady Caroline exhibited no evidence of physical injury from her escapade at the race-meeting two days previous, and appeared already to have forgot the sad despatching of the black colt.

"—Drowned, preferably, as the Other was," she persisted. "I tried to allow the waters to o'erwhelm me, as he sailed on, indifferent—but I was cheated of Death. O, to be dying!"

"—or at the very least, declining," Mona returned cordially. "On the whole, I think you should prefer *declining*, my dear—I really do. It is less absolute than death, and therefore offers greater scope for the imagination—one might persist in one's decline, with periodic episodes of rallying—one might alternately raise and dash the hopes of such gentlemen as place wagers on these things at White's, from week to week. Whereas with death, you know, the curtain is rung down quite definitely on your drama."

"Catherine Twining is dead, and all the world can talk of nothing but her," Caro said petulantly; "Catherine Twining is *Leila*, and George is forever writing verses to her! I wish I were *dead*."

"I should like to slap you." Mona's tone was all bored indignation. "You have only to hurl yourself into the sea, you ghoulish creature, without Swithin there to save you, to make an end of it. But tell us what we wish to know, first. You might then be comforted in your final moments, in the knowledge that you have been the *salvation* of Lord Byron. We shall promise to tell everyone so."

Caro Lamb turned doe eyes, brimful of tragedy, upon the Countess. "You are excessively unkind. Why do you *hate* me so, Mona? Why does the *entire world* hate me? Is it because I was fortunate enough to have been *loved* by him?"

We were perched on a scattering of uncomfortable chairs, done in the Chinese stile with hard wooden backs, intended to suggest bamboo, in a small saloon that faced a prettyish wilderness running down to the shingle. It was a bright morning, and a stiff wind tossed the branches of the trees; Lady Caroline had adopted a pose by the French windows, and kept her profile turned firmly to best advantage.

"Not at all," Mona replied cheerfully. "I expect it is because you are so *tiresome*, Caro. Now, you will have heard that his lordship has been taken to Brighton Camp, where he is held under armed guard, pending the next sitting of the Assizes—which in this part of the world are to be in two weeks' time. The magistrate, Sir Harding Cross, has told Swithin that he should not have taken his lordship up, but for your testimony—your insistence at the inquest, Caro, that his lordship was in your rooms for the better part of Monday night."

"Tuesday morning," I interjected.

"Very well," Mona said crossly. "You take my point, I hope. It is because of your ... *embroidering*, your ... penchant for the high dramatic ... that Sir Harding may insist Lord Byron was at the Pavilion. Which is the very *last* place any of his friends should wish him to have been."

"Why?" Caro demanded in a throbbing accent. "Why, Mona? Because they are *determined* to despise me, and my love for him? I am not ashamed of it! I am not ashamed of having felt that pure, elevating passion which ..."

"Can you apprehend *nothing*, you wretched woman, but your own interest in this affair?" the Countess cried in exasperation. "It has nothing to do with you, Caro, excepting in that you have lied—and Byron shall certainly hang because of it!"

Lady Caroline's gaze slid back, unseeing, to the windows. "I did not lie."

There was a palpitating silence. Mona turned a puzzled look upon me, and lifted her shoulders in mute interrogation.

"I should never lie where Byron is concerned," Caro murmured dreamily. "That should be to dishonour the sacred nature of our bond."

I rose, and crossed to where she stood. "You insist upon his lordship's having been here in the early hours of Tuesday morning?"

Caroline Lamb smiled at me, then—a faint, absent, half-crazed smile. "Of course he was," she said. "Why do you think Catherine Twining ran away, all by herself, without the slightest escort? It was because he followed her here, of course—and the goosecap was terrified of him."

CHAPTER TWENTY-SEVEN

A Matter of Questions

"I SHOULD HAVE KNOWN SHE WOULD NOT LIE ABOUT anything to do with Byron—and that Scrope Davies *should*." Mona spoke gloomily as we quitted Caro Lamb's rooms. "Swithin said Davies would do anything to save his friend's skin—*stand buff* was the revolting Eton-schoolboy phrase he used."

We had persisted in talking with Caro Lamb for a quarter-hour after her flat declaration, in an attempt to shake her from her appalling ground, but she would have none of it—nor of us. Her narrative consisted of the following:

Of *course* Byron had quitted the Assembly at her appearance; he could not bear to see her dancing—particularly if the dance was a waltz, and as she recalled, a waltz was being struck up within minutes of her arrival. She had expected Byron to lie in wait for her, however—or for Catherine Twining, it made no odds—because he could not bear to allow Caro the triumph of driving him out of Society, and must always have the final word. By adopting Catherine—of whose existence Caro had known already from her spies, as Lady Oxford had not—she had ensured that Byron would follow them both. And indeed, his lordship had braved the Pavilion itself—where Prinny had never yet invited him, due to their mutual dislike—on the strength of his acquaintance with Lady Caroline. Byron merely informed the footmen who awaited the late return of the Regent's guests that Lady Caro had pressed him to drink tea with her after the Assembly— and as Lady Caro had already brought Miss Twining up to her boudoir, the footmen assumed Byron was expected as well.

"Was it not brave of him?" she suggested in her habitually ardent tone. "But in truth, I believe he would brave *anything* when the desire to see me overtakes him. Tho' he professes to hate my very existence, he cannot quite live without me, you know—he is continually answering my letters, and stealing away to see me, under the very nose of my repulsive mother-in-law, Lady Melbourne. I believe it is the challenge he enjoys, as well as the delicious deceit."

I reflected that her ladyship understood the motives of her erstwhile lover very well; and decided to ignore, for the moment, Byron's intentions on that evening. Of greater import were his *actions,* and the approximate times at which they had taken place.

"At what hour did his lordship put in an appearance?" I asked.

Lady Caroline shrugged. "I could not possibly tell you the time. Time is mutable; it expands or contracts depending on the degree of boredom one suffers; in Byron's presence, it is precious—and horrifyingly fleet."

Desdemona sighed. "Give over, Caro, do—this is *important.*"

Lady Caroline lifted her shoulders once more. She was still directing her speeches to the French windows.

"You quitted the Assembly at one o'clock in the morning,

near as makes no odds," I said. "Byron left the King's Arms half an hour later, according to the publican's assurances, which I myself received. His lordship is supposed to have reached Scrope Davies's lodgings at a quarter to two—the same time at which Catherine Twining was observed by an undergroom to be crossing the Pavilion grounds alone. In order to credit your explanation, we must believe Mr. Davies to have lied—but recollect the evidence of his servants. Not *all* of them may be paid off, in a matter of murder."

"You appear to have a higher regard for a menial's sense of delicacy than I," Caro told me, "but even if you *will* have them all be honest, I see no great difficulty. Recollect you are speaking of a *publican's* clock, in stating the moment of Lord Byron's departure."

I stared at her in puzzlement an instant, until comprehension dawned. Mr. Tolliver's clock should never run so true to the hour as the Regent's great instrument above the stables, which should be calibrated with a precision unequaled anywhere but at Greenwich. Tho' the King's Arms clock be wound of necessity each day, it must lose time over the twenty-four hours, and was thus, as was common among publick-house instruments, generally set a quarter-hour *ahead*, so that guests might not miss their stage-coaches, nor Tolliver his hour of closing. When Lord Byron and Scrope Davies thought themselves to be quitting the Arms at half past one, they were undoubtedly doing so at a quarter past—or thereabouts. Miss Twining, however, had certainly quitted the Pavilion at a quarter to two. Nobody, at the inquest or thereafter, had considered of the customs obtaining among publick-house clocks.

"We have been very stupid," Desdemona observed.

"I had assumed it to be a habit with you," Caro replied distantly. "Take the statements of the servants, for example. Undoubtedly they were asked when their master and his guests returned home; and undoubtedly they told the time as they knew it—conceiving of the *guest* as being proved in the fact of George's valet. Where George himself might be was none of *their* concern; it is not their place to know. I think the matter readily explains itself."

Undoubtedly, we must speak with Scrope Davies, I thought despairingly; there remained his insistence that he had sat up drinking wine with Byron until three. I should have to employ Henry or Lord Swithin—who knew him best—in the task of wringing out the truth. But that was another interview; we were still confronting Lady Caroline.

"What occurred when Byron ascended to your boudoir?"

For the first time, her ladyship quitted the windows. She settled herself on a divan, crossing her legs beneath her and taking up a gentleman's long clay smoking pipe, in which she proceeded to tamp a bit of tobacco. The Countess and I were forced to endure a tedious interval while Lady Caroline engaged in all the business of lighting this, and encouraging it to exude an acrid blue smoke, which she then deeply inhaled, closing her eyes with bliss as she did so—until the eyelids fluttered open once more, and the huge, light-coloured orbs settled upon me unerringly.

"He came to beg Catherine to hear him, of course—full of abject apology for having spirited her away a few days before; he had attempted much the same sort of interview at the Assembly, of course, but she would not attend. She begged me to save her from his clutches, and being no fool—having not the *slightest* interest in promoting the *affaire*—I made a show of hurling myself upon George so that she might reach the door in safety. The little idiot ran straight down the passage and out of the Pavilion, without a word to anybody—and nothing more was known of her until the maid screamed bloody murder, as I understand it, at the King's Arms the following morning."

"And Byron?" I asked steadily, tho' I hated the indifference with which Caro spoke of Catherine's murder.

She blew a cloud before replying. "He would have followed her, of course, until I observed that a man with his limp and a girl of her youth were decidedly ill-assorted. If he could not *waltz* with me, he should never *race* with Catherine—she should be safely tucked up in bed by the time he achieved Church Street."

"Clever Caro," Desdemona said acidly. "And so he stayed with you?"

"Of course. Once caught in my toils, he never *has* found the strength to break them. He loves me, you know—in defiance of all he says in publick or private, in defiance of his own reason." She was suddenly serene as she lay upon the divan, an acolyte at a private altar. "He began by ranting against my passion—by warning me he was *unsafe,* and that if I could not cut him out of my heart it might end in tragedy for more than myself—but I assured him I had already lost everything of worth to a lady of my station. I am cut dead by my oldest acquaintance, called mad by my own family, and must look on as my husband's dearest friends urge him to divorce. There is nothing more Byron may strip from me—no further tragedy I may know."

Lady Oxford had been correct, I realized, when she described Caro Lamb as possessed of a brilliant understanding; it was unfortunate in the extreme that her intelligence had been incapable of subduing the wilder excesses of her emotions.

"And when his raging was done?" Desdemona persisted.

Caro's eyes closed again. "George was very tired. He has been working quite hard at his verses, you know, and I fear the efforts of Genius exhaust him. He took a little wine. Put his head in my lap, and allowed me to stroke it. And then he began to recite his poem to me—*The Giaour.* It is quite fine; something *quite* out of the ordinary way. And to hear the words in George's voice—" Her own throbbed. "I crave his voice, his touch, his look, as another might the transports of opium."

I could well believe it; Caro spoke and moved as one still in the grip of phantasm. The man could summon a diabolic power; I had felt it myself. "We talked of the customs of the *hareem* for at least an hour," she sighed. "We smoked"— she gestured here with the pipe—"and then he begged me to dress in my page's clothes, so that he might conceive of his Leila in Turkish dress."

"And this would have been . . . perhaps three o'clock?"

"Time, time!" she retorted petulantly. "I told you—when one is in the presence of Byron, time means nothing."

"And then?"

"And then—there was nothing for it, I was dressed as a page and the idea of taking a boy excites George profoundly—we went to bed, of course."

I had never in my life encountered anyone like Lady Caroline Lamb. Her frankness—her lack of embarrassment or shame—utterly silenced me; I could not summon a word. But Desdemona was otherwise; she had lived in Caro's world from birth; as had been true of Lord Harold, there was nothing she could not hear or say without complete equanimity.

"Naturally Byron would admit to none of this at the inquest, for fear of being laughed at," Mona said thoughtfully. "I see how it was. He has made such a publick parade of hating you—he could admit nothing so intimate without damage to his reputation. Very well—when did he leave you?"

Caro shrugged. *Time,* again. We were beyond saving.

"Was it light or dark, you tiresome girl?" Mona demanded.

"That lovely hour when the world entire is grey—and the birds commence their singing," she said dreamily.

"We shall put it down as dawn." I rose to leave. "Thank you, Lady Caroline, for your confidence. We are in your debt."

"I should say, rather, that George is," she returned quite calmly. "Provided he escapes the gibbet, of course. Perhaps you will nod to me now, Mona, when we pass each other in Hyde Park?"

"Perhaps, Lady Caroline." And Desdemona curtseyed with quelling stile.

WHEN WE HAD BEEN RELEASED BY A FOOTMAN INTO THE courtyard sweep fronting the Pavilion, the Countess halted in her steps, and looked to me appealingly.

"This will utterly *sink* poor Jane Harley. First Catherine Twining—and now the *impossible* Caro Lamb. I declare, had I never known my beloved Charles—I should believe all men heartless."

"Say rather they possess *too much* heart—it is fidelity that is lacking," I returned. "But I am not convinced Lady Oxford must be told. The outcome shall depend upon our success or failure, Mona—for if we discover the *true* murderer, Byron need never stand trial. And if he does not come before the Assizes, Lady Caroline's story may remain exactly that: one of the fantastic tales dreamt up in her bower."

The Countess glanced at me narrowly. "You still believe him innocent?"

"If we are to believe Caro, then we must believe her wholly; we cannot pick and chuse which bits of evidence to credit. Therefore, if we accept that Byron was here, and left her at dawn, it is impossible for Byron to have drowned Catherine Twining—for she cannot still have been alive at such an hour as half-past five o'clock. She was killed within moments of leaving this place—else she should have achieved her home, and lived to dance at another Assembly. By dawn poor Catherine was already drowned and lashed into Byron's hammock. She must have been carried to the Arms in the dead of night—when all the intimates of both Pavilion and publick house should be deemed to be sleeping."

"Caro wasn't sleeping," Mona interjected darkly.

"The risk of being heard at dawn," I persisted, "—or indeed, *seen* by a member of Tolliver's household, as the culprit exited the tunnel in one bedchamber and thrust the body into Byron's empty rooms next door—should be too great. It cannot have been Byron who did all this."

"As you say." Mona drew on her gloves. "Then who killed her, pray?"

At that moment, the great clock in the stable block's tower to the west of us began to toll the hour; Catherine Twining's service must be over, and it was already noon. The striking clock put me in mind of something I had nearly forgot.

"Mona," I said, "all that we have discovered derives from what the magistrate and coroner neglected to *ask*. Do you not think that the key to this tragedy lies in how one puts the questions—and to whom?"

"Very well," she sighed, "I shall rephrase mine. Pray, Jane—*who killed Catherine Twining?*"

"There was one other person abroad that night who may very well know. Are you incommoded by the smell of the stables, Countess?"

She drew herself up. "You forget. I have been accustomed to ride with the Quorn."

"Ah—but can you converse with the undergroom?" I wondered, and walked purposefully towards the Regent's sixty horses.

THERE WERE, OF COURSE, A DOZEN UNDERGROOMS, AND even two who bore the name of Jem; but we very quickly established which of these was cousin to my chambermaid, Betsy—by enquiring of the Regent's Head Groom, a very august gentleman in buff and blue livery. We expressed nothing more than a desire to convey a message from one servant to another, and if the Head Groom thought it odd that two ladies, one of them in mourning, should embark on such a trivial errand, he was far too well-bred to say so.

We found Jem in a beautifully-appointed loose box which held a fine-boned mare and her foal—a filly but four days old. The undergroom was concocting a warm bran mash for the mare, and murmuring foolish nothings to the foal, who lay flat on her side lost in sleep, her fragile ribs rising and falling with every breath. The box was warm with the heat of the animals and the strong smell of them, overlaid with the sweetness of the straw bedding and the hay in the feeding racks. I have never been much of a horsewoman—a family lack, which may be put down to our straitened circumstances. My elder brothers hunted with the Vyne—our local pack in Hampshire—whenever our friends the Chutes were willing to mount them; but there was no gentle riding hack for my sister, Cassandra, or me. That does not mean, however, that I am afraid of horses, or do not enjoy being near them. I lacked Mona's easy familiarity, however—she had no hesitation in leaning over the half-open door of the box, extending her gloved hand, and clucking softly to the mare—who stepped delicately over her sleeping foal and thrust a soft nose into Mona's gloved hand.

"She hopes that I have brought her sugar," Mona said, "but I am a rank cheat, you beauty, and have nothing to offer. What is her name, sirrah?"

"Rapunzel, on account o' her long tail, my lady." The undergroom lifted his hand to his forehead in respect, and stared at us.

Mona stroked the small Arab head. "And does she like to run?"

"Aye, but she's no hunter. A neat little mount for a lady, when she's not to foal. Granddaughter to Eclipse, she is—no better blood in the Kingdom."

"I believe it. Pray—go on with your bran mash. We have no wish to disturb you at your work. I am the Countess of Swithin, and this is my friend, Miss Austen—who is acquainted with your cousin Betsy."

The undergroom coloured, and dropped his gaze. "The lady'd be a guest over to the Castle?"

"I am—and was a friend to the young lady who met her death by drowning a few nights ago. Betsy said you spoke of her, at the inquest; I am glad to hear it. You have done a good deal towards apprehending a murderer."

"Arrested Lord Byron, they did," he said warily, and began stirring his bran with vigour.

"But you know that to be nonsense."

Jem glanced up at me swiftly, but said nothing.

"You saw Lord Byron enter the Pavilion that evening?"

"Aye, and he did."

"And then Miss Twining left it? When the clock chimed the three-quarters?"

He hesitated; it was probable he wondered what right we had to put such questions to him—but the habit of submitting to authority prevailed. With a slight grimace, he nodded.

"Was Lord Byron with her when she quitted the place?"

"No, ma'am."

"Did he pursue Miss Twining once she was gone?"

Another hesitation. "I was inside the box here with the mare, after the young lady—Miss Twining as it was—left. I stepped outside for just the short while, like, to fetch a rope— I had to slip it round the foal's head, and help the mare to birth it—and that's when I see her. I didn't see much more than that."

"When was the foal born?" I asked.

"Ten minutes past two, by the stable clock, and thank the good Lord for it—the foal would've been dead if she'd taken much longer."

I gazed at the delicate ribs, rising and falling with blessed air. While the foal drew her first breath, Catherine Twining drew her last. It was a bitter conjunction.

"And afterwards? When the mare and foal were comfortable?"

"I stood outside and looked at the stars for a bit," he answered, "then went to my bed. There were but a few hours till dawn, and foal or no, I'm expected at my work by six o'clock."

"Did anyone else cross the Pavilion grounds while you looked at the stars?" I asked.

"Nobody but the Colonel."

"McMahon?" Mona said quickly.

He shook his head. "Colonel Hanger. He's an odd one, and no mistake. Never sleeps, playing cards until all hours, or striding about the grounds as tho' all the imps of Satan be after 'im. Many's the time he's sat down on a barrel with Mr. Davy—he's the Head Groom—day or night, to talk of horse-flesh or race-meetings or such hunts as he's had. But Mr. Davy was gone to bed. There was only me to talk to the Colonel that night."

"And did Colonel Hanger stay long?" I murmured, to keep the flow of reminiscence unstinted.

The mare had abandoned Mona and was prodding Jem's shoulder with her nose. He poured the bran mash carefully into a feedbag, and strapped it to her head before speaking again.

"At first I thought he'd met with an accident, so wild did

he look—tramping into the stable block with his boots and pantaloons soaked to the knees. But then I saw as how he was grinning, so all was well. *Colonel Hanger,* I says, *you gave me quite a turn.* He clapped me on the shoulder and laughed out loud, as tho' he'd just won a packet at hazard or cards; and then he gave me a sovereign. To celebrate the safe delivery of the foal, he said."

His boots and pantaloons soaked to the knees.

"Was it raining that night?" I asked pensively. "I cannot quite remember."

"No, ma'am. He'd fallen into the sea, he said, while walking along the Marine Parade after the Assembly. Lucky for him the tide was well out. He was foxed, I suppose—but the cold water soon put him to rights."

Mona and I had gone very still. I do not think either of us moved a muscle for an instant, or bothered even to breathe. *The tide was well out.* No one had even thought to remark upon the tides, at the hour of Catherine's death. I had dismissed Caro Lamb, even, as unable to brave the water. But Catherine's killer had *walked* out to Byron's yacht, and fetched the hammock, with only a shallow depth to concern him.

"What did the Colonel want here in the stables?" I asked, as casually as possible. "Surely he did not mean to *ride* at such an hour?"

Jem grinned. "No, ma'am. Not that night—tho' I've known him to gallop the Downs in pitch black before, and a wonder it is that either the Colonel or the horse came home. No—it was a large needle Old Hanger wanted, such as we use on the horse blankets—a needle and good, strong thread."

CHAPTER TWENTY-EIGHT

Sentry Duty

"OH, WHAT I WOULD NOT GIVE FOR LORD HAROLD AT THIS moment," I said to Mona, compound of frustration and despair. "*He* should have known what sort of man Colonel Hanger is, and how he must be worked on!"

We had thanked Jem for his interesting conversation with a shilling pressed into his palm, and an unspoken hope that he did not share our interview with Colonel Hanger—lest his life enjoy a very *brief* duration. I suspected, however, that without the posing of pertinent questions, Jem's knowledge should remain locked in the stables; he was not the sort to offer intelligence unsolicited.

"To be sure Uncle was acquainted with Hanger," Mona said with a visible shudder. "They were both second sons, you know, and that is apt to make for fellow-feeling—tho' I do not think you could find two more *dissimilar* men the length and breadth of England! I confess I cannot see my uncle emerging from the sea at dead of night, and requesting a needle and thread from the undergroom, so that he might sew up a dead body."

"But that is just the point, Mona. I *can*," I retorted. "And it is for *that* reason I wish devoutly he were with us still! There is nobody I should rely upon more to confront a villain. Lord Harold may have been the consummate gentleman, but he was capable of *thinking* like a rogue—and therefore, outwitted the worst of them."

She studied me with an oddly arrested look. "You were often in danger when you were with him, were you not? It was not all a pleasant turn around the Park?"

"Your uncle was an agent of the Crown," I said, taken aback. "I cannot recall that it was *ever* a pleasant turn around the Park. But what is that to the point? I am not Lord Harold, and I shall be reduced to a quaking jelly by a man of Colonel Hanger's kidney; I knew it from the first moment I saw him, intent upon ravishing poor Catherine in the Regent's conservatory. The fellow is evil, Mona."

At her exclamation, I supplied the history of our entertainment at the Pavilion, and the Colonel's readiness to draw Henry's cork, or challenge him to a duel. She listened acutely, evidencing neither shock nor dismay.

"It is everywhere known, of course, that Hanger used to engage in very rum behaviour—procuring women for Prinny when they were both thirty years younger," she observed. "It was he who helped to make the illegal marriage with Mrs. Fitzherbert, poor lady—only think of having such a man as witness to one's wedding! And I do not doubt he has pulled Prinny out of countless scrapes that, were they made publick, should have greatly tarnished his honour. But I cannot think even Hanger should be fool enough to prey upon a child of fifteen, of good family—and drown her when she fought him, Jane."

"Someone certainly did so—and if not Hanger, then *who*?

Recollect what the undergroom saw, Mona—and what he gave Hanger."

"Very well," Mona rejoined, with her habitual air of calm amidst lunacy, "let us go and ask the villainous Colonel what use he found for needle and thread."

I stared at her.

"I have known George Hanger this *age*," she said impatiently. "I shall simply send in my card at the Regent's front door, and enquire whether the Colonel is at home to visitors. If he remains as rapacious for a glimpse of the fair sex as you say, he is unlikely to send us away unanswered."

Her confidence was cool enough to suggest her uncle, after all; and thus I followed her without a murmur from the stable yard to the Pavilion's entry. But George Hanger was not at home; he had gone, so we were informed, to play hazard at Raggett's Club, and none could say when he was expected back again.[23]

It was impossible for any lady to penetrate the sacred fastness of Raggett's; we should have to wait for the Colonel to return the Countess of Swithin's call.

"It is a pity he prefers dice over cards," Mona said thoughtfully as we achieved the Steyne, "else we might have set Swithin upon him. I can do nothing about that however, until we meet at dinner—and I am able to tell him all. No doubt he will think of something; I believe Swithin managed fellows of Hanger's ilk with great success, when he was about the opium trade in China."

"I am sure of it," I said. "But meanwhile, Lord Byron sits in Brighton Camp, under armed guard, for a murder he undoubtedly did not commit. We have no evidence to support our suspicions that Hanger drowned Catherine Twining and

---

[23] Hazard was a form of gambling with dice that led eventually to the present game of shooting craps.—*Editor's note.*

brought her corpse through the wine cellar's tunnel to the King's Arms—not a pair of trousers with the stains of salt water to their knees, nor a scrap of thread in Hanger's pocket, that might be shown to match the hammock's. We have no motive beyond the fact that the man is an unconscionable roué. In sum, Mona—we have nothing that exonerates Lord Byron! Indeed, we have sunk him to his neck by forcing Caro Lamb to place him in the Pavilion itself, within moments of when Catherine Twining was last seen! I cannot think we have done your friend Lady Oxford any singular service."

"But that was never your object, Jane. You are animated by a desire for truth; and *that* we shall achieve—I feel certain."

"Whether Truth is the same as Justice, remains in doubt."

We proceeded towards the Castle, where I must part from her, but she stopped me at the entry.

"Jane, do you not think it remarkable that Byron failed to *follow* Miss Twining that night? I observed him, you know, throughout the evening—because of my particular concern for Lady Oxford's heart. Byron was single-minded in his efforts to speak to Miss Twining. She was forced to elude him by dancing without cease. Not even the presence of her father at the Assembly could dissuade him. Captain Morley proved her protector for a time; and indeed, it was only after he exchanged words with his lordship that Byron desisted. And then, when Caro Lamb appeared, his lordship quitted the Rooms in high dudgeon—packed up his things at the Arms—and repaired to Caro's rooms. *He went so far as to invade the Pavilion*—he succeeded in achieving Miss Twining's presence—and yet, when she flew from him, he abruptly abandoned pursuit and proclaimed his verses to Caro Lamb instead! It is incomprehensible; in every respect, incomprehensible!"

"He is hardly the most *consistent* of men—" I began.

"But at present, he is very likely to be sober," she said

owlishly, "and that is so out of the common way where
Byron is concerned, we ought to take advantage of it. Do you
not agree this is the perfect time to speak with him—while he
languishes alone in gaol, entirely without an audience? What
do you say, Jane, to exercising my chestnuts?"

AND SO I COMMITTED MYSELF ONCE MORE TO THE PERILS
of the Countess's beautiful horses and perch phaeton, and set
off up the Lewes road in the direction of Brighton Camp. The
team was decidedly fresh, having been eating their heads off
in their stalls since Wednesday's race-meeting; the equipage
bowled along at a spanking pace through the bright noonday
sun. We encountered considerable London traffic, and as
Mona never hesitated to give the pair their heads, and pull
out to pass the odd gig or farm cart, I expected at every moment to be overturned in the ditch. Apprehension throughout
the whole quite robbed me of enjoyment, and I was for the
most part unable to speak; but the Countess maintained a
pleasant flow of conversation. This was purposefully innocu-
ous, as she had her groom up behind her; within twenty minutes, I daresay, we were pulling up in the Camp. The groom
jumped down and held the horses; he intended walking them,
I believe, while we were occupied amidst the Barracks.

"We ought to beg permission of the Camp Commandant
to visit the gaol," she said conversationally as we strolled
along the muddy lane that served as main thoroughfare, surrounded on every side by red coats. "But I could not say
where he is to be found. At Catherine Twining's funeral, possibly—or about some military business."

"I should not like to violate the Hussars' principles," I
replied, "but I think it should prove more efficient if we simply suborn Byron's guards—and beg ignorance of convention
later."

"I feel sure that is what Uncle would have done," Mona agreed. "Let us enquire the way to the gaol."

She approached the first young officer we encountered, with remarkable boldness; but as she carried a hamper of provisions over her arm, and had changed her straw-coloured gown for a bottle-green carriage dress and matching high-poke bonnet, she looked suitably demure. I, in my mourning clothes, hovered on the fringe of the conversation; and as the officer raised his hat, and strode on, Mona turned to me with satisfaction.

"Only think—that is young Norton, Lord Raleigh's second son. I am a little acquainted with the family; what a lucky chance I should meet with him, first off! They are cousins eight times removed."

If there was a well-placed family in England to which Mona was *not* related, I should be very much surprized. "But does he know where Byron is to be found?"

"His lordship is being held in the cells reserved for the drunk and disorderly. Young Norton says Byron's arrival in the Camp last night was all that was extraordinary—once the constabulary were gone, several of the officers of the 10th gathered outside his lordship's cell to toast his health, and Byron consented to declaim a number of lines of poetry. There is nothing like the Hussars, after all, for knowing how to live."

We hastened in the direction young Norton had indicated, passing in our way the chapel where Catherine Twining's funeral had been held. It appeared emptied of life at this present, and I concluded the cold collation so essential to every passing must be laid out in Mr. Smalls's quarters—or perhaps, as general interest in the family was so great—in the Officers' Mess. There was no sign of Henry.

Mona hesitated at a crossing of the way, then turned left. The cells for the drunk and disorderly were housed in a low-slung brick-and-stone building set apart from the barracks themselves, with a set of stocks raised before them. Two sentries stood at attention on either side of the sole door; narrow slits served for windows, placed high up in the walls, and they were barred. It must be airless and uncomfortable; but perhaps Lord Byron took consolation from his verse.

"Jane," the Countess murmured as we paused before the stocks, eyeing the sentries, "did your acquaintance with my uncle ever run to the penetration of gaols?"

"On several occasions," I admitted.

"Excellent. You shall know, then, how to go on."

I might have informed her ladyship that I had never breached a *military* gaol, but that seemed mere pettifogging at this point. So I drew breath and walked forward to attack the sentries. Mona followed with her hamper of food and wine.

"Good afternoon, sirs," I attempted.

Both sentries continued to stare straight ahead. Neither returned my greeting.

"This'll be another of 'em," the sentry on the right muttered to his fellow on the left.

"Sure enough. Like flies to cream, ain't it? I think I'll be takin' up poetry, I do. Nothing beats it for the ladies."

I glanced in consternation at Mona. She fluttered her hand, as tho' encouraging a bashful bride to the altar.

"I am Miss Austen, and this is the Countess of Swithin, whose husband is attempting to free Lord Byron. We have come this afternoon with food and . . . a quantity of writing paper . . . to succor him during imprisonment."

"A quantity of writin' paper!" the sentry on the right spat out, and at last his eyes met mine. "Aye, his-prating-lordship has *that* enough. Whole rolls of the stuff've been sent through the wicket in that door, ma'am, with the compliments of near every lady in Brighton—in the 'ope as a sonnet'll come back out, inscribed to *Louisa* or *Elizabeth* or *Airy-bell*. 'Nuff to turn a man's stomach, it is."

"The paper is merely by-the-way," Mona said indifferently. "If his lordship does not require it, of course I shall take it back again. But the provisions must be useful, I am sure. May we present them to his lordship?"

"Present them?" The sentry on the left turned his head indignantly and glared at Mona. "The gentleman is wanted on a charge of murder, your la'ship! He is *not* a lion-tamer out of Astley's Amphitheatre, nor yet the darling of the London stage! If you wish to see 'im, you cannot buy tickets—but by all means *do* attend 'is 'anging!"

At those words, to my astonishment, Desdemona abruptly began to sob. So overcome was she, that the hamper was nearly dropped from her nerveless hands; she swiftly covered her face and cried her heart out. I moved to comfort her, my arm about her shoulders, and looked to the sentries in reproach. "Heartless! How can you speak so, to a lady that has known his lordship from the cradle!"

The two men looked uncomfortable enough at the sight of Mona's weeping; my words only increased their chagrin. "Beggin' yer pardon, ma'am, but you've no notion how many young ladies—shameless camp followers, most of 'em—'ave dallied by this sentry post and offered any amount of money or favours to be admitted to his lordship, private-like," one said.

"Some o' the things they're promising would tempt St. Peter, they would," the other echoed.

"That is not our object," I said sternly—there is some benefit to being an aging spinster dressed in black; the sentries quailed as tho' I had been their mamma—"our sole concern is Lord Byron's health. He possesses a most delicate constitution. If you intend to hang him, you had better ensure that he lives long enough to stand his trial. Now, be sensible—and convey that hamper into his lordship with the compliments of the Earl and Countess of Swithin."

The sentry on the right—who could be no more, I guessed,

than eighteen—saluted me as tho' I had been an officer, and scurried to retrieve the basket from the ground where it lay. Carrying it gingerly, he first unlatched the wicket, and peered within Lord Byron's cell; then said, in an aside to his fellow, "Writin' again. 'E's all over ink. And 'e'll be askin' to 'ave 'is pen mended again, just you wait an' see. No pen-knives allowed the prisoners," he added, for my benefit.

"Naturally not," I agreed with quelling coldness.

The sentry unbarred the door, and carried the hamper within. After an interval of several moments, he reemerged with a packet of paper in his hands.

"The prisoner thanks ye kindly fer yer consideration," he said, as tho' having got the words by rote, "and asks that you convey these pages to Lady Oxford. If he is to hang, Lord Byron says, it would be something to know as his verses is published."

I held out my hand for the pages; they had been enclosed in a cover, and sealed clumsily with the wax from Byron's tallow candle. A letter? Or more lines from *The Giaour*?

Mona subdued her sobbing to a few dying sniffles.

"You have my gratitude, dear sirs, for your exceptional kindness," she breathed with trembling sincerity. "You will be blessed, I am sure, in Heaven!"

Such a picture as she made, with her tear-stained cheeks delicately overlaid with rose, that she might almost have been another Sarah Siddons—and I recollected, for the first time, that her grandmother had tread the boards of the Comédie-Française.

"Lord, Jane," she said as we walked with dignity back towards the barracks, "I was all of a quake lest they look inside the hamper. For beneath the roast chicken, the Gloucester cheese, and the lemon tart, is of course a pen-knife—for how could I neglect to send Byron one?"

CHAPTER TWENTY-NINE

The Viscount's Tale

FRIDAY, 14 MAY 1813
BRIGHTON, CONT.

~

WE HAD NOT ACHIEVED OUR OBJECT—TO CORROBORATE
Caro Lamb's tale, and enquire of Lord Byron why he had
failed to follow Catherine Twining from the Pavilion on that
fatal night—but we had in our possession a packet that might
prove a love letter for Lady Oxford; and this was no end
cheering to Desdemona, whose heart was softer than mine.
Lady Oxford, she informed me, had taken to her bed on the
strength of Byron's imprisonment—and must be cheered by
some word from him.

"Tho', do you know, Jane, that he had the presumption to
charge her with *unfaithfulness* at the Assembly last evening!
Was there ever anything more unjust? —When she has sacrificed so much for Byron's sake—and even now remains in
Brighton solely out of consideration for him!"

"Lady Oxford had better consider of her children," I
retorted, "for I assume her husband has long since been
forgot."

"The Earl is not very memorable, that is true," Mona said

doubtfully, "but whatever Jane Harley's sins may be, neglect is not one of them. I am sure that has all been on the *other* side, for Oxford is very well cared for, and never troubles himself about Jane's *affaires*—as he has had countless High Flyers in keeping!"

On such a point of mutual disagreement, as to the nature of marital happiness, it was as well to keep silent. I could only be thankful that Mona's domestic arrangements were not patterned along Harleian lines.

We emerged into the main thoroughfare of the Camp, and espied the Countess's groom walking her team and phaeton to an admiring audience of common foot soldiers. Among them, however, I noticed a glossy charger commanded by a captain with a familiar face—Captain Viscount Morley. The blond god who had danced his last with Catherine Twining at her fatal Assembly looked haggard this afternoon; a riband of black crape was tied about his right arm. Had he attended Catherine's obsequies that morning?

"Thank you, Hinch," Mona said as she approached her groom. "Pray go to their heads."

"Allow me to assist you, Countess." Morley had dismounted, and tossed his reins to a brother officer; now he stood by the phaeton, offering his hand, and Mona, accepting it, sprang lightly into the carriage. Immediately, he turned to me with a smile, and offered to spring me into the other side. As Mona fingered the reins and the team tossed its heads, the Captain observed, "A lovely pair! I envy you up behind them."

"You should not, if you saw how the Countess drives," I murmured.

Morley smiled. "I have often observed her, in Hyde Park of a spring morning; and tho' I admit her to be a very dashing whip, I cannot think you in any danger, Miss— Forgive me, I have forgot your name."

"Austen," I said. "And you are Captain Viscount Morley, I believe?"

"Got it in one." He glanced at me ruefully as I ascended into the equipage. "I must do better, next time we meet, Miss Austen. That was unconscionably rude."

"Not at all," I assured him. What boy of four-and-twenty, as I judged him at most to be, should concern himself with the name of a spinster seen once in a crowded room, whose dress proclaimed the dowd, and grieving mourner? "But if I may presume upon our chance acquaintance—I observed your armband—may I ask whether you attended Miss Twining's funeral this morning?"

His gaze dropped. "I did, so help me. To think that such a perfect being is laid into the earth—but forgive me. I should ask rather whether you knew her."

"Pray, do not hide your sensibility on *my* account. I was a little acquainted with Miss Twining."

"Ah! I had thought you a stranger to Brighton—a guest of the Countess's."

"A visitor to Brighton only, to be sure—my home is in Hampshire—but I first met Miss Twining on the road from London, at Cuckfield."

I deliberately tried this information on the Captain to see how he should react; and the change his countenance underwent was remarkable. He first paled, then flushed red.

"Miss Austen—" He hesitated. "I collect that the Countess is intent upon driving home. Should you mind if I rode a little way beside your carriage? A dawdling escort might encourage her ladyship to curb her horses."

"Then you shall earn my undying gratitude," I returned with a smile, "and any indulgence you might name!"

The Captain remounted, Hinch swung himself up behind the phaeton, and the mettlesome chestnuts, given their heads, sprang forward with a lurch.

Until we were well out of the Camp, the talk must be all on Mona and Morley's side—of horseflesh and auctions at Tattersall's; the fate of a mutual acquaintance's hunters, when that acquaintance lost everything at loo and was forced to sell his stable. "Six hundred guineas, Swithin says old Jepson paid, for that rawboned young'un," Mona exclaimed. "We must hope it's up to carrying Jepson's weight."

"Do you hunt, Miss Austen?" Morley politely enquired. We had achieved the main Brighton road, and he was obviously dawdling, keeping his handsome charger at something between a trot and a walk; I had never enjoyed a ride in Mona's phaeton so much.

"Sadly, I do not," I replied, "although I have many brothers who are addicted to sport. I rather wonder at your finding time to enter the field, Captain—do not your military duties take you much from England? I had heard you were at Talavera."

"I had that honour, yes." He dropped back from the carriage, and came round to ride beside me. "I was used to hunt with the Duke of Beaufort's pack—but it has been at least three years since I have enjoyed a meeting."

"—Having been perpetually fighting with Wellington in the Peninsula, I collect. Miss Twining also had a brother in the 10th, I believe—Richard Twining. Were you at all acquainted with him?"

"Indeed I was. We were tent-mates for a time. I thought poor Richard the best of fellows, and as fine a cavalry officer as ever lived. He was but nineteen when he was killed. I saw him fall."

Mona gave a soft exclamation of sorrowful sympathy.

"It is extraordinary, is it not, that General Twining has lost both his children?" I said thoughtfully. "Almost as tho' he had been marked out by Fate—or an avenging Fury."

"There are some men who draw misfortune as surely as carrion draws the vulture," he said in a taut voice. "I valued

Richard Twining exceedingly, Miss Austen—but if his father should meet with the most painful death imaginable, I should greet the news with relief, and raise a glass to Heaven on the strength of it! I say this, tho' he *is* a senior officer."

"Strong words indeed, sir," I said imperturbably. "What has the General done to inspire such implacable resentment?"

"He had a wife, ma'am, before he possessed his children—and the misery he brought upon her head cannot fail to move any who once knew her, tho' she is many years now in her grave."

I bowed to the Captain; his words were laden with honest emotion, and I detected no attempt at dissimulation, no effort to disguise his passionate disregard for the General. If this young man *were* determined to be the agent of his family's revenge upon the Twinings—and had sought to destroy the father by extinguishing first his son, a companion in arms—and then his daughter, so trusting and young—Morley was exceedingly clever. A man who had much to hide, should have affected a careless cordiality towards the General—and I should have suspected his motives instantly. By exposing his unvarnished enmity, Morley appeared guileless; and I suspected him the more.

"But I blame myself for Miss Twining's murder," he said, in a lowered voice. "I spoke too freely, when I should not—I sought to protect and shield her. Instead, I served only to incite her murderer to violence."

"Unless you held her head under the waves, Captain, you cannot possibly claim guilt."

He looked at me in swift dismay. "I, drown *Catherine*? You will acquit me of such an atrocity, I hope, Miss Austen, when I tell you that it has been many months since I have known she was the only creature on earth capable of ensuring my happiness—and that, tho' she shrank from openly proclaiming an engagement, until she should be of age, I may say with confidence that she felt the same depth of regard for me."

"Good God!" I said blankly. "Do not tell me that the Earl of Derwentwater's estates lie somewhere near *Bath*?"

"My family has long been established in that part of the country, indeed," the Captain returned with a faint air of curiosity.

Thus did my brother Henry's predicted appearance of a gallant Unknown, devoted to Miss Twining, come to pass— and as I had feared, entirely too late. A host of impressions swept over me. *Catherine in love with a young officer. Catherine, sent home from school. Catherine, going in fear of disclosing her beloved's name.* But Morley was speaking, and I must attend.

"The fact of her brother having reposed his trust and friendship in me, early supported my suit; but many months of mutual esteem, and increasing knowledge of one another's character, established the true bond."

"Then you have all my sympathy, Captain," I said; but I studied his classic profile in some doubt. "How did you come to meet? Miss Twining was much of the year at school, I believe, in Bath?"

"She was—but at such a remove from the General, Catherine naturally felt herself to be free of inordinate restraint. She might receive visitors, under the eye of Miss Addams, the Headmistress. I first called last November, to deliver a letter I had long held in keeping—the final one penned by her brother. Richard had told me much of his beloved sister during our long campaigning in Spain."

"Of course," I murmured.

"From that beginning," the Captain continued in a voice that wavered only a little, "our attachment was constant and fervent. The knowledge that I was to be garrisoned in Brighton—where Catherine made her home—only increased our happiness—but we taught ourselves discretion, so as not to excite the animosity of her father."

"You only danced the one dance with her, at Monday's Assembly," Mona observed.

The Captain turned his head. "All subterfuge must be abhorrent; but I knew the General should make Catherine's life a misery if he suspected our mutual regard. An ancient scandal lies between our two families, which renders any marital tie repugnant to the General."

"You were aware he intended to marry her to Mr. Hendred Smalls?" I asked.

"The Company chaplain? Catherine had spoken of the General's threats, but did not regard the union as imminent; she pled her tender years, and the unfortunate Smalls is an elderly gentleman. He might, after all, be carried off by a putrid fever at any time," Morley said, with the unconscious arrogance of youth, "and had he pressed his suit—or the General forced the union upon her—we should have been ready to fly to the Border at a moment's notice."

He was pensive a moment, the charger skittering sideways, and I observed that his pallor was extreme. "To think that it should be *my darling*—in all her freshness and bloom—who should be lost, and as a result of my unguarded tongue! I do not exaggerate, Miss Austen, that when I learnt of her death—of the wretched manner in which she was found—that I very nearly made away with myself. Only a consciousness of what was due to my father—to all my family—preserved me. I would not have it said that a *Twining* was the ruin of another generation's hopes!"

"*Your unguarded tongue*," Mona repeated, all anxious concern. "What can you possibly have said, Morley, to bring such guilt upon your head?"

"I told his lordship too fully, and too freely, what I thought of his manners in abducting my Catherine."

"His lordship being—Byron?"

The Captain nodded. "I upbraided him at Monday's Assembly. I was careful throughout the whole to suggest only the indignation of a *gentleman,* rather than of Catherine's betrothed, lest I betray too great a partiality. I informed him that by making a sport of Catherine's virtue, he had exposed her to all the burden of her father's anger—and that the General's rage had undoubtedly found expression in physical abuse. In short, I accused Byron of blind selfishness, that had occasioned harm to the very being he professed to love. I believe that I so shamed him—and that, in publick—that he found Catherine in her way home from the Pavilion, and—"

"Killed her."

His hands must have clenched on his mount's reins, for the horse jibed.

"You do not credit Mr. Scrope Davies's assertion, then, that Byron was with him the remainder of that night?" I said nothing of Caro Lamb.

"Davies is Byron's friend," Morley said simply.

"You believe all this," Mona cried, "and yet may play at *cards* with his lordship? I will never understand the code of gentlemen. Never!"

"I have no proof, and the coroner had effectively acquitted Byron. When I learnt the inquest verdict, I was beside myself—and might have called him out, then and there. But my family has a wretched history where private vengeance is concerned," he said, with a faint smile.

Point to the Captain, I thought ruefully; his performance was exceedingly well done.

"I chose to shadow Byron," he continued, "in order to engage him in conversation when I might, over cards or a glass of claret—in the hope that he might betray himself, so that I could then lay information before the magistrate. But happily, Sir Harding Cross arrived at his determination before I was required to act."

"It is so difficult to untangle the events of that evening." I sighed. "I was not in attendance at the Assembly myself; but I *had heard* that the principal actors came and went at such confusing times! Byron quitting the Rooms as Lady Caroline Lamb entered them; Lady Caro quitting them in company with Miss Twining; and the General, who was said to be so jealous of his daughter's virtue, departing hours before she did! Do you not think it odd, Captain, that so scrupulous a parent should have left his daughter alone at a ball where two men he despised—Lord Byron and yourself—should be paying her marked attention?"

This was plain speaking indeed.

"I should, had I not learnt the cause of the General's early departure within minutes of leaving the Assembly myself," the Captain answered calmly. "He had been invited, as I was, to drink Port and play at hazard with Colonel George Hanger, at the Pavilion."

"With Colonel Hanger!" I glanced at Mona in surprize and consternation, and saw the same mirrored in her looks. "But the General claimed to have gone home that night!"

"It is possible he did not wish to admit of an acquaintance with Hanger, particularly in the company of Mr. Hendred Smalls," Morley said drily. "But it is common knowledge within the 10th that Hanger and the General—who was but Major Twining then—served together years ago, during the rebellion of the American colonies. Indeed, Hanger was Twining's second, in the duel that forever divided our two families."

"Then what were you about, in Heaven's name, drinking Port with the pair of them?" Mona demanded, scandalised.

The Captain's mouth curled. "Hanger remains a senior officer, Countess. A fellow in my position does not idly ignore such invitations—which must be received uncommonly like orders."

"At what time did you join Colonel Hanger?" I recollected that the undergroom, Jem, had received Hanger's sodden visitation at about half-past two o'clock in the morning.

"I reached the Pavilion when Miss Twining did," he replied without reservation. "Indeed, I waited until she had quitted the Assembly with Lady Caroline—and then followed, by prior agreement. I escorted the ladies across the Steyne, and parted from them in the front entry. I was shown to Hanger's rooms, and found General Twining already established in a chair. He did not remain above a half-hour, however, having already been at Hanger's mercy some time; he stayed only long enough to twit me on my parentage and family history, with undisguised contempt; to belittle Wellington and all our efforts in the Peninsula; and to speak with indescribable bitterness of the loss of his son, and the unusual survival of others—meaning myself, of course, whom he should have preferred dead. I might have said such words to him *then* as should have justified him in calling me out—for a Captain offers a General disrespect at his peril, you know. But I thought of my friend Richard—and more of my beloved Catherine—and kept a still tongue in my head."

"And so, by your calculation, the General left you at half-past one?"

"Or a little earlier, perhaps. I did not linger alone with Colonel Hanger long. The General was no sooner out the door, than Hanger must be abusing him—and all his family. The affair of the duel was dragged forward, with Hanger describing the morals of Catherine's mother in such terms as I should blush to repeat; and then—" Morley hesitated, his blue eyes flicking to meet mine, and a dull red colour suffusing his cheeks—"went so far as to drag Catherine herself through the muck."

The charger's head jerked back; the Captain had clenched unconsciously at the reins. "He knew of Byron's persistent suit—knew, as well, of the attempted abduction, I know not how. His contempt for Byron was immense; he seems to regard all poets as weaklings and—forgive me—sodomites; the fact of Byron's lameness only inflamed his derision further. I did not waste my words in defending a man I regarded as my enemy; but Catherine—Hanger seemed to believe that Miss Twining *encouraged* Byron's attentions—that like her mother, she was, as Colonel Hanger put it, *soiled goods,* no better than a *common doxy, not worth the bullet fired to defend her honour.*"

Mona uttered a shocked exclamation of sympathy.

"You may imagine how I felt," Morley said in a low voice. "Indignation—outrage—on the point of personal honour, and family pride— Had he been anyone but a senior officer, I should have thrown my glove in his face. As it was—I bade him goodnight with the barest civility and showed myself out of the old blackguard's rooms.

"I loitered in the Pavilion's foyer a moment, in the hope that Catherine might descend, and require an escort home. I wish to God I had waited longer! I must have missed her only by moments."

The Pavilion footman responsible for the door that evening should of course corroborate this, did we ask.

"But Catherine did *not* appear, and I had no business disturbing Lady Caroline. I recollected I was expected on the Parade Ground to train some raw recruits early the next morning, and slipped regretfully out the door. The stable clock had just finished tolling the half-hour."

"And General Twining was nowhere in sight?"

Morley hesitated, then continued with marked distaste. "In fact, he had lain in wait for me, if you will credit it. He stepped forward out of the shadows and offered me such abuse—the sort of violent obscenities only a man in his cups should utter—that I so far forgot myself, as to knock him down. No doubt that was his very object, that he might have the pleasure of calling me up before a court-martial."

"You struck the General?" Mona cried gleefully; she seemed to regard a mill as excellent sport.

Morley smiled at her sadly. "He was excessively foxed, I fear—Hanger is notorious for a deep drinker, and the General had been keeping pace with his old comrade. Indeed, he was so unsteady as to take the blow full on the chin, and lose his footing—and once he fell, appeared senseless. I was horrified enough at the result of my actions to search for a pulse— satisfied myself that he breathed still—and then left him. My feelings were so uncharitable towards General Twining at the time, that I had no interest in aiding him—and hoped he should suffer acutely from the head-ache in the morning."

Mona laughed delightedly, and her team seemed to take some of their excitement from her—slipping into a canter that hurtled the precarious phaeton down the road towards the sea.

"And then?" I gasped, clutching at my seat as Mona sawed at the ribbons. The chestnuts dropped back into a walk.

"I returned to the Castle, where I had stabled Intrepid," Morley said, patting his charger's neck. "We must already have achieved our road home when Catherine—when she quitted the Pavilion, entirely alone. . . . How Lady Caroline can have allowed it . . ."

"As to that," Mona began—but I pinched her near arm and she shot me a look of enquiry. I gave my head the slight- est shake. There was no need to inform the Captain of Byron's appearance in Caro Lamb's rooms. Morley appeared in ignorance of it, and I had no wish to heighten his conviction that Byron was a killer.

We had reached the final descent into Brighton when the Captain drew rein, and doffed his hat.

"Will you not dine with us this evening, Captain?" Mona asked, at her most engaging.

"I should enjoy nothing better," he said, "but must decline the invitation—I do not have leave. Indeed, I have neglected my duties already too long. I shall be fortunate not to be thrown in the stocks! But I could not resist the chance to speak of Catherine to a few who knew her—and wished to thank you, Miss Austen, for having saved her that day in Cuckfield. Would that she had never known a greater danger!"

He wheeled Intrepid, and galloped away from us then, but not before I had seen an unexpected rush of tears stain his cheeks.

"It is remarkable," Mona told me sombrely, "that such gentlemen may cut their way through scores of French—and yet return home possessed of hearts enough, to mourn the loss of a green girl."

"He makes no mention of meeting Byron as his lordship entered the Pavilion, tho' the timing was such, it is extraordinary their paths did not cross," I observed. "Do you think we ought to believe him, Mona?"

CHAPTER THIRTY

The Giaour

SATURDAY, 15 MAY 1813
BRIGHTON

A REVENGE TRAGEDY, LADY OXFORD HAD SAID OF THE verses Lord Byron was presently writing. I had thought that she referred to her lover in this—that it was Byron who sought revenge, for Catherine Twining's murder—but as the phaeton swiftly descended towards the village by the sea, and the beautiful youth who was Captain Viscount Morley disappeared behind us, I asked myself which of the gentlemen might have had cause to feel the spurs of jealousy more.

A man I knew for my enemy, the young captain had said of his lordship; and who could blame him? Morley had, in retrospect, shown remarkable restraint while playing at cards with Byron the previous evening. Was this a testament to the quality of his breeding—or the depth of his satisfied revenge?

"I wish we had been able to speak to Byron," I fretted, as Mona pulled up at the meeting of the Lewes and London roads.

"It is a pity," she agreed as she headed her team south.

"Had we been able to put Caro's story to him point-blank, he might have confessed the whole—and we should then be saved the embarrassment of interrogating poor Scrope Davies. I shall make Swithin do it, of course; he will manage exactly the right blend of sympathy and sternness. He is forever adopting that tone when my modiste's bills prove shockingly high, and we are forced to engage in an uncomfortable interview in his book room. Shall I set you down at the Castle, Jane? I confess I should prefer you to come back with me to Marine Parade—I do not like to face Lady Oxford alone."

"Mona," I said, shaking the sealed packet of paper, "if this proves to be a letter from Byron to the Countess, you shall be greeted with joy."

"And if it is not?" she countered. "Pity me, Jane!"

I glanced at her sidelong. "I believe all this fresh air has given me an appetite. I should be happy to partake of a nuncheon in Marine Parade—and shall *stand buff* as heartily as Scrope Davies, should you require it!"

Lady Oxford still kept to her room.

We discovered her established on a settee, in fetching dishabille, with a pretty lace cap covering her light brown hair and a pair of spectacles on her nose. She was reading Volume the Eighth of her history of Rome.

"We intend a trip to Sardinia, you know, in June," she told me carelessly as she set aside the book; "or perhaps we shall simply stay at Naples. Oxford hopes to find some antiquities there—his friend Lord Hamilton is forever singing the praises of Naples for such treasures, and if watching poor labourers dig in the dirt will make my lord happy, I find no cause to complain."

"—Provided Vesuvius does not erupt again," Mona murmured. "Jane—we carried a hamper of provisions to Byron this morning, but the sentries at the Camp would not allow us a glimpse of him. He sent this to you by way of his gaolers."

"At last," she breathed. "A communication."

She reached eagerly for the packet, broke the seal with impatience, and began to scan the first page.

I observed her with interest and some apprehension. Closeted in her rooms without the benefit of dress, hair, or such touches of powder and rouge as a fashionable London lady must always employ, she looked all her forty years; and the recollection of Byron's haunting visage and vigourous frame, despite the club foot—proclaimed all the disparity of the five-and-twenty-year-old. Theirs was a misalliance, undoubtedly a misalliance—and as I studied the Countess's face, I guessed that she apprehended the same. Without Byron's overwhelming presence, she might better command her reason.

"What effrontery!" she exclaimed, casting aside the sheet she had been reading. "Only look at it, Mona, and tell me whether I have not been exceedingly ill-used!"

"It grows late, and I should take my leave—" I began, but Mona had already perused Byron's words, and with a snort, thrust the page into my hands.

A Song

Thou art not false, but thou art fickle,
To those thyself so fondly sought;
The tears that thou has forc'd to trickle
Are doubly bitter from that thought.

"Shall we sing it together, Mona, you and I?" Lady Oxford jeered. "Or shall we cast it into the fire, as cold fuel for forgotten warmth?"

The Countess of Swithin stared despairingly at her friend. "Indeed, I am truly sorry—he is an uncouth yokel, my dear, and unworthy of your love. He shall repent of his harshness, however, given time."

Lady Oxford threw back the light shawl that had covered her ankles, and got up from her settee. "I have given Lord Byron too much of my time already. I believe I shall return to London, Mona—if I set out within the hour, I might arrive in time to kiss my children goodnight; at the very least, I shall sleep in my own bed, and may awake next morning prepared to embark on all the preparations for Sardinia. Oh, to see the blue of the Mediterranean again! I am wild to pass Gibraltar! There is nothing like travel, after all, when one is broken-hearted!"

She had cast aside the remainder of Byron's packet with her shawl, and the pages were scattered on the floor. I bent to retrieve them.

"Lady Oxford," I attempted. "There is more he has written here—a further communication—"

She glanced at the sheets I held, and her lips curled. "It is only the last of that wretched poem to his dead Leila," she said. "I suppose he has been scribbling away at it, under the light of a single oil lamp, at Brighton Camp. Here—" she moved swiftly to the writing desk placed beneath her bedroom window, and gathered a sheaf of pages together. "Here is the entire work, fresh from the Genius's pen. Keep it, if you like, Miss Austen—sell it, if the spirit moves you. I shall not look into *The Giaour* again."

AND SO TONIGHT, AFTER A *MOST RESTFUL* DINNER WITH Henry, I curled up in bed to read Lord Byron's epic poem, of a *hareem* maiden drowned alive in a canvas sack, for the crime of loving another than her master.

A revenge tale, Lady Oxford had called it, but the opening lines gave little hint of this. They were rather a paean to

Greece as it must once have been, before the yoke of Turkish rule.

> *Fair clime! Where every season smiles*
> *Benignant o'er those blessed isles,*
> *Which, seen from far Colonna's height,*
> *Make glad the heart that hails the sight,*
> *And lend to loneliness delight.*

I sighed.

There was a great deal more of such stuff, about the Tyrant's bitter lash, and the Eden of the Eastern Waves that once was Greece, and so on. I had an idea of Byron looking about him during his travels in Attic climes, and seeing only what he could despise—a race of men far different from himself, that he might ennoble in his verse, and yet regard as undoubtedly inferior. My Naval brothers, Frank and Charles, had been sailing about the globe for most of their lives, and the excellent sense of their observations, in the letters each faithfully sent home, was greatly to be preferred to *this*. However—I could not imagine a roomful of young girls, only just embarked on their first London Season, swooning at the excitements of my brothers' letters; while they should certainly suffer palpitations at:

> *Though like a Demon of the night*
> *He passed, and vanished from my sight,*
> *His aspect and his air impressed*
> *A troubled memory on my breast,*
> *And long upon my startled ear*
> *Rung his dark courser's hoofs of fear...*

Yes, there would be countless young girls who should take the dark courser's hoofs of fear to bed with them, and read long into the night by their flickering candles—if Byron lived to see *The Giaour* published.

I could not think it entirely certain that he *would*.

"You will hardly credit it, I know," Henry had said over dinner, "but the *Regent* appeared at Miss Twining's funeral, and so far condescended as to spend a half-hour over the cold collation in the Officers' Mess."

"As I understand it, His Royal Highness is the very *last* man to forgo a meal," I retorted, "however melancholy the occasion. Did he have anything intelligent to say on the tragedy?"

"Only to assure the General that Justice should be served as soon as may be, and the *scoundrel Byron* punished for his sins."

"—Lest he cast a shadow of murderous doubt over the sanctity of the Pavilion, and its unmentionable tunnels. So Lord Byron is to be assumed guilty until proven innocent, in the best English tradition. And General Twining?" I enquired keenly. "How did he appear?"

My brother hesitated. "I must suppose that grief takes each of us in different ways—and that it is impossible for any man to judge another's heart—but he looked very oddly, Jane. Cold, and severe, and as tho' he stood in judgement upon the remains of the poor creature going into the earth before him. One might have thought he *blamed* Catherine for having been murdered—that the manner of her death *embarrassed*, rather than destroyed him."

"I should have expected little else."

"He almost hurried the attendant company out of the churchyard when poor old Smalls had done—the man fairly sobbed his way through the service—and seemed impatient the full hour he was required to converse with the mourners at the collation."

"How dreadful," I mused, "to be the sort of man to take

consolation solely in his *pride*. All else may be sacrificed—human warmth, love, compassion in the face of weakness. I begin to think we were very fortune in our father, Henry. However little of wealth or station George Austen may have possessed—he did not set himself up as God over others; and there must be a good deal of temptation in that way, for a clergyman."

Later, as I read Byron's verse by candle-light, I found *The Giaour* had much to say on the matter of Judgement, and playing at God; and as I had not yet come to Leila, and was growing sleepy, I determined to push on. It had been a shockingly wearisome day.

—And here was a description of the poet's jaded heart. Had Lady Oxford read it? I wondered. And was it meant for her—or Caro Lamb—or Catherine Twining?

> *The lovely toy so fiercely sought*
> *Hath lost its charm by being caught,*
> *For every touch that wooed its stay*
> *Hath brushed its brightest hues away,*
> *Till charm and hue, and beauty gone,*
> *'Tis left to fly or fall alone.*

All that I had read thus far had been written long before the events of the past week—the description of Hassan's court, and the scented gardens with their plashing fountains where Leila reposed; the flight of the brooding Giaour, whom Leila had loved at her peril—

> *For she was flown her master's rage*
> *In likeness of a Georgian page,*
> *And far beyond the Moslem's power*
> *Had wronged him with the faithless Giaour . . .*

Yes, there would be innumerable mammas forbidding their daughters to read anything remotely penned by Byron in the coming winter, lest the rage for dressing up as a young boy should overcome an entire generation. . . .

And here was the murder.

Sullen it plunged, and slowly sank,
The calm wave rippled to the bank;
. . . .
I gazed, till vanishing from view,
Like lessening pebble it withdrew;
. . . .
And all its hidden secrets sleep,
Known but to Genii of the deep . . .

I shuddered, and closed my eyes. Byron had certainly written these lines *before* Catherine Twining was murdered. Unlike the scraps Lady Oxford had shown me a few days before, or the ones lately delivered to her boudoir, these pages were penned in fair copy, without correction, and thus must represent finished verse. He had written it, and then the drowned girl had been delivered, in her sack, like Leila to his bed. . . .

The conviction grew stronger within me that the *revenge tragedy* was not of Byron's seeking; it had been visited upon him, by one who hated him profoundly—or, hated, perhaps, *the victim*. . . .

I turned over the successive verses. There were more than a thousand lines, by my estimation, most penned in black ink. But here, at the bottom of the pile, were words less neatly scrawled—lines penned at random, in the discomfort of a gaol, with much crossing out and revision, written in *blue ink* . . . and on the very last page, the word emphatically placed:

FINIS

He had finished it, then, on the day of Leila's funeral.

I worked through these final pages, struggling to pick the sense from the alterations—the true words from the discarded—the rhythm and flow of poetry from amidst the lumber-room of Byron's mind. For a writer such as myself, accustomed to reading pages that were fitful starts at best, before the typesetter's art gave a neater appearance to my prose, it did not prove *too* taxing; but my eyes were growing tired in the poor light of the single candle.

And then, about line seven hundred and sixty-five, as best I might judge, I stopped dead—and reread the verse, my heart pounding.

I had not mistaken; it was there, buried in the middle of *The Giaour,* as Byron had shaped it in his gaol—an accusation of murder. In his poem, he had all but named Catherine Twining's killer.

I stared at the lines, wavering in the candle-flame, and felt a cold dread. Then I began, unthinkingly, to bundle the pages together—as tho' by squaring the edges I might make sense of them. It was well after midnight; would Henry be asleep? Or if I braved the draughty passage of the inn, would he open his bedchamber door? I had a decided need for human conversation—and the counsel of my brother.

Outside, in the darkened street below, there was a sudden chaos of shouting, and the cantering of a horse—unusual for Brighton of a Friday, when no Assembly was held and most of the world established at card tables or private parties. Obeying instinct rather than reason, I hastened to the window and threw up the sash.

"Murderer!" the messenger on horseback was shouting as he galloped towards the Marine Pavilion. "Byron the murderer has escaped!"

CHAPTER THIRTY-ONE

Poetic Justice

"Henry!"

I stood in the private parlour that divided my bedchamber from my brother's, holding aloft a fresh candle—the one I had employed for reading being almost guttered—and knocked at his door. *"Henry!"*

After an interval, he peered out, looking rather absurd, as I thought, in his nightcap and silk robe. I should rather it had been flannel, tho' in general I despise the stuff—there is something profoundly comforting and home-like about flannel.

"Did you hear the messenger?"

"What messenger?"

He groped towards one of the parlour's chairs, eyes still blinded with sleep; he had not wasted so much time as to light a candle.

"In the street below. A mounted rider—from Brighton Camp, as I presume, and bound for the Regent's people. Byron has escaped!"

"Oh, *Lord*." Henry rubbed ineffectually at his head, loosing the cap and raking his grey hair into tufts. "He'll have the whole country roused against him now! Men on foot with torches and dogs, constabulary horsed—and Byron cannot even run! What is the fool about, to be limping towards liberty?"

"I only hope that he did not employ Mona's pen-knife in his escape," I fretted, "for she should never forgive herself."

"Mona's pen—? No, do not explain—I should rather remain in ignorance," Henry said. "But consider, Jane, how ill-advised—Flight cannot impress the magistrate with his lordship's innocence!"

"I think it may be *guilt* Byron prefers," I said frantically. "A murderous aspect—particularly when it is assumed in the name of Justice—appears so much more *romantic* than a helpless one."

"What are you talking of, Jane?"

"I know where Lord Byron will have gone."

"If he has any sense, he'll have stolen a horse and raced up the London road by now."

"That is exactly where he shall *not* go. He means to avenge Catherine Twining's murder—like the Giaour of his poem."

"The what?" Henry demanded blankly.

"Never mind." I thrust the telling sheet of paper into Henry's hands. "Read this—and be so good as to put on your clothes. I mean to thwart his lordship, and I cannot go out in the dead of night alone."

MORE THAN OURSELVES WERE ABROAD BY THE TIME MY brother roused the Castle's porter, and pled with the bewildered fellow to unbolt the door. The lackey would not promise to wait up for our return, until Henry informed him sternly that it was a matter of life and death—and pressed a guinea into his hand. Then we were out into the night.

A party of horsemen were collecting on the Steyne; and as predicted, torches flamed about them, casting a livid glow upon cheek and brow. Rising behind them, the bulk of the Marine Pavilion showed lights in many windows, and the riding stables were also illuminated; was Caro Lamb aware of what had occurred? There was much hallooing and barking of orders from the assembling search party; and some of the common Brighton folk had gathered on foot to observe the bustle. I glimpsed the undergroom, Jem, with his arm about the shoulders of my chambermaid, Betsy—both looking watchful and expectant.

"Wait a moment, Jane," my brother said. "It would be as well to learn the latest intelligence."

He crossed swiftly to one of the mounted constables, and conversed with the man briefly; then, with a shrug of his shoulders and a faint laugh, turned back to me.

"It seems his lordship was aided in his escape by a page from the Pavilion, who rode up to the gaol dressed in the Regent's blue and buff livery," Henry explained hurriedly. "The boy claimed to bear a reprieve for Byron, direct from His Royal Highness—and the sentries, upon reading it, released his lordship immediately. It was only once the Camp Commandant learnt what had occurred, and demanded to see the paper, that the Regent's signature was perceived to be a forgery. By that time, of course, the two had cantered away."

"Caro Lamb!" I exclaimed. "That is *entirely* like her! She should commit every crime in the Kingdom to save her Genius—and never give two snaps of her fingers for what the Law might say."

"But to forge the Regent's signature," Henry returned in tones of shock, "must be a *treasonous* offence."

"She should argue, with complete *sang-froid,* that to do anything less should be traitorous to the dictates of her *heart*—and might even win clemency from a Prince who saw fit to marry two women bigamously. But enough about Caro—We must *hurry*, Henry, or it shall be too late."

As we achieved Church Street, I observed Scrope Davies's lodgings to be as well-lit as tho' for a ball. That would be, no doubt, where the little page in blue and buff would be regaling her court with her adventures. No doubt Caro had expected a flight by water, in Byron's yacht, perhaps—the two of them sailing romantically out into the darkened sea, their destination Greece or Turkey. It had not turned out like that; but then, Caro's plans rarely bore fruit, and never corresponded to the elaborate phantasies she spun. She would be busy already, I guessed, at spinning another—

We were bound for a different abode, one that stood still shuttered in darkness, but for the faint glow emanating from a side window, that suggested *one* was awake, and keeping vigil at the house's rear—

Henry strode up the path to General Twining's door, and pounded on the oak. To our surprise, it gave way with a reverberating shudder—it had been ajar, and trembled on its hinges. My brother glanced at me wordlessly; I nodded, and he stepped across the threshold. The entry hall was in darkness.

"General Twining!" Henry called.

"Suddley?" I attempted.

No answering voice came. But there were footfalls—a curious, sickening, *dragging* gait that betrayed the club foot. It was approaching us.

I clutched at Henry's sleeve.

He groped, in turn, for a taper that ought to lie on the entry hall table. But there was no way to light it.

A dark head, faintly backlit by the pale glow spilling over the threshold of the rear room, appeared suddenly before us;

I was reminded of General Twining's habit of materialising at the far end of the passage. That must be where his book room lay.

"The General will receive you now," Byron said with a bow, "but do not expect to speak with him overmuch; he is unequal to all explanation."

I could not make out his countenance or read his looks in the darkness of the passage; but in the throb of his voice, in the very current of suppressed violence his still form conveyed, I read the truth. Every pore of my being was alive to his; that was Byron's inimitable power. "Dear God," I whispered. "You have killed him, then. We are too late."

Byron advanced towards us silently; Henry raised the taper as tho' it were a weapon. His lordship stopped perhaps a yard from where we stood. At last I could see his eyes glittering in the faint light, and the pallid gleam of his countenance.

"Killed him?" he repeated contemptuously. "He did not die by *my* hand. That was unnecessary; there are such men on earth, Miss Austen, who are mortal to themselves." He stepped closer, all the intensity of his look fixed upon mine, and my rebellious pulse quickened. "But how did you come here?" he demanded. "What unknown seraph whispered my truth into your ears?"

By way of answer, I drew breath and recited the words I had read only a half-hour before, in the comfort of my Castle bedroom:

Thy victims ere they yet expire
Shall know the demon for their sire,
As cursing thee, thou cursing them,
Thy flowers are withered on the stem.
But one that for thy crime must fall,
The youngest, most beloved of all,

Shall bless thee with a father's name—
That word shall wrap thy heart in Flame!

"Ah," Byron said acidly. "*The Giaour*. It is an excellent tale, is it not? So replete with exotic detail—so vivid with Attic life! All of London shall read it, and exclaim at the barbarous customs that obtain in the East!"

"And in Brighton," I supplied.

"Exactly so, Miss Austen. And now—if you will forgive me—I stand in need of whiskey." He made as if to limp past us, but Henry seized him by the arm.

"You cannot quit this place, Byron," he said wonderingly. "Are you out of your senses? The entire town is raised against you!"

"If the *entire town* wishes to speak with me, I shall be at Davies's house," the poet said wearily. "In the meanwhile, you might offer the *entire town* the General's last letter."

He shook off my brother's hand, and pushed his way through the open door.

We let him go.

Then we glanced at each other and walked side by side towards the faint light spilling from the back room.

General Twining was in dress uniform, seated at his writing desk as tho' sleeping, his head resting on his arms; but a pool of dark blood flowing from one temple shattered the illusion of dreaming peace. His eyes were open, and dreadfully fixed; their last sight, I must suppose, had been the portrait of a young officer of the 10th Hussars that hung over the mantelpiece—his son and heir, Richard, killed in the Peninsula.

"Observe, Jane." Henry reached for a folded sheet of hot-pressed paper, which had been sealed with wax and the General's ring. "It is inscribed to Sir Harding Cross."

"His confession, no doubt." Another sheet had lain beneath it—and this hand I recognised. It was Byron's.

Yes, Leila sleeps beneath the wave,
But his shall be a redder grave;
Her spirit pointed well the steel
Which taught that felon heart to feel.
I watched my time, I leagued with these,
The traitor in his turn to seize;
My wrath is wreaked, the deed is done,
And now I go,—but go alone.

CHAPTER THIRTY-TWO

The Corsair

HENRY INSISTED UPON REMAINING WITH GENERAL TWIN-
ing's body, the letter replaced in its position on the desk,
while I walked swiftly back in the direction of Marine Parade
in order to rouse the Earl of Swithin's household. It was for
Charles Swithin, we thought, to inform Sir Harding Cross
that his case of murder was done—so that the magistrate
might have the reading of Twining's sealed letter before anyone else should find it. That it had been dictated to the General by Lord Byron, and probably at gun point, I never
doubted; whether his lordship or the General's hand eventually despatched the pistol's ball into the General's brain, I do
not care to consider over-long. The duelling pistol was the
General's own—and antique enough to have accounted for
the death of his wife's lover, nearly fifteen years since. It was
found on the floor near the General's chair; and coupled with
the confessional letter, was enough for Old HardCross to
proclaim the death self-murder, and to acquit Lord Byron of
any charges in the drowning of Catherine Twining. As for

Byron's part in the General's scandalous end—so far as Sir Harding knew, his lordship had never been more than *near* the place, having repaired to his friend Mr. Davies's lodgings the very instant his amorous page effected his release from Brighton Camp.

When the contents of the General's letter were related to me the following morning, over a late breakfast at No. 21, Marine Parade, they were much as I had suspected: The General confessed to having drowned his daughter in a fit of drunken rage. After Captain the Viscount Morley knocked him senseless outside the Pavilion's doors, the General had regained his wits in time to observe Lord Byron entering the Pavilion. When Catherine exited a few moments later, in evident agitation, her father had followed her out of the courtyard. He had confronted her on the Steyne with his suspicions—that she had disgraced herself like a common trollop with Lord Byron. He then informed her, with evident glee, that her indiscretions should never dishonour her father again—that he had agreed that very night to give her hand in marriage to Mr. Hendred Smalls. In return, Catherine declared that her heart already belonged to Captain Morley— and that she should *rather be dead* than marry anyone else.

It was this honest expression of feeling that inflamed the General against his own flesh and blood. In his right mind, of course, he might only have struck the girl, and carried her home to live out a miserable existence confined to her rooms. In his drunken state, however, he was deaf to all reason. He had declared that she should have her dearest wish—and dragged her towards the shingle, where he thrust her head beneath the waves.

It was a dreadful history; and I suspect that the General's old friend, Colonel Hanger—in having plied his former comrade with Port that night—bears much of the responsibility for Catherine's death. I am certain it was indeed Hanger, discovering the corpse in one of his solitary midnight strolls, who hit upon the excellent joke of sewing Catherine Twining into a shroud formed of the *Giaour*'s hammock—and deposited Catherine in what he assumed to be Byron's bed.

The Colonel, of course, cannot be accused, approached, or touched—he remains the Regent's friend, and enjoys a Royal protection. But I confess I hate the very sight of him.

What might have been the General's sentiments the following morning, when he awoke to a brain restored from drink, a full sense of the horror of his crime, and the intelligence that his daughter's remains had been discovered in *such* circumstances, can only be guessed at; his confessional letter is silent upon all points. His cowardice, however, in allowing another man to bear the brunt of suspicion and guilt, to the very threshold of the gibbet, must acquit the world of the slightest impulse towards sympathy.

"I must say, Jane, that you are very poorly repaid for all your efforts on Lady Oxford's behalf," Mona observed as she crumbled a roll and sipped at her tea, "for she left Brighton last night before Byron's escape was even heard of; and never thought to thank you. I am ashamed of Jane Harley, I confess; tho' in truth I cannot *blame* her. Lord Byron would try a saint."

"Then let us hope Lady Oxford exerts her considerable energies in sailing past Gibraltar," I replied, "and that Lord Byron is left to enslave another lady with his verse and his caprice." If I felt a slight wistfulness at failing to bid the poet *adieu,* I ruthlessly suppressed it. I did not approve Lord Byron, I should never judge his character as worthy of respect—but it is something, indeed, to have won the esteem of such a writer. I shall not judge myself *too* harshly for exulting in his privileged knowledge—or his flattering regard.

"If Lady Oxford does not know how to repay Jane's exertions," my brother interjected, "I certainly *do.* You came here for the restorative powers of Brighton; and thus far, have enjoyed none of them. Tomorrow you shall bathe in the sea, with the aid of a dipper and a machine—"

I confess I *squeaked* at this, from both pleasure and dread.

"—but today, you will spend the whole morning at Madame La Fanchette's, in purchasing a modish gown in any colour *but* black. There remains a quantity of winnings that must be spent."

Lady Swithin clapped her hands, and I jumped up to hug my brother; he truly is such an *excellent* Henry.

SILK THE COLOUR OF WINE, LORD HAROLD'S GHOST HAD urged; an opinion seconded by Mr. Forth, the redoubtable Master of Brighton, who had gone so far as to name the wine *claret*. Madame La Fanchette possessed no less than three bolts of a suitable shade—one a sarcenet, one a French twill, and the last a silk so gloriously rich I might fancy myself a figure in the Regent's Chinese gallery, as precious an *objet d'art* as the porcelains he collected. My practical soul counseled the selection of French twill—as serviceable as it was fashionable; I reluctantly weighed the claims of stout sarcenet; but another voice—neither Lord Harold's nor Mr. Forth's—whispered me *nay*.

Let it be the taffeta, my dearest Jane.

And I caught a snatch of laughter tinkling as bells, remote and beguiling as birdsong.

Eliza. She was with me still, and I was returned on the instant to Sloane Street, her soul flying away from me without a backwards look. My eyes pricked at unexpected tears, despite the blandishments of Madame La Fanchette, the furls of cloth sliding between my gloved fingers, the dulcet chatter of Lady Swithin as she turned the plates of a fashion magazine. My breath drew in on a sob, quickly stifled.

Forgive, the butterfly shade murmured. *You know what Byron is. You felt it, I am sure. The response, so involuntary, of every nerve. A woman might sell her soul for such an instant of glory.*

Of course I had felt it.

Regret. Regret.

Forgive.

Of course you are forgiven, Eliza—and never forgotten. Never.

"Jane?" Mona said gently. "Are you unwell?"

I blinked back my tears, and fumbled in my reticule for one of Manon's black-edged kerchiefs. It was Mona, however, who handed me her own—embroidered with the flourishing script of entwined initials, Wilborough and Swithin.

"In all this bustle of murder and accusation," she said softly, "I had almost forgot you were mourning."

I smiled at her. How extraordinary it was that I should find again this acquaintance of long ago, this connexion unlooked for to my roguish lord; how extraordinary that in Eliza's passing, I should discover a *friend.*

"I believe," I said firmly, "that I shall take the claret-coloured silk. A ball-gown with demi-train, in the very latest mode, Madame—and a headdress to match."

Eliza should have countenanced no less.

It was as we were leaving Madame La Fanchette's some three hours later—I, smug in the knowledge of having ordered a becoming gown for evening wear, Mona in possession of a *very* fetching carriage dress that should become her dashing perch phaeton to perfection—that we espied Lady Caroline Lamb, bound for the New Road.

She held the reins of a showy pair whose coats exactly matched the tint of her own cropped curls; her landaulet was piled high with baggage. A diminutive tyger was mounted behind—no more than a child—in the chocolate and maroon livery the Lambs favoured. Her ladyship pulled up at the sight of us, and inclined her head; and Mona—when put to the test of acknowledging the reprobate, or offering the cut direct—deeply curtseyed.

"Bound for London, Lady Caroline?"

"Naturally—for Byron has already gone, you know." The Sprite's mobile countenance—so often captured in dreaming or fury—was woebegone today. Byron had escaped her toils again; her pallor was extreme, her glance feverish, her eyes encircled with darkness. She had not slept from the moment the wild plan of impersonating the Regent's page had overtaken her, I judged; and now that her god was freed, her costume thrown off, her drama run—she was cast off, by Regent and poet both. Poor Sprite! So like a child in her passions and tantrums, and a lost child now in her misery, lips trembling and fingers clutching at the reins. The smouldering fire of life was doused—Byron, in all his intensity and chaos, had fled. "There is nothing else in Brighton I should stay for," she said petulantly. "I quite despise the sea, and this town is grown impossibly stuffy—all quizzes and dowds! Besides, my poor William will be wondering where I have got to."

Poor William, I thought, should more likely be enjoying the first peaceful interlude he had known in nearly ten years of tempestuous marriage; but it should not do to say so aloud.

"I almost forgot!" Caro cried. "I have thought of the most cunning thing—only look at the buttons of my tyger's livery! I mean to have *all* my servants sport the same!"

We approached the carriage at her ladyship's behest, and leaned closer to study the boy's buttons. Engraved on their face was the Latin inscription *Ne crede Byron*.

Do not believe Byron.

"The Regent's silversmith engraved them for me," Caro

confided, "and is not the phrase apt? —For you cannot believe a *word* his lordship says. It is all poetry. George assured me, when I rescued him from that horrid gaol, that he meant to remain in England all the summer; and now I find he intends to sail to Sardinia, in pursuit of that tiresome Jane Harley. Byron, of course, insists it is to gather impressions for his verses—having done with *The Giaour,* he means now to embark upon a long narrative entitled *The Corsair,* and must therefore put to sea at once. I am sure it will be *vastly* exciting, but I dread the effort of persuading poor William to embark. I may be forced to abandon my home. Do you think," she enquired dreamily, "that I should look well in the garb of a pirate? Or perhaps a pirate's jade?"

Mona and I exchanged glances, then stepped back from the landaulet.

"Walk on," Caro commanded her pair; and with a flick of her whip and a nod of her head, moved briskly up the New Road.

"Jane," Mona said faintly, "I stand in need of a good, stout nuncheon; and then I must look into Donaldson's. I have had enough of poetry. I require a dose of prose. I shall spend my remaining hours in Brighton established on the sopha, with a volume of *Pride and Prejudice* in my hands. Do you think it at all likely the authoress has commenced a third novel?"

"I *had heard,*" I answered cautiously, "from sources I should judge unimpeachable, that such a work is undertaken—but is not yet launched upon the unsuspecting publick."

"It does not, I trust, deal with piracy?"

"I believe the subject is Ordination." I glanced at her with considerable apprehension, to learn how so fashionable a member of the *ton* should receive such a tedious topic.

Mona closed her eyes in relief. "Thank Heaven. My dear Jane, should you care to join me at Donaldson's? We might enquire the title of Miss Jennings. She is certain to know it."

"With pleasure," I said; and linking arms, we strolled off in the direction of Marine Parade.

A FEW QUESTIONS FOR
STEPHANIE BARRON

Q: *Your ten-book series about Jane Austen as detective has carried readers through more than a decade of the novelist's life, from December 1802 to what is now the spring of 1813 in* Jane and the Madness of Lord Byron. *How closely do you follow the historical record of Austen's life, and how much of the series is pure fiction?*

A: Some of the books are so faithful to Jane's letters that I've used the actual calendar of her week as the structure of the novel—and included everyone she mentions as a character. But others, like *Jane and the Madness of Lord Byron*, are complete invention. Although Jane chose Brighton as the site of Lydia Bennet's infamous elopement in *Pride and Prejudice*, there's no record of her ever having visited the town, for example, and certainly none of her having met Lord Byron. And to be fair, the man was never taken up for murder in 1813. But I knew Jane had seen almost every major town on the Channel Coast over the years; I knew she read Byron's poetry—she refers to several of the poems in her letters, and in her novel *Persuasion*—and they had acquaintances in common. It was just within the realm of possibility for them to meet. I like the realm of possibility; it's the bedrock of all my writing, and far more interesting than the known world. When I saw that Byron was writing that spring about a doomed love affair and a drowned girl—and that he made a habit of sailing in Brighton—I knew I had to place Jane in the town. And remarkably, at Byron's death in 1824 he was laid in state *not* at Westminster Abbey, which refused to have him—but at the London home of Fanny Knatchbull, Jane Austen's niece. No one has ever explained why.

Q: *Brighton seems like the last place Jane would be comfortable. In fact, she derides it in* Pride and Prejudice.

A: True. But she was always happy to go anywhere a friend was willing to take her, which is why her brother Henry is so vital to the story. Henry was fashionable and ambitious and well connected to people in the Prince Regent's set, who would have descended on Brighton by April for the Royal birthday. Henry would absolutely *love* the frivolity and display, the pretty and available women, the horse races and the crowd of gamblers at Raggett's Club. Given that he was in mourning—and that we know Jane spent both late April and late May in London with him—it seemed logical to send them off to the seaside during the intervening weeks, to recover from the death of the incomparable Eliza.

Q: *Was Byron as promiscuous as you suggest?*

A: He was far more promiscuous than I suggest! He seemed to require constant sexual stimulation, from a variety of women—usually twenty years his senior—and young boys. There's a suggestion he forced himself on Lady Oxford's eleven-year-old daughter while staying at her estate, Eywood; and he certainly had an incestuous relationship with his half sister Arabella, and fathered one of her children. When he eventually married Annabella Millbanke—a cousin of Caro Lamb's—the relationship lasted barely a year. Although she would never disclose what Byron had done to her, Annabella was probably physically and sexually abused. Byron was not a mentally healthy man.

Q: *Byron is called a mad poet in this novel, but frankly Lady Caroline Lamb seems a bit more unhinged. How faithful to the actual woman is your portrait?*

A: Oh, my goodness—I was probably far kinder to poor Caro than she deserves! I think today she'd be diagnosed as manic-depressive. Or possibly a narcissist. Or both. She was certainly volatile in her moods, violent in her rages, compulsive in her attachments, and extreme in her self-destruction. A few months after *Jane and the Madness of Lord Byron* ends, in July 1813, Caro put herself completely beyond the pale of good society by attending a waltz party at the home of one Lady Heathcote. She encountered Byron in the dining room, and when he avoided her, she smashed a wine goblet and tried to slash her wrists with the shards of glass. She had to be carried screaming from the party, and from that moment forward, she was rarely invited anywhere again. William Lamb, her husband, nearly divorced her that time—but he found it impossible to abandon Caro. He sent her into exile at his family's country estate instead, which for Caroline Lamb was probably a kind of death-in-life.

Q: *Speaking of death-in-life, how deeply attached was Jane to her cousin and sister-in-law, Eliza de Feuillide, whose death opens the book?*

A: I think Jane was one of the few Austens, other than Henry, who truly loved her. Jane was witty and sophisticated enough to enjoy Eliza's essential nature, which was frivolous, fun-loving, and profoundly of the moment. Eliza connected Jane to the Great World, and her kindheartedness and intelligence would more than make up for any French pretensions she persisted in displaying. The rest of the Austens seemed to mistrust Eliza as a bad influence. But her amusements were so tame—she never appears to have hurt Henry in any way, and added greatly to his consequence and comfort—that one wonders whether there was not a bit of envy at the base of the family's poor opinion.

Q: *And yet Jane and Henry go on.*

A: You had to go on, in those days. People died left and right. In the course of her life, Jane would lose four sisters-in-law, most in childbirth. She lost her father, of course, and her close friend Madame Lefroy. And eventually the Austen family would lose Jane herself, far too young. To be a citizen of the world in 1813 was to be intimate with death.

Q: *You make use of a very convenient tunnel in this book. Is that an invention too?*

A: Actually, no. The Prince Regent liked to get around Brighton without being seen—particularly in his later years, when he was obese and somewhat crippled by his size. He had a number of tunnels built to and from the Pavilion, and three of them survive in the present-day Royal Pavilion complex, connecting modern concert and public performance venues erected in the former stable block.

Q: *What's ahead for Jane Austen?*

ABOUT THE AUTHOR

STEPHANIE BARRON is the author of the stand-alone historical suspense novels *A Flaw in the Blood* and *The White Garden,* as well as the Jane Austen mystery series. As Francine Mathews, she is the author of the Nantucket series, as well as acclaimed standalone novels, including the thriller *The Alibi Club.* She lives in Evergreen, Colorado.

A: She's going to travel to Kent in the autumn of 1813, for a protracted visit to her wealthy brother Edward. At this point in her life she's publishing her third novel, *Mansfield Park*, and gathering material for *Emma*, which she's forced to dedicate to the Regent! Kent is another secure and comfortable world full of rich and famous families; but the Pilgrim's Way to Canterbury Cathedral also runs through Edward's estate, Godmersham Park. A mysterious stranger will find his end there, in *Jane and the Canterbury Tale*.